DRAKE THOMAS

-BOOK 1-

RISE OF GRIMDOR

TYLER SVEC

JORDAN SVEC

Copyright © 2025 by Tyler Svec / Jordan Svec

CITIOFBOOKS, INC.
3736 Eubank NE Suite A1
Albuquerque, NM 87111-3579
www.citiofbooks.com
Hotline: 1 (877) 389-2759
Fax: 1 (505) 930-7244

Ordering Information:
Quantity sales. Special discounts are available on quantity purchases by corporations, associations, and others. For details, contact the publisher at the address above.

Printed in the United States of America.

ISBN-13:   Softcover   979-8-89391-587-7
                    Hardback   979-8-89391-588-4

Library of Congress Control Number: 2025905581

Other works by Tyler Svec

<u>The Kingdom</u>

<u>Crunch</u>

More at svecbooks.com

To Anthony,
who is without a doubt my biggest fan.

DRAKE THOMAS
-BOOK 1-

RISE OF GRIMDOR

TYLER SVEC
JORDAN SVEC

RISE OF GRIMDOR

DRAKE THOMAS : BOOK 1

Chapters

<u>INTRODUCTION</u>

The story that you're about to begin, is a very old story. The first versions of the story go back almost 13 years now.

It was shortly after I finished the original version of what is now the *'Kingdom'* trilogy that I felt led to create another fantasy adventure. This was a daunting conquest at first because it is very difficult to keep things fresh and not revert to the same story arch that I used previously.

After I had sufficiently mulled over ideas for several months I decided to ask my brother to join me in writing this story and it has been a rewarding, fun, but sometimes challenging venture in the years that have followed.

Many of our friends who read earlier editions of this book have compared it to J.R.R. Tolkien's *'Lord of the Rings'*. I take it as a compliment, and as a side note, I love the *'Lord of the Rings'* and other related works.

I like them because although they are called 'high fantasy' at the heart of them they are an allegory for something greater. It was in that spirit that we set out to compose our epic tale.

There were a few things we wanted to focus on, and some things we wanted to do differently from others in this genre. One thing we tried to focus on was depth. Depth of the characters, the land. Everything should have a backstory. That is one thing that I feel is largely missing in the modern era of writing, is a deep history. I think it's mostly because society for the most part is just not interested in the origin of things these days. But it is important, and therefore history had to be prominent for the world of Drake Thomas to work.

This did get a little complicated when planning, simply because we would spend twenty minutes, talking about the background and culture of one town, and in the end not that much necessarily made it into the final text.

It was also important to us, that the books wouldn't just follow one moment in time. In so many books or movies the character has a great adventure, but you never see beyond that. They live happily ever after...

However, I always find myself wondering, what happens to the characters afterward? Where did they go? What else happened to them? Did they change? As such, this series isn't going to be a story just about Drake Thomas at one point in his life. It will be about his life.

Admittedly, this was not the plan at first. The first and second were written together, and then we added the third book a year later. Then they sat on my computer for six or seven years, and when I read through them again I said to myself *for a book that's called Drake Thomas...we don't learn that much about him.*

So the fourth book and beyond were added a good 12 years after the first book was completed.

What you're reading now, is effectively a second edition of the first book. This was partially due to when you add books 12 years later, things change or become developed differently, and at times you have to go back and tweak things just a little bit.

So now, this tale will be much longer and more involved than it was intended to be, but it should better tell the story of Drake Thomas, as well as give you a sense that you're stepping into a larger story, in which Drake Thomas's tale, is just a small part.

One of our big goals was to use Bible stories within pages. To create a world where we could bring those to life in a way that would make sense.

Some think the Bible is a bunch of children's stories, to which I say that the people who say that...have never read the Bible.

This is where the historical part became essential because if you know your history, the Bible makes a lot more sense and everything becomes very clear.

Included in the back of every book, we'll have a stories/references section to show you which stories we used in the book and where to find them in the Bible. In some cases, we tried to recreate the culture within our fantasy world so that it would become more clear for readers.

Tyler & Jordan Svec

A DISTANT PAST

A crimson moon filled the sky, blanketing the world in red. The heavens were opened to the eyes of the three Elves. The only sound permeating the silence was that of their horses, who stood tall and proud, easily traversing the sandy dunes. They rode in silence, with an un-suppressible sense of wonder and awe stirring within their hearts.

A trail of dust lazily drifted through the air, turned red by the rays of the moon. They crested another sandy hill, only to find an empty vale lying before them with another sandy dune waiting on the other side.

Despite the bleak desert before them, they pressed on, certain that they were close. They looked to the stars once more, seeing the sign that so many had so easily overlooked. Never before in the history of the Earth had the world seen anything like this. This was not just the beginning of another day; it was the dawn of a new age.

Ishamel pulled on the reins, and brought his horse to a stop; his two brothers flanked him on either side. They all smiled when they spied the city known as Masada. It glistened in the red moonlight, inviting them forward.

The slumbering city lay before them. The only sounds of life were the armor-rattling footsteps of a few guards that walked the walls. Otherwise, the city was as still and silent as a tomb.

Of all the cities in the world, the city of Masada was anything but grand and glorious. The city was an armory, but its name was nearly forgotten by the world and the ancient scrolls.

A foul voice whispered in the air and with it came the desire to return to their home. For the first time, Ishamel questioned the sign that was written in the heavens. The sight of the city both beckoned to them and urged them to turn away.

Aware of the shift, Ishamel cursed the voice. As if recoiling a hand from a burning flame, the voice departed and their minds became clear.

"At long last the city we have searched for has appeared in our sights," Berdin replied. Ishamel smiled.

"Alas, it remains hidden from others," Ishamel lamented. "Though it lays right in front of them. The significance of the city will be overlooked for years to come."

"A night of such importance, yet they sleep?" Merken asked.

"Forget not, my brothers, that we too wandered in darkness," Ishamel said. "Long ago the rulers of this nation, and many others, offered their hearts to the darkness that took too strong a hold on them. As such, the citizens of Farndor and other nations alike have been blinded by the cruel, hardhearted rulers of the world. We see the sign of Lathon in the sky, but they have not. Few in Farndor will remember this night for what it is. A holy night."

The name of Lathon was known all across the Earth. Lathon had been the greatest ruler who had ever lived and certainly the greatest of the Elves. The nations of Men hated the Elves because of him and had turned him into nothing more than legend and a mythical king who had never lived.

"The hearts of Men may not remember, but we will make certain that the Elves do. This is our chapter in the great history that will be remembered for ages to come. The heir of the Lathon is waiting within the walls of this city. We must be vigilant. We are in the dominion of Men now, not Elves. We will not be welcomed warmly."

"We follow your lead brother," Merken replied. Ishamel nodded, coaxing his horse towards the city. The dust from their horses announced their presence to the soldiers on the wall. Ishamel restrained himself from checking to see if his sword was ready.

The bleak and dreary gates stood before them, and the wall itself stretched thirty feet high. The guards atop the wall came together, watching with a keen yet bored interest. The sentries who stood outside of the gate stepped in front of them. At once, the three brothers stopped their horses.

"Who seeks to enter the city of Masada at such an unearthly hour?" the guard on the right questioned.

"Weary travelers from a distant land," Ishamel answered.

"And your business?" The guard replied in an irritated tone from the obvious evasive answer.

"We request to speak with your king about things that are for his ears only. We come in peace not war."

"I find that hard to believe," the guard remarked. His tone not changing with continued annoyance.

"Believe what you will, but truth does not change. We wish to speak with your lord at once, no matter what inconvenience it will cause. Haste is of the utmost importance."

"Elves visiting in the middle of the night? I'm curious about this myself." The soldiers chuckled to each other. "I'm not sure I would wake up the king at this hour, but it may be amusing to see how he reacts. We will awaken His Majesty if the matter of your visit is truly that important."

"Do as you have said! Thank you for your cooperation," Ishamel commended. Everyone shifted uncomfortably.

"What are the names you go by? I would guess by your wardrobe and your horses that you are of importance in the Elven world, but Men in these parts do not stay well educated on your type. What names are we to give?"

"I am Ishamel, and these are my two brothers Merken and Berdin. We are kings of Ariamore; the Elven kingdom, long forgotten in the world of Men. As proof of our claim, here is our signet ring!"

Ishamel slipped if off his finger and handed it to them. Though Men were often uneducated on their type, they would recognize the symbol etched onto it. The men shifted uncomfortably again, as if they now perceived the Elven Kings in a different light.

"Farndor does not trust Elven kind to walk the streets alone, as such you will be escorted to the main palace by an armed guard. We will send messengers to wake His Majesty. I would warn that he may not be pleased about being awakened at this late hour."

"That will be our risk," Ishamel replied. The guards nodded and the orders were given. Finally, a dull grinding noise was heard from the other side. The portcullis was lifted and the two wooden doors were opened. On the other side, a company of horse-ready troops waited.

Ishamel guided his horse through the gates, with his two brothers not far behind him. They stopped when instructed and the mounted soldiers wrapped around them. The gates shut and the portcullis lowered, leaving them no escape.

The minutes dragged on and faded into an immeasurable amount of time as the company was led deeper and deeper into the city of Masada.

At length, they came to the palace. Giant stone columns greeted them, looming ominously over the rest of the city. Its sharp curves and dark shadows created an atmosphere that repulsed them.

The leader of the company motioned them to dismount. They did so and then were led to the palace steps, where they met a seasoned man with hard narrow eyes and a glare that spoke of great hatred towards Elves.

"I am Captain Midelba. By order of Erode, son of Meron, the ruler of Masada, you are to leave your weapons at the door. You are forbidden to enter his presence otherwise. He is aware of the historic scrolls and is wary."

They removed their weapons, which consisted of swords, daggers, and knives alike, all of which were housed in beautiful sheaths. They laid them on the ground near the Captain's feet.

For a moment, everything was silent. The eyes of the captain shifted nervously from one elf to the other. Though he glared he also seemed to be studying them with keen interest. Finally, as if he had learned everything he could by observing, he motioned them to follow.

The palace doors opened before them, revealing a dark corridor illuminated by torches. They followed the captain for several more minutes through the palace until finally, they came to a set of intricately carved doors. Scenes of war, supremacy, and the gods of Farndor covered every inch of the large doors.

Midelba, gestured for them to stay as he entered the room and announced them.

A dark red carpet marked the path before them, leading to a platform where a throne sat. The beauty of the throne was little, stolen away by lines of age and decay. Seated on the chair was a shadow of a man, his crown was dull and tarnished and little else about him stood out. Still, the king's eyes narrowed as they walked forward.

The ancient scrolls had spoken about this night, but never had they imagined such evident signs of gloom and despair. Of all the nations that Shedaros could have been born into, why had this one been chosen?

They stopped when they reached the chair of the king and the raised platform that it sat on. The three brothers fell to their knees bowing low, waiting to be spoken to. The king watched them closely.

Silence blanketed the room and dampened their spirits like a wet towel. The three elf kings remained bowed low, determined to outlast the silence that was growing heavier.

The silence was shattered by laughter from the king.

"You may stop bowing you pathetic fools," King Erode derisively told them. Ishamel held his breath and said another prayer as all three of the Elves stood tall and proud in front of the king.

"On behalf of the Kingdom of Ariamore, I would like to thank you for agreeing to meet with us at this late hour."

"Don't thank me. The only reason I agreed to meet with you was because of the nature of your visit. There haven't been Elves in these borders in nearly a hundred years. I had to see it for myself. It is a sport to kill Elves in my kingdom, perhaps you were unaware."

King Erode's eyes drilled them for a moment, glancing from one to the other, illuminated by a deeper concern that, as of yet, remained concealed from them.

"The business that brings us here is worth such a risk," Ishamel responded.

"You Elves are strange. You vanish into your borders for a thousand years, and then out of the blue, you will show up and expect to speak to a person like myself. For your sake, this had better be good."

"We are certain that it will be," Merken calmly stated.

"Get on with your tale. I was having a most pleasant sleep in the dead of night as men, in these parts, usually do. What is it that brings you to the nation of Farndor at this unearthly hour?"

"We are kings of the Elven nation of Ariamore. My name is Ishamel and these are my two brothers, Merken and Berdin. The business that has brought us here is of the most importance."

"So you say," Erode remarked.

"A star has brought us to your doorstep, and more specifically, to your city. A star that has announced the birth of our Savior."

"*Your* savior? May I remind you that you are in *my* kingdom?"

"You need not remind us," Ishamel answered. "The star is the sign from Lathon. It has shone brightly in the sky, far too bright to be written off as any accident. There is no doubt in our hearts that this star is indeed the sign that was prophesied."

"And what was prophesied?" Erode inquired.

"An elf king," Ishamel answered. Laughter immediately followed.

"An elf king? You mock me. If you are looking for an Elven king you might try looking in the mirror. I can lead you to one if you so desire. Or perhaps you have forgotten that you are Elven-kings?" Laughter again filled the hall.

"An Elven king has long been spoken of by the prophets. At last, the silence between Lathon and the Elves has ended. This star in the sky has offered us hope. We have set out on this journey and now we are here to pay our respects to the long-awaited one."

"Do you not remember me telling you that it's sport to kill your kind in Farndor? I can assure you that no Elven kind exists in this nation, and if they did they would have been slaughtered long ago. You study the stars and say they have meaning when in actuality the only meaning they have is to taunt us with what we cannot grasp. The stars have no more meaning than you do to me. Go back to your homeland and wallow in self-pity where no one has to look at you. Your trip has been for nothing. "

"We know that there are no Elven kind in the nation of Farndor my lord, but that is exactly what brought us here. For if there was an Elven child born in your city, whose parents were also Elvish then what would be so significant about that? They would be no greater than any other Elven child, living and dying as people do."

"You admit that your trip was a waste?" Erode mocked.

"Our trip has not been in vain," Merken admonished.

"Then what am I missing? What would make this supposed 'king' so different from yourselves?"

"According to the scrolls and prophecies, Sherados has been born into your nation, is Elven, but born of two parents who are human." Erode's face stiffened. "For such a miraculous act to occur would be beyond explanation. The only explanation that would make any logical sense would be that this *is* the heir of Lathon. In our tongue he is called, Shedaros, and he is coming to right the world of its injustice. Would you have another explanation for such a phenomenon?"

"What you search for is impossible and you will only cause yourself more humiliation by searching for this supposed child."

"We have traveled far. We do not doubt. We do not fear. We trust in the word of Lathon as given through the prophets. We humbly ask for your permission to search out the city for this child."

Erode stroked his chin for a moment, leaving the Elven-kings standing in front of him for an uncomfortable amount of time. The silence continued, and the king's eyes narrowed in on them.

"Perhaps, my Lords, we may yet come to an agreement. I wish to discuss this matter with my private council?" Erode asked. "I have many historians, magicians, lore masters that are experts in all matters. I wish to check your information with my records and test the validity of your tale. If it holds up, I shall correct my scrolls and give you my blessing and make sure that you are not harmed in your quest for the child."

"We do not take offense at such a request," Ishamel replied. "We would be concerned if you didn't discuss this with your advisors. This is a historic night."

"Yes, indeed it is," Erode stood up and looked at them again. "Would you by chance be able to tell me *when* you first noticed this star in the sky?"

"We noticed the star two years ago for the first time. We wrote it off at first as nothing more than a star, but with each night that went by we became certain that it was not there by chance. It was put there by Lathon."

"I shall consult with my council and together we will consider your request. For the moment, I shall have you escorted to some guest quarters while we deliberate. You have my word that you will not be harmed. I will send someone to you."

Erode walked out of the room.

"I must say that went better than I thought it would," Merken replied.

"It went, but should we say it went well?" Berdin asked. "I have a strong leading that King Erode only agreed to see us because we were Elven and had made it through this much of Earth alive."

"Either way it was a step in the right direction," Merken pointed out. "If he gives us permission to search the city, my heart warns against whatever condition comes attached to it."

"We shall follow our hearts and trust that Lathon will guide us in our decisions."

A door opened on the far side of the room and they were greeted by a servant who led them through the dark twisted corridors until finally, they entered a large and spacious waiting room. They took a seat on the soft couches and chairs. The gravity of the situation struck them as they waited for the king's word. The Elven race had long awaited this day. Despite the uncertainty that loomed, a sense of peace filled them.

Erode stood at the head of the chamber. His sleepy-eyed council members stared ahead blankly. For ages, the Elves had stayed within the borders of their nations, and now they ventured out?

The nations of Elves and Men had long been enemies in war. The intellect of the Elvish kind was renowned in the wide world, just as much as it was loathed. Despite multiple attempts to destroy the Elvish people as a race, from the earth, there had never been a successful campaign.

Admittedly, the Elven-kings unnerved him. Showing up on his doorstep was one thing, but they claimed a prophecy named his city as the home of their 'savior'. He had no interest in sharing his kingdom with anyone, let alone an elf.

Finally, the last people staggered into their seats.

"Thank you for answering my call. I do apologize for the late hour of this gathering but there is a situation that demands that we meet at such an unearthly hour. On this night, three Elven-kings from the nation of Ariamore have arrived in this city." The council awakened from their stupor with cries of indignation.

"How they managed to get through our borders and to this city unnoticed and unchallenged I can't even begin to guess, but that is not what I have brought you here to discuss. They insist that they have come to pay their respects to a *savior* that has been born in this very city!"

Now the entire assembly was in an uproar. Erode held a hand to silence them.

"They claim they are looking for an Elvish king; Shedaros." A murmur went through the now alert council members. "They also suggest that this 'king' was born of common folk. If their story is true, the child could belong to any of us. I ask you, the wisest in the land, about the matter of the Elvish prophecies. They claim that the birth of this 'Elven' child has been foretold for thousands of years. Do these Elves speak the truth?"

The room was silent as everyone considered what was being asked. Erode shifted his gaze from one member to the next, hoping to gain insight from their expressions. At last, a man stood and made his way to the front of the assembly. He was a tall, proud, learned man, named Rohemir.

"This is disturbing news for Your Majesty," Rohemir started. "For unless I am very much mistaken, Elven children look no different from the children of Men until they are three years old, give or take a few months. With that being said, I conclude that Your Majesty is right; the child could be anywhere, even within the walls of this very city."

"So the prophecies have validity?" Erode asked. Rohemir nodded.

"In Elvish lore, there is much said about an heir of Lathon coming to live among us. I speak for everyone when I say that my heart is troubled by this."

"Do you know the prophecy they refer to?"

"Yes, my lord."

"Please recite it, so we may share in your knowledge and better guide our course of action," Erode replied.

Rohemir opened his mouth but never got any words out as one of the guards began speaking boldly. His hair was brown and, his shoulders were broad. Emerald light shone from the man's eyes as he stepped into the light. His face was flawless and his build was that of a warrior.

"The prophecy says...

'And you oh Masada, in the lesser nation of the Earth shall not be forgotten by the prophets, or by Lathon. Your nation will stand tall and proud in the final days, and yours will welcome in Shedaros who shall take the throne and restore the land to the beauty it once was.'

As you can see the prophecy is true."

"Precisely as I was going to say, my lord!" Rohemir exclaimed.

"I have no doubt," Erode said coldly. "However, please elaborate on how it is a simple guard is so educated? Last time I checked a person of his rank should not be here."

"My sincere apologies Your Majesty. We will thoroughly examine him after this meeting has concluded to see how much he knows. Although we might wait for a more reasonable hour to do so." A few snickers went through the assembly. "Nonetheless, that is how the prophecy reads. If the elf kings are here to pay their respects to their king then perhaps they know something that we do not."

"Are you implying that he *is* in this city?" Erode asked. "I will not bow to Elven kind, whether it be a child or the grown Elves that are waiting outside these doors. I would sooner take my life than bow to them."

"We understand," Rohemir said. "But we might benefit from having these Elves in the nation. They know something that we do not. If their blood is what you seek, as well as the death of Shedaros, then I suggest you permit these Elves to search this city for the child. Ask them to return and tell you where to find him so that you may worship the child. For an elf king being born into the nation of Men is unique and therefore you could say that you are curious."

"That sounds like a reasonable plan," Erode replied, thinking it through. "They must be followed. As soon as the child is found, that person must report to me. We can marshal the army and blockade every gate. The elf kings, as well as Shedaros, will be trapped within the walls and will be butchered like animals."

"An excellent resolution, my lord!" Rohemir concluded. "Sedric, come forth!" The guard who had spoken earlier came into the center of the room. Fear washed over the man's face. "You know more than a guard of your rank should, which makes you a wanted man. However, if His Excellency agrees with my proposal, you may walk freely through this nation. You will follow the Elves and report their findings. If you fail to do so, death will hunt you for the rest of your very short life. If you succeed, your understanding of things that are not meant to be known will be overlooked for the time being."

"I understand," the man said.

"Thank you everyone for your assistance," Erode said. "You are to spend the rest of the night in the guest quarters of the palace. If something goes amiss, I will need your help again."

Erode left the room and then sent for the elf kings once again. The sound of the door announced their arrival. The three Elves strode forward. As much as he hated the notion of letting them live, he knew that Rohemir was right. If he wanted to kill this child, he would have to leave these three alive for the time being.

"Rise, my friends," Erode greeted. "It seems that I have reached a decision about the situation at hand, and I will agree to let you search the city for the child."

"Thank you, your majesty," Ishamel replied.

"Think nothing of it. However, I do have one favor to ask in return," Erode started. "This situation and the prophecies are so unique, I am curious. When you find this child, I would very much like you to tell me where to find him, because he is truly worthy of praise if everything you claim is truth."

Merken bowed low. "We are mere visitors. We will agree to do as you request. We are at your mercy."

"In that case, I send my blessings with your search. Be on your way and I look forward to your return," Erode replied. The elf kings were led out of the room, vanishing from his sight. He turned to one of the messengers who stood along the wall and beckoned him closer.

"Silently marshal the army. We must be swift and we must be quiet. I want everyone ready for action in ten minutes." The messenger nodded and ran out of the room. Erode looked towards the doors, his mind filled with malice and hatred.

FLIGHT OF THE ELVES

The clomping of hooves on stone unavoidably echoed through the empty streets. Ishamel reflected on their short time in the palace. They were wary of the king's motives, but they took hope in what they would soon find.

A solution to their problem. A person the world could put their faith in.

Compared to what Shedaros would have to deal with, their problems seemed insignificant, as though they were nothing more than a speck of sand on the shoreline.

Having received their weapons again, his two brothers took either flank as they rode three abreast through the streets, allowing the minutes to pass without care. The child that they were seeking would be unlike any the world had ever seen, and would ever see again.

In unison, they brought their steeds to a standstill, a voice whispered in their hearts as they looked down the street on their right. The houses here were less grand than the ones that they had passed up to this point. They were simple houses, constructed out of mud bricks, with straw roofs.

They passed house after house until they became aware of a specific house on the left side of the street. The house appeared no different than the others, except that this one had a lamp on inside and a man watching them through the window.

They dismounted as the man moved from the window and the house went dark. They opened their saddlebags, each removing a package of great value.

Each of them had brought something for the child, a mere token to display their gratitude and loyalty. They confidently strode to the door, passing by a table and chairs as well as the tools of the trade for a carpenter.

The prophecies had said that he would be overlooked by the world, and forgotten by his own kind. Never had they imagined that Shedaros would humble himself, to not come into the world as the king he was, but by that of an ordinary person.

They knocked on the door and it was cracked open a moment later. A man appeared, his features disfigured and clouded by the darkness. His eyes darted from one to the other and then finally back to Ishamel at the front of the company.

"What do you want?" the man asked defensively.

"We mean you no harm," Ishamel told the man. The man shifted slightly.

"What do you want?" the man asked again.

"We have come to pay our homage to the king of the Elves that few will recognize."

"And how do we know that you're telling the truth?" the man asked.

Ishamel smiled. "We are three of the Elven race in a nation of Men. We have traveled far and are weary."

"Rare happenings," the man mumbled to himself.

"Such things will become more common in the days ahead."

"Words spoken like a friend. They shine brightly in the darkness. I knew you were coming but I wanted to be sure."

"You knew we were coming?" Ishamel asked, curious. "How?"

"I guess you could say it was intuition," the man answered. "You may enter, but only you three."

"Except for our horses, we are all that is here and I don't think that anyone in their right mind would bring a horse into their house."

The man chuckled and opened the door, welcoming them into his home. A lamp was lit bringing into focus a modest house.

The man studied them warily for a moment or two, looking at their ears which were slightly pointed, and then moved to a closet on the far side of the room. He opened the door and whispered to a woman who was inside. She came out, tentative and shy. A child was in her arms. She sat the child down on the floor and bowed to the three of them.

"You do not need to bow to us," Ishamel told her. "It is us who need to bow to you. You have done what no one else in this world was capable of doing. We know how this came to be and we thank you for everything you have done. What are your names?"

"I am Joseph and this is my wife, Marion," Joseph answered. Now that they were in the light, the elf kings noticed how he was built like a carpenter. His hands were calloused and his face was rough. He stood tall and proud in his home with shorter black hair covering his head. The woman, Marion, came only up to his shoulders and had long wavy brown hair. Her eyes pierced into their souls searching for answers to the questions they had. They held her gaze for a moment before they turned their attention to the child on the ground.

He wasn't as young as they had expected, clearly being a year and a half old. They fell to their knees and bowed to the king before them. So mighty and so worthy of taking the throne. They had seen many babies and a lot of princes in their lifetimes but nothing compared to this. Their hearts were undone and a few stray tears slipped out of their eyes.

"Our king and our savior," Merken said in a whisper. They looked back to Marion and Joseph. "This is not your child is it?"

"It is...but it isn't. I was a virgin when it happened. I still was when the child was born. I had never known a man before. I was engaged to Joseph and he still took me as his wife...but it is not our child."

"For reasons, that our hearts do not understand, we were chosen to bring the child into this world," Joseph said. "Until this happened, I was not familiar with Elvish writings and prophecies...now I believe them with all my heart. We know that he will save this world from the trouble that lies ahead "

"You will certainly be rewarded for the suffering you have gone through, and will go through in the days to come," Ishamel replied. "We fear that time is short, so we must give these gifts to show our appreciation while we have the chance."

Ishamel removed the silk cloth that was wrapped around the small chest that he had brought and knelt before the child. "For my savior and my king, I have brought a token of my appreciation...a gift of gold. Valuable and beautiful, worthy of being held by royal hands."

He stood and his brother Merken came forward and bowed down. "For my savior and my king, I have brought, as a token of my appreciation...a gift of frankincense, only to be held by the richest of people."

He stood up and the last brother Berdin came forward and knelt before the child. "And finally, for my savior and my king, I have brought as a token of my appreciation...a gift of myrrh. The finest perfume that exists in this world. Though these gifts may not be much where you come from, it is the best that we can do in this world." Their breath was taken away as the boy seemed to nod at them as if he were thanking them for the gifts they were bringing.

"We have for our king, one final gift," Ishamel announced. He removed a sword and sheath from his belt. The sheath was beautifully decorated, fitted with various jewels and stones of unimaginable value. The hilt of the sword was decorated the same with a single ruby embedded in the center of the cross guard.

"This sword was made especially for this occasion. It was made from the finest forge in the entire Elven nation, and certainly the greatest in all of the Earth. We present the gift of this sword to the king, Shedaros! May he use it wisely in the days to come."

All three of them put a hand on the sword and lowered it in front of the child, trembling as they did so. They set the sword on the ground and looked into the child's eyes.

The world changed before them, showing them glimpses of what lay ahead. For a moment they were unable to pull away as the baby held their gaze. Each of them laid a hand on the child, praising Lathon.

They stood as a knock came at the door. Joseph held up a hand and carefully crept to the window looking through the thick curtains. He nodded that everything was alright, opening the door. A man quickly darted inside.

The man was in a royal guard's uniform with the crest of King Erode on his breastplate. Joseph and the man embraced before he turned his attention to the baby in the middle of the room. He opened his mouth but no words came.

"Who is this man, Joseph?" Ishamel asked.

"This is Sedric. He works for Erode, but is a loyal friend."

"All this time and Shedaros was right in front of me," Sedric reflected. "I can't believe it."

"You know of the prophecy?" Merken asked.

"Known and waited for," Sedric answered.

"It is reassuring to know we have friends," Ishamel said.

"That is why I'm here," Sedric replied. "Erode is setting a trap. He sent me to follow you to Shedaros. I am to report back to him and give him the location of the child so that he can kill him."

"But you-"

"I am risking my life," Sedric answered. "Not all people in this nation are loyal to King Erode. I will not bow to the king of this land. His mind is clouded by the very lust for power that his ancestors held in their hearts. I am loyal to the Elves and Shedaros. There are many more like me in the king's service. That being said, I fear that Erode suspects my loyalties are elsewhere, and had me followed. I did my best to lose whoever I thought was following me but I can't guarantee success."

"We're running out of time?" Marion asked. Sedric looked into her eyes and then nodded.

"He's already barricaded all the gates and alerted the infantry. But if you'll allow me to explain my plan to you, I think we could all get out of here alive," Sedric said. Everyone nodded and he continued. "There are two companies within the ranks that will fight for Lathon and the Elvish nation. At most, one hundred men. It's not much, but it might be enough for us to create a distraction and provide the cover and manpower we need to take down whatever stands between us and the southern gate."

"Why the southern gate?" Joseph asked.

"Because it's the closest to the border. You will only have to ride a couple of days south to get to Idumea. You'll be safe there."

"Be realistic Sedric, you know no horse can run for two days without stopping. I'm sure we'll be followed and, in the end, we'll be caught."

"As soon as I get the gate open, I'll take a horse and head in another direction and try to draw them to me. If you time your departure right, they might not even notice you."

"How long will it take you to alert your friends and open the gate?" Berdin asked.

"Give me ten minutes and then start coming. I know the back alleys and roads of this city better than anyone. Your Majesties' should leave in a different direction, to pull the troops towards yourselves and away from the house. Once it is clear, Joseph, Marion, and the baby can sneak out."

"What horse shall I ride?" Joseph asked. "I don't have a horse."

"We came with three, but we have no further need for them," Ishamel answered. "They are fast and graceful, capable of running for days on end without food and water. Keep them for your good use and may they serve you well."

"Thank you, but how will we ever be able to pay you back?" Joseph asked.

"Make it out of here alive, and raise the child to the best of your ability. When he comes forth, it will be the best kind of payment that we could ever ask for."

Joseph and Marion hastily gathered the supplies they would need while trying their best to hide evidence that they had been living here at all. When they were ready, Joseph and Marion hid in the closet taking the baby and the gifts with them.

Ishamel and his brothers headed towards the door followed by Sedric who closed it behind them. They stood in the shadows, listening for any sign that anyone could be waiting for them in the streets. Silence passed between them until they heard the clattering of armor.

A company of troops came around the corner and stopped when they spied Sedric and the elf kings. The Elves rested their hands on their swords. Sedric looked at the Elves one last time and nodded his head in respect. Without hesitation, he bolted across the street, vanishing into the darkness.

Ishamel and his brothers stepped out from the shadows, gathering the attention of the soldiers who stood at the street corner. Apprehensively, the company assembled into an orderly line.

Drawing a deep breath, Ishamel and his brothers drew their swords and waited. Their blades glimmered in the moonlight, reluctant to hand out death and judgment. The soldiers in an effort to bolster their resolve, let out a cry and rushed to attack the three Elven Kings.

The brothers raised their blades, defending themselves with the speed and poise that Elves were renowned for. The elf kings took on one challenger after another, as soldier after soldier were slain and fell to the ground. As the final soldier fell, the street became silent.

Sheathing their swords, they ran until they were about ten minutes from the house that Joseph and Marion were still in. As they ran, Ishamel pulled a horn from his side and put it to his mouth letting it ring through the silent air.

Sedric crept into a narrow alleyway, remaining perfectly still. Another company of soldiers passed by the lane and came through the street just ahead. The group passed him by and were soon out of sight.

After a while, he came out of his hiding spot and continued to the north until he entered the street at the end. His heart nearly stopped as he bumped into a general, leading his soldiers. The general's expression quickly turned sour.

"What do you think you're doing soldier?" the general asked. Sedric struggled to form a response, stuttering awkwardly for a moment. A mischievous smile came on his face as he turned and ran back the way he had come. His heart pounded inside his chest as he became well aware that everyone was now chasing him.

Sedric tried not to panic as he darted into a small narrow lane, only to have it come to a dead end fifty feet later. Erode had constructed walls within the Masada, meant to keep commoners out of the more beautiful parts of the fortress. He jumped up on a small wagon, hoping to grasp the top of the wall with his hands. Sedric hesitated as the commanding voice of the general called out, he turned to see recurve bows aimed at him.

Sedric jumped behind the small cart. The arrows flew overhead and embedded themselves into the mud brick wall. At once, Sedric leapt onto the cart and scaled the wall, using the arrows as a ladder. The soldiers cried out and their general furiously yelled out orders.

Sedric reached the top of the wall, rolled to his feet, and took off running along the top of the barrier. He frantically studied his location, attempting to chart the course he needed to take. From behind, he could hear the soldiers reaching the top of the partition.

Arrows sailed by him, but he forced himself to continue. His heart was filled with unease as ladders were erected and soldiers appeared in front of him.

Beyond the soldiers, the barricade ended and gave way to huts and lesser buildings. A gap stood between him and the other side. To Sedric's relief, a few more arrows flew past him and struck the soldiers climbing up the ladder.

Sedric hastened to the now empty ladder, giving it a shove and clinging to it for dear life. He landed safely on the flat-roofed building on the other side. Willing himself to move forward, he ran across the top of the buildings, jumping gaps when he had to. The soldiers, only momentarily slowed, managed to keep close to him.

Sedric jumped another gap, tumbling onto a different section of the barrier wall. Unlike the previous barrier, this one featured a large temple that was built into it. Had it been daylight the steeple of the temple would have displayed lavish colors and priceless gems that glistened in the desert sun.

He knew from experience if he could traverse the steeple and get to the other side, he could drop into the alley he was looking for. With little effort, he jumped onto the balcony of the steeple.

The steeple room itself was only twenty feet across and wasn't that interesting to look at. He hastily grasped the rope and swung himself across the gap. The bell clanged noisily.

Sedric jumped the railing and dropped onto the steeply sloped roof. He slid uncontrollably towards the alley, his only relief coming when he landed in a pile of straw. He was buried in the straw and remained there for several minutes until the general peered down into the alley.

"Where do you think he went?" another soldier asked.

"Check the temple and all the surrounding buildings. Something about this is not right."

An Elvish horn rang through the air, the note different from that of the human race. Every soldier in the city would be drawn to the sound, giving Sedric the opportunity he desperately needed. Without delay, the pair turned and headed back the way they had come.

Sedric climbed out of his hiding place and carefully turned into a series of side streets and alleys, which at times were nothing more than footpaths between the rows of buildings.

Relief came over him as he came to his destination. A small narrow house, pressed between two buildings waited for him. He carefully shimmied through the open window.

Without warning, Sedric was shoved against the wall, and the cold blade of a knife pressed firmly against his neck.

"Give me your name soldier!" the man ordered.

"You know my name," Sedric replied. He was released and the knife was put away and a lantern was uncovered, allowing the light to chase away the darkness.

His friend Malachai stood in front of him. He was a rough-looking character with a beard that did not have a hint of grey in it. His hair was short and well-trimmed while his face and hands clearly showed that he was a hard worker. The woman behind him was his wife. She was tall and slender, a dark green dress covered her, matching her sparkling green eyes and her dusty blond hair.

"What brings you here through the window instead of a door like a civilized human being?" Malachi asked.

"I cannot stay in this city much longer."

"What's going on?" Bethany asked.

"So, it's happened?" Malachi asked. Sedric nodded.

"It happened two years ago! The baby is almost two years old!"

"What's he talking about Malachi?" Bethany asked.

"He's talking about Shedaros," Malachi answered. Her eyes also lit up at the mention of the title. "He's been born into this city?"

"Yes, and Joseph and Marion are the lucky ones who get to raise him."

"Joseph and Marion?" Malachi laughed. "Well, those are two people I never would've guessed.

"Me either, but they've been discovered and we need to get them and myself out of this city as fast as we possibly can, or else it will all be for nothing."

"What do you want us to do?" Malachi asked.

"There are three elf kings in this city who are risking their necks for us by drawing the troops to them. Send reinforcements. Then we have to get to the south gate as fast as we can and get it open so that when Marion, Joseph, and the baby come they don't run into a dead end."

"Alright. You and Bethany head to the stables on the south side of the city and wait for me. I'll alert the companies loyal to us and I'll meet up with you to get the gate open."

"Do you think that this is a position a woman should be joining us in?" Sedric asked. Malachi smiled.

"No, but you try keeping her back."

"You might find that a little challenging," Bethany taunted as she pulled a dagger out of the small table next to their bed. "I don't like being left behind."

"We'll probably have to leave the city as well," Malachi said. "It won't take long for word of our treachery to reach the ears of the king. I want to be as far away from here as possible when Erode finds out."

They helped Bethany grab a few things before the three of them entered the alleyway.

"I'll meet you at the south gate stables in five minutes," Malachi said, giving his wife one last kiss. He was soon lost from sight, leaving them alone.

Sedric and Bethany reached the stables without incident, finding horses that would suit them well. Finally, Sedric laid his eyes on two massive black stallions, which were alert and awake even though all the others paid them no mind.

They were saddled and ready to go as Malachi entered the stables. They mounted their steeds, Bethany and Malachi on one while Sedric took his own. Malachi held a hand up and they fell silent. The sound of shuffling feet came from outside the doors.

"He went in here," A voice whispered. Malachi gave Sedric a look as he kept one hand on the reigns reins and moved the other to the sword around his waist.

"Are you certain?" A voice asked, a little gruffer than the first one.

"I'm sure. He's the one responsible for the soldiers that are rebelling against the king's army."

"He'll pay for that," the rough voice said. "Get ready, they could be anywhere in here."

"You ready Sedric?" Malachi whispered.

Sedric nodded and rested his hand on the pommel of his sword while grabbing the reigns with the other hand. The stable doors were opened and the soldiers paused, trying to process what they were seeing as they laid their eyes on Sedric and Malachi.

Together they kicked their horses in the side, sending them into a full gallop down the aisle. They ran straight towards the bewildered men, who scrambled out of their path.

They rode to the north, long enough to throw off anyone who might be following them, before heading to the southern gate. When they arrived, Sedric wasn't surprised to find the gate blocked and guarded by ten soldiers. Catching them off guard, the three of them drew their swords and charged toward the soldiers.

One by one, they fought the men, and one by one they fell until they were victors. Hiding their horses, they hastily pulled the fallen to the side and acted as if they were the guards. Time seemed to drag on as they stood waiting for Joseph and Marion to arrive, hoping that there were no issues.

"The portcullis is controlled by that winch just to your left. The doors after that are relatively balanced. One person should be able to get it open far enough," Malachi informed.

The sound of hooves echoed through the street. A single horse with two riders came forward, followed by a company of mounted soldiers. Sedric was the first to jump out of their hiding spot, running to the winch that held the portcullis shut. It consisted of a large wheel that stood a foot or so off the ground. With effort, they were able to move the iron grate up a couple of inches.

They pushed again and again until the portcullis was all the way open. The horsemen raised their bows, sending a volley of arrows at them. Malachi cried out as an arrow struck his back. He stumbled and his eyes went wide. A distraught Bethany ran to her husband's side, leaving Sedric to hold the gate open himself.

Sedric looked to Marion and Joseph and the baby who rode with all the speed that the horse could muster. He uttered a prayer as his legs trembled as he struggled to hold the winch in place. The portcullis had slipped down a few feet, but it was still plenty high for them to get through without a problem.

"Open the door! I'll hold the gate!" Malachi yelled as he found strength and stood up. He was soon struck by another arrow to the back, but Malachi's resolve seemed to grow instead of wane.

Sedric did as instructed, allowing Malachi to take the winch. Sedric undid the brace and sent the right gate swinging open, revealing the vast empty desert. Marion and Joseph disappeared out the city. Relief flooded over Sedric.

"Get out of here!" Malachi yelled. "Get her out Sedric!"

Conflict filled Sedric as he ran to Bethany, grabbed her around the waist, and pulled her backward until they were in the darkened alley their horses waited in.

"No!" Bethany yelled starting to run to her husband, who received another arrow. His body went limp and fell to the ground. The winch rotated for a moment and then rested against his chest holding the gate open six feet from the ground.

He put a hand over her mouth and restrained her, despite her efforts to get away from him. "We have to get out, Bethany!" Sedric yelled.

"No! My husband!"

"This is our only chance or we're both going to die!"

"Then let us die!" Bethany screamed as the troops were getting closer.

"If we die, then he's sacrificing himself for nothing!" Sedric yelled. "Get on the horse!"

"No!"

Sedric grabbed Bethany and threw her on the horse in front of him. He held her from getting off as he took the reins in one hand and spurred the horse forward at full speed.

They galloped out of the alley and made for the opening, narrowly missing arrows that were aimed at them. Sedric drew his sword with one hand and cut the rope holding the portcullis. The winch came loose and the iron grate fell to the ground, narrowly missing Sedric and Bethany as they slipped through. Their attackers were forced to stop as they rode away.

Sedric turned east and pushed the horse as fast as he possibly could, trying to block out the pain of Bethany's crying as it carried through the night. They looked to the south, seeing a faint trail of dust.

Ishamel fought with a ferocity that the race of Men had never seen. All three of them were appreciative of the extra help that had been sent to them. They fought, having faith that everything would work out the way they had hoped. Had Shedaros escaped the city? The question was answered by a whisper in their hearts.

Joy filled them as they knew it was time to leave. Ishamel yelled to his brothers and nodded. All at once the Elven Kings pulled out their horns and blew into them. The sound pierced the heavy air that had settled over the city, permeating through the hearts and minds of the men attacking them and keeping them from attacking until the sound stopped.

Three black shapes appeared in the sky, striking fear into their attackers who scattered. Three Taruks dropped to the ground. The soldiers scrambled, frantically trying to prepare for the new threat.

Arrows flew through the air but missed their targets as the Taruks easily maneuvered through them. The men looked upon the menacing creatures, who gracefully landed in front of the elf kings.

The Taruks growled and bared their teeth in a deadly grin. They pawed the ground, ripping up the stone road as they did. The company stood unmoving, too afraid to attack. Each elf king made their way to one of the Taruks and climbed on.

With a single command the great beasts took off, soaring high into the sky.

The fighting and the sounds of the city disappeared from their view as they looked to the desert landscape. Two faint trails of dust could be seen. One heading south and the other heading the direction they were heading...east. Ishamel looked to his brothers.

"Farewell, heir of Lathon. May we see you again when your glory is revealed to the world," he whispered. They flew off into the night, never to be seen in the nation of Masada ever again.

THE MAN BY THE RIVER

A pale sun rose in the east, gently waking up the sleeping land with its rays of light. It had been twenty-three years since that night the elf kings had visited, and for many the truth of the matter had been reduced to myth and lore.

Rohemir had spent countless years pondering the events that had transpired. For anyone who had lived through it, it was forever etched in their minds. The last time Rohemir heard tell of the child had been on that night long ago. Now all he could do was sit back and wonder how long it would be until Shedaros revealed himself.

After the elf kings had escaped, Erode declared that throughout Farndor, all babies under two years of age were to be killed to ensure that the 'King of the Elves' would die. The mourning of the country had been great, and the rule of King Erode was dimmed in the eyes of his people. The memory of Erode would never again be a fond one, instead, it was likened by his subjects as a foul taste they wished to spit out of their mouth but were never able to.

A few weeks later Rohemir resigned from the king's council, left the nation, and had never gone back. He had wandered for many weeks, till he had arrived at the borders of what remained of the Elven nation of Ariamore.

It was no secret that in the land of Men, Elves were despised, rejected, and shunned. He had entered their woods expecting death, but to his eternal confusion, he had been offered life.

He had been taken to their stronghold, a city named Belvanor where he found many things were not as he would've thought. There were thousands of people like him...ordinary people who had decided that they wanted a better life. They earnestly believed in the ancient prophecies and were content to wait for their king to come forward and wipe away all evil from the face of the land.

His mind formed a picture of the flawless landscape, unaffected and unchanged by the gates of time that ruled over everything. He was proud to call the Elven nation of Ariamore his home now.

The distant waterfall pounded into the earth, creating endless foam as the water washed over itself. Bordering the river on each side were oak trees, which offered shade to a weary traveler like himself.

Rivers had always amazed Rohemir. They seemed to appear out of an endless spring and continue, unbothered by the landscape that they met. They always reached their destination and overcame whatever stood in their way. The ages came and went and still, the stream continued as though there was nothing that could stop it.

Rohemir looked ahead, his eyes focusing on a dark shape. As he neared, it was easy to see that the shape he had noticed was a person. Rohemir came alongside the man and dismounted his horse.

He knelt on the ground and carefully turned the man over, holding his head so it wouldn't hit against the rocks that the man rested on. Rohemir checked the man's pulse confirming that he was alive.

The man's hair was dirty blond in color and his face was pale. If he had been standing he would have been just under six feet tall. His clothes were torn and tattered beyond recognition. The man himself, whoever he was, was covered with dozens and dozens of scars and gashes. His blood was washed away by the water which occasionally lapped up against the shore. The waterfall in the distance offered at least a partial explanation for the man's condition. It was a miracle he was alive.

Rohemir moved his arm, his eye-catching something on the man's palm. An unusual marking covered the palm of his hand. It was pale and consisted of three white slashes each separated from the other by an inch.

The sign of Lathon.

Rohemir returned the man's hand, being mindful to place the symbol face down. He was a student of the ancient scrolls, reading and studying them. He had read hundreds of scrolls but had only come across that insignia a couple of times.

Great fear filled Rohemir, but with the fear also came an excitement that he hadn't felt in a long time. He stood, choosing to leave the man where he was. In one swift motion, he mounted his faithful steed and spurred it forward. The animal snorted and then took off north, down the riverside as he instructed.

The landscape flew by them. The stallion was one that the three kings had left in the city. Faster and far more graceful than any he had ever ridden, the stallion carried a rider with surety and the lightest foot imaginable, barely leaving an indentation in the ground, no matter how wet or dry the ground was.

Being an Elvish horse, many had passed up the opportunity to own a noble steed such as this. When it was clear that no one was interested, Rohemir had taken the beast as his own.

He turned to the right and entered the forest along a narrow trail, which was a shortcut to where he wanted to go. Two hours passed before the trail exited the forest and opened into a large clearing.

The logging community of Nariven waited for him. Rohemir slowed to a gentle trot as he approached the fenced perimeter. The guards at the gate stopped him and asked him a few questions before he was allowed to pass. He rode up and down the streets, ignoring the skeptical glares. To the untrained eye, people would know this horse was different, but they wouldn't know how.

At long last, he came to an inn. The inn was long, two stories tall, with a pub in the middle of it and the rooms off to either side. Rohemir dismounted, hardly sore from the incredibly smooth ride.

He entered the smokey pub, surprised to find it already full despite the early hour of the day. He studied each of the faces in the room and spotted his friend sitting in the corner, the hood of his cloak concealed most of his face. He held a drink in one hand and had his arm around a beautiful woman next to him.

The woman smiled when she saw him and nudged her husband enough to point to where Rohemir was standing. The man caught his gaze and then nodded, acknowledging his presence. Rohemir entered the long hall of rooms until he found room fifty-six, which he knew to be unlocked.

Rohemir took a seat in a chair that looked better than it felt as he patiently waited. The seconds passed, each one feeling like an eternity. Finally, the door was opened and the woman stepped through.

The woman ran to Rohemir, smiling from ear to ear. The cloaked figure stepped through behind her and closed the door. The cloaked figure took down his hood, revealing himself. Sedric stood in front of him and Bethany took her place by his side.

"Good to see you, my friend!" Sedric exclaimed.

"It is good to see you both," Rohemir agreed. "It's been a long time. I'm not sure how it's possible, but you Bethany, seem to get more beautiful every day."

"That's possible," Sedric acknowledged. "However I have a hard time convincing her of that." Bethany blushed. "To what do we owe this honor? It has to be five years since we've seen you in person."

"A most unusual event. I was riding along the Charenella River just this morning and I came across a man lying on the bank, unconscious but alive."

"You seek us out to tell about a man you found along the river?" Sedric teased. "That's a bit of a wasted trip don't you think?"

"He bore an impression on his palm. A symbol that would send chills down your spine if you had seen it yourself."

"What kind of symbol?" Bethany asked.

"The sign of Lathon."

"Lathon?" Sedric asked. "Are you certain?"

"Completely. There also seems to be something familiar about this man. I can't put my finger on it, but it seems as if our paths may have crossed in the past."

"You think he is the child?" Sedric asked.

"Yes I do," Rohemir answered. "We helped Marion and Joseph flee with their baby, who we know *was* Shedaros. There is no doubt in my mind that this man *could* very well be the baby we helped escape so many years ago."

"I do not think so," Sedric stated. Rohemir studied him trying to figure out his thought process and failing miserably. "The ancient scrolls tell of *two* people that will usher in the new age. One will be Shedaros and the other will be called *Elyay* or 'messenger' in the tongue of Men. It is said that Elyay will prepare the way *for* Shedaros. He will be the one to recognize the king when he comes forward."

"So which one is he?" Rohemir asked.

"He may be neither," Sedric suggested.

"He must be one of the two," Rohemir persisted.

"Have you been watching the borders of Grimdor as of late? Even distant travelers like us have heard the Borags are growing restless within their borders. The ancient scrolls warn of a leader who will rise and will lead Grimdor in conquest to rule all the Earth."

"Are you suggesting that this man could be an impostor?" Bethany asked.

"I think all possibilities need to remain on the table."

"But suppose this man is one of the two that the scrolls speak of. What are we to do?" Rohemir asked. His two friends were silent in reflection for a moment.

"Nothing," Sedric answered, decidedly. "If this man is Sherados, and is to unite the races of Elves and Men, or if this man is Elyay and will first recognize the Heir of Lathon, then we must let him be what he will be, without any of our influence. By doing so we will answer our questions."

"If this man is not Shedaros himself, where do you think Shedaros is? We never even found out his name twenty-three years ago when we helped them escape?"

"Who knows where he is?" Sedric stated. "For all we know he could be one of those men working in a little shop."

"Do you think that he knows? Do you think that he knows about the night that unfolded so many years ago?" Rohemir asked.

"I think he remembers the night even better than we do," Sedric continued. "While we try our hardest to keep the events of history in order, we are mortal, and our memory fails us. Truth turns to legend, and legend into myth, until the very core of the truth is nothing more than fairy tales. My heart tells me that he remembers that night. However, why he has not come forward yet, I cannot say."

"Maybe he does not wish to have the throne?" Rohemir suggested. "Why else would it take him this long to come forward?"

"You're asking questions I cannot answer," Sedric stated. "I cannot make any better a guess than you can. After all, who would have thought that Shedaros would come into the world as he did?"

"That is one thing I've never been able to come to peace with. Why would the heir of the greatest king who ever lived come into our world, born into a family of common folk? I loved Joseph, but he was nothing more than a carpenter."

"The lines of kings have long been corrupted by every kind of evil imaginable. Perhaps Shedaros wished to come into the world by way of people who were pleasing in his eyes. Lathon is humble, perhaps he was trying to show it," Sedric suggested. "That being said, I do agree with you that it would make logical sense for a king to be born into royalty. I have a hard time seeing how Shedaros is going to get himself into a position to do any good if he wasn't born into power."

"Do you suppose that the baby we helped escape, was not Sherados, but instead, Elyay?"

"At the moment, the answer is unclear. Nevertheless, we should prepare for Shedaros and wait for him to come forward, regardless of who this man is. War is coming and we'd best be ready for it. In which case we must hide what must be hidden and trust that this man, whoever he is, will find his way to our nation without our influence."

"I agree, though I am saddened that this is the last time we'll see each other for quite a while," Rohemir asked. Sedric nodded.

"Unfortunately it must be that way. I have things to do before I vanish into thin air. However, I think you should remain in the area and keep an eye on this man you discovered."

"I had already thought of it," Rohemir said. "If he is one of the two the Borags will not stay idle long. If rescue is needed we may intervene and offer him refuge in the Elven nation of Ariamore."

"You are very wise my friend, it's unfortunate that we have to bid you farewell after such a short reunion."

They embraced and said their goodbyes before Rohemir left them and departed the village. His mind wandered between the present and the past, as all the events of the past twenty-three years flashed through his head.

At length, he came to the spot where he had found the man only to find him missing. He noticed two sets of tracks and then three sets of tracks as the man had gotten up and walked with whoever had found him.

The familiar sight of the Charenella waterfall brought innate feelings of nostalgia. The trees, the birds, the way the torrent of water churned at the bottom of the cascade. All these things combined to form the most beautiful sensation that Lily hadn't seen or heard in a long time.

Lily was an elf. She was tall and slender with long black hair, often worn in a single braid, and eyes sparkled like diamonds. Her face and skin were flawless, and her ears were slightly pointed. Her graceful walk displayed all the features the Elves were known for.

A dwarf named Ellizar walked next to her, standing no more than four feet tall. He had an unruly brown beard that covered most of his face and big bushy eyebrows that would have looked like a forest on most people, still for whatever reason it seemed to suit him. His hair was just as much the same as his beard but had been rarely seen on their trip as he had worn a helmet nearly the entire time.

People had never understood their friendship. Considering hostility usually separated the two races; for a dwarf and elf to be friends was uncommon. The Elves always thought of themselves as more wise and sophisticated than the Dwarves, who spent their days digging tunnels and looking for treasure.

In the same token, she was reminded that Elves were hardly on good terms with any race on the Earth. They were despised, rejected, and often participated in petty debates and divisions among themselves. Elves had never been highly respected when she had been growing up and sadly she doubted the relations with other races had improved in her absence.

As much as being treated differently had caused her pain, she couldn't deny that through it she had found a determination and a strength that wouldn't have existed otherwise. Still, as many difficult times as she had faced, she felt they would pale compared to the moment she both wished for and dreaded.

She was going to her parents' home for the first time since she had left so many years ago.

Despite her anxiety, she was acutely aware of an undeniable whisper growing in her heart, hinting that today would be the beginning of a great adventure. She chided herself for thinking such thoughts, after all, adventures only happened to people that were in fairy tales and even those could hardly be believed.

Beside her, Ellizar jumped at a sound and pulled the axe from his belt. A moment later the source of the sound was revealed to be an overgrown squirrel scampering through the trees. Lily couldn't help but laugh at the sight of her own private soldier.

"Something scare you, Ellie?" Lily asked. The dwarf jumped again.

"Only the disturbin' sound ov someone callin' me by somethin' other than my name!" Ellizar exclaimed.

"I'm just shortening it," she countered. The dwarf narrowed his eyes on her and her into his. Moments later they both smiled.

"Just shortenin' it?" Ellizar asked with a laugh. "That's a good one! Perhaps I should just call yeh Lil if that's the case."

"You call me Lil and I'll personally, rip your hair out, and feed you to the vultures."

"What a nice friend yeh are," Ellizar retorted. "I suppose if yeh did that I'd just have to put my axe teh good use!"

"I still don't understand why you brought your axe, or for that matter why you wore your helmet and armor when you knew it was going to be this hot and we were going to be traveling for this long."

"Fer protection. I couldn't let yeh wander all the way home by yerself without protection ov some kind. I'm the only soldier that could do the job! After all, have we been attacked once since we set out? I think not!"

"So you're the best there is?"

"Blasted elf kind! Always twistin' yer words around before yeh even get em out of yer mouth."

"I didn't twist anything," Lily insisted. "Seriously though, was it really necessary to bring the axe? We're going to my home town and they're going to find it strange enough that I have a dwarf with me. You look like you're ready to go to war."

"A dwarf is ready fer everythin'. Look at the bright side, should somethin' awful come out ov the trees and attack us, we'll be perfectly fine."

"And what might that be, a bear? There are no bears in this part of the country," Lily pointed out. Ellizar frowned.

"Maybe not, but if one should happen teh show up he'll be sorry he did when the wrath ov Ellizar is unleashed upon him."

"The wrath of Ellizar? That sounds more like a bad fairy tale than something that could happen. Besides, the title should be the 'Wrath of Ellie' it's got a much better sound to it don't you think?"

"I think yer crazy, and if I've told yeh once I've told yeh a thousand times that my name is Ellizar! How many times do I have teh tell yeh that?"

"One more apparently," she answered, spotting something in the distance. Ellizar looked ahead trying to focus on what she had seen.

"Could yeh help me out here Lily, what are we lookin' at?"

"There's something along the river," she said, pointing ahead.

"There is?" Ellizar questioned.

"Yes."

"Your elf eyes must be better than mine. I can't see anything."

"Maybe if you didn't have bushes for eyebrows," she replied. If he had uttered a reply, she didn't answer him and instead began running down the shoreline leaving Ellizar standing where he was.

"Blasted elf kind! Always runnin' off, why can't they walk?"

Lily quickly dropped down to one knee next to a man who was lying on his stomach. His clothes were torn and tattered. Blood and dirt matted in his hair. She had already turned the man over on his back by the time Ellizar caught up with her. She looked into his motionless face, noticing that the man's chest rose up and down with his breathing.

He was alive.

She grabbed his hands, surprised to find them warm, indicating that he hadn't been in the water as long as some people they had discovered in the past.

She turned his hand over looking at the palm, seeing an insignia she hadn't seen on anyone before. Three slashes were across the man's palm, seeming to shift and move as she looked at them.

Lily held her breath and showed Ellizar who became as white as a ghost. Questions danced through both of their eyes as they exchanged glances.

"What do you think Ellizar?"

"I think we've stumbled upon a most rare find," Ellizar decided. "That's no ordinary mark!"

"My family might not think I'm crazy or delusional if they saw what we're seeing right now."

"If I wasn't seeing it with my own eyes I might already think you are delusional," Ellizar said with a smirk.

"But still, it's here right in front of us, on the hand of a normal human being. Why would a symbol like this, be put on the hand of a common man?"

"Only Lathon would know. After all, why does anythin' happen the way it does? We were meant teh find this man, now what are we goin' teh do with him?"

"I don't know," She answered standing up and pacing in the river. The water splashed as she walked ankle-deep in the water. Ellizar meanwhile, in an attempt to make himself look taller, was standing on a rock right next to the man. "My family already hates me for what I've done, I doubt they'd forgive me if I brought home a man that would offend them at first sight. Let alone, I'm bringing a dwarf with me too."

"I'm assuming this means yer family still doesn't approve ov yer belief?" Ellizar asked.

"My family is too absorbed in themselves to give a thought about what might be the purpose in life. They have their money, and they have their status; that's enough for them."

"Well, at least one ov yeh had the sense teh realize the truth. I always wondered why yeh didn't live with yer family."

"I do not live with them because I am not wanted."

"If yer not wanted, then why have we been traveling fer so long to get to yer hometown?"

"Because I cannot help but cling to the hope that someday they might want me back. They might one day look into my eyes and see their daughter and not some stranger from the street. My love for them is deep and I will hold out as long as I can. I have to believe there is hope, that they will see the error of their ways. My family is nothing I can explain in a short conversation. I'm sure when we get there many things will become clear."

"If I've traveled this far, I will surely travel with yeh the rest of the way. I cannot let yer family look down on yeh as though yer a slave. I can't believe how far I've come. We have covered many more miles than I thought it would be, Dwarves are not known fer travelin' like this."

"We both defy our races."

"It seems we do. Now what do we do about him?" Ellizar asked. Silence passed between them.

"Wake him up and see what his story is?"

"I suppose so." Ellizar held his axe to the side as she knelt near the man once again. His face was calm and expressionless with a twitch in one eye. Perhaps they wouldn't have to wake him at all.

The man slowly began to stir. Lily helped him sit up. The man covered his face and rubbed his eyes, groaning. Ellizar dropped down off his rock.

"Don't make any sudden movement sonny, or they'll be the last ones yeh make," Ellizar declared. The man looked at the axe and then at the person holding it before looking in her direction. A thousand questions filled his eyes.

"Are you alright?" She asked. The man looked at the trees and then at the thundering falls.

"Where am I?"

"The man's a bloody idiot!" Ellizar whispered.

"He's not an idiot, he just woke up."

"Say what yeh want, I still think he's a bloody idiot."

She turned her attention back to the man. "How about we start with an easy question? What's your name?"

"My name?" the man asked, repeating the question several times.

"You do remember your name don't you?" Lily questioned. Ellizar moved close to her.

"Idiot," he whispered to her.

"You, my friend, are the Idiot, Ellie."

"Blasted elf kind, always tryin' teh outsmart people."

"You're not much of a challenge." The man laughed lightly, before wincing and grabbing his side. "What's your name?"

The man thought hard for a moment. "Drake Thomas."

"Where's Thomas?" Ellizar asked.

"That's my name. Drake Thomas. Is something wrong?"

"Told yeh he was a bloody idiot!" Ellizar said. "Have yeh ever heard ov a town named Thomas?

"What do you mean?" Drake asked.

"What he means is that people only have one name, and then where they are from. For instance, I am Lily of Fiori and this is Ellizar of Jermin. I can't say I've ever heard of a place called Thomas."

"You don't know where I'm from?" he asked.

"No, Sorry," Lily replied, exchanging confused glances with Ellizar who seemed to have no better idea of what to do. "Do you remember anything else?"

Drake thought for a second.

"My memory fails me. Where am I?"

"You're in Epirus," Lily answered, warily. "Do you truly not know?"

"I reckon yeh took a tumble off that bridge up there." Ellizar pointed to a covered bridge that spanned the river above the falls. The bridge wasn't straight, but instead warped and twisted with old age and moisture.

"That's quite a fall."

"It's a wonder that yeh've lived teh tell the tale."

"Do we have any way to find out where I came from?"

"Can you tell us what you were doing before we found you?" she asked.

"I'm terribly sorry, my memory seems to have failed me once again. I don't seem to remember much of anything. I couldn't tell you where I am or what I was doing, or where I was going for that matter."

"And the mark on yer hand?" Ellizar asked. Drake shot them both a puzzled look before looking at his hand. He looked at it, seeming to be mesmerized by the sight. No one spoke until he finally turned back to them, a familiar light in his eyes.

"Something about it is peculiar. I almost get the feeling that it could frighten some people."

Ellizar let a chuckle escape. "Do you know about the Elven beliefs?"

"No," Drake admitted.

"Despite all yeh've forgotten, yeh seem teh have gotten somethin' right in this area."

"What do you mean?"

"Ellizar means, this is a symbol we've seen only a handful of times, each of them on an ancient scroll or parchment. Each telling about the time of confrontation."

"Confrontation?" Drake asked, sounding both amazed and alarmed at the same time.

"It's a little hard to explain in a short amount of time," Lily answered.

"Based on what I can remember I have nothing but time," Drake said with a pleasant smile tugging at his lips. She watched him most carefully, her anxiety dissipating. Whatever unusual circumstances had brought this event to her and Ellizar, she believed that Drake was telling the truth.

"What do you think happened to me?"

"We have no way of knowing," Lily answered.

"Can you help me?" Drake asked.

"We might, but not right now," Ellizar stated. "We're on our way somewhere."

"I see," Drake said looking around. "In that case, if you could just point me where you think I'm supposed to go."

"You are coming with us," Lily decided. Ellizar expression questioned her without speaking. "I can't exactly make things any worse. My family already hates me."

"Aye, but yeh won't make them any better either," Ellizar reminded.

"We need to do this Ellizar," Lily insisted.

"You speak as if I'm dangerous," Drake noted.

"Only to some people," she concluded. "You're right when you say your scar could frighten people. If our suspicions are true, then you can count us among your friends."

"I'll pretend Ito understand what you're talking about."

"That'll do for now," Lily said. "You're coming with us, you can stay in our house until you either remember where you came from or find where you belong."

"I've got no better idea so I'll go with it." They started walking.

"What if I never remember anything?" Drake asked. Lily sighed heavily, having wondered that herself. "What if I fall asleep, wake up, and never remember what's happened today?"

"We'll take it one day at a time and worry about that bridge if and when we get to it. For now, you'll stay with us."

"Thank you." His eyes drifted all around them looking at his surroundings. "This place is beautiful."

"Yes it is," She agreed. "This land is far older than it might look, yet it seems to hold its poise and beauty as it did in the old days."

"Word of warnin' teh yeh, Drake, I wouldn't try arguin' with an elf. Yeh'll never win an argument."

"You might win an argument if ever you were arguing about something right Ellie."

"Oh yeah, and I might add that they also call yeh by names other than what yer name is!"

"I sure hope I remember all of this."

"Don't worry yeh'll be just fine now that yer with us," Ellizar assured. They continued walking eagerly trying their best to make him feel a part of this world that he didn't remember. They walked towards the falls and approached a steep wall of rock at the base.

Carved into the rock was a narrow staircase that wound through the inside of the cliff. Small square holes peppered the wall and let in light and air.

They walked up to the top and entered the green grass-filled land in front of them. Lilies bloomed as far as the eye could see. They came to the old covered bridge they had seen from the bottom of the falls.

"Does any ov this look familiar teh yeh?" Ellizar asked.

Drake shook his head.

"Well just so you know, we are heading southeast to my hometown of Fiori, we still have a ways to go but we should be there by tomorrow. Fiori is mostly a town of Elves, although there are some Men there." He nodded and they walked across the bridge, swallowed by the forest on the other side.

Drake felt like he was walking in a dream. They had traveled throughout the day with little rest. The trails were easy and Ellizar and Lily set a relaxing and comfortable place as if they didn't have a care in the world.

Ravines, pastures, vales, small villages. The world was both familiar and strange; new and different. Each trail, each tree, seemed different from the one before. In the dying light of day, he wondered about his past and stared at the scar on his hand.

They traveled until the light became too minimal to continue. As Drake allowed himself to fall asleep he listened to the sounds of the forest, mesmerized and haunted by everything he didn't remember ever seeing and hearing before.

It was as if he was in a completely new world.

He awoke to the sound of Lily and Ellizar starting a fire; cooking some fish they had caught in the river. To Drake's relief, he could remember everything that had happened the day before. Bits and pieces of memories stole his attention. Largely the memories were the same, filled with flashes of light and water.

They resumed their travels as soon as they finished their meal; for hours as the trail lazily meandered through woodlands and rolling countryside. Some of them were quite steep and resulted in Ellizar complaining about the weight of his helmet, to which Lily cheerfully suggested that he should leave it, and perhaps a wild animal would find it a suitable home.

Lily and Ellizar were a funny pair to observe. They both laughed and carried on as though they were family, though they seemed as different as night and day. Drake watched them closely, wondering just how these two had become friends.

"Smells like we're getting close," Lily concluded.

Drake took a sniff of the air, unable to detect the smell of smoke.

"I don't smell anything."

"Elves have several abilities that are *unnatural*," Ellizar replied with a ridiculous expression. Drake laughed at him.

"Perhaps Elves have better senses than we do?"

"I think she's bluffing," Ellizar said, now in a whisper. "Better senses, bah! She can't smell a fire from this far away."

"I can hear what you're saying," Lily piped in.

"Blasted elf kind! How in the world can yeh possibly hear that?"

"She's Elvish," Drake pointed out. Ellizar frowned. "Where are we going, and can you actually smell it?"

"Fiori, and yes I can," Lily remarked confidently, striding ahead.

"She can't smell nothin'," Ellizar whispered, quieter this time.

Drake didn't respond, as they walked for another half hour. His attention was divided between listening to Lily and Ellizar, and taking in the beautiful scenery. Finally, they came over the crest of the a great hill.

Below, a hundred brick buildings were neatly arranged in the valley. Small trails of smoke wafted from the various shops and houses. The air was cool and the breeze was light. Children happily played in the streets and everyone carried on taking no notice of the travelers on the ridge.

Lily Turned to face both of them.

"This is it," Lily said, sounding more wearied than pleased. "Point of no return."

"Is something wrong?" he asked. Lily sighed heavily, and Ellizar seemed to understand whatever she was feeling.

"Fiori is a very...interesting town," Lily answered. "Try to keep your palm from sight as much as possible."

"What is so unique about this insignia? If you don't mind me asking."

"My town won't likely welcome it," Lily told him, her voice still filled with apprehension. "Also, Drake, let's not tell anyone about your second name right now. You're from Jermin like Ellie here."

"That's Ellizar yeh blasted elf! Make sure that yeh get that right when yeh introduce me!"

"And you behave," Lily warned. "My people are just as afraid of Dwarves as they are of Men. You blow this and I'll be calling you Ellie for the rest of your days."

"Yeh already call me Ellie. It can't be that much worse," Ellizar pointed out. "Don't worry I'll behave, teh the best of my ability."

"You two are interesting, the way you argue," Drake observed.

Ellizar and Lily both gave him a questioning look.

"We're not arguing," Lily stated.

"If you're not arguing then what are you doing?"

"Well let me put yer heart at rest Drake, we are not arguin'," Ellizar declared. He turned to Lily. "What are we doin'?"

"We're....pointlessly debating?" Lily suggested.

Ellizar laughed and nodded. "Yeah, that's it! We're pointlessly debatin'. If we were truly arguin' then yeh would know it."

They entered into Fiori, which consisted almost entirely of Elves. The bright colorful eyes and the pointed ears were the clearest identifiers. Drake quickly noticed their skin to be smoother and their hair to have a sheen to it. Their walk was distinct and they carried themselves with poise and stature, no matter their age.

Lily in contrast, did not look as though she belonged in the town. The hem of her dress was covered in soil from their travels, and her hair was slightly rougher by the standards of Fiori. Despite all this, she walked confidently and the Elves of the little village seemed weary and worn down by some great burden.

There were a few Men in the town, but, they appeared even more burdened than the Elves.

As they continued their way through the little town, it became evident that they were attracting a great number of glances and stares, from the hard judgmental eyes of the people. Ellizar walked stiffly, seeming both shy and timid, which Drake perceived was not normal. Discerning their unease, Lily paused in her stride and took each of them by the arm.

"You're doing good boys," Lily whispered, forcing a smile to her lips. "Seldom have new faces come into Fiori since it was built twenty years ago. I moved away five years ago."

"Is that a good thing or a bad thing?" Drake questioned.

"You might find that my family and I don't quite see eye to eye."

"Wonderful, so we're going teh be in the middle ov a war zone?" Ellizar asked.

"Let's just say it's a good thing you brought your axe," Lily commented.

"Yeh see, it *is* a good thing I came along...fer protection purposes that is."

"I heartily agree. Perhaps, my family will be more civil, if I have guests with me. Although, Lathon knows they wouldn't approve of me bringing home a dwarf and a man."

"Why wouldn't they?" Drake asked.

The question was never answered as they continued on their way. The whispered and hushed tones of the conversations seemed to intensify. Mostly they spoke Elvish, but that did little to curb Drake and Ellizar's unease.

"Why are they starin' at us?" Ellizar asked.

"I think it's your four-foot height," Drake remarked. Lily smiled and Ellizar frowned.

"Yeh stick out just as much as I do!" Ellizar exclaimed.

"Alright boys, behave. We're almost there."

They rounded what Drake thought was the last corner and instead came to a broad road, lined entirely with Anil Trees in full bloom. The blossoms were full of vibrant purples and blues and a sweet aroma lay over the lane.

At the end, a large mansion lay waiting. Three stories tall, and twice as wide as it was tall, the wealth and splendor of this estate was not in question. A dozen different kinds of flowers bordered a meticulously designed path that led to the grand entrance. Once the flowers reached the threshold they split in two and wrapped around the manor. The grass was green and a wooden picket fence enclosed the entire property. The throng of people who had followed, now surrounded them, lining the fence and remaining silent.

After a moment of agonizing silence, the richly decorated doors silently opened, and three people stepped out into the warm sunlight. The gathered crowd seemed to hold their breath as their footsteps echoed on the stone courtyard.

The first was a taller elf with shorter black hair and eyes that could cut through the most powerful darkness like a knife. His expressions were hard and calloused and watched each of them with a suspicious eye. The elf moved to the side and a woman (who Drake assumed must be his wife) moved forward and examined the three of them with the same calloused expressions.

Drake shifted his attention to the person who followed behind. Her hair was an auburn color and her eyes were sparkling green. After a moment he caught of glimpse of her ears, which were not pointed. In the silence, she shifted anxiously and as she caught his glance, he perceived that she was not treated kindly.

The woman was wordlessly commanded to come forward. Without speaking or making eye contact of any kind, she opened the picketed gate for her two masters.

The Elves exited their estate and the crowd watched with anticipation. At once the two Elves smiled wide and then began laughing. They embraced Lily, who seemed taken aback by the affection. They turned her to face the throng of people that had gathered.

"Ladies and Gentlemen of Fiori! I present my daughter. Lillyana!" The male elf said. The crowd cheered and then quieted down. "Our daughter has come home, and tonight we will celebrate her unexpected return. Songs will be sung and many tales will be told! Certainly, with her guests, there is be a most riveting explanation!" A few chuckles went through the crowd and Drake could see that Lily was trying to stay composed. "Tonight we feast and dance such as this town has never seen! Be here tonight at eight o'clock, for a party that won't soon be forgotten!"

The people cheered and happily dispersed, not turning another glance to the three new arrivals.

They turned back around as the man left his daughter and stood next to his wife. The woman with the auburn hair stood a few paces behind the two of them, looking at the ground.

"This is a sight I thought I would never see!" her father exclaimed, smiling from ear to ear. "The word was brought by a servant that my Lillyana was coming through the streets, but I did not believe until I could see it with my own eyes."

"Better is the one who believes without seeing," Drake blurted out before he had time to think. Drake held his breath, but for the moment it seemed as if the comment had been unheard.

"Never in our lives did we think we'd see you return to us." They embraced their daughter again.

"Yes. Well, we're only here for a visit," Lily said as they separated. Immediately, the smile disappeared from her father's face.

"Only a visit?" her father asked sternly. Lily nodded. "I was hopeful you had given up your foolish ways."

"We can stay for a couple of months and then we must be getting back before winter comes."

"Yes, I suppose," her father said rather dismissively. "However, I wish I had known this before I promised to host a party. I have no real interest in throwing a celebration for a family member that is dead to me."

"I'm sorry you feel that way, Father."

"Let alone bringing two strangers with you!" her mother snapped.

"You would have no problems if they were Elven," Lily said.

Her mother frowned. "If that was the case, we would hope that you were getting married to a wealthy Elvish Lord who could talk you out of the delusional state that you're in. May these months go quickly, so you can return to your fairy tale land."

A tear slipped out of Lily's eyes as her father and mother stared at her with more contempt and prejudice than Drake ever thought possible. If looks could have killed he was certain that Lily would be dead. They turned their attention to her traveling companions.

"Who are they?"

"These are my friends, Ellizar and Drake." The man and the woman shook their heads in disapproval.

"I wish I could say it was a pleasure," the woman replied. "My name is Brida and this is my husband Rulov. This is our slave Gwen." She pointed to the auburn-haired girl who was fighting back tears. "She will do whatever you ask, but conversing with her is forbidden. We don't need your poison filling her mind as well."

"We didn't come to argue with you over philosophy or religion we came to visit and have a good time. We aren't going to try and argue with you," Lily stated.

"Good, I suggest you keep it that way. Your father and I have a reputation to uphold."

Without speaking, the two of them turned and motioned for Gwen to follow. The auburn-haired woman looked sorrowfully at them. She gave a weak smile. The three of them were left alone as the trio entered into the mansion.

They began walking around to the back until they came to a small covered gazebo, which was also bordered with flowers. They sat down on a wooden bench, while Lily sat on the railing.

"Congratulations, you made it through meeting my family."

"A bitter bunch, aren't they?" Ellizar asked.

Lily nodded. "They've never approved since I left."

"What's so bad about what you believe?" Drake inquired.

"Our religious views are vastly different. Mine, as well as Ellizar's, are based on the ancient scrolls and teachings of the prophets of Lathon. All Elves used to believe in them, but in certain parts of the world, the teachings are taught as myths rather than facts. Some Dwarves, Giants, Men, and Elves still believe though. Most of them live in the Elven nation of Ariamore. I'd love to live there someday. Ellizar and I still believe in the ancient scrolls and prophets."

"But your family doesn't?"

"Correct. My family, first settled this town to remove us from the teachings of Lathon. They gave up believing that the words of the prophets would come true. Since then they have tried to earn their way into the hearts of Men, which are normally quite bitter towards Elves."

"Why?"

Lily shook her head. "I'm not entirely sure, but the two races have never peacefully coexisted. They will be united one day, but not for a while."

"The two races will be united?" Drake asked confused. "I might not know too much, but it seems like thousands of years of anger and hatred couldn't just be melted in a matter of years."

"You're right and you're wrong," Lily replied. "Do you know anything about that scar on your hand?" Drake shook his head. "That, Drake Thomas, is no ordinary scar. There is a lot more to the story and a lot more we can't explain."

"I don't understand," he said with a weak smile. "Don't suppose there's a chance you could educate me on this matter. Does it have anything to do with your parents and their beliefs?"

"Let's just say we don't want them to notice. I wish there was more time right now, but we'd better try and fix things with my parents so we don't feel like exiles the entire time we're here."

"You will tell me right?"

"Yes, we'll tell you, but for now cover it with a piece of cloth," Lily answered. "Perhaps tomorrow morning when everyone else is drunk and sleeping, the three of us can explain it to you."

"Three of us?"

"The slave, Gwen, thinks the same that we do except she is unable to leave because my parents have not released her from their service. If she left without their permission she would forfeit her life."

"Yer family sounds like a happy bunch," Ellizar replied, grimly.

"Oh yes, we're just one big happy family."

"I'm glad to learn yer full name."

"Please, call me Lily. Lillyana puts a bad taste in my mouth."

Ellizar nodded. "We are not yer parents, but I understand all the same."

After a while Lily gave them a tour of the grounds. The entire place was immaculate and meticulously cared for, with each new section prettier than the previous one. Woods and a river stood as a border against the entire estate and in the field just behind the manor they could see the beginnings of the preparations for dinner that was supposedly for them.

The treatment Drake and Ellizar received upon entering the manor was hardly worth noting, in fact, the two of them felt like they didn't exist at all. Feeling like unwanted baggage, they kept to themselves and shared stories and lore to pass the time. Drake's contribution to the conversation was limited as he only remembered a few things of interest and even those tales seemed distant and unreachable.

Lily did her best to mingle with her family but still came back every so often, trying to make them all feel better about the current situation. The more they tried to fit in the more it seemed like they were shunned for trying to do so.

Drake felt like an unwanted piece of baggage and after that encounter neither he nor Ellizar could find anything to say, choosing instead to blend into the surroundings as Lily's mother and father came and went, paying the three of them no mind.

The servant Gwen came by every once and a while and looked at all three of them, a glimmer in her eye. She was suffering just as much as they were and it became clear, she couldn't speak to them without being ordered to. Anger began to fill Drake as he watched the servants and housekeepers walk by, forced to keep quiet and not say anything.

In the backyard, an enormous tent was erected. The peak itself was twenty feet high, and how they had managed to construct it so quickly, he hadn't a clue. It was white with red coverings on the poles that stuck into the ground. On the edges of the canvas, deep purple patterns added some color, while still a large insignia of a sort, adorned in deep oranges and reds, covered the top inside and out.

When it was finished, they were told that the tent was so large that the entire town would be able to sit beneath it, with plenty of room for a dance floor, food, and all the servants and staff that Lily's parents owned.

Having been given some fancy clothes, he felt more presentable than he had earlier. Lily's black hair was done up nicely and she wore a thin light blue dress that seemed to compliment her.

Ellizar had brought some nicer clothes with him and looked quite well, if not a little unnatural without his helmet on.

Despite having been shunned for most of the day, the townspeople, who had no idea what had happened in the Manor after they had gone back to work, were friendlier to them, though still distant.

Ellizar, Lily, and Drake sat at a table near the outside of the pavilion watching the crowd, feeling as though they couldn't join the festivities for fear of ruining them.

"This has to be the worst party I've ever been at," Ellizar said to Drake in a light whisper.

"Me too, and I don't remember having ever been to any parties before this."

"I'm just glad that my parents let us do this much," Lily said. "Granted, they only continued with the party because of public ridicule if they didn't, but at least we get to be dressed up and sit here. I feel a little more welcomed than I did earlier."

"If there's ever a day when I can fix this kind of treatment then I'm going to do it," Drake stated. The others looked at him surprised. "Even if it's the last thing I do."

"If yeh try anythin' now I can pretty much guarantee it'll be the last thing yeh do. People will throw yeh out ov here faster than yeh can run," Ellizar replied.

"Let's not stay out too late; Gwen said she'd meet us down by the river tomorrow morning, and then we'll discuss what needs to be discussed."

"She's allowed to come talk to us?" Drake asked.

"Yes," Lily answered. "But only because everyone else is drunk and sleeping off the party. Gwen and I would often meet down by the river before anyone else is up. Despite how my parents treat her we've been good friends for years."

"You're friends with a dwarf, a man with no memory, and a slave?" Drake asked. "Some would say you have interesting choice in friends."

"So they would," Lily concluded. Drake turned his attention to Gwen who stood on the North side, serving drinks and food alike. She was dressed in a bland outfit of beige that was identical to every other servant's outfit.

The servants did their job but no one seemed to notice or care as they drank their wine and ate their food, shunning all they didn't care to approve of. Drake's blood boiled as he watched the servants and the way they were being treated.

No one should be judged because of their station, or in Drake's case because he wasn't an elf. He thought about his past. wondering if he had been like these people in any way. He desperately hoped not.

"Come Ellizar, we must dance!"

"Dance? Bah! What kind ov a dwarf would I be? I couldn't be caught dancin', let alone with an elf. What a ridiculous idea!"

"You're coming then?" Lily asked, standing.

"Yes I'm comin'," Ellizar said. She extended a hand to him.

Drake couldn't help but laugh. "So much for it being a ridiculous idea." Ellizar shrugged his shoulders.

"If yeh can't beat them join them!" Ellizar took her hand and led her into the dance floor. Drake smiled to see the two of them with her being at least two feet taller than he was. Still, at least they had someone to share their good times with.

Drake searched over the happy crowd, hopeful that at least one would catch his attention and trigger a part of his memory. Right now he felt like he was alone in this world. Granted Lily and Ellizar had gone out of their way to make him feel accepted. If nothing else, he was glad to have at least two friends in this world he didn't remember.

The flap of the tent moved and it seemed no one noticed a man joining the celebration. He searched through the masses of people, with a stoic expression on his face.

Gwen strode to the man and offered him a drink but then seemed to speak to him. She had her back turned to Drake so he couldn't even hope to read her lips, and he wasn't close enough to hear what was being said.

He rose from his spot, weaving his way through the people, they hushed themselves as he came close, making his curiosity even greater.

"Good evening, sir. Is it not a wonderful night?" the man asked, holding a hand out. Drake shook his hand, looking into the man's eyes and wishing that he would recognize this man. The man stood just a little taller than Drake with a neatly groomed beard and nicely combed hair, both of which were graying.

"Yes, it is," Drake replied. "I was hoping to talk to someone. Most people here seem to ignore me."

"Yes they tend to do that to people like us," the man said.

"Like us?" Drake asked.

"Those who are not of the Elven race," the man answered. Drake's eyes moved to his ears, noticing that they weren't pointed like everyone else's were.

"Where are my manners, my name is Rohemir. Rohemir of Hammna."

"Drake Thomas," he said. A light grew in both Rohemir's and Gwen's eyes as they heard his name.

"Drake Thomas?" Rohemir asked, saying the name aloud as though he was searching his memory. "That's an unusual name. Are you from around here?"

"I'm new to these parts."

"As am I. I have met Ms. Gwen but other than that, I'm afraid I don't know a soul here," Rohemir said.

"Yet you still came?" Drake asked.

Rohemir nodded. "I do love a good party. Mostly I came because I fear there is something that's going to happen."

"What do you mean?" Gwen asked softly. Drake couldn't help but notice how pleasant her voice was.

"I'm not exactly sure," Rohemir answered. "All I know is that I like to be where things are happening, so I can help out in any way I can. People can think just about anything if the situation is right. I like to be there to set people straight if you take my meaning."

"I don't, but I'll take your word on that," he replied.

Rohemir excused himself and left him and Gwen standing together. "How do you know him?"

"I meet up with him every once and a while and he brings me scrolls and books from a library. Please don't tell anyone! Servants aren't allowed to read and write and if they find out I could be killed-"

"Gwen!" Brida scolded from a distance. "Stop talking and get away from that man now or we'll have you lashed within an inch of your life!"

"Sorry my lady," Gwen responded, lowering her head. "Please don't tell them anything I told you."

"I won't tell anyone. I've got my own secrets to worry about."

"Your name right?" He nodded.

"Gwen!" Brida reprimanded. Gwen's smile disappeared and she immediately shrunk back and resumed her work.

For the next few minutes, Drake wandered around the festivities listening to some of the conversations that were being said, most of which were about him and Ellizar. Though not *all* of the conversations were bad, the vast majority didn't exactly make him feel comfortable.

After a while, he spotted another man looking at him from the far corner. The man casually sipped a glass of wine. His hair was nicely combed but his wardrobe seemed to suggest that he hadn't bought any new clothes recently.

Perplexed by his appearance, Drake made his way over to the man, who at once looked away.

"Excuse me sir, but could I sit down?" Drake asked.

"It would be an honor," the man replied, looking up from his glass of wine. Drake puzzled over the man's choice of words "How are you doing this evening?"

"Not bad," Drake answered, shaking the man's hand and sitting down. "Do you live around here? I'm not sure I've seen you before just a couple of minutes ago, and I've been here all day."

"That's because I haven't been here all day. I just showed up about ten minutes ago. I had a feeling that this is where I needed to be."

"What's your name?" Drake asked feeling a little uneasy.

"My name?" the man asked. A smile came across the man's face and a strange light entered his eye. "It seems I can't remember it at the moment."

"You can't remember your name?"

"My name's not important. However, who you associate yourselves with *is* important. I saw you were talking to a man named Rohemir."

"So I was."

"He is not a pleasant fellow," the man said. "If you knew his past you might not want to be a part of his circle of friends."

"I don't understand," Drake admitted, the man smiled.

"He's a murderer," the man explained. "Murdered more people than I can count; seen it with my own eyes. He killed my brother, my entire family."

"Murdered your family? Why would he do a thing like that?"

"It doesn't matter, it still doesn't change who or what he is. I would like nothing more than to kill him right here and now, but I must wait for the time to be right if I have any hope of living to tell about it. If he has any idea of my plan I'm dead right from the beginning."

"It seems you couldn't be more right," a voice said from behind the two of them. Drake turned to see Rohemir standing at the side of the table. He couldn't help but notice a dagger, made of solid gold, concealed beneath Rohemir's robe.

The man staggered out of his seat vanishing into the crowd.

"Do you know who that man was?" Drake asked.

Rohemir nodded. "Yes, but I do not wish to know him. If I'm right he'll be back and when he does you'd better flee. People like him don't deserve to live."

"He said you had murdered his family. Is that true?" Drake asked. Rohemir didn't say anything else and Drake wouldn't have noticed if he had. Just to their right, A beautiful young woman came into the tent. Her hair was golden and flowing and she wore an exquisite yellow dress. As she approached, she bowed in the customary way. Drake was immediately taken by her beauty.

"The night is young, sir," the woman greeted. "Would you care for a dance?" She held out her hand.

"Don't take her hand," Rohemir whispered. Drake looked at Rohemir seeing a strange light in his eyes.

"Why not?" the woman asked. "Is he not allowed to dance with whoever he chooses?"

"Not if it means he's dancing with death," Rohemir answered. He stood and drew his dagger. The woman shifted uncomfortably and backed away. She looked at Drake with an anxious expression.

"What's going on?" Drake asked, positioning himself between the lady and Rohemir.

Drake was thrown aside by Rohemir who lunged at the lady with his weapon. Drake was blinded by a searing light. The woman had produced her own knife from the folds of her dress and had stopped Rohemir's blade from piercing her.

The music abruptly stopped. Panic took hold, as guests ran and screamed. Rohemir grabbed Drake by the collar, lifted him to his feet, and shoved him toward the exit.

"Get out!" Rohemir yelled. Drake scrambled out of the tent and around the corner, watching through the crowd of people as Rohemir and the woman fought viciously. Rohemir thrust his dagger forward and pierced her breast.

Light poured from the woman's chest, getting brighter and brighter with each second that passed. Rohemir grasped the knife and out-muscled the woman, twisting the knife as he did.

The woman screamed and the voice changed until it was that of a man. Drake blinked to make sure his eyes weren't playing tricks on him as a fog surrounded the woman and she transformed from the beautiful woman she had been to the man that Drake had been talking with before Rohemir had arrived.

The man cursed Rohemir, struggling to keep Rohemir from pushing the knife in any further. The light coming from the man's chest increased and then began to spread over his body as if it was starting to break out from his skin.

The man vanished into a cloud of fog and mist that had a bluish color to it, spreading through the tent. It wound its way around the people and between their feet, none of whom seemed to notice it.

The mist and fog moved past Drake, and In an instant, the fog came back together, taking the form of the man once again. He pulled the golden knife from his chest and dropped it on the ground. In the blink of an eye, the strange man mounted a horse and was lost from sight.

Drake crawled over to the knife. The blade glowed and steam rose from it. Unable to resist, Drake reached for the blade but was stopped as Rohemir placed a foot on the weapon. Without speaking Rohemir grabbed the knife and began walking away.

"What just happened?" Drake asked.

"Your life was just saved," Rohemir answered. "Stay out of sight and try not to cause too much trouble! The man won't be back for a while now. He's been wounded beyond his own repair." Rohemir began walking away again.

"Are you a murderer like he said?" Drake asked.

"Judging people does not define who they are, it defines who you are. Do not be so quick to judge people or come to a decision."

Rohemir mounted a horse nearby and rode away. Drake was startled from his thoughts as Lily and Ellizar ran up behind him, soon followed by Gwen.

"What just happened?" Lily asked.

Gwen looked in the direction Rohemir had departed. "We'll find out in the morning."

A CONSPIRACY REVEALED

Drake was shaken awake. He opened his eyes, looking into a face he didn't recognize. The man was tall and though he had the pointed ears of an elf, something didn't seem to fit.

"Come, you must go now!" the man said. He hardly had a moment to react as the man grabbed him by the collar of his shirt and pulled him out of the bed.

"What's going on?" Drake asked frantically. The man threw clothes at him and then looked out the window.

"There is a great danger coming and I am sent to make sure you get out of here alive!" the man exclaimed, striding to the other side of the room.

"Who are you?"

"You may call me Michael," the man answered abruptly. "No more questions, just do as I say and I'll keep you alive."

"I don't understand," Drake cried out.

"I know!" Michael exclaimed. "Come!" Drake hesitated, looking out the window, trying to see the threat that Michael felt.

"Come now!"

Drake still hesitated. Michael strode forward and pulled him by the collar again. He shoved him out the door and down the hall of the third story. A moment later the room he had been staying in erupted in flames. Within seconds fire was quickly spreading through the hall.

Explosions shook the house and soon multiple fires were burning out of control. Michael stayed behind him, urging him forward. Blue mist, like had been seen at the party rapidly moved through the fire.

"Get to the river!" Michael ordered. "Do not go into town! I repeat do not go through the town! Go!"

In an instant, the blue mist raced towards the stairs and took the form of a cloaked warrior. Michael jumped in the way, fighting off the attacker with skills that Drake could only envy. A moment later the cloaked warrior had been forced off of the stairs, clearing the way for Drake.

Heeding Michael's warning, Drake descended the flight of stairs to the second level. More explosions shook the mansion and within seconds flames had cut off his route to the next flight of stairs.

He jumped the railing, dropping to the ground floor. Ellizar appeared out of a flame-filled room, he struggled to walk under the weight of an unconscious Lily he carried over one shoulder.

"Ellizar!" Drake called. Ellizar looked in his direction and relief passed over his face. "Allow me!"

With a single motion, he swung Lily over his shoulders and they ran out of the mansion.

"Where do we go?" Ellizar asked. Horror came over them as the sky was shrouded in blue mist, every one of them rapidly descending towards the manor. A moment later the blue mist struck the manor without mercy.

Michael's words came to his mind. "To the river. Get to the river!"

"That's going to be a hard task!" Ellizar cried out. In front of them as far as the eye could see, a line of grey formed as a vile sort of creature methodically began approaching the manor which was fully enveloped in flames.

Drake and Ellizar ran around the building to the front, but they were not comforted by the sight that awaited them there either. Thick black smoke billowed from the town beyond the trees and more of the wretched beasts closed in on the mansion.

"Drake!" They looked to see Gwen in a barn to the side of the burning mansion. They made for the barn and Gwen hastily closed the door once they were in.

"Is Lily alright?" Gwen asked. He laid Lily on the ground, her black hair was singed and part of her dress was badly scorched. Drake lowered his head to her chest, hearing her heartbeat.

"She'll live," he said. "Ellizar see if you can wake her up. We're safe for the moment, but not for long!" Drake moved to the door where Gwen was looking out through a crack. The yard around the house was now overrun with strange grey creatures. On their hands and feet, they had long cruel claws and their features were angular and harsh.

"Borags," Drake said through gritted teeth.

"Never heard of them."

"I've only seen them a couple of times. They're far and few between at home."

"Where is that?"

"Don't remember," he admitted, pausing as he realized he *did* know what these creatures were. "What is this place?"

"The stables," Gwen answered, embarrassment staining her voice. "I'm not allowed to sleep in the house."

"Praise Lathon, she's awake!" Ellizar exclaimed. He held Lily tightly, helping her to sit up.

"What's going on?" Lily asked.

"I have no idea, but we need to leave," Drake answered. Lily stood to her feet.

"Gwen, get some horses ready!" Lily called out. "Ellizar come with me!"

Lily and Ellizar disappeared to the back of the stables while Drake and Gwen quickly saddled two horses. Ellizar and Lily came back moments later with weapons.

"Where did you get these?" Gwen asked.

"My father always kept a secret stash, in case they were needed!" Lily exclaimed. They each took whatever they knew how to use. Gwen grabbed a simple bow and a short knife, while Lily took a sword and a recurve bow. Drake claimed one of everything, strapping them to himself within moments.

They mounted their horses, Gwen with him and Ellizar with Lily.

"Where should we go?" Gwen asked.

"The river!" Drake exclaimed.

"What about the town?" Lily asked.

"The town is destroyed."

"Destroyed?" Lily asked in disbelief. The door opened on the barn and Michael came through, leaving the door wide open."Yes, and you will be too if you do not leave now!"

Drake spurred his horse forward and Lily rode alongside. They turned sharply to the left and galloped towards the forest. The Borags were now huddled around the manor and the town, blind to the fact that anyone had been in the stables.

They entered the thick woods that led to the river. Beneath the canopy of leaves, the forest was dark and cool, unaware of the chaos behind them. The ground was bare, with minimal vegetation except for a lone fern or small tree that had taken root.

A few more minutes later they came alongside a river that flowed gently and calmly. They rode for nearly an hour in complete silence before they stopped. They dismounted and remained silent for a while longer as the gravity of the situation fell on them.

"Do you think anyone survived?" Lily asked.

"Not likely," Drake answered. Lily wept bitterly into Ellizar's embrace. Even from where they were the sky was dimmed by smoke that rose high into the sky.

"Lathon be praised that we made it out!" Ellizar exclaimed. "I thought I had lost you all."

"I didn't think I would see any of you again," Gwen remarked. "I admit I stayed in my barn because I was afraid for my life."

"We're alive now, that's the bigger point," Drake encouraged, though the words felt empty to him.

They led their horses along the winding river for some time, each lost in their thoughts. As if they had fallen under some kind of spell, the birds fell silent, numbing him to everything around them.

Drake flexed his hand, which was now growing cold. It became white and slowly turned to ice. He tried to speak but found himself unable as the cold numbed his mind and began to consume his body. He walked and stumbled, falling to his knees.

Lily turned and ran to him, crying out to him, but he found he couldn't hear anything she said.

The sounds of the world around him were muted and distant. A soothing voice penetrated his mind. The voice was dark and seductive and spoke in a language that he couldn't comprehend, but still, the words resonated in his heart.

The world around him vanished and faded before coming to him again. This time he was looking down on himself and the others, from the sky, as though he were in someone else's body.

His vision returned to his own as a cloud of blue mist struck the ground in front of them. Their horses were frightened and ran from the scene. Both Lily and Drake were paralyzed with fear as they stared at their attacker, cloaked and hooded. He held a sword in one hand and a dagger in the other.

Ellizar gave a great cry and sprung forward, axe in hand. Their attacker seemed to smirk at the dwarf and instantly Ellizar fell to the ground unconscious.

Their attacker drew back his arm and threw a knife towards them. Lily and Drake dove out of the way, and it landed harmlessly in the mud of the river bank.

An arrow flew overhead but it passed right through the man as though he wasn't there. Gwen had shot the arrow, but before they were aware, another dagger appeared in the man's hands and he threw it at her.

The blade pierced her arm. Instantly, Gwen's eyes faded and rolled back in her head and she collapsed on the ground. They were forced to turn their attention to the veiled attacker who approached with yet another knife in hand.

The same foul voice from earlier entered Drake's head again.

A knife was thrown from behind them and shimmered in the grey light. The dagger was gold like the one that had been used the night before. It struck into their attacker's chest, instead of going through as the arrow had.

The warrior cried out, unable to remove the weapon. Light flooded from the point of impact. The light grew brighter and a small explosion filled the shoreline. The wall of air from the explosion was greater than they expected, sending them tumbling backward where they toppled onto the ground.

Drake's sight and hearing returned, the voice disappeared from his head, and warmth flooded back into their souls. Lily lay a hundred feet downriver from him, while Gwen was lying on her back with a knife sticking out of her arm.

Drake and Ellizar scrambled to their feet. He was able to easily move now that the cold had vanished. Ellizar hurried to Lily's side.

Drake knelt next to Gwen. Her face was white and her skin was cold. Her eyes were covered with a dark blue film and foam bubbled from her mouth. She gasped for each breath. He reached for the handle of the knife but when he touched the handle, fire consumed his mind and he was thrown twenty feet backward. Lily scrambled towards Gwen.

"Don't!" Drake yelled, stopping Lily. "Don't touch it."

"Why not?" Ellizar asked

"Trust me, it's not normal!" he exclaimed.

"It looks normal!" Ellizar replied.

"He's right!" They turned to see a man standing behind them. He was fairly tall with a graying beard and hair. His eyes were kind and he wore a robe. Drake recognized him as Rohemir, the man from the night before. "That is no ordinary dagger. If you touch it you will be killed."

"It didn't kill me," Drake pointed out.

"You only held it for a second. Hold it for much longer and you'll die, unless, of course, you are different from the ordinary person." They exchanged looks.

"How do we get it out of her arm if we can't touch it?" Ellizar asked. Rohemir came forward.

"Carefully," Rohemir answered. He reached into a pocket of his robe, grabbing a stick from it.

"How are you going to get it out of her arm with that little stick?" he asked. Rohemir looked at him and smiled.

"Sorcerery does have some uses." Rohemir pointed the wand to Gwen's arm and the dagger promptly removed itself. Rohemir ripped off a piece of his cloak and laid it on the ground, where it was set down. Rohemir covered it at once and looked at Gwen's arm.

"Can you do anything to help her?" Lily asked

"This cut is worse than I can heal," Rohemir concluded, after a minute of examining the wound. "I can heal the skin, but I am powerless against the poison. I'm not sure how far the poison has gone into her blood."

"Poison?" Ellizar asked.

"I've come across only three blades like this in my time. The blade is Borag made. If you aren't a scholar of Borag forgery, they have discovered the secrets of crafting indestructible blades."

"Nothing is indestructible," Lily replied. "Everything has a breaking point of some kind."

"I wish I could find the breaking point of these daggers. They are a weapon from a bygone age," Rohemir started. "They are made from the hardest sort of metal I have come by. Seemingly immune to heat as well as destructive forms of Magic. How you destroy them I'm not sure. If the blade pierces your skin it will eventually kill you."

"How is yours different?" Drake asked. The image of the golden dagger was burned in his mind.

"My dagger kills the body and entraps the spirit of the person inside. Here they can do no harm except to each other."

"You mean the attackers live?"

"Within the blade, yes," Rohemir stated, with a rather grim tone to his voice. "Though their flesh is destroyed, their souls live on." Small amounts of chatter could be heard, it was still unintelligible but all of them knew that it came from the dagger. "The attacker at the party last night was not destroyed. He was a Spirit and it takes more to kill them because they can take any shape or any form. They could turn into a tree and wait for you if they wanted. Some Spirits are weaker than others and don't take as long to kill, which is why this Spirit was promptly destroyed."

"They live within the blade forever?" Lily asked, unbelieving. "Isn't there a way to destroy them for good?" Lily asked.

"None that I've found," Rohemir answered. "I've tried every bit of alchemy that I can think of."

"Magic as you use it is frowned upon by the Elves," Lily said.

"I don't use it lightly. To use necromancy, in any form, offers your soul to something other than yourself and certainly something other than Lathon, but if used sparingly and carefully it does come in handy. For example, I would not have been able to remove the weapon from Gwen's arm had I not used sorcery. She would have died and now she has the chance to live. I use such devices for emergencies only, and even then I am very cautious."

Lily fell silent and Drake still sensed there was more she wanted to argue.

"What's going to happen to her?" Lily asked. Gwen's auburn hair fell to one side. Her skin and lips were colorless.

"The poison of these daggers works slowly. The victim will stay exactly like she is now. Each day that passes a part of her heart and soul will fade from her eyes. She will be tormented by visions that only she can see. She will be able to see them but she won't be able to stop them. This kind of healing is beyond my knowledge. Only the Elves can heal her the way she needs to be healed."

"Do yeh know ov anyone that might be able teh heal her?"

"I might," Rohemir said after thinking for a moment. "Either way you can't stay here, you must keep moving.

"Where are we supposed to go? We can't exactly go back!" Lily reminded in frustration.

"The nations of Men and Borags are of no protection to you. You have only one choice and that is to make your way to the Elven nation of Ariamore. They know the ancient prophecies and believe in them. You will be welcomed and protected."

"How long does it take to get there?" Lily asked.

"Longer than Gwen has I'm afraid. She has maybe two weeks, while it can take well over a month to get to Ariamore."

"What are we supposed to do, fly?" Lily snapped.

Rohemir thought for a moment. "I don't know. But you cannot stay here. She is not the only one who is in danger."

"What do yeh mean?" Ellizar asked.

"It's me isn't it?" Drake asked after a few moments of silence passed. "Does it have anything to do with this?" Drake showed his scar to Rohemir who seemed to ponder it for a moment.

"I believe it does," Rohemir answered, "But I can't be sure. Things like this are hard to explain. The recent events are even more complex."

"It is about me," Drake decided. "I'm sure of it."

"You're sure of it?" Rohemir asked sounding interested. "How can you be sure of it?" Drake hesitated, the images of a dream flashing in his mind.

"I just know," he stated. "Even now I have a vision. The kind that feels so real it just might be. I see a veiled, shadowy figure. He wants me dead. I know it."

"But how can one understand one's dreams?" Rohemir asked. "Few can understand dreams for what they are. Who says you interpret it correctly?"

"Because above the cloaked figure is one who is greater. He's uncloaked, a great staff is in his hand. The light shines from him. It is he who is speaking to all of us."

Rohemir sat up straighter as if understanding something he hadn't previously. Silence passed between them and they watched Rohemir closely. Finally, he spoke.

A vision shall fill his eyes,
And a whisper shall fill his head
A light that walks the darkness
Will light the path ahead.

Though the world shall be blind,
This one man shall see
Shedaros on his throne,
As he is meant to be.

The world will despise them both
But continue on they must
Or else everything dear to them shall fade to dust.
The Will of Lathon they must trust.

"The words I have just said were long told by the ancient prophets about the coming of one who would recognize Shedaros for who he really was. This is your prophecy."

"My prophecy?" Drake questioned. "I can't have a prophecy, I'm just a normal person."

"No you aren't," Rohemir corrected. "That scar on your hand proves that you are no ordinary person. The events of the past several days only back up my claim! That mark on your hand is the symbol of Lathon. No one receives it by accident. It has the power to make you famous or despised by the people of the Earth, it has the power to change the way people think."

"I'm not even sure how I got it, all I know is it's there."

"Perhaps I can shed some light on the subject," Rohemir stood and began pacing in front of them. Gwen's gasping and breathing had steadied some now, but she was still as white as a ghost and as lifeless as a feather.

"Thousands of years ago there was a great elf king named Lathon. In those days the world was perfect and as such there was a need for only one king. Fast forward nearly a hundred years and it was nearing the end of the First Age and there was a great war between the people of the ancient world.

"The world was then divided into two kingdoms. Elvish kind, and the kingdom of anyone who didn't agree with Lathon and the Elves. They named their nation Grimdor. Together the people who had separated themselves destroyed the land they had created, and it quickly became the desolate place that it is today. There is no vegetation, it is a forest of rock and dry land with an occasional stream that goes through it. The people of the Grimdor became lost beyond hope, having sworn their very hearts and souls to the person they follow."

"Who is that?"

"What his true name is I cannot guess. The visitors that came this morning, as well as the one who attacked you last night, were Spirits. Servants to the dark king of Grimdor, who keeps himself hidden behind the veil of darkness that he calls his home.

"Not much is known of whatever happened to their leader. After all this time people have come to assume he is dead, but I suspect that his Spirit wanderers the earth able to take form if he wishes.

"As the history unfolded Lathon became disappointed in the people of the land, hating what they had done to the paradise they had lived in. Lathon vanished in the night, promising to return to set things straight and rid the land of evil.

"People asked how they would know when he came and Lathon said that he would send an heir to take his place. He would be marked by the very symbol that is on your hand. Three slashes represent the three marks of history: the past, the present, and the future. Lathon also said he would come to the world in a way people wouldn't expect.

"I was there twenty-three years ago when this very child was discovered. Many people helped the child escape with his parents. Where they are now? I couldn't tell you."

"You're saying I'm Shedaros?"

"No! That's not what I'm saying at all. There were two prophecies, one about Shedaros himself, and one about the person who would first *recognize* Shedaros and lead the people to him. It is written that he will be the first to see what others have not. Together he and Shedaros will unite the land of Elves and Men and march against the armies of Grimdor who are building their forces once again."

"They think they are doing this in secret, but I know better. The Spirits last night and this morning must have learned of the mark on your hand and therefore have been assigned to kill you. To keep the Elvish prophecies from coming true. This is the only explanation that I can come up with for these events."

"What are we teh do?" Ellizar asked.

"Grimdor isn't far from here and if the Borags should choose to invade Epirus in hopes of finding you then nothing can stop them." Rohemir paced in front of them. "When you were attacked this morning did anything unusual happen to you?"

"The world went mute", Drake started, not wishing to relive the experience. "My head was filled with a voice that wasn't my own. I wanted to hide from it, but it still found me. Does that mean anything to you?"

"The only thing that I can conclude is that the voice you heard was the Spirit of the dark lord. He was telling himself what you looked like, your features, where you were located. If you were ever in danger you are in greater peril now. You must leave before something or someone can return to finish what this Spirit tried to do."

They were all silent, realizing what was being asked of them.

"Where do we go?" Drake asked.

"Are any of you familiar with the location of the town of Bucklebeary?" Rohemir asked.

"It's northeast, isn't it?" Lily asked.

"Yes. Go there and I will come with help shortly, someone who will know how to heal Gwen, for there are those who are better versed in the lore of herbs and medicine than I am.

"We will get some supplies and make way for Bucklebeary," Lily said.

"Good," Rohemir replied. "Keep to the country, go into towns only if you have to. Now, waste no more time, speed will be your best friend at this point."

UNEXPECTED ALLIES

After everything that had transpired in Fiori, the next five days felt like paradise. The wind rustled the branches of the trees gently and methodically. The air was warm but not hot, and at night it seemed to get no cooler than was comfortable. They kept to the river, occasionally going off the path and cutting across the countryside, dotted with charming little farms and villages. Lily claimed these were shortcuts although sometimes Drake wondered if it actually was.

Still, to her credit, they hadn't seen another Spirit since they had left Fiori.

Lily and Ellizar rode on one horse next to him, while Gwen remained in front of him, tied to the saddle to keep her from falling when Drake wasn't holding her. Her eyes were blank and lifeless and her skin grew colder by the day.

"What's that I smell?" Ellizar asked.

"Smoke," Drake said. Ellizar's face lit up.

"Does that mean we're gettin' closer teh this blasted town?"

"It's a possibility," Lily answered.

"Possibility?"

"I've never been there before. I know the general area but as far as an exact location I don't know it."

"Yeh bring us all this way and yeh don't even know where the town is?"

"We've got to be near," Lily reasoned.

"I'll be glad teh get off this beast. Never in my life have I traveled by horseback and if I have anythin' teh say about it, I never will again. It is unnatural fer a dwarf teh ride on a horse."

"It's unnatural for a dwarf to do anything that makes sense," Lily teased.

"I've had just about enough ov yeh," Ellizar started. "It's a wonder I've stuck around this long.

"Like you have any say in the matter," Lily teased.

"Drake! If we ever have teh travel by horse again I'm ridin' with yeh."

"Just relax Ellizar we're only trying to broaden your horizons," he replied.

"My horizons are broad enough."

"What is that up ahead?" Drake asked, pointing to an object.

"I wouldn't know, I can't see past the elf in front ov me," Ellizar remarked, trying to glance over her arm by leaning over.

"Looks like a boat's run aground," Lily observed. "Someone is lying on the shore."

"How can you see that?" Ellizar asked.

"Elf eyes are better than Dwarves?" she taunted. Ellizar frowned but seemed to smile with his eyes.

"Ah, I see him!"

Without warning the horse reared up, throwing Ellizar off. He tumbled to the ground, quickly stood, and brushed himself off. None of them could suppress a laugh.

"That was graceful," Lily said.

"Yeh paid the horse teh do that!"

"Of course not," she remarked, circling around and holding out her hand.

"If it's all the same teh yeh, I think I'll walk since we're hopefully close."

"Have it your way," Lily said. She turned and galloped next to Drake who was nearing the boat and the man. Ellizar muttered to himself and caught up to the two of them who had now dismounted their horses.

"Is he alive?" Ellizar asked.

"Yes, weak though," Lily replied.

"This doesn't make sense," Drake commented.

"Why not? He came from the boat," Ellizar reasoned.

"Kind of a strange place to run aground don't you think?" Drake asked. "The river's got to be twenty feet away from the boat."

"Strong storm?" Ellizar suggested.

"Possible, but the boat doesn't look like it was in a storm. The ground's not wet, there's no tree damage. Nothing. There's not even a sign that there's been any kind of rain."

"I don't even see footprints, aside from our own," Lily observed.

"Yeh sense a trap?" Ellizar asked, his hand gravitating to his axe.

"We should leave."

"What about him?" Lily asked. Without warning, the man who had been lying on the ground lunged at them, pulling a knife from his side. He swung at Lily, catching her across the chest. Lily clutched at her chest, her hand reddened with blood. The man swung again but she nimbly, twisted out of the way, grabbed hold of his arm, and twisted it back at him. The knife pierced the man's chest. He vanished into a cloud of blue mist, which scattered into the forest beyond.

"Spirits!" Drake cried. They mounted their steeds and were, soon thundering down the riverbank.

"How do you think they knew where we were?" Drake yelled.

"Maybe it has something to do with the poison that's affected Gwen? Maybe there's something in it that they can sense."

They both pushed their horses harder, noting that the smell of smoke that Ellizar had detected was getting stronger.

"We're going teh have company!" Ellizar exclaimed.

They looked behind, a stream of blue mist circling through the air. The Spirit hit the ground, taking the form of a horse and rider.

The rider pulled out a sword and ran alongside them. The Spirit swung at Drake but was unable to inflict any damage as he repeatedly blocked with his sword.

The trio of horses rounded the corner, Bucklebeary now in sight. A heavily reinforced wood wall was built around the town.

The rider dropped back and dissipated into a cloud of blue mist once again. It flew past them and burrowed into the ground, sending chunks of dirt flying into the air. The Spirit was joined by two more who twisted and churned the ground in front of them.

One of the Spirits took form, wielding a sword and taking a swing at Drake. He dodged the blade but lost his balance and slipped off his horse. In a panic, he flailed and grabbed Gwen, pulling her limp body to the ground with his. They rolled to a stop as the horse ran in another direction.

Lily and Ellizar rode towards the open gates of Bucklebeary, pausing when they noticed Drake was no longer behind them.

"Get to the gate!" he yelled throwing Gwen over his shoulder and running. Laughing filled the air as the Spirits circled them. They came closer and closer, blocking Drake's vision.

In an instant, the sound of water rushing reached his ears, and then a sound like an entire ocean. The Spirits fled, lost in the forest somewhere.

The water in the river had vanished, all coming together and taking form into a breathtaking living watery sculpture. It was plain to see the being holding a great staff in his right hand, but all other features were distorted by the movement of the water. Either way, everyone looked on in awe, as the magnificent being looked like nothing they had ever seen, yet struck a cord in his heart.

At once six Spirits came out of the trees and took the form of the black-cloaked figures Drake recognized all too well. They brandished their swords and screamed in a dark and hideous language.

Then it seemed as if the watery being was laughing at the Spirits. The creature opened its mouth and let out a cry that shook the entire river bank. The trees trembled and Drake's fear grew as he ran towards the town, whose gates were now closed. The creature roared again and then dove towards the Spirits. In the blink of an eye the Spirits were consumed and the water raged on.

The water overcame him, swallowing both him and Gwen. They surfaced a hundred feet later, completely at the mercy of the fast-flowing water. They were thrown towards the wooden wall and came to an abrupt stop against it.

The water churned, shoving them underneath. Drake clung to Gwen, his lungs burning as the water continued to wash over them. When they managed to surface Drake struggled to keep them both afloat. A rope came down from the top of the wall and Drake managed to grab it with his free hand, while his other arm was fastened around Gwen's limp body.

They were pulled from the water as the men drew in the rope. They were pulled over the top and both he and the unconscious Gwen ungracefully collapsed on the other side. The water receded and within a few moments, it was back in the riverbed as though nothing had happened.

Drake started to sit up but stopped as swords were drawn against them. Stern faces, hardened by years of experience greeted him.

"Is this it then?" At once, the men surrounding them withdrew their weapons and parted revealing a man who was taller and sterner than the others. His eyes shifted to Gwen. "What's the news with her? Is she dead or playing dead?" A moment passed. "Answer me or I'll have you both killed."

"She's not dead, she's ill," Drake answered.

"Very well," The man held his gaze for a moment, finally withdrawing. He turned to a soldier next to him. "Take their weapons and we'll figure out what to do with our new guests."

"She's ill!" Drake urged. The man's expressions softened, displaying at least a little empathy.

He turned to one of his men. "Take the woman to the doctor and try your best to help her. She is a prisoner, so keep two guards at all times! No matter how sick she is or isn't, she shall face the same fate as the other three."

Drake didn't get another chance to respond as his weapons and anything that might pose as a weapon were taken from him and thrown into a large barrel that was left on the wall.

Drake was forced down the narrow wooden staircase to the ground, which was filled with soldiers. He was shoved next to Lily and Ellizar who were tied and restrained in the middle of a large group.

"It seems we are graced with the presence of a dwarf, an elf, and two humans. A bit unusual for a traveling party don't you think? I am Morgrin, first in command of this town. It seems you have managed to get yourselves into quite a mess. I now hold your life in my hands. Who are you and what is your business?"

"My name is Lily of Fiori. We are travelers from the village of Fiori, seeking aid for our friend who was wounded in a similar attack to that which was seen today."

"If this kind of attack has been seen before, you are a curse and I should dispense of you where you stand. People who bring evil must be evil. Am I wrong to assume this?"

"Yes my lord, you are," Lily asserted. "We came seeking aid, that is all. We were told that there is someone in this city who could heal our friend."

"Whether there is or isn't is irrelevant to the fact that some great evil has now come to our doorsteps. An evil that I have never seen, nor do I wish to see again. Many would say that you should be killed in hopes that whatever attacked will not come looking for you." He turned to his men. "Execute them and lay their bodies in front of the gates, when their attackers return they will see the bodies and leave us be."

"What of Gwen?" Drake asked. Morgrin became interested.

"The fair maiden has a name? She shall suffer the same fate as you. Kill the woman and lay her body next to theirs. Execute them on my count of three. One." The men drew their weapons back. "Two…"

"Stop!"

The soldiers parted and another man stepped forward, he was clothed in a dirty old cloak and looked as though he had been through a thousand wars. His face was hard but kind and showed concern and interest as he looked at Drake from beneath his hood.

"You cannot kill these fair people," the man said.

Morgrin seemed reluctant to restrain himself. "And what right do you have to keep these 'fair people' alive?"

"The right that you have denied them. The right to tell their whole tale and leave nothing out. Only then, when you see everything can you begin to understand and therefore carry out justice that is just and right."

"I could have you arrested for stopping my orders!"

"I have not stopped you from killing them, I have only asked you to look at these people with a desire to know what you cannot see from the outside. If I am wrong, you may kill me where I stand."

Morgrin shook his head conceding that the man was right. "It seems that your lives have been spared for a few precious moments. This man is right to say that I acted with haste and did not learn all the details as I should. Therefore answer my questions and perhaps I shall change my decision. Start with your names, all of you. I know the elf's name. You're next dwarf."

"Ellizar is my name, and if yeh should decide teh kill us I might warn yeh that Dwarves can be rather stubborn and will not go down without a fight."

"Trust me we've been traveling with him for a week. He's no picnic," Drake said. The comment got a few laughs from the men surrounding them and a look of annoyance from Ellizar, though he too seemed amused by the jest.

"Very well then. How about you? Is there anything about you that we should know?"

"My name is Drake Th-... My name is Drake."

"You paused as if though you were hiding some great secret."

"I hide no secret. I was speaking the name of the town I am from. I stopped myself only because I sensed that you did not care," Drake fibbed.

"Who sent you and what were you fleeing from?" Morgrin asked. "There are many magicians in this world, but never have I seen a display like that. Keep in mind I have seen a lot."

"You saw no magicians," Lily started. "We believe them to be Spirits. Other than that we know nothing."

"What is their business with you?"

"We do not know. But we fear for our lives. They attacked our friend-"

"The ill one?" Morgrin asked. She nodded. "When?"

"A week ago. We were sent here."

"Sent by who?"

"Rohemir, as we know him unless we've been greatly deceived." Morgrin's eyes shifted to the man with the cloak.

"You sir, seem to know more than I do, therefore I leave the decision up to you. If you know a man named Rohemir and if you think these three people are telling the truth then spare their lives, otherwise they will be dead as I said they would be. Do they speak the truth?" Morgrin asked the cloaked man.

"Their story is truth, whether you're too pigheaded to believe it or not," the man said. "I know the man Rohemir and I have come to heal the woman. Therefore I must do so."

Morgrin nodded. "Your lives are now his responsibility. You have been spared for the moment. If anything is out of line you will all pay for this."

"Understood my lord," the man with the cloak answered.

"Release all three of them and give them back their things." He looked to the man in the cloak. "You may take them to your house we will fetch the woman and bring her to you." The men carried out their orders and slowly dispersed back to their stations.

The man who had just saved their lives led them away from the soldiers. They entered the busy and crowded streets, where the people went to and fro, seemingly unaware of the situation that had transpired beyond their walls.

The people were cheerful and pleasant to look at, which couldn't be said of the rest of the town. The ground was hard and barren, with little to no grass within the fortified walls.

The alley's became narrow and twisted, though the man in the cloak seemed as if he could walk the path blindfolded, Drake was completely unsure of which direction they were heading.

At the end, there was a small house pressed between two others. They were faded grey from years of wind and rain. All things considered, it was one of the better-looking structures they had seen in Bucklebeary.

The cloaked man opened the door and motioned them inside. The doors were closed, and the curtains were kept drawn. The mysterious man didn't speak to them, instead choosing to build a fire. They were left to awkwardly fill the silence as they looked around the dwelling, too nervous to speak.

The dwelling was plain and simple, with several unique mugs on a rack over a wash basin. Aside from a cupboard, beds, a fireplace, and a single chest on the far side were the only items of interest that filled the one-room house.

Several minutes passed before a knock came at the door. The man opened the door and three guards came in, one of them carrying Gwen's pale and limp body in his arms. To Drake's surprise, one of the men in the company bowed as they crossed the threshold. The other two guards, though they didn't bow, carried themselves in a way that suggested they highly respected this strange mysterious man.

As directed, the soldiers took Gwen to the couch and set her down. With another bow, the soldiers left and the man with the cloak pulled down his hood.

His face was more pleasant than they had expected it to be, with kind eyes, longer brown hair, a neat and trim beard, and a face that put them at ease. His hands were calloused and his skin was tanned, and from the state of his boots and cloak, it was evident he did a great deal of traveling. He came and sat next to them, pouring some tea into crudely made cups.

"Drink this. It'll refresh you," the man told them. They drank, finding that even with a little sip of the drink they felt more relief than they had felt the entire trip.

"Who are you?" Drake asked.

"The one Rohemir sent to heal Gwen, My name is Adonai. You may call me Aiden."

"You are not Elvish?" Lily asked, searching for any sign that he was. His hair came down over his ears. "Rohemir said that Elvish healing was needed to cure Gwen."

"I assure you I am well accustomed to the Elvish methods of healing and that is what I'm here to do. If I had other intentions I would have let Morgrin carry out his sentence."

"How do yeh know Morgrin?" Ellizar asked.

"I only met him a few days ago. I received Rohemir's message and came at once. Morgrin was reluctant to let me in, but thankfully he did."

"Why?" Drake asked.

"Because rumors are rampant, and many scouts have been reporting Borags straying from their boundaries. He was suspicious, as he should be in regards to his job."

"I suppose," Drake agreed. Aiden began throwing other herbs and spices into a pot of water he had started over the fire. As he stepped into the light they noticed his pointed ears."Where do you come from?"

"I hail from the town of Avdatt to the north."

"Ellizar and I have been to Avdatt many times," Lily said. "It's a very nice city."

"Yes, it is. Though I may spend a bit of time there, I do not have a town I call home, instead, I do what I can to help people, no matter the cost."

"Can you heal Gwen?" Lily asked. Aiden stole a glance in her direction.

"I can heal her, but it will take some time. It'll take a week for her to be completely healed and frankly, I'm not sure we have that long."

"What do yeh mean?" Ellizar asked.

"The Spirits that attacked you will return," Aiden started. "Overall, Spirits hate to come into a town like this but they came very close today. The fact that the Spirits have attacked twice, so openly, is a surprise, but I think there is more waiting for us yet."

"What are we to do?" Lily asked.

"We must get Gwen healed and get you out of this town and on your way to Ariamore. You will be safe there. Spirits fear the Elves, but most of all, they fear that Men and Elves may join forces once again."

"They've worked together before? The two races."

"Indeed and they were a powerful combination. It happened during the first age. Since that time a rift has been between them. They do not work together. According to ancient scrolls and prophecies, the two nations will join forces again and destroy all that is evil."

"What would make them join forces after all this time?" He asked.

"People like you and me," Aiden answered, throwing more ingredients into a pot over the fire he had started. "You are Drake Thomas, a man with two names, which is unusual in itself, but you are to make the way for Shedaros, the one who will forever unite the two races and make a force that no one can destroy. The Spirits know this and are afraid. They seek to kill you so that you will not fulfill this in any way."

"I don't know anything about this world other than the fact that I washed up on the side of a river. I'm not even sure how I got two names! How am I supposed to unite these races?"

"You must learn to let things happen the way that Lathon means for them to happen. You'll see that everything will transpire as the prophets have foreseen. The will of Lathon is sometimes a mystery to Mankind and Elves, but only because we cannot see the end. If we try too hard to do something or make something happen the way we want it to, we only get in the way. You have to have a little faith."

"Faith?" Ellizar asked, Aiden looked at them knowingly.

"Faith is what unites a group of people, or even one person to another for that matter. It is the belief in something that you cannot control. It is trusting that in the end, everything will work out the way it's supposed to. The way Lathon wants it to. Faith is something this world doesn't have and because of it, it is falling into ruins. Worry is practically atheism and will get you nothing but a headache. To give up faith means that you're alone."

Silence came over them as the pot that was cooking over the fire started whistling. Aiden got up and poured some of the liquid into a smaller bowl, which he then took to Gwen, putting some of it into her mouth. She gagged, but slowly drank the liquid, which seemed to not affect her. After a few minutes, he stood up and moved over to Lily whose blood stained her dress. He grabbed a cloth and dipped it in the liquid and then dabbed at her chest.

Hissing filled the air as her skin was heeled and the blood that covered her vanished in an instant. They all watched as within a couple of minutes no sign of her being injured could be seen.

"Incredible!" Ellizar exclaimed. "We should just make that stuff up by the bottle and carry it with us."

"Good idea, but not the greatest idea," Aiden said, taking a seat again. "You have to serve this liquid hot or else it turns poisonous. Almost killed myself a few years back when I tried to make it for the first time."

"What's in it?" Lily asked.

"Plants, and a few herbs. Some of them hard to find, others so common you could walk down the street and find them."

"Do you think the Spirits will return before Gwen is healed?" Drake asked.

"Yes, but we must wait and see what will happen." Aiden stared into the fire as though he was drawing some great wisdom from it. "On the third day, we need to move, no matter what kind of shape Gwen is in. Borags from Grimdor are likely the allies of the Spirits at this point. We're not far from the border, they could be here within a day. Morgrin and his men will stand a much better chance against Borags than they will against Spirits."

"Why do you say that?" Drake asked.

"They can't change form like the Spirits can. However, they are faster at running than most humans or Elves. Their feet and hands have claws like talons that make it easy for them to scale large cliffs and everything else that stands in their way. They can also tunnel underground. When you are in Grimdor you'll rarely find a city that you can see."

"You've been to Grimdor before?" Lily asked.

"Once or twice. Only passing through, taking a shortcut. It's faster but more dangerous to go through. I'm not sure which way Rohemir will want you to go, but I would take my chances in Grimdor. The best place to hide is right under your enemy's nose."

They talked for several more hours. Something about Aiden seemed different from anyone they had ever met while another part of him seemed to be just like they were. Whether he truly was a person they could trust or not, none of them could deny that Gwen looked better already. Her skin was now warmer than it had been previously, and although she was still pale and limp it was progress enough to instill a sense of hope in all of them.

They were given a nice meal and then were shown the town by Aiden who seemed to have some other motive in mind.

Eventually, the day faded and the shops closed sending everyone back to their houses for the night. Aiden turned up their covers and brought out new garments to replace their well-traveled ones.

They accepted these graciously and remained talking for several hours as the night deepened. Everyone found sleep, but for Drake, it lasted only a few hours as he awoke, unable to turn his mind off. He lay there awake, and his eyes shifted to Aiden who was stooping over Gwen once again. He had more of the medicine made up and was putting it down her throat. Drake watched and, listened to the song he was humming, unable to understand the words.

It was a beautiful song, whatever it meant. His mind was confused, but his heart embraced it with open arms. The song put him at ease and seemed to bring a sense of security that he hadn't felt since he had gotten here.

He slept more soundly after that, only waking up on one more occasion, but both times it was Aiden's voice as he sang to Gwen. Curiosity stirred in him as he wondered what he had been singing. His mind drifted briefly to the future as he wondered what lay ahead but then remembered Aiden's words and tried not to worry about the future.

VII   THE HUMBLE HOUSE

Lily was awakened by a hand clamping over her mouth. She relaxed once when she realized it was Ellizar. He held a lantern in one hand and held a finger to his lips. She sat up and followed his lead as he motioned for her to get dressed. Soon everyone was awake and dressed as she was.

Aiden sat by the window, studying the darkness. Clouds filled the sky, bringing with it an uncomfortable silence.

"What's going on?" She asked.

"Morgrin just came to the door five minutes ago and informed me that several of the guards that were posted at the front gate were found dead," Aiden told them.

"Dead? Who did it?"

"That's a question I cannot answer. I have guesses, but that's all they are. I am certain they are looking for you."

"What about Gwen?" Ellizar asked. They looked in her direction, noticing that she was up and dressed, but moving slowly. It had been three days since she had first begun taking the medicine that had been curing her illness.

"We don't have a choice. She won't be any good in a fight yet, but she can run and think on her own. I'll start leading you towards Ariamore on the road that Rohemir would have chosen and hopefully, we'll meet up somewhere along the way."

They put their weapons on, ready to depart moments later. Lily drew her sword, but Aiden took it and threw it on the ground.

"What are you doing?" Drake asked. Aiden moved to the end of one of the beds and opened a trunk. They huddled around, seeing weapons of every kind.

"It would be better for all of you if you would use these weapons," Aiden said carefully taking them out of a heavy wooden box. They each took one of the swords and drew them, the pale light flickering off the blade.

"Something is different about these, but what it is I cannot say," Drake commented.

"I can't begin to explain in the time that we have, but I've managed to make swords that will never dull and never break. This is the most deadly weapon you could carry. If you respect it and allow it to do its work, these swords will never fail you. I used no magic to craft these weapons."

"That's not possible," Lily replied, admiring the weapon.

"I've had my sword for the past five years and never have I had to get it sharpened or repaired in any way." Aiden turned, handing another sword to Lily, who quickly strapped it to her waist.

"Why's the elf get two blades and I only get one lousy axe?" Ellizar asked.

"Because she's an elf and you're a dwarf?" Drake suggested. Ellizar frowned.

"One of them is for Gwen when she can wield it," Aiden answered. He left the room and then came back a few moments later with another steaming cup of medicine. She put it to her lips, cringing as the hot liquid went down her throat. Aiden turned towards Drake and handed him a flask.

"Keep that close to you. It's her medication," Aiden told him. "You have to heat it to a boil for a few minutes before you can even think about giving it to her. You'll kill her faster than you can blink an eye if you don't."

Aiden strode to the front door and then put out the lantern. "Morgrin has agreed to help us escape. The front gate will be guarded. We're going over the back wall. As long as we don't run into any unfriendly people between now and then, we'll be fine. Follow me."

Lily calmed her breathing and kept her hand on her sword as they slipped out of the house and started down the silent streets of Bucklebeary. Several minutes passed and still, there was no sign of anyone that might be looking for them.

Aiden turned another corner and then backtracked. The reason why was answered by a thick arrow that whizzed through the air and struck a nearby building. They instinctively flinched as more arrows scattered to either side of them.

They scrambled into another alley and panicked when three dark shapes appeared in front of them. Aiden didn't hesitate, engaging and quickly dispatching one of them. Drake and Ellizar took the other two until all three were on the ground.

"What are these things?" Lily asked, having never seen such creatures before. If they had been standing they wouldn't have been much over five feet tall, with rough skin that seemed as hard as chain mail. Their ears and their noses were pointed and their eyes were dark and small. Their body structure was bony, with claws instead of fingers and toes.

"Borags," Aiden stated. "We don't have much time now."

They twisted through the alleys, to the point that Aiden seemed to be the only one who knew where they were. The company turned around one last corner and then across a street, pointing to the left where a group of Borags crossed the alley. The vile creatures took no notice of them, though, and they continued on their way, at length coming to the back wall.

Two hundred yards to their left were the stairs that would take them to the top. A strange deep sound rumbled through the night air.

Ellizar's face washed white. "That's not good is it?"

"We've got trouble now!"

More horns called through the forest around them. Inside the city bells began ringing almost immediately, calling the people of Bucklebeary to arms. The city came alive as men and children who were old enough to wield swords came out of their houses to defend themselves.

They scaled the stairs coming next to Morgrin. Their hope withered as they looked out at a solid line of grey circling the entire city. Crude weapons of war were cast in eerie light from the torches the Borags carried as they approached the city.

"I had horses waiting in the forest, but I'm sure this filth has claimed them!" Morgrin exclaimed.

"Just get us over the wall."

"You still wish to try your luck?"

"We must," Aiden said with such conviction that Morgrin nodded and let the rope down the over the edge, near the southwest corner of the wall.

"I am sorry I was hard on you when you first came. I can see there is more to you than meets the eye."

"We are united in our belief in Lathon, May Lathon protect you."

"The same to you. Go now!" Morgrin urged. "They are not in bow range yet."

The soldiers of the enemy marched towards the city on each side, undaunted by the feeble defenses of Bucklebeary.

Aiden was the first to slide down the rope. Everyone followed, though Drake had to hold tight to Gwen who was unable to get over the wall with her illness still plaguing her.

Aiden led them away, turning towards the river. They carefully wadded through the water and entered the trees on the other side. Legions of Borags passed by them on either side but seemed to be unconcerned with the five travelers.

Lily's heart beat wildly as they unavoidably drew closer to the enemy line. Aiden motioned them to stop, as a line of soldiers came over a small hill in front of them. Fear took hold of her thoughts as more Borags came behind them.

Aiden slowly and carefully drew his sword as their enemies halted, seeming surprised to see the five travelers. Aiden's stance remained resolute and if he felt fear Lily could not tell. He turned to look at each of them. Despite the overwhelming odds, Lily felt calm.

Aiden let a great cry escape and charged from his spot in the forest, rushing toward their foes. Lily and the others found their courage and followed suit, joining their voices to the battle cry. The Borags paused and made no other move as if they were trying to process what was happening in front of them.

They flanked either side of Aiden with Gwen right with them. For the moment Gwen appeared to have been brought out of the fog that had clouded her mind.

Lily swung her sword at the first Borag that came to her and then watched in horror as the blade pierced the skin as though it was nothing more than a thin, frail fabric.

She swung again, this time the curved and jagged blade of the Borag blocked her attack. Her opponent swung but Lily sidestepped the blade. She swung wildly, but it was swiped away and she failed to escape the counterattack. Instead, she received a cut in the shoulder of her dress, though by some miracle it did not cut her skin.

Finally, she brought the Borag to the ground. She watched him fall and then stared at the blood on her sword. She had been trained in swordsmanship since she was young, but never had she imagined she would have ended a life as she was doing now.

The events of the past two weeks played through her head. She readjusted her grip, understanding that she had no choice but to continue to her next opponent. Lily focused her mind on survival, carefully calculating every move that she was making.

She kept close to Ellizar, who seemed to have an advantage because of his height, able to confuse his enemies who looked at him in surprise. They probably hadn't expected a dwarf to be with two Elves and two humans.

As they fought Drake's skill with a sword surprised her. He remembered nothing about himself or the land that he was in, but he fought like a seasoned warrior, with a skill that she could only dream of.

"Lily!" Aiden cried out. The forest now burned and everyone began running towards the next line of Borags that was approaching. This group was thinner than the previous one, but still, her hope wavered. Aiden turned to face them, once again instilling her with a confidence that otherwise would have eluded her.

"We're almost out of this, but this line will be the hardest yet," Aiden told them. "Once we're through we're going to have to run for our lives and hope that we can lose them. Are you ready?"

They nodded and Aiden boldly led them into the line of their enemies. Time faded, each second blurring into the next. For each Borag they slew, there seemed to be another one to challenge them.

The soldiers suddenly paused and sniffed the air. They looked up to the hills as horns called through the night sky. A strong clear note, and it didn't belong to Borags.

The sound of hooves beating on the ground thundered through their hearts. Cavalry appeared behind the enemy ranks and took out many as they rode through the Borags. After a moment, several riderless horses came up to them and stopped.

Lily was relieved to see Rohemir sitting tall and proud on his horse. They each mounted one of the horses. She pulled Ellizar up as she had many times over the past week. Aiden was the only one who did not mount a horse.

"Aren't you coming?" she asked.

"My place is here."

Rohemir wasted no time in spurring his horse onward, the others followed behind. Lily looked over her shoulder watching Aiden as he grabbed an empty horse and then rode towards the city.

Flames lit the sky, but they soon became a distant glow. The sounds of the battle vanished and they were left alone in the darkness.

Gwen and Drake were right next to her, and Lily couldn't help but notice that Gwen seemed to have gone backward. She was once again pale and looked weaker, as though the battle had sent more poison through her veins.

The time passed and soon daybreak was nearing and light started to flood into the sky. The birds of the forest began to wake. After several more hours of riding they halted.

It was now midday, but none of them cared as they found a little outcropping in the hills and curled up to sleep. She closed her eyes, her mind filled with the horrors of battle.

Now she wished for only sleep as her fatigue caught up with her. Her eyes fell shut, welcoming her to dreams that offered peace not war.

The group slowly plodded their way through the wilderness. Drake struggled to focus on anything other than Gwen. She rode behind him now, but though she tried, she was visibly fading. Her speech was slurred at best; the poison had taken a powerful hold on her with their 'activity' in escaping.

Lily and Ellizar rode together and carried most of the conversation, though a great deal of their unspoken thoughts was wondering what had happened to Morgrin, Aiden, and Bucklebeary. At the head of their procession, Rohimer rode in studied silence, finding the path they didn't know.

Not long after the sunrise they entered into a forest of willow trees. Despite Drake's objections, Rohemir insisted they rose two hundred feet in the air. Regardless, they were the largest trees he had seen since waking on the side of the river.

Their thick, large branches hung down and sheltered them from the sunlight that managed to break through in only a few places. The willows swayed in the breeze, their branches sometimes rubbing together in a way that almost sounded like music.

Drake looked up at the magnificent trees in wonder, trying to imagine how old this forest was. It felt as if it was torn out of a page of history, surely filled with great stories and adventures in its past.

They slowed to just a gentle walk due to the ground beneath the willows, which was confusing and twisted with their roots. The day continued and then faded into night and they stopped along the side of a brook that meandered through the trees.

They started a fire and gave Gwen her medicine. After supper, they took turns bathing in the brook. which in some places was deep enough to get in up to your waist. Eventually, they all came back to the fire and said nothing as weariness overtook them and they fell asleep a while later.

Drake was awakened by the light of the fire. He sat up, sore from riding in the saddle for so long. Rohemir sat against a tree, staring straight ahead. His lips moved slightly but his eyes were full of mystery.

"Can't sleep?" Drake asked.

"Our situation demands that I stay awake."

"You can't go on without rest," Drake said. "I've been sleeping better than ever, yet I still feel like I could sleep a thousand years."

"I'm sure. But I must figure out which road we must take to Ariamore. We need to get out of this Epirus and we have to get out of here fast. But which road we should take eludes me."

"How many different ways to get to Ariamore are there?" Drake asked, a smile came to Rohemir's face.

"There are many roads we could travel by, but there is only one that is right and the best one to choose. My vision on this matter is still clouded."

"What are the options? If you don't mind telling me."

"I have no problem telling you Drake, after all, you're the one that's a wanted man. The fastest way would be to make for the seaport of Tyre. It's a fishing town back on the coast of Epirus. From there we could board a boat and then it would be a couple of weeks sailing through the hardest part of that ocean. If you don't mind the sea you'll do just fine."

"I can't remember if I like the sea or not. So, from that standpoint, I can't see that it would bother me."

Rohemir chuckled. "True enough, my friend, true enough. That is, the fastest way, but I'm not sure that it's the best. It's fast, but we would have to go through or near numerous towns and cities, which I fear would be places that the Spirits or Borags would be watching.

"The other option is the one that I'm in torment about," Rohemir continued. "It would require riding south for a day. From there we would enter the borders of Grimdor, which is the domain of the Borags. Dangerous, from that standpoint, but considering the Borags tunnel most of the time, there would be few places where they would spot us. We could be relatively safe. In about a week we could cross the narrowest part of the nation and then enter into the land of Men, which would be ideal because they are not yet looking for you. We would travel another week through that country before we would reach the seaport of Revly which could take us quickly and safely to Ariamore."

"Which one would you suggest?" he asked.

"Which one do you want to take?" Rohemir countered. "You are the one they want more than any of us."

"If there's no city above ground that seems ideal, but then again if they could track us then it's no good."

"Tracking wouldn't be much of a concern. We would have to be very careful though. The nation of Grimdor is nothing more than rocks. Large rocks that are three times the size of you, and then other rocks that are small and seemingly insignificant until you put them all together.

"There is no vegetation that grows at all. Every sound echoes through the air as though there was a loud explosion. Footsteps, conversations, everything. We would have to leave the horses behind because of this, plus the Borags have an incredible sense of smell and would likely pick up the scent of the horses before they would smell us."

"Is that the best way to go?"

"I have traveled through Grimdor before on several occasions, and I would lie if I said there was nothing unusual about the place. The air seems to be heavier there and the rocks wear down your soul and your spirit. The more time you spend within the borders of Grimdor, the more you lose yourself to the Borag's influence. You slowly fade until you find that you are nothing but one of them, hopelessly trapped and unable to get out. I don't suggest going that way just to go that way, nevertheless, I fear it might be the only way to go," Rohemir answered. "Life is full of hard choices and temptations and this will be no different. If we choose to go that way then we will live with the results of that choice for the rest of our lives. So Drake Thomas, what will your choice be?"

"Let's go through Grimdor," he decided. Rohemir's eyes showed surprise."That's my choice. I'll live with the results no matter what they will be."

"It is done then," Rohemir agreed. "You have saved me many hours of thinking. We'll have to double Gwen's medication to make sure that she's as strong as she can be when we reach the border. Grimdor is not for people who have no backbone or conscience. Now get your rest and for the first time since Buckleberry, I shall get mine. Tomorrow we will arrive at the border of Grimdor."

The night went faster than Drake had wished, and they soon found themselves hours from the border that they feared more than any other. Gwen had improved greatly over the evening, now well enough to speak and do almost everything. She and Drake talked for hours as they rode on the horse together.

Their world had turned upside down and now they each wondered what lay ahead. What would happen when they reached Ariamore? Drake couldn't answer the question, but the unknown lingered in his mind.

He had no memory of his history, let alone the land. For the first time, he hoped everyone was wrong about him. He held his hand out in front of him, looking at the unusual scar that was on it.

Three slashes, which at times burned like fire and other times were cold as ice. What did they mean? What was he supposed to do? He was supposed to prepare the way for Shedaros, but what did that mean? What would that require of him?

He wished the scar on his hand would fade with time and he would be no different from any other person. He could be normal and live happily ever after.

The landscape changed as the day passed. The forest of willows had been lost behind them and so had their sense of security. The sun beat down on them, and light wind moved through the open fields. They walked now through open meadows and fields which, according to Rohemir, were signs they were close to Grimdor.

Trees had vanished since they had emerged from the forest. and since then the vegetation had been diminishing. The grass grew shorter than it had previously, now coming only to their ankles as opposed to their knees. The flowers had vanished and it seemed so had everything else they had been enjoying over the past couple of hours. The houses became sparse and they were left to themselves as they wandered closer and closer to the border.

A few small brooks and creeks wound lazily through the empty countryside, which was so desolate they wondered if there were people anywhere, this close to Grimdor.

Clouds began to fill the clear blue sky and the air seemed to become heavier, weighing on all of them as though they were carrying some invisible burden.

Their thoughts changed for the better when they spied workers in a large field on their left. Despite the barren landscape that they had been traveling through, this estate was a beacon of wealth and splendor. The servants happily greeted them, sending messengers ahead to inform their master of visitors.

They continued on the path coming into the presence of a large manor three stories tall and as beautiful as anything they had seen. It appeared as if it was made for a king.

"Do you know whose house this is?" Gwen whispered as they approached the front door.

"No. It's familiar though, almost like I should know who lives here."

"Do you think we should keep going?" Lily asked, leaning closer. "We don't know that we can trust these people. What if this turns out to be a setup and all of these people are Spirits waiting to attack us?"

"Fer once I agree with the elf," Ellizar said. "I don't like the feel ov this place. We should just keep goin' right now."

"Patience my friends. If they were Spirits that wanted to attack us then they would have done it by now," Rohemir interjected. "We have little choice in the matter. We are low on supplies that will be crucial if we are to get through Grimdor with ease. I have a strong leading that we will find rest here."

Rohemir knocked on the door; the sound echoed through the house. The door was opened immediately by a woman in a comfortable dress, which was clearly made of the finest material. Her hair was a deep brown color and her eyes shone like diamonds chasing their fears away. She stood tall and proud, but not arrogant like Lily's parents had.

She was joined by a man of greying hair. His hands were rough and calloused, and his complexion was tanned as if he had been working in his fields all day, which Drake felt was unusual for people of their status.

"Greetings fellow travelers," the man greeted. "What brings you to our door?"

"We are seeking rest for the night before we set out to cross the nation of Grimdor."

"Very well," the woman replied. "You shall stay with us for the night, and before you try to refuse might I just warn you that I can be a very persistent woman and I won't likely lose an argument."

"There's a big surprise," Ellizar said. A chuckle arose out of all of them.

"Careful Ellie, they might not allow a dwarf to come in if you talk like that," Lily whispered.

"Yeh call me Ellie again and I'll be happy teh sleep outside!"

The man and the woman laughed. "You are all welcome in this house, I can assure you of that. Do not worry, your horses will be well cared for," the man said. Immediately servants came and led the horses away to stables that were across the yard.

"Welcome into our home," the man greeted. They entered the house, finding it was not decorated for royalty as they would've expected. Inside they found that it was furnished like any other house.

Drake's mind went back to Lily's parents, remembering how rich and lavish their house had been and yet they had seemed to be the most unhappy people in the entire town. Now as Drake looked at this house and its owners he realized that possessions, in the grand scheme of things, didn't matter if you were miserable all the time.

The woman disappeared into another room as the man led them to the nearest sitting room, where chairs and a few benches were waiting for them. They put their packs down against one of the walls and then took a seat as the woman brought out a tray with a tea kettle and some cups.

"You must certainly have a tale to tell, for it is not often that a dwarf, an elf, and three humans come walking through this part of the country. What are your names and what are your adventures? We love a good story."

They introduced themselves and recounted their stories, leaving out certain facts that might cause them trouble if these two people turned out to be untrustworthy. The minutes passed and soon an hour had gone, and their servants informed that the meal was ready.

They moved into the dining room which was once again decorated as though no one special lived here. They took their seats at the long table, surprised to find that all the servants also sat down at the table and it was the man and the woman who served them.

Everything about these two people seemed to go against what Drake had seen so far. These people served guests and servants alike, with a selfless attitude, and seemed to be far more humble and likable than Lily's family had been.

"We have told you our tale and our names but we have yet to learn yours," Gwen pointed out as they finished their meal. The man and the woman nodded, taking a drink from their cups.

"Indeed we have not, and for that, we are very rude. My name is Joseph and this is my wife Marion. This is our house and we've lived here for many, many years."

"I thought that's who I was looking at," Rohemir said with a laugh.

"Yeh know these people Rohemir?" Ellizar asked. Rohemir looked at the couple, a smile on his face.

"We have not met each other face to face until now, but I aided them once, along with a friend of theirs to help them escape a city a long time ago."

"You did?" Marion asked as if trying to remember. "Who was it you assisted in getting out of this 'city'?"

"A man named Sedric." Light shone in their eyes.

"Well, I must say that after all of these years, it is nice to learn who was connected to that escape so many years ago. Sedric told us that he had some help from inside the city, but he never said who."

"I hope the meal is to your satisfaction," Joseph told them. "We will have all your supplies replenished for your trip across Grimdor. Foul place to be crossing, what is your reasoning behind crossing in such a place?"

"We need to get to Ariamore as swiftly as possible. We are putting to test, the old saying 'the best place to hide is right under their nose'.

Joseph laughed. "Unusual tactic, but it might just work. But I would be wary about traveling with such a large group. Grimdor is empty and barren, sounds echo through the hills for miles on end. It's next to impossible to know if the sound you are hearing is a mile away or a hundred miles away. You can easily get lost or go insane."

"Aye, but we cannot sit back and not try," Rohemir defended. Joseph and Marion both nodded their agreement.

"Best be on your guard with an elf in your company," Marion said. "We all know that the Borags hate the Elves with a passion, as do most people these days."

"Why's that?" Drake asked, unable to hold the question back.

"Don't you know?" Joseph asked. Drake shifted uncomfortably and looked at him with interest and curiosity. He took a sip of his drink and leaned back in his chair. "Unless you're from the far southern nations you should know that tale yourself."

"I'm-"

"From one of those far southern nations," Rohemir interrupted.

"According to history when the great king Lathon, formed this world as we know it, there were some who never got along with him. Lathon treated them all equally, and for whatever reason, certain people thought that they were entitled to more, or better treatment than the rest of the nations and races.

"After they voiced their displeasure the people of the earth became un-content. The people moved over the earth, each to their own region. However, those who didn't agree with Lathon held malice and hatred within their hearts.

"In their contempt for Lathon, they devised a plan to raise the Tower of Seru at a place called Uzal. A tower of such might and prosperity that it would prove their greatness over Lathon. But when Lathon saw their hearts and knew their intentions, he confused their languages. The people scattered, each to their own language, and the Tower of Seru was never finished. I am told that it still stands within the vastness of Seredath, but I will never see it.

"What happened next?" Drake asked.

"They cursed him and formed Grimdor. They swiftly destroyed all that was good in the land, creating the wasteland it is today.

"From among the nations of the earth Lathon chose the Elvish people of Ariamore as his chosen people, which would only make sense because, after all, he was the king of Ariamore. The greatest king to ever live.

"Where do the Borags come into the picture?" Gwen asked.

"The Borags are a mixture of all races, Dwarves, Elves, Men, Gogs," Joseph explained. "It is rumored that these people intermixed with spirits and souls of much stranger origins. It corrupted them to the core, that is the history of the Borag race. Now they sit inside their borders, waiting for their moment to strike Shedaros down before he has a chance to do any good."

"Can they do that?" Lily asked. Joseph nodded.

"They can try. I think that as hard as they may try they cannot interfere with the plan of Lathon. Nonetheless, it has become evident that Grimdor suspects something."

"What makes you say that?" Rohemir asked.

"My wife and I have heard movement from inside Grimdor lately, about a week ago was the last time we heard anything. No idea what they were doing, but they were certainly above ground and on the move."

"That must have been the group that attacked us!" Ellizar exclaimed.

"Perhaps," Joseph replied. "Although I think you left out that part of your tale."

"Please forgive us," Rohemir interjected. "We work on a need-to-know basis, we don't mean to upset you or compromise your trust."

"There's no need to apologize, everyone has their secrets and I'm sure that if I were in your situation I would do the same thing. Although I still don't know why you're on the run from them."

"And if it doesn't offend you we will keep that to ourselves for the time being," Rohemir said.

Joseph nodded. "It doesn't offend me at all. I have my own secrets that I keep hidden for safety reasons. I must say, though, that you are an interesting traveling group. No wonder the Borags have taken an interest in you."

The meal ended and they were shown to their rooms, which were large and decorated like the rest of the house, simple but beautiful. Lily and Gwen took one room and Ellizar and Drake took another. Rohemir stayed up talking with Joseph and Marion.

The morning came too soon and Drake, felt like he could have slept for an eternity. A knock came at the door as it opened slowly. Lily and Gwen both stood around the corner, already dressed.

"Drake if you wouldn't mind waking the silly little dwarf," Lily started. "Rohemir says we have to be on our way within the hour. Breakfast will be served before we leave."

"Is it safe to wake a dwarf?" he asked. "Especially one who sleeps with his axe a foot from the edge of the bed."

"There's nothing to it. You just do this." Lily came into the room, grabbed Drake's pillow, and smacked Ellizar who was sleeping peacefully. He cried out and reached for his axe but never got the chance as Lily scooped it up.

Ellizar looked around the room for a moment before realizing what had happened.

"Blasted elf!" Ellizar exclaimed. "All the different ways yeh could wake me up and yeh choose teh do that?"

"Yes, you know why? Because it's the funniest way."

"We'll see how fun it is when finally I get teh wake yeh up. I'll smack you with a pillow and see how you like it."

"Bring it on Ellie!" Lily teased.

They dressed and made their way down the long corridor until they entered the dining room once again. Rohemir was already sitting at the table talking with Joseph.

"As soon as you eat your breakfast we will be on our way," Rohemir told them. They ate the food gratefully, knowing that it would likely be the last decent meal they had for a while.

"Your packs are ready, and I wish you the best on your journey," Joseph said once they had finished.

"Thank you for your courtesy, you've been a very gracious host."

"You don't have to thank us for anything," Marion replied, putting her arm around her husband. "Just be safe and we'll call it payment."

"We shall certainly try our best," Rohemir started. "How far from Grimdor are we?"

"You might have two hours of traveling before you get there. That depends on how hard you ride. It might interest you to know that you're a little farther west than you might have thought. You were hoping for five days of crossing at this point, but you're likely to have nine days of hiking. I hope that doesn't come back to bite you too much."

"That makes two of us," Rohemir said. They said goodbye and mounted their horses, and waved as they rose into the sunrise.

Silence came over them as the vegetation became less, with the grass appearing to be stunted and growing no more than a couple of inches tall. No trees or shrubs grew as far as the eye could see. Not long after, the vegetation ceased altogether. Just the bare dirt was visible, and each step the horses took kicked up a cloud of dust that trailed through the air.

Feelings of gloom came over the group as they pressed on for another half hour, the ground becoming dry, and cracked from the lack of moisture. Only slightly cracked at first, but soon they were large cracks, nearly a foot or two wide that wound through the dirt like snakes.

They dismounted, took all their supplies, and released the animals. The horses turned and ran, disappearing back the way they had come. They continued, having to watch their footing as the ground became worse yet.

Drake strained his eyes seeing a sea of grey on the horizon, which was matched by dark storm clouds that were above. Thunder sounded in the distance and streaks of lightning lit up the sky. The ground beneath changed to a dark grey rock as they crossed over the border. He looked again at the sea of grey, which rose and fell slightly until it formed a set of mountains in the distance. Gloom and despair filled them all as their footsteps echoed through the barren landscape.

"Welcome to Grimdor," Rohemir greeted. Thunder crashed through the sky and a new sound reached their ears. Rain began falling in sheets, making the rocks slippery and darker. They set off across the desolate nation, trying to keep their footing as well as their bearings as they traveled into the unknown.

The rain soaked through their clothes until they felt as if they might as well have been walking through the rain naked for as wet as they were. The hours passed as they continued into the gloom.

VIII GRIMDOR

The rain continued to pour down for the next three days. Grimdor, an endless sea of stone, became more dangerous than anything they had encountered so far. The water pooled into the valleys and didn't drain, instead, small lakes formed, forcing them to go around. The stone became like ice, and the lower ground was ankle-deep at best.

They walked in a line, barely speaking. The rain pounded loudly on the rocks and lightning and thunder filled the sky and shook the ground. Each moment led their souls further into a dark place.

The end of the third day grew near and much to their relief so did the rain. They managed to find a large plateau of rock that wasn't buried underneath water. They opened up their packs and laid out their belongings on the rocks to dry in the sunless sky.

The air was cool, and the sky never seemed to change even as the lakes (or runoff) receded until there were only a couple of inches left in most of the area. As much as everyone wished to light a fire, they refrained, not wanting to risk alerting anyone to their presence.

Each one of them nodded off to sleep, but Drake soon awoke. Faint and muffled crying was heard to the east. He stood and only had to go a hundred feet until he found Lily hiding behind an outcropping of rock. Her feet hung out over the edge of the plateau and tears soaked her face.

Drake took a seat next to her, but neither of them spoke. When she finally turned to him, her eyes showed both surprise and humiliation for crying so openly in front of someone.

"I'm sorry. I hope I didn't wake you," Lily said.

"What's on your mind?"

"My family, Fiori, everyone who lived there. It's hard to explain exactly what my emotions are. They never approved of my decisions, and I've never had their *blessing* for anything. I've felt like a stranger in their home for years. I have every reason to not care that they are dead. But I feel sorrow for them, I really do."

"Maybe that's a good thing," Drake said. "It proves you care, and are focused on others. From what I gather you went on this trip to try and make things right with them. You aren't as hard-hearted as they were."

"I wish I truly understood why they had a problem with me." She shivered in the cold night air, pulling her blanket tighter around her.

"People are a hard thing to understand. But maybe they were the ones with the problem, not you. It seems like some people can work for their whole life trying to win approval from other people and they never get any closer. You could have tried to win your family over but unless their hearts are open to that, your efforts would've been in vain," he said thoughtfully.

"Yes, but what made them that way?" Lily asked. "There had to be some defining moment that changed them. Could I have done anything different to change their fate?"

"I can't even remember my past, so how I'm supposed to help you with yours I couldn't begin to guess. But if there's one thing I have learned since that day you found me by the river, it's that there's only one moment we can do anything about and that's the one that we're living in right now. We can't change the past and we can try to change the future but the only way we can *live* is by changing the present."

The clouds thinned and a ray of moonlight illuminated the water around them.

"I envy you, Drake."

He looked at her and studied her far-off expression. "Envy me, why?"

"Because you cannot remember your past. You can't remember the hurt and the pain that you have or haven't felt; for that I envy you."

"I wish I did remember. Maybe then I would feel more like a normal person. Like you, I wonder…why haven't any of my memories returned?"

"Perhaps you aren't meant to remember anything. What if some higher power intentionally took your memories away because they would get in the way of what you had to do? You have that scar for a reason. Maybe Shedaros himself is among us right now and will need you for something in the future."

"You think so? That I'm meant for something greater?"

"Yes I do and not just because you bear the mark of Lathon," Lily told him. "There's something about you that is different, and even I'm not sure what it is. We all see it. You wish to be different, but you were given this privilege and with that comes specific things that you must do whether you want to or not. Perhaps your definition of normal is just a little different." They both laughed and then sat together in unbroken silence.

"Where does all the water go?" Drake finally asked. "This place is all rock, it must go somewhere right?"

"Maybe the Borags have drainage tunnels that allow them to use the water underground."

"Perhaps," Drake agreed.

"Borags are by far the weirdest creatures I've ever heard of, as well as the most dangerous."

"I would say those Spirits were pretty dangerous," Drake replied with a laugh.

She smiled. "Indeed, and nothing is quite as scary as a dwarf."

After a while, they grew tired and returned to the camp. A splash was heard behind them, but they saw nothing as they walked back to the camp and lay down on the cold, hard rocks, hoping and praying that the dark clouds wouldn't bring rain anytime soon.

The next morning Drake was so tired he found it difficult to walk in a straight line. The world spun around him and the air seemed to be heavier than before, weighing him down physically and mentally.

Their hearts continued to be dampened by the dark clouds above, which always seemed to forebode a great storm that would destroy them. To their relief and eternal thanks, no such storm overtook them.

They navigated the sea of rocks, hoping that Rohemir had an idea of where they were and knew where they were headed. The day passed and gave way to yet another night, which offered sleep but not real rest as they had hoped. When the dawn came, the water had receded completely, allowing the company to travel in relative ease.

When he couldn't sleep, Drake found himself away from everyone else, staring out at the endless ocean of rock. Drake carefully slipped off his shoes, which were in bad condition, but his feet were far worse, covered in blisters.

"My feet are the same." A hand gently touched his shoulder and he looked to see Gwen's sparkling eyes. She sat down and removed her shoes.

"I'd say yours are worse," Drake concluded.

"Shoes of a slave," Gwen replied grimly. "All I got was the worn-out clothes and garments," Gwen admitted. "Never had any of my own."

She threw what was left of the dilapidated shoes over the edge of the cliff, (which was no more than seven feet tall) where they landed with a dull thud. Drake thought about objecting but they were in terrible shape, and would likely only hurt her more.

"We'll get you some new ones," Drake promised. Gwen seemed to take comfort in the idea, even if they both knew she would be going barefoot for a very long time.

A soft, dull clicking echoed through the land for only a moment before the wind changed and carried the sound away. Immediately afterward, Drake drew his sword as someone hastily approached.

Ellizar jumped back in fright, throwing his hands up in surrender.

"Blasted el-human kind!" Ellizar whispered.

"Sorry," Drake apologized putting his sword away.

Ellizar motioned for them to come quietly. "Rohemir says we have teh move immediately."

"Now?" Drake asked. "It's the middle of the night. If we wander through this darkness without a torch we'll kill ourselves, and we can't exactly take a torch for fear of being seen."

"I'm not sure the how or why, all I know is that Rohemir said teh find yeh quickly," Ellizar replied. They scrambled back to the camp which was a flurry of activity. Rohemir was busy throwing everything into their packs.

"What's going on?" Gwen asked.

"I fear we're going to have company in a short while," Rohemir answered.

"How do you know?" Lily asked.

"I heard clicking on the rocks."

"We heard it too. Is that bad?" Gwen asked. Drake quickly stuffed his belongings in his pack.

"The enemy may already know we are here!" Rohemir exclaimed. "The claws of the Borags, hitting the rock is the source of the sound. Borags are near, and we all know what they want." Every eye shifted to Drake who rested his hand on his sword.

"My life is never going to be boring is it?" Drake answered.

Gwen started to reply, but Rohemir held up a hand to silence them. They stared ahead to the hills beyond. They had camped on a large enough rock to give them some advantage, but overall their large rock sat in a natural vale, and now they were regretting it.

The vile creatures, as they had seen in Fiori and Bucklebeary, crawled over the crown of the surrounding rocks. Everyone gripped their sword in anticipation as the Borags closed in.

"Any ideas? Gwen asked. Drake watched Rohemir who didn't say anything in response.

"They are surrounding us on three sides, but not four," Drake noted.

Only a few torches illuminated the small army that closed in around them. In the dim lighting, Drake guessed there were eighty warriors. Lily and Gwen strung an arrow to their bows and immediately the procession stopped.

"They can see well in the dark," Drake commented, though Gwen was the only one who heard him. An uneasy silence hung over them like a wet towel. The Borags made no move, while Drake and their company held their breath.

A single Borag stepped out from the horde of warriors.

"The commander," Rohemir whispered. The commander spoke harshly, in a language Drake was hopeless to understand.

"You will not take us alive! So you might as well attack!" Rohemir cried. Every head in the Grimdorian ranks turned to look at the commander who again spoke and summoned his soldiers to attack.

"Fight!" Rohemir yelled as he ran back to them.

The army rushed forward, uttering unintelligible curses at them as they thundered into the valley. Ten or fifteen soldiers broke off from the main group and sprinted ahead engaging Drake and the others.

Drake swung his sword as quickly as he could, each movement seeming more natural than the next. After the first few were easily slain by either him or Rohemir, the Borags withdrew slightly, sending five or ten at a time to challenge their opponents.

They fought the beasts endlessly, helping each other when they could. The Borags wore armor, but only helmets and chest guards. Drake marveled at the Borag's tough skin which made their swords, though they were sharp, feel dull and childish as they bounced off the rough, calloused skin. Their skin could be any number of colors. Though the ones that had attacked Fiori had been mostly grey, these seemed to be brown or black with spots of grey on their legs.

Lily cried out and all of them turned to see that she had slipped and fallen. Drake rushed to her aid, taking out her opponent who was ready to finish her. Drake helped her to her feet. To both of their surprise, Lily was now covered in a strange, foul-smelling oil.

"What is this?" Lily asked. Rohemir hurried over and stooped to the ground. He put a taste of the oil to his lips and screwed up his face.

"What is it?" Ellizar asked, despite fending off his opponent.

"Blulen oil!"

Drake twisted out of the way, narrowly avoiding a sword aimed at his neck.

"In the old days, Borags used this to kill their enemies, first by dumping this on the ground around them. They would engage their enemies and then quickly retreat. As soon as the last soldier was safe, they would light the oil with fire. Their enemies would be trapped and suffer a horrible death."

Drake stumbled and fell backward, his sword clattering from his reach.

"How did it get here?" Lily asked, defending herself.

Drake lunged for his sword and grasped it, but an arrow struck his attacker in the throat. Gwen quickly strung another arrow as Drake stood.

"We haven't seen anybody," Drake pointed out.

"Through Grimdor the dark arts are plentiful. They could've hidden themselves with a spell."

"Why not just kill us in our sleep, if that's teh case?" Ellizar asked.

"You know nothing of the Sorcerer or what he is like," Rohemir said grimly. The seriousness in his voice took all of them by surprise and each of them second guessed anything they had imagined about Grimdor.

"The Sorcerer?" Drake asked. "The king of Grimdor is a Sorcerer?"

"We do not have time for this conversation!" Rohemir reprimanded. "We don't want to be trapped in this oil."

The two sides continued to clash and the night was filled with cries of pain and the sound of swords and armor.

"I'm not sure how long we can hold out!" Gwen yelled.

"Get off the cliff I have an idea!" Drake ignored the voices of warning and instead barreled into an unsuspecting Borag carrying a torch.

The torch fell to the ground, rapidly igniting the oil that covered the rocks. They all sprinted away from the flames, dropping over the edge. Ten feet later they landed on the rock and began to follow Rohemir who led the way as they ran into the unknown.

When Drake looked back he guessed that thirty Borags had made it out of the blaze alive. The fire still burned in the distance, lighting the darkness like a beacon in the night.

"What are we supposed to do?" Lily asked.

"Run and hope that something good comes out of it!" Rohemir said.

The chase continued for nearly an hour as the light filtered into the sky before them. Their hearts pounded inside their chests and their lungs screamed for air that they were currently being deprived of. To their wonder, the Borags continued to fall behind.

Just when they were beginning to think they were gaining an advantage, their hopes and spirits were shattered. In front of them, a sea of black rushed to intercept them. They changed course, but their enemies changed course to match them.

"We're not making as good of time as we thought we were," Rohemir exclaimed, pressing forward. "It appears that they somehow signaled another group of Borags."

"How did they manage to do that?" Lily asked. "They can't send a message that fast can they?"

"Their speed astounds me and frankly I'm confused by the speed at which they organized an interception party. The company behind us never intended to catch us," Rohemir cried.

"They'll be on us in a few minutes! What are we supposed to do?" Gwen asked. Rohemir didn't answer. The sound of the Borags grew nearer and they could now hear the harsh and confusing language.

A cry went up and they turned to see Ellizar, who lay flat on his back. Borags grabbed him, tied him up, and then sprinted away.

Lily cried out and chased after them, but Drake stopped her as all of the Borags. swiftly vanished from sight. She tried her best to get free but was unable to. When they were far enough away he let go of her. She fell to the ground and slammed it with her fist.

"All that time and we were running into a trap!" Drake said.

"I should have known better!" Rohemir exclaimed.

"We have to keep following them or else we'll never stand a chance at getting Ellizar back alive!" Lily cried.

"Don't worry Lily, we'll find Ellizar," Rohemir assured. "It seems that although I may not know much of their language I do know a little bit. After they had captured Ellizar I heard the word Duhma mentioned."

"What does that mean?"

"In the common tongue that means silence or death, but at any rate in Grimdor it's the name of a small city, one of the few that's above ground and it's only a day and a half from the border of Idumea, much further east then we wanted to go. If we can make it out of the city quietly then we'll be in good shape."

"Why didn't they take us?" Gwen asked. Drake's eyes drilled him with the same question.

"I thought the Spirits wanted to kill me, wouldn't the Borags want the same?"

"Perhaps there is some other motive behind all of this that we fail to see. The Borags were able to call for support easily and quickly. They are fast creatures but not that fast."

"Maybe the Spirits and the Borags are working together," Lily suggested her breathing still labored.

"The Spirits chased us close to the border and then the Borags have been chasing us ever since," Rohemir pointed out.

"If they had a Spirit with them, it could have taken the form of a Borag and we would never know the difference," Gwen added.

"Indeed. That whole other group that was coming right at us could have been Spirits that took the form of Borags," Drake said. "How are we supposed to fight someone who's constantly changing their appearance? They could become one of us and we'd never know it."

Rohemir was silent, thinking about everything. "For whatever reason they want Drake alive. Otherwise, they would have killed us with arrows moments after we tried to escape. If they want you alive they'll keep Ellizar alive, to question him about where we were going, and for bait in case we show up. We have to start making our way to Duhma,"

Their course was uncertain as none of them knew where they were anymore. They had run so far in a short amount of time that even Rohemir himself seemed to have lost his bearings. Still, he led them through the confusing maze of rocks, hills, and valleys, all of which offered nothing different from the last one they had gone over.

IX · THE RESCUING OF ELLIZAR

The dawn came and with it a new sense of hope. The company pressed forward with Rohemir in the lead. He walked with certainty as if he now knew where they were going.

A few hours later, they were forced to slow to almost a crawl as they became mired in fog and light rain once they entered a large rock field. Previously the rocks had been large and smooth, but now they were rough and smaller, with pointed edges.

They wandered for a day inside the rock field only briefly stopping for rest. The rain increased in intensity, and by day's end, (in some places) they were trudging through a foot and a half of water.

In addition to the rain, the fog also became thicker, forcing the four of them to tie a rope to each other in order not to leave someone behind. A damp wind swept through the barren land and chilled them to the bone as it chewed through their clothes and numbed every nerve in their bodies. Rohemir lit a fire that night, having to use magic to do it. Lily didn't seem comfortable with the idea, but even she didn't object as they huddled around for warmth.

Another day came and went and the weather became worse in a different way. The rain had stopped, the fog had lifted, and the cold wind had ceased. The clouds were gone from the sky.

Now, heat unlike anything they had ever experienced beat down on them, grilling them alive. Their skin became sunburned and dried out, peeling off in long flakes. The water vanished from every corner of the rocks. Their flasks of water also dried up, leaving them nothing to drink as they pressed forward.

Every day they walked in the same formation, with Rohemir leading the way, Lily close on his heels, and Drake and Gwen pulling up the rear. Drake observed Lily with a keen interest. She was second in line and everyone knew she was only second because she didn't know the way.

The terrain quickly became the toughest stretch of land they had ever been through. Hills, cliffs, valleys, and flatland. Every bit of it was rock, with not one plant to be seen seen. Each mile brought the same view, an endless sea of rocks and sweltering heat that threatened to melt them down to nothing.

Their skin blistered in the sun and the sweat rolled off of them as they blindly followed behind Rohemir. Their clothes were now shabby and tattered, appearing as though they had been worn for a century. Their sweat from the sweltering heat had stained them beyond repair and then dried becoming hard and stiff, making them the most uncomfortable things that Drake had ever worn.

They all made modifications to their clothes to help battle the heat, but it seemed futile as every minute became more and more unbearable. When asked, Rohemir hadn't said much except that someone was trying to make the trip more difficult for them, trying to wear them down to nothing before they reached the city.

When they asked who would possibly have the power to do something like that, Rohemir was silent and refused to answer. The only consolation was that they were hopefully getting close to the city and one step closer to Ellizar.

Drake wondered what Ellizar was going through. He knew Ellizar was tough and would likely have plenty of spirit if they tried anything, but the thought crossed Drake's mind that he could be dead. What if all this traveling was nothing more than a plot to offer them hope, only to find that there was none? They could be walking into a trap.

The next day came and went and so did the next night. The trip had already taken two days longer than they had expected, due to the extreme heat which was taking its toll on them.

Eventually, the rain started again, this time joined by a wind out of the north, which did nothing to raise their spirits. They filled their flasks and found a small cave to use as a shelter for the night.

In the morning they detected the familiar smell of smoke and as such Rohemir picked up the pace. The torrent of rain had subsided to a comfortable rain allowing them to make better time. A while later they stopped at the edge of a vale, looking at a city that lay in the distance, on top of a hill.

"Welcome my friends to the Fortress of Duhma," Rohemir announced.

Drake was at a loss for words as he looked at the impressive city before them. The walls were constructed out of a course rock that was grey to the glance, but also with a sheen on it that made it hard to see. If it hadn't been for the fact that they had been looking for it, Drake felt as if they would've passed it right by.

Torches illuminated the city, leaving shadows at every corner. The might of this city was not in question as they could vaguely make out catapults, watch towers, spires, and battlement-filled walls which stole any hope they had been hanging onto.

A pool of water surrounded the entire city, whether it was meant as a defensive tactic or not, was unclear. A single draw bridge led right up to iron gates and on either side a statue of some hideous beast from ages past stood to welcome them.

"How are we supposed to get in there?" Drake asked.

"The only way to get in there is to walk in through the front door and pose as prisoners," Rohemir suggested.

"We're not Borags. We can't just walk in."

"There are humans and some of the other races that work with the Borags and the Spirits, let's just hope that they're foolish enough to believe the charade."

"I don't know about this!" Lily exclaimed. "Do you have any idea where they might be keeping Ellizar? This seems hopeless."

"My dear elf, he is probably in the tallest spire, directly in the middle of the city."

"You serious?" Gwen asked. Drake too questioned it.

"Borags build their prisons very differently from the way any other nation constructs theirs. Although it is difficult to break people out from a below-ground prison, it is harder to take them from the highest point."

"Are you sure this charade will work?" Gwen asked.

"I am unsure about a lot of things these days. But of this, I'm quite certain! You three will be my prisoners and I will be the one in charge. We'll have to leave our weapons behind if we're to make it believable."

"Let's just give them all to you and then we can take them from you, and overpower you," Lily mentioned.

They took her idea and found a way to place all the weapons on Rohemir, which made him look more intimidating. They left their packs where they were for the moment. Before tying themselves at the wrists with some rope, Rohemir had brought in his pack.

Rohemir marched them down the slope and across the drawbridge, with little more than a glance from the guards. Once they had passed into the city, they each let out a sigh of relief.

Several minutes later they found themselves at the foot of the spire, which was crudely carved out of a dull grey rock. The base of the spire was wide, becoming narrower as it wound up into the sky. Torches illuminated the tower, most of them unaffected by the rain that seemed to be getting heavier again.

Rohemir opened the front door and shoved them through, speaking harshly in the Borag tongue. They silently slipped the ropes off their wrists as another Borag entered the room, speaking in his dark and hideous language. Rohemir exchanged a few words with them, but it quickly became clear that the general believed whatever Rohemir was telling him. A moment later the Borag left.

Lily jumped to her feet, rushing towards the small door that would lead them up the tower. She stopped when she realized that none of them had followed.

"We have to get to Ellizar!" Lily exclaimed.

"I have a better idea," Rohemir started. "You take care of getting Ellizar out of here, we'll go back and get our bags and meet you on the far side of the city. Once word of this attack gets out they'll be looking for four of us not two."

"How is that a good idea?" Drake asked. "We'd be sending her in there alone."

"You will have to trust me on this," Rohemir said. "They want you more than they want her or Ellizar. We have to get you out, which means we need to leave together while we can."

"Go! I'll be fine," Lily said. She vanished from their sight and the rest of them reluctantly stepped into the rain which had gotten heavier while they had been in the building. The streets were now flooded with an inch of water.

Rohemir bounded into the rain, and within moments the rain became so thick that Drake and Gwen fell behind. When they looked again, Rohemir was gone. Desperate to stay together, Drake and Gwen held each other's hands so they wouldn't lose each other as they stumbled through the streets, unable to see more than a few feet in the dense rain.

They wandered, hoping that at any second they would see something they recognized, but with each corner, their hopes were dashed. A horn called through the city, above the noise of the pounding rain.

They turned around another corner, fear coursing through them as they were staring at a company of Borags. Gwen hastily pulled Drake into the alley on their left and despite their best efforts, they were met by a group of three Borags.

Drake and Gwen were overpowered as Drake was knocked to the ground, momentarily submerging him into the cold water. When he resurfaced one of the Borags held Gwen by her hair, a thick, cruel knife to her throat. Her captor growled and spoke harshly. Drake's heart pounded in his chest as he understood.

A flash of light appeared in one of the spires and the Borags turned their heads for a split second. Drake pulled a knife from the enemy closest to him and sent it sailing through the air. It caught the hand of the Borag who was holding Gwen.

The Borag cursed loudly and released his hold on Gwen. All three of their enemies rushed in and then stopped in their tracks as a shrill note rang through the sky. At once two of the Borags rushed away, leaving only one for them to overpower. Drake and Gwen rushed their captor and swiftly overpowered him.

The soldier was submerged in the water that had risen to their knees. Unable to get a footing the Borag was swept away in the current that was growing stronger. They slogged their way to the end of the alley. Borags moved all around them on the higher levels. And in the distance, a fire burned in the tall spire that Ellizar and Lily were in. They vanished into the rain.

Lily rushed through the first door and hurried up the winding staircase, skipping one or two steps at a time. Cells lined each side of the steep, (and at some places impossibly narrow) stairwell. Despite the size of the stairwell, there were only a few torches and lanterns to light her way.

She came to an abrupt, small landing with a door directly in front of her. She grasped the handle and only got it open a couple of inches before a hand shoved it closed from behind her.

A Borag said something in his language but never got any further as Lily kicked her leg backward. The Borag gasped for breath and fell backward, tumbling down the steep stairs. His cries were only heard for a moment as he struck his head on the bricks and went unconscious.

She flung open the door and was greeted by three more doors. She slowed her breathing down and tried to focus as she hoped to pick the right one. She listened to the silence suddenly hearing something that she didn't expect.

Music?

She crept to the door on the left hearing a merry tune coming down the stairwell. Lily found the door unlocked and warily began climbing the stairs. The music grew louder and the smell of food reached her. Her intrigue occupied her thoughts until at last, she came to the cell with Ellizar in it.

Ellizar sat on the floor with a bottle of ale, happily refilling the cups of the guards who were all laughing and having a good time. Ellizar winked at her and motioned her into the unlocked cell.

With a mischievous smile, Ellizar pushed one of the guards over. He knocked his head on the cement and was out like a light getting a round of laughter from the others. Ellizar laughed.

Lily stepped into the cell and grabbed a piece of bread from the plate in the middle, as the other two guards didn't even take one look at her for several minutes. When they finally did they sat there dumbfounded before stumbling to their feet and struggling to pull out their weapons. Their attempt failed and they passed out on the ground at her feet. Ellizar held a cup out to her and filled it up as he did his own.

"I guess you didn't need my help after all?" Lily said taking a sip of the drink. Ellizar laughed.

"A dwarf needin' an elf's help? Now there's a laughable concept."

"You, my friend, are a laughable concept. I don't know how you managed to get them all in here and drunk, but good job. Don't suppose you have any way to get out of here."

"I do. I figured yed be along so I had a little something prepared just in case yeh did. I had them bring me rope. They were drunk enough that they didn't even ask why, which worked fer me. It seems I also had them loosen this grate on the window. They're very stupid when they've drunk teh much."

Ellizar put both hands on the metal grate and pulled it out of the wall. "My plan is we tie a rope teh one of their arrows and then send the arrow through this grate and shoot it at that tall buildin' over there. They've been braggin' that their arrows pierce rock. We hang on teh this and slide down and drop onto that buildin' over there. Good idea?"

"Brilliant actually," Lily admitted. She quickly did as he had suggested grabbing the rope and tying it to one of the Borags' arrows and then looping it through the grate. She looked out into the rain, pulled back the bowstring, and let the arrow fly.

The arrow sped towards its target and struck into the building, embedding itself deep into the rock. Ellizar secured the other end of the rope to the cell door. They both climbed up into the small window, grabbing hold of the grate, which was looped through the rope.

"Ready when yeh are," Ellizar said. Lily took a torch from the wall and dropped it into the barrel of ale that had been brought into the cell. The barrel ignited and she grabbed onto the grate and they pushed off, sliding down the rope.

"Say when," Lily yelled as they picked up speed.

"Now!" Ellizar yelled. They let go of the grate and fell onto the roof of another building. Ellizar and Lily ran until they reached the edge, unsure of where to go next. Fire had filled the tower they had just come from and horns sounded loudly through the air.

Lily cut the rope that they had just slid down and they both grabbed on and jumped over the edge of the building, letting themselves swing down to the watery streets below. They splashed their way through the flooded city streets now pushing through nearly two feet of water.

They glanced behind only long enough to notice a volley of arrows streaming toward them. Ellizar shoved Lily out of the way, sending her down into the water but in turn missing the arrows that landed where she had been standing.

He took Lily's hand and the two of them took off running as fast as they could. They floundered around the vacant street for close to ten or fifteen minutes, the water becoming to deep for them to stay on the ground. Accepting defeat, they climbed to the top of a building.

They stood for several lonely seconds, the water getting dangerously close to coming over the edge and flooding the rooftop. They whirled around to the sound of water splashing. To their relief it was Drake and Gwen who had also climbed on this building for refuge.

"Any ideas?" Drake asked, the torrential rain and rolling thunder forced them to yell.

"Not one," Lily answered. "Is Rohemir with you?"

"We got separated," Gwen exclaimed.

"What if the outside is flooded too?" Ellizar asked. "Then we're really stuck."

"I'm not sure it is," Drake answered.

"Why do you say that?" Lily asked.

"They know we're trying to get away so if they can contain us to the rooftop by flooding the streets why wouldn't they do it? I think they've sealed up the city gates and are holding the water in."

"What purpose would that serve?" Gwen asked. "They'd just be flooding themselves as well."

"Unless they know something we don't," Drake suggested. "Rohemir himself said that most Borags live underground and they tunnel. For all we know the only people that live here are soldiers. I'm sure that if they were going to flood the city, they all knew about it and had a plan as to how to get rid of us and the water."

"And the water?" Ellizar asked. "Are yeh suggestin' that they have a way teh drain the city?"

"It would make sense wouldn't it?" Drake challenged. "They need water below ground. Whenever it rains this much they would open a drain and all the water would run through tunnels that would take all the water below ground so they wouldn't die from thirst."

"It's genius actually," Lily admitted, starting to get chilled by the rain. "But how is that going to help us?"

"They have to eventually open the drain." Chills swept through all of them as the rushing of water reached their ears. The water was now mere seconds from covering the top of the building and they could see it had a current.

"Looks like they opened the drain," Gwen stated. "How is this going to help us? We'll just end up underground."

"I'm sure they can't take all the water at once, they must have a holding area. I say we jump in, once we're in the holding area we'll be able to swim to shore."

"If the currents are not so strong that it sucks us in any way," Lily pointed out.

"I'm not sure I like this idea!" Gwen exclaimed.

"It's the only one I have," Drake answered. They exchanged glances and nodded their approval of the plan. They cautiously moved toward the edge of the building where the water had picked up speed. Already the water level had dropped a few inches. They all took hands.

"On the count of three, we jump!" Drake exclaimed. "One...Two...three!" They pushed off from the building, submerging themselves in the rushing water. They were swept away down the streets, picking up speed and surfacing a couple hundred feet later.

Drake forced himself to breathe; the water felt like ice slowing their reflexes. They were pulled through countless streets and around corners by the current which was increasing in speed. The rain still thundered down above them.

They could faintly see the shape of the Borags standing on top of the buildings emptying their quivers as they tried to kill the four of them. The arrows splashed into the water, harmlessly floating past. They rounded another corner, and a dark cavern appeared ahead of them.

"There's the tunnel!" Drake yelled pointing ahead. Gwen grabbed onto his hand as they were swept towards the entrance. The dark tunnel swallowed them and they were lost to the darkness, struggling to stay above the water.

"Get down!" Gwen yelled. They dove beneath the water swimming for a few feet before they resurfaced finding that they were now on the other side of a baffle that had stood in their way.

"Good call!" Drake exclaimed.

Torches lit the shaft and they could see dozens of tunnels on either side of them, all filled with archers. They dove beneath the water, staying under for as long as they could as more arrows splashed into the torrent of water. When they came back up for air they were in darkness again.

"Where's this holdin' area yeh thought we would find?" Ellizar asked. A faint light appeared.

"Right there!" Drake exclaimed pointing towards the light. Their fear grew as they were swept towards the opening and then shoved out by the water. The ground disappeared beneath them and they found themselves free-falling into a massive body of water as they exited out of the tunnel. Seven other tunnels had joined, bringing water from other places in the city. They cried out as they were forced underwater. They sputtered their way to the surface.

"This way!" Drake yelled, swimming as hard as he could for the shore. Despite their best efforts, they began fading as the current threatened to swallow them.

Then in the darkness, a long line of silver became visible. Drake grasped a rope that was extended into the water. He wrapped a firm arm around Gwen's waist and held to the rope. A second rope came and Lily grabbed on and held Ellizar, from being swept away. The ropes became tight as the current swirled.

To their surprise, they were not pulled out of the current but rather held in one place while the water receded. Eventually, the current became weak enough, and the water level low enough that they could stagger to their feet and walk to the end of the rope.

The ends of both ropes were tied to a large column of rock that jutted out of the Grimdorian landscape. Rohemir smiled as he came closer.

"Welcome back everyone," Rohemir greeted.

"Nice rope," Drake complimented.

"Thank you, found it in your packs. Good thing to bring with you on a journey."

Drake nodded and racked his brain; he didn't remember packing rope.

"Where have you been?" Drake asked. "We thought you had deserted us."

"I didn't realize you weren't behind me until you were far out of my sight," Rohemir replied. "I was out of the city and gates were shut. I knew eventually they would have to open their drain tunnels. I'm just glad that you figured out why the water was moving. We're only two days away from the border. Once we're there we should be perfectly safe and out of this nation. One step nearer to our destination."

"Can't argue with that, lead on," Lily answered. They walked into the rain, blindly following Rohemir's lead. Eventually, the rain stopped but the sky didn't get any brighter as the dark clouds continued to dampen their spirits, then just as it had the first time, the heat came. Their thoughts were fuzzy and they stumbled through the hot and dry land. Hope faded in their minds.

Two days later they stepped out of Grimdor and into the sunshine. Warm, lovely sunshine. Trees waited in the distance. The ground below them was grass-covered, but short and stunted. They walked and the vegetation grew taller, just as it had before they had entered Grimdor more than a week ago.

A couple of hours passed and the sun began to set in the west, creating a sunset that brought rest to the weary company. They made camp on the edge of a forest that had been recently cut down, feeling better than they had felt in a long time.

MEETINGS IN THE DARK

Drake squinted as he opened his eyes to the midday sun. The sound of a hundred horses caught his attention and to his surprise. The horsemen seemed to be riding directly towards them.

The soldiers atop the horses, called out to each other, quickly surrounding their little camp. He reached and shook Gwen awake, though everyone else woke up but never got a moment to speak.

Drake looked for Rohemir, who was nowhere to be found. A horse and rider made his way through the ranks, pushing through the circle that had been formed.

"Do you know where you are strangers?" the man asked. He had greying hair and his voice carried authority. He sat tall on his painted mare and his headgear was more elaborate than the others.

"No," Lily answered.

"You're in the nation of Idumea," the man answered. "You look most unusual, and could no doubt, spin an interesting tale if I wished to hear it. I do not wish to hear tall tales. I am interested only in learning the truth. Who are you and what is your business? Choose your words wisely. They may be your last."

"I'm not sure I understand what we've done that puts us on thin ice," Gwen said. The man's eyes bored into hers for a moment.

"You are in the middle of a cut-down forest. This forest was not authorized to be cut down by anyone. The king did not order it and we've been after the thieves for months. In the night, they come into our beautiful forests and cut down *our* trees, and are off with them before we can even hope of catching them.

"We have spotted large numbers of Borags breaching the long-peaceful borders. Until now, we thought the Borags were the ones finding our forests, but apparently, we were mistaken and we have spies in our midst."

"We're not spies!" Ellizar answered. "We're escapees from Grimdor."

"I don't believe it for a second. You fit every stereotype of a spy there is, no denying that. You are seemingly in the middle of nowhere and on the edge of death. You have barely any clothing or food, which would stimulate feelings of sorrow and pity in our hearts and therefore affect our decision."

"We're not spies," Drake said once again. The man laughed.

"Do you have anyone who can vouch for that? I see no reason to believe you unless you have someone that I know and trust to validate your claim." He turned to face the soldiers. "Do any of you believe them? Or should we show them what a blade of Idumea can do to a traitor's neck?"

"Aramen you old fool put down your weapons and leave these poor people alone!" The soldiers divided and Rohemir came into view, carrying rabbits in hand.

"Rohemir?!" Aramen greeted. His face lightened as Rohemir came closer, eventually, he began laughing.

"You are a mystery," Rohemir replied. "You can face down the largest army that might attack, but one look at me you break out into laughter."

"I can't help it, your face-"

"Be careful now," Rohemir warned with laughter in his voice. "You do not need to worry about these people I am certain that they are not spies of any sort. They are as they have said, and I've been traveling with them. I'm afraid however that we might have gotten lost and I no longer know where we are. We are trying to get to the seaport of Revly. Perhaps you could point us in that direction."

"Indeed I could, but if that's where you were headed you're far from there,"

Aramen answered. "You're a good week away by horseback. Heading southwest will get you there the quickest, though not necessarily the easiest path. You could go a different route but it would be far longer."

"Speed is of the utmost importance to us."

"Have you seen Borags lately?"

"Not since we entered your borders. Have you?"

"We believe that they are responsible for the deforestation that has taken place. Our forests have been disappearing faster than we can blink an eye. The king himself has ordered that we patrol and kill anyone we find that may appear to be suspicious especially if they are Borags."

"What would the Borags want with your forests?" Drake asked. Aramen shrugged his shoulders.

"It is a question we do not have the answer to. The king seems to be lost and confused in all that has been happening, having no clear sight of where he is sailing this great ship. I fear there is a storm coming on the horizon."

"As long as we're alive there will be hope," Gwen answered. "We will not give into them."

"I wish everyone had the determination you had." He turned to his men and yelled to a couple of them. "Give them all horses and a fresh set of clothes and all the food and drink that they want. If they are going to be crossing to the sea they will need provisions. You can't be expected to be taken seriously about anything in clothes and conditions as you are in. Our patrol is heading back southwest as it is so we can ride with you for a few hours. If you wouldn't mind the company?"

They gladly accepted all the provisions even though the clothes weren't perfect fits, they would do for now. They mounted their horses just like they had a couple of weeks ago with Gwen and Drake on one horse and Ellizar and Lily on the other.

The day faded and the sun dipped out of the sky. The company made camp, quickly setting up tents and starting fires, preparing food. They ate the food feeling more and more relieved as the food replenished their bodies. The others talked and laughed but Drake found himself unable, too occupied with his thoughts as he replayed the events in his head.

Leaving Fiori was supposed to help them stay safe and so far they had been chased, attacked, and nearly killed. What was going to happen when they finally reached the nation of Ariamore? He was supposed to be safe if they could make it there, but in Drake's heart, he had doubt.

The next morning they rode to the southwest. Aramen and his company eventually headed to the east, having business elsewhere.

Drake lost all track of time as one day blended into the next, separated only by a few hours of darkness which brought much-needed rest to the weary travelers. The days were long but pleasant for the most part. They rode through the wilderness enjoying the many things that had been lacking during their time in Grimdor. Birds, wind whistling through the trees, the sounds of their horses plodding through grass. All of these things combined brought Drake a peace that he hadn't felt since he had been awakened on the side of the river.

"Rohemir?" Drake asked. "What's going to happen to me when we get to where we're going...you know to Ariamore?"

"Any number of things could happen, but which one will occur is beyond my knowledge and foresight. If I could see the future then I would gladly tell you the answer."

"But still you must have some idea...some inclination."

"Under normal circumstances, you would be interviewed before the council of Ariamore and then they would make decisions from there. However, I think the situation with your memory will likely wipe out that possibility. That's beside the fact that the council usually frowns on interviewing people."

"Why is that?" Gwen asked. "Wouldn't the council want to interview people?"

"Yes, but doing so has its disadvantages. You see if someone is brought before the council, it is a possibility that they could lie to the entire council at once and no one would know the difference. What the council usually likes to do is have a couple of members of the council, seemingly run into the person they wish to interview and ask them the questions they need to know. People are often much more forthcoming if they don't think they're being interrogated."

"What are the other options if that one isn't likely to happen?" Drake asked.

"You could be considered insane and thrown in prison until they can figure out what they're going to do to you. Also unlikely if you ask me. I have sent many messages to a friend of mine in Ariamore who is keeping everyone updated on our progress and situation. The council will not be surprised by your arrival.

"The other option which in my opinion is the most likely is that they will let you live as normal of a life as possible while they discuss the unusual events that have transpired."

"You mean my arrival?" Drake asked. Rohemir shrugged his shoulders.

"You're arrival is not the only happening that is unusual Drake Thomas. The Borags are straying from their boundaries and cut down forests that do not belong to them. Several other things are a bit strange, but I will keep my secrets for the time being. Just know Drake, that it is unlikely that you will ever live a completely normal life. After all, you bear the mark of Lathon, and that in itself will lead you on another path."

"I wish I knew what the path was," Drake asked. "How am I supposed to prepare the way for Shedaros when I don't even know who he is?"

"Don't worry about the future for it is not for you to worry about. When the time comes I suspect that everything will become clear."

"Do you know who Shedaros is?" Drake asked.

"I only have suspicions," Rohemir said. "And as I have stated previously I shall keep them to myself. I don't want to make any assumptions that might be wrong and mislead people. If you take my meaning."

"I understand."

The next few days passed just like the first ones with nothing of any importance to say. Lily and Ellizar had been constantly teasing each other which proved to be amusing for everyone who was listening.

Before long they had left the familiar surroundings behind them and had entered into a forest that seemed to be older than time itself. The trees stood high above them, and they were just as wide as they were tall. The sun was blocked out completely during the day, but none of them complained.

Instead, they took solace in this strange forgotten forest. The sounds within were unusual and carried them away with their thoughts as they imagined what the world must have been like when Lathon had first created it.

Before long a road appeared, They joined the road which was now heading steadily south, with the traveling being harder than they wished as the formerly flat road, turned into steep hills and ravines and narrowed, at times, until they couldn't ride two abreast.

Eventually, the road did level out, and when it did they were joined by two other roads. The activity picked up immensely and the road became wide and broad, before eventually turning to small little stones that were neatly arranged together.

They crested one final hill and came to see the city of Revley, which was thoroughly squished into the ravine of three adjoining several large hills, that Drake thought could've passed as small mountains. An old stone wall, no more than twenty feet high ran the stretch from hill to hill, with most of the wall facing the sea, creating a perfect defense or levee in the case of rough seas. The harbor and docks were filled with ships and countless others anchored in the harbor, waiting to unload their precious cargo.

The road was now filled with carts, horses, and citizens, and all were brought to a stop as the sentries at the gate questioned everyone. They waited patiently until it was their turn. To Drake's surprise, the guards were smiling and seemed in a pleasant mood.

"Good afternoon travelers," the guard on the left greeted. "What business do you have in Revly?"

"I see there are many ships in port, we seek to hire a vessel to take us home."

"Is that your only business?"

"Yes," Rohemir answered.

"In that case, welcome to Revly. I'm sure you will find what you seek. Be informed though, that no ships are likely to be leaving port for several days. You may be spending more time here than you would like."

"Thank you very much," Rohemir answered. The guards moved out of the way and they passed into the city. Nothing about the city stood out as grand or glamorous, but it was easy to see that it was a very proud city.

The citizens were a range of different kinds, though Men were the vast majority. The buildings were tall and grand filled with intricate carvings and designs, many no doubt, depicted the gods of Idumea or other great historical things that had transpired throughout Revly's history.

They carefully found their way through the streets and byways until they found a decent inn with vacancies. The building itself, looked as if it was older than the city, built out of hundreds of small stones, which had been happily taken over by moss and lichen due to the excessive moisture from the sea.

They entered into a happily chaotic dining hall as the people talked, and laughed, and many couples danced in the large open floor between the tables. A roaring fireplace sat on one end, with a long bar and many patrons filling every nook and cranny that wasn't reserved for tables.

"Good day fellow travelers!" They turned to see a wirey sort of fellow, with a thick mustache and a balding head coming towards them. "Welcome to the

Moss Haven. Are you looking for accommodations?"

"Do you have any?" Drake asked.

"Last room is yours if you want it."

"Do you have stables for our horses?" Lily asked.

"Yes, mam. Stable fees are Included with the room. Twenty Fettels a night."

"We'll take it," Rohemir said, pulling some coins from his pocket and stuffing them into the man's hand.

"Always glad to have a new customer! The name's Baron, I'll show you to your room in just a minute." He turned to face someone else and spoke in a hushed tone. Baron had their horses brought around to the stables out back and then led them away from the happy chaos to a long tight hall with several rooms.

"Here you are, travelers. I hope you'll enjoy your stay with us Mr?"

"Rohemir."

"Ah, yes, I thought you were!" Drake felt himself tense up at the exclamation. The others felt it too, though Rohemir didn't seem surprised. "I had this to give to you."

Baron pulled an old worn envelope, with a red wax seal from his pocket. Rohemir quickly took it and stuffed a few more fettels into Baron's hand in return. "I was never here."

"Of course not," Baron said with a smile.

"Thank you very much." Barron left and they closed the doors.

"What was that."

"Nothing. Pay it no mind," Rohemir insisted.

Despite their best effort, they were unable to get any more information out of Rohemir about the envelope. Wash basins, several beds a small table and two chairs were the accommodations of the room, but even those meager offerings made them feel like royalty with their recent adventures.

Rohemir patiently waited until everyone had fallen asleep. He grabbed his cloak and exited their room, quietly making his way into the now dimly lit dining hall, where only a few couples and shady characters kept to the darkened corners.

He stepped out of the Mossy Haven and was relieved to see that the city was finally sleeping, and Revly was as quiet as a tomb. A few torches burned on the street corners, breaking up the thick darkness. A dense fog had rolled in off the sea thoroughly muffling any sounds that he made and hiding him from unsavory eyes which could be at hand.

Torches burned creating pale light in the streets. The city was nothing more than a confusing maze of shadows and strange shapes that seemed to lurk around every corner waiting for his arrival.

He took his time making his way through the city, which had become mired in the thick fog. The streets were now a confusing maze of shadows and strange shapes, but having, lived here for a year or so, Rohemir knew this city better than anyone.

He kept a close eye and his ears sharp as he was careful to circle back every few minutes to lose anyone who might be following him. Time crept on and still, there was no sign of the coming dawn.

He looked up at the street sign which was hanging crudely on a worn and weathered metal post. The sign was old and faded, with rust having taken over most of it. Only the last four letters could be made out anymore E-M-I-R. He turned down the alley entering into a forgotten part of the city.

Without warning, the buildings ended and he entered into ruins. An old wooden house, decrepit and decaying, sat in front of him. Vines and thorns as well as several trees had grown up through the ruined house, The weight of the branches caused them to droop down over the building, hiding it from view.

When he was convinced that he was safe and undetected he continued, moving to the left and vanishing beneath the first tree that had grown up and over the ruins.

He knelt and studied the ground and then followed one set of footprints until they disappeared. He grabbed hold of a handle and pulled open a trapdoor, revealing a dark tunnel.

When the door closed, Rohemir was left in the darkness, forced to feel his way down the stairs. He muttered a simple spell that brought light to his hand. The tunnel was carved out of the dirt, reinforced in areas with wood and rocks.

Old portraits hung on the wall, covered by years of dust and grime which almost completely blocked out the pictures that were held within. Rohemir considered the situation for a moment knowing that several people could be compared to these pictures.

The dirt and the grime covered the only good part of a person's soul to the point where they forgot about what was good because everyone else only saw the dirt and the grime. It had been his life for years to point out what was wrong with someone else's life while failing to realize his own was screwed up.

The past filled his mind for only a moment but he pushed it away and focused on the path ahead. He came to a fork in the path and stared at the two tunnels in front of him. Eventually, he took the path to the right, leaving the gaping dark hole behind him.

Light began to appear at the end of the tunnel and grew until it became clear that he had reached his destination safely. He put his wand away and walked more confidently now as warmth filled the tunnel and the walls became cleaner as did everything else. The pictures in the picture frames were now clearly visible.

He stepped into a large room. A roaring fireplace was in the corner, a large pot of something bubbling over it. He stepped forward and then cried out in pain as he was thrown through the air.

He landed hard on the floor and whipped out his wand. An uneasy silence consumed his thoughts and his heart told him things he did not wish to know.

"Sorry old friend. It seems I thought you were someone else." An elf stepped out of the dark cave and came into the light. Atruss strode forward elegantly, a long black robe coming down to his feet, the man's hair was long and brown. His piercing green eyes shattered everything they looked at. His ears were pointed indicating that he was an elf

"You look much different than the last time I saw you."

"Wearied and traveled by the rough world we live in."

"You shouldn't have come here," the man said.

"I had no other choice," Rohemir answered. The elf looked at him skeptically.

"There's always another choice Rohemir. You and I both know that."

"Yes, well things unfolded differently than I wanted them to. Besides I'm not the only one who shouldn't be here."

"Your messages have been increasingly intriguing as well as terrifying. Furthermore, I had pressure from several other people to make the journey here. Several council members among them."

"The council members wanted you to meet me here?"

The elf nodded. "Indeed they did. Skander, Willard, and Miles are in the city as well. It wasn't in my power to stop them from coming. As much as I might not have liked the threat they posed I had no choice. You can't say no when you think of their situation."

"No argument there."

"We have much to talk about and I'm not sure how much time I have to sit and dilly-dally," Atruss warned. "I can't be sure I've made it here without being seen. Tell me about your travels. You sent word when you left Fiori and I have heard nothing else since. It's been over two weeks. If I know you, you've run into something interesting."

"Why did you send him?"

"Because I trust him with my life and he's the only one who could heal Gwen. You know that."

"Of course, I know that, granted I hadn't been able to find a healer capable but still you shouldn't have sent *him*. You know I don't like him."

"Aiden is a good man Rohemir. I've never figured out what you don't like about him but maybe you should put aside your differences and try to befriend him. I'm sure when you do that you'll find a friend like you've never had before."

"My heart warns me of him."

"Then perhaps your heart needs to be corrected. There is nothing wrong with Aiden. He is as good as they come, he wanted to help and so I sent him."

"In my own opinion, you have been deceived by him. You can't deny that Aiden is very persuasive."

"He did not persuade me of anything Rohemir! I agree with everything that he stands for. Why don't you trust him?"

"Your guess is as good as mine," Rohemir answered. "Perhaps in my heart, I still hold a little of the prejudice that stands between Men and Elves. I met him a couple of years ago in a small village. He was talking with a few blacksmiths. Something about that turned me against him. He could be a high-up figure, yet he was talking with common people. It's not the way of things."

"No but perhaps it's the way things are meant to be," Atruss pointed out. "He is a breath of fresh air in this musty world."

"Perhaps the main reason I distrust him is because he walks as though he knows something everyone else doesn't know, yet it's not an arrogant walk. It's just different and I'm not sure how to describe it. Despite his casual and normal attire, he carries a broad sword. I feel uncomfortable around him."

"Hopefully time will unravel the mysteries surrounding Aiden and the truth will become clear as to his identity so that you may see that you are wrong," Atruss replied.

"Something about Aiden is different. The fact that he is elf-kind already foils one of my thoughts about who he could be."

"Indeed that was my first thought, but Marion and Joseph are not Elves. If Aiden was Shedaros then I think we would most definitely see it in him. This world is changing before our eyes," Atruss replied.

"If we're unprepared then we're dead!" Rohemir exclaimed. "I know that Ariamore is known to be a peaceful nation but what is going to be said when armies show up on our front doorstep?"

"Your concern is dually noted, and the council has authorized that an army should be formed. They have seen the signs in the world; they know it's coming. Little do they know that war is nearly on their doorstep. If Grimdor has a leader, then Shedaros has to be around here somewhere."

"I'm sure he is, but who is he and when will he come forward?" Rohemir asked. The question hung in the air. "Ancient scrolls and my and Sedric's account of what happened that night can only go so far. How are we to know Lathon's timing?"

"Seeing that he created all of this in the first place, perhaps we're not meant to know Lathon's timing," Atruss pointed out. "Maybe for the time being we should just sit back and let things unfold the way they will."

"I think that would be wise, although it would probably kill me, or at the very least my curiosity would."

"If I may entice you, I have come up with another theory. One that might change the fortunes in the future that is before us," Atruss started. "It is no secret that I think that Aiden has the material to be Shedaros, yet he is, in fact, an elf. We both know that Shedaros was born into Marion and Joseph's family. The race of Men."

"Are you suggesting that Shedaros could be human?" Rohemir asked.

"I would say, it's plausible. In which case I would suggest that Drake Thomas himself could be Shedaros. He bears the mark, he is human. He seems interested and concerned about the world around him. Even though he has no memory past the last month everything else seems to fit. From your letters, I gather that he's excellent with a sword. It all fits."

"It's an interesting thought, I'll give you that. But there's one problem with your theory," Rohemir started. "We stopped at Marion and Joseph's house before we entered Grimdor."

"Yes?"

"Wouldn't they recognize their son if they saw him face to face?"

"Yes, but at the same time we both know that Marion and Joseph have tried their best to keep the boy hidden so that he could live a normal life. Maybe they just pretended not to know him because they knew something greater was going to happen. They wouldn't want to reveal the truth to the wrong people."

"I'm unconvinced," Rohemir replied. "Marion and Joseph have always kept to themselves. Of course, I guess that's to be expected when you look at what they've been through. What we've all been through for that matter. If Drake Thomas is by some chance Shedaros then things are about to get very interesting."

"They already are."

"Perhaps you would be interested in a theory of mine?" Rohemir paused gathering his thoughts. "Have you ever traveled through the nation of Grimdor?"

"A couple of times. Not in many years though."

"I have passed through the nation so many times that I can barely keep count. We went through Grimdor this time and experienced weather unlike anything you've ever seen."

"Grimdor is known for having bad storms," Atruss pointed out.

"They haven't had storms like this I can assure you. We were in torrential rain for days on end. We walked through so much water and were soaked for so long that we might as well have been naked for the good our clothes were doing us. Then we experienced heat. I've never felt anything like it. The combination of the two was total disaster and we looked like we had been through a hundred wars by the time we reached the other side. But here's where it gets interesting.

"I've traveled through Grimdor on several other occasions and had no problems. Nothing more than a sprinkle or a few drops here and there. Never pouring rain, and certainly not heat like what was felt. I did make a slight navigational error and we ended up in a place where it would take us more than a week to cross Grimdor. Not the widest part of the country, but certainly not the shortest.

"I have come to suspect that people in Grimdor knew we were there and I also suggest that there might have been some great Sorcerer present and they were conjuring up these storms."

"You are suggesting that the entire storm you went through was a well-thought-out trap? You think they meant to kill you?"

"Maybe not to kill us, but perhaps just to get us off track. You see if we had gone directly across the area we were in, like I had planned, we would have come out right into the city of Omar. We ended up nowhere near the city. I think that whatever was controlling the storm was trying to turn us off our course to keep something hidden."

"Do you have any proof that they're hiding anything?" Atruss asked.

"When we came out of Grimdor we were greeted by a company of soldiers and an old friend of mine who informed me that their forests were being cut down in the middle of the night. They think the Borags have been doing it but they have no proof. Marion and Joseph have also said that they could hear large numbers of Borags moving."

"Grimdor is certainly hiding something," Atruss agreed. "But what Sorcerer would be strong enough to conjure up storms that last for days on end? That's a power I've never seen. Through Lathon, I can do many things, but I can't do magic like that. Maybe it was Spirits, taking the form of storms that were helping him."

"Possible, but if the Borags and the Spirits are working together as we suspect, then they've been united by a power far *greater* than us. I propose that this power knew that we were in the nation and I propose that he knew we were near whatever he meant to hide. He created the storms to hold us up and push us off track and when those efforts failed he had one of us kidnapped so that we would have to go out of our way and further from what he was hiding."

"I don't like the sound of this Rohemir," Atruss replied. "I don't like the sound of this at all."

"But you must admit there is some shred of truth to what I am suggesting."

"I admit there is, and that is what frightens me the most. With these findings, I know the council will be happy with their decision to approve the creation of an army. There are still a lot of unknowns though. Do you think Sedric would recognize Shedaros if he saw him?"

"Maybe, why?"

"Even if it is my own theory, I'm not entirely sold on the idea that Drake Thomas is Shedaros. Maybe he is, maybe he isn't. I'm sure that Sedric would recognize his nephew if he saw him face to face."

"He probably would, but I'm afraid that's out of the question," Rohemir reminded.

"Why?"

"Because Sedric and his wife Bethany are wanted people just like I am. They are now in hiding, protecting things that must be hidden if a great Sorcerer has united the races of Spirits and Borags. We can't ask any of them to come to Ariamore just to identify one person."

"Unfortunately you're right," Atruss admitted, losing himself in his thoughts for the moment. "From the way you speak, I assume that everything went according to plan."

"Yes. They are now safe, hiding in a location that even I do not know."

"And everything is hidden with them?"

"Yes, it is. If the object should turn out to be authentic."

"Then it appears there is not much left to be said," Atruss concluded. "Everything seems to be unfolding, but where the path leads I cannot be sure. The only thing any of us know for sure is that war is coming and Drake Thomas is going to be the center of attention for a while. If Borags are attacking cities in other nations, in addition to cutting down trees from Idumea then we have problems. Big problems."

"We will make it to Ariamore as fast as we can. Do you know of anyone in the area that could that could give us passage?"

"No. At least no one with a boat that is worthy of traveling the path you will want to travel. I have money for you to hire one, but that end of it is up to you. If I wasn't going so far out of my way I would give you a ride myself."

"I only hope that I can get something arranged soon. I'm getting nervous with all of us just sitting here in plain sight. I'm sure by now we're wanted people."

"At the very least you are, my friend."

"As long as I can keep my identity hidden for a few more days then we'll be fine, if not then I'm not sure what we'll do."

"Take your time and do things right. I'll get the council to put out an open call for anyone and everyone who's interested in being part of the army to come forward. You have a couple of months if you want it.

"I understand."

Atruss turned to leave. "Be careful getting out of the city, however, you do it."

"Don't worry about me I know how to get out of this city in one piece," Rohemir replied with a wink. "You're the one who has to be careful."

"Thanks to the adventures I've had with you," Atruss replied with a laugh. They said their goodbyes and he vanished into one of the tunnels.

Rohemir made his way back the way he had come until he reached the top of the stairs and looked into the ruined house. The memories flashed through his head and still haunted him.

Rohemir sat down in one of the chairs, relieved to find that it held his weight. He looked around remembering what had happened and knowing that he shouldn't be here. Time passed and he stared into space, processing everything that had happened in the past couple of weeks.

There was a chance that Drake Thomas was Shedaros, but no one would know for sure until the day finally came when Shedaros would come forward. Spirits, Borags, Sorcerers, Shedaros. Everything was rushing towards the inevitable. A war was coming...and they were going to be right in the middle of it.

XI A WANTED MAN

The gentle touch of lips pressing against her own made Gwen not want to wake up. She reveled in the sensation, wishing this to last. But soon her eyes fluttered open and her tired eyes brought the surroundings into focus chasing the dream from her mind.

The smell of the ocean as well as smoke from the chimneys wafted in through the open window where Drake sat reading a book. Outside, the sun said it was mid-morning and the noise of the city reminded her they were not sleeping in the wilderness for once.

"Look who's finally awake," Drake greeted looking up from his book.

"And no one's trying to kill us?" Gwen asked, both she and Drake smiled at that. "Where are the others?"

"Rohemir left a note, saying he would be back later. Ellizar and Lily went to the dining hall. I didn't feel right leaving you here all by yourself."

Gwen climbed out of bed and got dressed, taking care to do her hair up a little more formally than she normally would. When she felt like she was presentable, she joined Drake by the window. A large featherless bird flew up to the window and perched itself on the sill. The bird cocked its head and made an eerie sound.

"How do you suppose it flies without any feathers?" Gwen asked.

"The wonder of Lathon's creation," Drake stated.

"You, Mr. Bird, are the most unusual one I've ever seen." The bird cocked its head again, studying both of them intently before turning its gaze to Drake who seemed mesmerized.

"Are you alright Drake? Drake?" Drake shook his head and looked at her with a strange smile.

"I've seen this bird before," Drake admitted. Gwen puzzled over his words.

"Where?"

"I'm not sure. It's familiar to me though. As if this bird has come to my aid in a time I can't remember."

The bird took flight and flew into the city.

"You are a fascinating man."

"Ready for breakfast?" Drake asked. She nodded and they left their room and entered into the long hall. At the end, they could see the light of day and smell the delicious food.

"What are you thinking?" she nervously asked.

"I wish I remembered my past."

"My past is less than glamorous. I wish I could forget mine," Gwen admitted.

"It would appear we both want what the other one has." He smiled warmly at her and she quickly turned away, pushing her auburn hair behind her ear. "So what does Gwen of Fiori want?"

"What do you mean?" she asked nervously. Drake casually played with a small knick-knack that sat on the table.

"I want my memory back, but you want to forget yours. What do you want to do...what is your dream?"

"I, uh, haven't really thought about it. Yet," Gwen said. For the most part, the statement was an honest one. Though she tried to suppress the emotion, a small part of her was glad that Fiori had been destroyed. For the first time in her life, she felt free.

"When you figure it out, let me know," Drake said. Gwen was somewhat intimidated by the request, but it went to her heart and for the first time in many years a twinge of joy began to take hold.

They entered into the dining hall, which despite the hour was just as full as the night before. Servers went to and fro carrying trays of hot food. Mr. Baron stood behind the counter, happily caring for all the customers. He smiled and waved them down as they entered.

"Good morning Mr. Baron," Drake greeted.

"Good morning to you to Mr. Thomas. Your party is right over there." Baron pointed to the far left corner where Ellizar and Lily sat at a table. "I'll be along to take your order just as soon as I take care of this fellow right here." He motioned to a man in casual attire sitting at the bar. The fellow was tall and lean, with a golden ring with a single purple stone upon his finger.

"Thank you very much," Drake replied. They weaved their way through tables and people.

"Hey! Hey! There's teh sleepy head!" Ellizar greeted. Gwen smiled at the comment and he hoisted a mug of ale in the air as if to drink in her honor.

"An ale at this time of morning?" Gwen asked.

"Their water tastes like twice-curdled milk mixed with vomit," Ellizar declared.

"Have experience with that?" Lily asked, mostly under her breath, allowing the comment to go unnoticed.

"It can't be that bad," Drake argued.

"Try fer yourself," Ellizar said, cautiously pushing a glass of water toward him. Drake put it to his nose and smelled it, and then as if he had decided it was alright, he took a swallow. He gagged and then spit it out.

"Then again," Drake said, setting the glass back down. "Perhaps ale is in order for this morning?"

"Did I hear you want some ales?" Baron said as he hurried to their table.

"Have yeh tried the water?" Ellizar asked.

Baron gave an amused smile. "There's a reason I don't charge for that."

"It tastes nasty!"

Lily smacked him in the side.

"It's true. I don't know what they did when they built the well...but it tastes horrible doesn't it?"

"I'm just glad yer ale is better!" Ellizar exclaimed. Baron smiled.

"That's makes two of us. I'll be right back with those ales." Baron hurried off as Drake and Gwen finally took a seat.

"When should we tell him we don't have any money?" Drake whispered.

"Once our food is gone," Lily remarked.

"I think tomorrow it's my turn teh sleep in," Ellizar said, taking another drink from his mug.

"You don't need to sleep in," Lily replied. Ellizar looked dumbfounded.

"Why not?"

"Whenever you sleep in you drive me crazy."

"I always drive yeh crazy," Ellizar replied.

"Yes, but it's like you've had fifty cups of coffee...all...day...long!"

"I take offense to that," Ellizar remarked. "I'm a dwarf. It's my job teh drive yeh out ov yer mind."

"And Lily's supposed to drive Dwarves crazy, so the love is mutual right?" Drake asked. Ellizar looked at him with a screwed-up face.

"Love? Yeh think I could ever love an elf? Ha! I think yer memory's gettin' worse Drake Thomas."

"Why did you assume that I was talking about romance?" Drake asked; Ellizar frowned.

"This is why I'm so short! I'm under so much stress from bein' around yeh three that I don't have time teh grow."

"Here are the ales!" Baron exclaimed, sitting them on the table in front of him. "Before I forget, Rohemir left this for you." He set an envelope on the table and excused himself as he took care of a nearby customer.

"What is it?" Ellizar asked.

"It's an envelope, duh," Lily replied.

"I know that. What is in the envelope?"

"Are Dwarves always this nosy?" Drake asked.

"Only this one," Gwen replied. Lily gave her a high-five, while Ellizar sat looking defeated.

"I'm done talkin' teh yeh two. Women, who needs them?" He turned back to Lily who was stifling a laugh. "So who's the note from?"

"There you go being all nosy again," Lily pointed out. She opened and quickly scanned the note.

"It seems Rohemir is going to be absent for a good part of the day," Lily recounted. "He says he will be speaking with the shipmaster, to book us passage. We're free to do what we want as long as we stay out of trouble. He also has provided money for food."

They ordered breakfast with the fettels Rohemir had given them and continued their conversation and bantering. Gwen's spirits were lifted as they talked throughout the meal.

Her mind drifted to daydreams of what the future might hold. She had dreamed of finding a perfect man and being a wife, but she had been a slave, and it had always been a dream.

Now as she watched Drake, she began to hope there could be something more. Her eyes followed his every move, hoping and dreaming like she had never allowed herself before. Gwen looked out the window consumed in her fantasies until their food came.

They finished their food and soon after left the comfort of the Mossy Haven. They walked all through the city, seeing as much of it as they could, each relieved not to be on the run for once.

Blacksmiths pounded away at metal and merchants eagerly tried to sell their merchandise, some of which included clothes, and others sold fish or meat of some kind. A butcher was on one corner while the other corner had another inn (The Scarlet Rope) on it.

"Hey Lily," Drake said, gently touching her arm. Ellizar and Gwen continued on for the moment, not noticing they had stopped. "How many fettels do we have?"

"More than we need," Lily said. "I don't know where Rohemir came up with so many. I thought we were poor."

"How much is a pair of shoes?" Drake pointed to Gwen had been without shoes since her previous ones had been destroyed in Grimdor. Lily smiled and happily handed him the pouch with the fettels in it.

"She's a size seven. Get her nice ones. She hasn't had that." Drake slipped in with another group of travelers, hiding from Gwen's line of sight as he slipped by her and into the shoe shop.

It was a quaint little shoe shop and certainly was smaller than he had expected from the outside. No matter where you turned there were shelves and shelves of shoes, boots, heels, sandals, every kind of shoe he could have wanted to buy.

"Can I help you sir?" an elderly lady asked. She shuffled around the shop as if she could walk it blindfolded.

"Anything in a size seven?" Drake asked.

"Size seven?" the elderly woman questioned. "Must be buying the shoes for someone else I think?" She smiled in a mischievous, charming way. Drake nodded.

"Yes ma'am."

"I thought so." The elderly woman stroked her chin thoughtfully. "I assume she's beautiful?"

Drake nodded again, and the old lady smiled wide and her eyes widened in wonder as if Drake had somehow awakened an old memory of hers, and she enjoyed it.

"I have just the thing!" She shuffled off to the far corner, bringing back fancy, but not over-the-top red velvet heels. "These no doubt would make quite a statement and enhance her beauty." Drake tried to hide his own smile.

"That is true ma'am, but I need something for adventure, not beauty.

We've been traveling a bit, you see."

"In that case, these might do the trick." She grabbed a durable pair of boots, clearly made for a small feminine foot.

"I believe they will! How much?"

"Three fettels." Drake dropped the coins into her hand. "Take the other pair too."

"Oh, no. I'm only buying the one pair," Drake explained.

"I insist!" The expression on the elderly woman's face hardened in a way that said arguing with her would be useless. "Don't go arguing with an old woman now!"

"Very well," Drake agreed. He thanked her again and hurried out of the shop and down the street until he caught up with everyone.

"There you are!" Gwen exclaimed. Drake held both pairs of shoes behind his back.

"These are from us," Drake said. Lily smiled when he held the boots out to her. Gwen was speechless and almost looked like she would cry.

"For traveling, and for sometime when we're not traveling," Drake said, bringing the other shoes out. She audibly gasped as she gently took the shoes in her hands.

"This is the best gift I've ever had." Gwen finally managed.

"Then let's get them on yer feet!" Ellizar exclaimed. Gwen carefully put on the boots and smiled widely as she handed the heels back to Drake.

"I'll try those on when we have good use for them." She smiled and he put them into a small pack that Lily was carrying.

"There's the bird again!" Drake exclaimed pointing down the street.

"What bird?" Lily asked.

"A bird is sitting on the sign at the end of the street."

"I don't see a bird Drake," Lily answered, hesitantly.

"You don't?" They all nodded their responses. "Surely you see it, Gwen. It's the same bird we saw this morning."

"I might have seen it this morning, but I certainly don't see it now," Gwen replied. Drake looked again, seeing a black bird resting on the sign. It was large, featherless and scraggly looking, just as it had been earlier. Why could only he see it?

The black featherless bird took flight, and throughout the day, Drake noticed the black featherless bird perched on various buildings, and still no one else noticed. Eventually, they found their way to the east gates of the city.

"Where should we go now?" Drake asked, eyeing a billboard to the side of the archway.

"I see some ruins up there. Made ov rock! Dwarves paradise!" Ellizar exclaimed.

"Would you like to go?" Lily asked. Ellizar happily nodded. They started walking. Drake remained where he was, hardly believing his eyes.

"Here's something I can't explain," Drake exclaimed. They turned around and walked to the large wooden board he stood in front of. Four pieces of paper were crudely hung, each one with an etching of a person's face and then a name. "Wanted" was written at the top of the paper and a price tag was written on the bottom.

At the top of the list was Rohemir, with an etching that was almost identical to what Rohemir looked like.

"What do yeh guys make ov this?" Ellizar asked.

"I wonder what he's wanted for," Drake said.

"What does it matter? He's a criminal."

"We don't know that," Drake replied. "I'm wanted by two different nations, and I haven't done anything wrong, except maybe taking my next breath. Maybe whatever Rohemir did or didn't do is just a misunderstanding as well."

For the moment they pushed the distracting thoughts from their minds, heading for the ruins that Ellizar wanted to see. They explored and investigated the ruins, which were larger than they had expected. It was easily the size of an entire city as if the port of Revly had been rebuilt after a great disaster had destroyed the first city. The day and afternoon went quickly and they lost all track of time, talking and enjoying each other's company until it was nearly dark.

"We've been down so many streets in such a large city, do we know how to get back?" Drake asked.

"That's what I'm fer," Ellizar replied with a laugh in his throat. Lily gave a look of amusement. "I can get us to the Mossy Haven, no problem!"

"Lead on my little friend," Lily replied. "Since you Dwarves are so good with directions."

"It comes naturally teh us," Ellizar replied. "A dwarf always knows exactly where we are and what dangers lay ahead of us!"

"Mr. Thomas." Drake's heart nearly stopped at the use of his name, and their steps faltered. They found themselves staring into the face of a warrior. The man was tall and lean, dressed in black with a flowing cape behind him. His armor glimmered in the pale light and looked completely unlike the uniforms of Idumea. A ring, with a single purple stone in the center, glowed on his hand. "It's a pleasure to meet you."

"Have we met before?" Drake asked. The man seemed to consider the question.

"No."

Six more men, dressed similarly, came alongside the first. Two of them carried bows, while all were adorned with swords of unusual design. In addition, each of the cloaked warriors wore a ring with a different colored stone that glowed.

"Who are you?" Lily finally managed.

"My name is Rade."

"And are you a friend or a foe?" Drake asked. Rade sighed heavily.

"Often we are portrayed as cursed souls. Nightmares sent to torment and steal away what little joy this life holds." Rade paused as if seriously thinking about his next words. "But I am not here for that purpose today."

"Why are you here, then?" Gwen asked hesitantly.

"We wish to help you, in your fight."

"Help with what?" Drake asked.

"You don't yet understand what chases you? Beyond Borags and Spirits, there is something else. Your enemy moves ever closer to finding you," Rade warned, in his eyes they could see a conflict and it was reciprocated by the other six men behind him.

"Who chases us?" Drake asked.

"A foe you don't want to mess with. An enemy that far too many people underestimate," Rade replied.

Though the words were spoken plainly, Drake could feel an underlying emotion or remorse in the words that came from his mouth. A breeze moved through the air and all the men circled around and looked out towards the city.

"Get back in the city while you can. We may be able to help you a little bit but we have our limits."

"What do we do?" Gwen whispered. Drake looked at Lily and took Gwen by the hand.

"Let's get back in the city. I'm tired."

Rade bowed and without saying another word. he and his six companions, turned and were lost from sight in the ruins.

"Did you recognize him?" Gwen asked.

"No."

"He kind of creeps me out," Gwen admitted.

"Let's just get back in the city like he said," Drake suggested.

They started through the ruins, which now seemed like silent grave markers in the dusk sky. Reminders of a city that had once been, as opposed to the great adventure their day had started with.

A whisper came across the wind, it was faint and tainted in every manner of darkness. Their thoughts became dark and cold, but then the feeling passed as quickly as it had come.

A different voice now came to them, soft, gentle, soothing. It encouraged them, though they didn't understand the words that it spoke. Compelled by the voice, Drake looked into the shadows behind. At first, he saw nothing, and then he glimpsed blue mist rising from the ground.

"Spirits!"

They fled through the ruins, only able to see a few feet ahead with the dying light. Unexpectedly, a building they had just passed was leveled by the blue mist that raced towards them.

"Run!" Drake exclaimed sprinting from the scene. They ducked down one alley and then another, losing ground as their enemy closed in on them. Suddenly they stopped, having run into a dead end.

The mist separated into two different entities and struck the ground at the same time. They both took form. One, a man, and the other, a twisted and deformed creature they had never seen before. The Spirit shifted as if analyzing his attack. The creature in front of them blocked their escape, but stood resolute, as if there was no doubt in his mind who would be walking away.

Both Spirits lunged toward them. Drake and everyone else threw themselves to the side, avoiding the powerful magic. The force of the Spirit knocked a hole in the wall, and Drake wasted no time leading everyone through the new opening.

Once inside it opened up to a large corridor with several rooms and hallways off to either side. Explosions and the crumbling of rock filled the air as the Spirits transformed back into the blue mist and sped through the walls, crisscrossing every direction.

Pieces of debris began to fall. One of the Spirits raced in front of them and dove into the ground, creating a crevice that opened up in the floor. Drake didn't hesitate, jumping across the divide that had appeared. The others followed, jumping without question, safely spanning the gap as they fled the building.

The building collapsed as soon as they exited, leaving nothing but a pile of dust and debris. They stopped and looked at the heap of stone.

Had the Spirits killed themselves?

They turned from the sight but never walked away, their resolve stolen by a low rumbling behind them. The pieces of rubble came together forming a rock monster that stood twenty feet tall, stealing every shred of hope that remained in them.

They ran but knew it was a useless gesture as the rock monster chased after them. They ducked down another street of abandoned and decaying buildings and abruptly dove to the ground as flames raced towards them. The plume of flames went overhead, followed by six more.

The flames struck the rock monster which then became consumed by them. The monster stumbled to the ground, breaking into a thousand pieces of flaming rock which were scattered everywhere.

A few moments passed and all that remained was an empty silence and smoldering rock pieces. When Drake looked, he saw that Rade and his six companions stood before them. The building that had been destroyed was fully restored.

"What happened?" Drake asked.

"Go," came the reply. Again Rade and his companions turned and walked into the fog.

Drake turned to face the city, fear once again taking hold as a wolf came into their path. Another wolf appeared in the fog and came closer yet until they were so close that they could've reached out and touched them. One wolf had reddish fur, while the other was all white with a black spot on its face. The wolves looked at them warily and then left, disappearing.

"How about we go back to our room?" Lily asked.

The others nodded their agreement and they quickly made it back to the Mossy Haven where they found Rohemir, snoring loudly. They changed and climbed into their beds, never having felt so relieved to be in a building. Drake tried to shut his mind off but found it nearly impossible.

The attack by the Spirits had awakened his mind and occupied every ounce of his attention. His mind pondered what Rade had said. Were he and Rade connected in any way?

Whatever the answer was, Drake finally managed to shut off his mind and fall to sleep, where his dreams haunted him and replayed the events of the past month or so. Drake woke up during the night and looked at the scar on his hand, for the first time wondering what he was destined to do.

XII TARUKAI

The sound of nervous pacing awoke Drake the next morning. The salty air came through the open window and the dark blue curtains billowed gently in the wind. Everyone except Rohemir was asleep. Rohemir muttered to himself and was already pacing in front of the room when Drake woke.

Rohemir muttered to himself and stroked his beard as if he alone could not figure out the answers to his problems. Drake sat up on the bed, wondering if he should say something or not.

"Good morning," Drake said. Rohemir was startled from his thoughts. "Where were you all day?"

"I could ask you the same question," Rohemir countered. "Where were you? Why were you out so late at night?"

"We ran into some old friends of ours."

"Spirits?" Rohemir asked. Drake nodded. "I had a feeling. We are in more danger than I thought. We shouldn't have come here."

"When are we leaving?"

"Not as soon as I would like. The shipmaster was none too helpful yesterday. A friend of mine gave me a hint as to a ship that might be willing to take us to Ariamore, but we may be stuck here for several more days."

"I don't think we have a couple of more days," Drake replied. "Not after what happened last night. The Spirits know we are here."

"I agree with you. In all likelihood, I doubt Spirits will attack a city of this size during the day. They prefer to have their target in seclusion before they strike."

"Why's that?"

"If a person is alone, they are an easier target. You're not as strong as you would be if you were with a crowd of people. Trust me, the Spirits will not bother you as long as we're within the city walls."

"And you can guarantee that?" Drake asked. Rohemir shifted uneasily. "We were walking around the city and we saw a poster of you. Is there something you're not telling us? Something we don't know?"

"Several years ago, I helped with an operation to get some friends out of the city. Spirits attacked us upon trying to depart. Part of the city is still untouched. The people have heard of that night and are too afraid to go near the house."

"Let me ask you one more question. Before we were chased and attacked by Spirits, we were warned by seven men. In the end, these seven men killed the Spirit that was attacking us." Rohemir's face washed white. "Are they Spirits? And if so, why would they do such a thing?"

"If they are here, then I am in just as much trouble as you four. You see, they were also involved in that escape from *this* city so many years ago. I have met them before and I am afraid of them, for they were not friendly to me."

Rohemir said no more and soon the others woke up and dressed, sharing a brief recount of everything that had transpired the evening before. Rohemir seemed to grow more anxious, but Drake was certain he was the only one who perceived the change.

"What are we going to do for the day?" Lily asked. "I'm a little nervous to wander these streets alone."

"You'll stay with me today," Rohemir replied. "You should come with me to the harbor. Then at least if anything happens we're all there together."

They walked for an hour before they reached the harbor and dockyards which brought them to numerous boats. Twice as many boats had shown up since they had entered the city just two days earlier.

They looked at the massive ships, their masts reaching into the sky. The strong powerful bows pointed towards the north, each one looking grander than the last. Some of them were so beautifully decorated that Drake was afraid to touch them for fear of damaging them.

The shipyard was a flurry of activity as crew and hired hands worked together to unload the enormous ships. In addition to what Drake expected was the normal activity, there was also a long line of heavily reinforced carts, pulled by no less than two beastly creatures with heads that were thick and broad, and shoulders that were even more imposing. The yokes around their necks made it clear they were meant for pulling heavy objects

"This will complicate things," Rohemir lamented.

"What are they doing?" Drake asked.

"The Mezutor have come to Revly!" Lily exclaimed excitedly. Nearly everyone else showed their excitement on their faces.

"Mezutor? What's a Mezutor?"

"Mezutor is just an old term that...I guess it would mean, a big race," Lily explained.

"You've never heard of Mezutor?" Gwen replied. Drake shook his head. "I've never been to it, but I've heard about it."

"I don't understand. What are they racing?" Drake asked.

"Taruks!" Ellizar cried.

"Taruks?"

"Bloody idiot! Let me get this straight you've never heard of Mezutor or Taruks before?" Ellizar asked. Drake nodded. "Are you even alive?" Lily smacked him in the side. "What?"

"Don't give him that much of a hard time. Not all regions of the world have Taruks in the first place."

Ellizar opened his mouth to speak but was stopped as Lily clamped a hand over his mouth.

"You've never seen a Taruk?" Lily asked, politely.

"No. Should I have?"

"I've never seen one either," Gwen whispered.

"Why would Mezutor be bad news for us?" Drake asked.

"For security reasons, they close the harbor for a couple of days while the festivities are going on."

"Why would they do that?" Lily asked.

"They used to leave the harbor open, but they had an unfortunate accident with one of the Taruks a few years back. It didn't listen to anyone who was in charge of it and broke free of the cage that it was being held in. It flew out into the harbor and lit one of the ships on fire. It went up in flames faster than anything you could imagine and everyone on the ship was killed. Since then they don't allow any ships to be manned during the races."

"So we'll be here for a couple more days?" Gwen asked. Rohemir nodded and then turned his attention to the ship that was docked in front of them. The sails were full and colorful, dark purple with a few other colors mixed in. The front of the ship read the *Sargon*.

A massive crate was lifted from the deck of one ship and then set upon a waiting cart. The box shook violently and a deafening roar (even when muffled by the crate) shook the shipyard. The ropes were undone and at once the cart began its slow, steady procession away from the harbor to another place in the city. As soon as they had left, another team pulled up to the next ship in line and the order of events was repeated.

"I take it that was one of the Taruks?" Drake asked.

Ellizar rolled his eyes. "Don't be ridiculous. What did yeh think it was, a kitten?"

"Speaking of ridiculous," Lily replied.

"Are yeh sayin' that I'm ridiculous?" Rohemir held up a hand to silence them as they swiftly moved to the side of the ship as the crew began exiting. Only the captain remained, standing at the bow.

"A friend of mine, says this ship is reputable. Leave the talking to me," Rohemir walked up the gangway and onto the ship where the captain was coming down a set of stairs.

"Good day, sir!" Rohemir called out.

"Can I help you?" the captain asked as they approached. He pulled his pipe out of his mouth and let a trail of smoke slowly rise into the air.

"I'm hopeful that you will," Rohemir started. "Allow me to introduce myself, my name is Rohemir and I am looking for a ship to carry me and my traveling companions to our home."

"And where exactly is that?" the man asked. "I don't usually give rides to strangers unless they agree to work the ship as one of the crew. A hard job if you aren't used to it."

"We are from Ariamore and wish to return there as soon as we possibly can." The man nearly dropped his pipe in laughter.

"Ariamore? You want me to take you to Ariamore? I wouldn't set foot in Ariamore if you paid me a thousand Fettels."

"We are not asking you to set foot in Ariamore, we are only asking you to give us a ride to the shore. Once we're close enough we could swim the rest of the way if you wanted."

"Well, I'm afraid you're out of luck mate. I'm not heading anywhere near Ariamore I'm heading to the seaport of Havren."

"If I'm not mistaken isn't Havren only a few days from Ariamore?"

"Yeah it is, but you see as soon as these 'festivities' are over I have one week to get from here to Havren. I can't waste any time, therefore I have no room to be making a run to Ariamore. Plus I have to buy all the supplies which will cost me a fortune."

"There is a way to get to Ariamore faster than anyone else and therefore get yourselves to Havren on time if not ahead of schedule," Rohemir told the man. The man frowned at him.

"Not as far as I'm concerned there isn't. This isn't just any ship, mate, this is my life! I wouldn't risk this vessel being destroyed just to get *you* there the fastest way possible. Anyone who passes through the stretch of water that you're talking about is a fool who deserves to die."

"You might be interested to know sir that I have crossed that part of the sea many times in my life, on ships nowhere near as large and powerful as this."

"Then go ask one of them to take you to Ariamore, because I won't do it."

"How much money would it take to persuade you? I know you have expenses and I wish to pay for all of them, plus some if you want it."

"More money than you have I can be sure of that."

"You might be surprised," Rohemir replied. The captain shifted uncomfortably for a couple of moments.

"Name your price and I'll tell you what I think of it," the captain answered.

"Seven hundred?" The captain laughed.

"Seven hundred hardly touches the tip of the iceberg, so to speak. This is a valuable ship if it should go down in the storm or we take any significant damage that won't satisfy me."

"Name a price then," Rohemir replied. The captain thought for a moment or two.

"For a thousand I'd do it, but I'd feel better with twelve hundred," the captain answered.

"Then twelve hundred it is."

Drake exchanged glances with everyone else. They knew all too well it was an outlandish price, but even at that Rohemir didn't flinch.

"I want to see the money before we leave the shore in a couple of days."

"I can pay you now." Rohemir reached out into his pocket and pulled out some coins and a wad of cash. He paid the man who counted it out and then stuffed it in his pocket, extending a hand to them.

"Welcome to the Sargon, you can call me Barnabas," the captain replied with a smile on his face. "Within two days from tomorrow, we'll be on the sea and on our way to Ariamore."

"Thank you, sir."

They shook hands and then made their way off the ship and back onto the dock where several more crates passed by them. They didn't speak until they had finally left the docks far behind them.

"How did you come up with that much money?" Drake asked. "Up until now, I thought we were poor."

"We are poor, but I had a meeting with a friend of mine yesterday and he brought funds. Of course, I don't think he'll be too happy that I managed to spend almost all of it."

"Why did you hire him if he was so expensive?" Lily asked.

"Because he was going somewhere near the place we needed to go."

"Yeah about that. What stretch of the ocean are we going through and why is it so dangerous?"

"Most people would take the slower, safer route sailing on the far side of Calamar, but the fastest way is a stretch of ocean between Calamar and the Revly called Behoman, or in the common tongue, the Sea of the Spirits."

"That name doesn't give me much comfort," Lily replied. "The very sound of the name makes my blood run cold with fear. Between all of us, I don't mind saying that I've had enough of these Spirits."

"Nothing says that they will spot us," Rohemir replied. The others laughed.

"Yeah, we're only goin' through a part ov the sea named after them; what would make us think they'd spot us?" Ellizar replied.

"Point taken, but you have to trust me on this. It's a rare thing when people pass right through that part of the ocean and if I'm guessing right the Spirits, and everyone else for that matter will be looking everywhere but where we are going."

"Sounds logical I guess," Gwen finally concluded. "What is this part of the ocean like?"

"The winds will be impossible and the storm will be enormous. I've never traveled through it in such a big ship before, even with that I wouldn't expect it to be a comfortable ride." Rohemir stopped and looked around the city.

"Would you guys mind enjoying the city by yourself for the day?" Rohemir asked.

"Why?" Drake asked.

"Given the recent developments, I have to contact some people who are mighty important if you take my meaning. Have a look around the city and enjoy the peace and serenity, because I have a feeling that it will soon be gone." They spoke a few more lines in reply and then he vanished into the city.

"Are Gwen and I the only two that don't completely trust Rohemir?" Drake asked.

"Careful," Gwen warned. Drake's heart stopped as a wolf stood in the middle of the street. They held their breath and carefully stepped back as the wild animal advanced toward them, letting out a singular bark, that felt more dangerous than it sounded.

No one else seemed to notice the wolf or even care that it was standing in the middle of the streets. Drake led the others away, but the wolf kept the same distance from them, never getting any closer.

"Alley," Gwen whispered. Drake nodded as they ran into a crowd of people and snuck into a narrow lane. They waited anxiously trying to both be quiet and blend in with the surroundings and citizens that lived here.

Not a moment later the wolf appeared around the corner, now running at them, teeth barred. They came to a sudden stop moments later when another wolf appeared and blocked their way.

They drew their weapons but then were astonished to see that the wolves stopped in their tracks and sat down, as though they were nothing more than soldiers who had just carried out an assignment.

A large silhouette of a man entered the alley. As he neared they became truly afraid as he stood ten feet tall, and each step he took shook the ground slightly. Both of the wolves looked at him.

"Good job Willard and Miles!" the man praised in a booming, jolly voice. "You found them far faster than I could have."

"Don't worry Lily, yer mighty protector will protect you!" Ellizar replied stepping between the giant and Lily, pulling out his axe.

Lily laughed. "Yeah, you do that."

"I've been waiting for this!" the man cried. Drake puzzled over the Giant's words, though Lily was smiling from ear to ear. The wolves moved behind the giant who now stood with his hand on his hips. "Is that any way to greet kin?

"Most certainly not!" Lily exclaimed. She ran forward and jumped into the stranger's arms. He twirled her around like she was a paperweight, and then set her back on the ground. They both laughed merrily.

"What's going on Lily?" Gwen asked. Lily turned to face them.

"Everyone I would like you to meet a very good friend of mine. This is Skander my-"

"Giant lover?" Ellizar suggested.

"No, this is Skander, my brother," Lily replied. Drake couldn't hide a smile as Ellizar's face displayed the shock they were all feeling.

"I didn't know you had a brother," Gwen stated, moving into different lighting so she could see the man's features clearer. One look at him proved that he was related to her. His build and facial features were the same when they stood side by side.

"You wouldn't likely know that I had one," Lily replied. "He was given up for adoption at the age of two, which was a year before you were brought to our house."

"Why was he given up for adoption?" Drake asked.

"You've met my family. When he was two years old and five feet tall, they didn't like having a 'freak' in the family. They exiled him and sent him to live with someone else. I didn't think I'd see him ever again until I moved a few years ago."

"Speaking of which, I heard about the attack. Do you think there's a chance that anyone made it out of the village alive?" Skander asked. They shook their heads.

"I think the only things that might have survived are the foundations of the buildings," Lily answered. Skander reflected for a moment.

"I might not have always agreed with them and for that matter, I may not have enjoyed being around them, but I can't deny that I feel sorrow at their passing. They were the only parents I had and for whatever reason I wasn't good enough."

"It's something we can't focus on Skander, it won't change what happened.

They weren't too fond of me bringing home strangers either. I felt as if I could walk through a battlefield and be safer."

"They could always make people feel like that. They either liked you or hated you and they would let you know which it was...At least you're okay," Skander said embracing her once again.

"How did you know of the attack on Fiori?" Lily asked.

"When I was old enough I wandered to Ariamore, won the favor of the leader, Atruss. He told me that you were alive. Not sure how he found out, but as soon as I learned he was coming in this direction, I convinced him to let me come along. I didn't know which seaport I should come to, but I knew I had to try. I'd have searched a thousand years if it meant that I found you, whether it would be dead or alive."

"It's nice to know I've got one person who cares about me, besides these three."

"Yeah, who are these three? I'm not sure I've met any of them before."

"Of course, where are my manners?" Lily asked. "This is Gwen. She was a slave in our house. This is Ellizar, but he's a dwarf so I'd keep your distance."

"Generally good advice from what I hear about Dwarves," Skander teased. Ellizar frowned.

"Yeh, two are definitely related!" Ellizar replied sounding both amused and annoyed.

"And this is Drake Thomas, a friend of ours whom we met along the way," Lily said. Skander's eyes seemed to light up as she spoke his name.

"Drake Thomas?" Skander asked, repeating the name to himself. "Sounds a bit unusual. Nice, but unusual."

"You don't know the half of it," Drake remarked. They shook hands, meanwhile, the two wolves still stood behind him.

"Are they yours?" Lily asked.

"Yes, they are. Bought them from a couple of traders a few years back. They like to roam around though, interesting things they dig up. Their names are Willard and Miles. Don't worry they're tame."

"Can we pet them?" Gwen asked.

"They've never bitten my hand off, go for it." Gwen and Drake approached the two wolves and pet them on their heads feeling the soft thick fur beneath their fingers.

"Which one is Willard?" Drake asked.

"The reddish fur one is Willard, the one with the black spot is Miles," Skander answered.

"Don't you want to pet them Ellizar?" Drake asked. Ellizar shook his head.

"I'm not pettin' anythin' that's the same size as me!"

"Willard, Miles, why don't you go give Ellizar a nice greeting," Skander told them. The wolves moved forward and circled Ellizar. They jumped up and put their two front paws on him licking his face. Ellizar mumbled something in Dwarvish as the wolves moved away.

"It's confirmed, that this elf, Skander *is* her brother. Only someone who was related would do somethin' ridiculous like that just teh freak out a dwarf!"

"What can I say? It runs in the family," Lily said. The two wolves left and disappeared into the streets, leaving them alone.

"Where are you three headed anyhow?" Skander asked.

"To Ariamore. A friend of ours has hired a ship, we're just waiting until the Mezutor is over so we can depart."

"Maybe I should sail back with you."

"That would be wonderful!" Lily exclaimed.

"Think there would be any problems with that?"

"I don't see why," Drake answered. "But be forewarned that we tend to be pretty good at finding trouble."

"Ah, it can't be that bad. Anyway, since we'll be here for the Mezutor tomorrow, do you want to go to the race?"

"Are you serious?" Lily asked, looking more excited than Drake had ever seen her.

"Of course I'm serious. Sorry, to say but that was half the reason I hoped I would find you *here*, because then in a celebratory fashion, I could buy us all tickets to the Mezutor."

"I still don't understand what a Mezutor is?" Drake asked. He couldn't stifle a slight chuckle when he saw Skander's face.

"Where have you been living all your life? Tomorrow is the biggest race of the year! Fifty racers from all across the world, competing for the most prestigious title of all."

"And that is?"

"He's joking, right? Please tell me he's joking!" Skander exclaimed.

"Don't worry yerself about what he appears teh not know Skander, he's a bloody idiot this one," Ellizar replied, Lily smiled.

"No, I believe that honor still is yours."

"At least we know he's good for something," Gwen said.

"Skander, this is a rough bunch ov people, I think we should just get out ov here and leave them teh their demise."

"You keep saying that but you never leave," Drake replied. Ellizar frowned and shook his head, muttering something under his breath. "What are they racing for?"

"To take home the award of being the best Tarukai in the world. There are races all over the nation during the year. Fifty of the riders are chosen by the Taruk Council and they are brought to the final race to see who's the best. They change the location every year. Can't wait to see the grounds."

"I can't wait to see a Taruk," Drake replied.

"The good thing is we don't have to wait any longer!" Skander exclaimed. "In about two hours the stable gates open and we can see the magnificent beasts for ourselves."

"Are you serious?" Gwen asked. Drake smiled at the elation on her face.

Skander nodded happily. "Every Taruk and Tarukai (Riders if you didn't know the term), will be there for talking and admiring alike! They don't usually want you too close to the Taruks though!"

They meandered through the city, casually joining a long line of people where they blended in and patiently waited until they could purchase their tickets for the race the following day. The stadium was to their left and was easily the tallest structure in the area.

They purchased their tickets and were directed out the north gate of the city to a secluded and well-kept paradise. Stables constructed of wood and brick with large iron bars on the front and backs of them, made up the housing for the Taruks, while a large lavish building provided housing for the riders. While it seemed some riders were just by themselves, others were accompanied by a large entourage of heralds, cupbearers, and blacksmiths.

Each of the stables housed a large Taruk, the likes of which Drake had never seen before. The Taruks stood nearly six feet tall at their shoulders and walked on four legs. The wings were folded up on their backs, but the others insisted their wing span was no less than twenty feet. They bore a tail, nearly ten feet long, which had a few spikes on the tip of it.

The neck was long and lanky, but despite this, every movement the Taruk made looked graceful. Their skin was covered in very short hair that could be any variety or pattern of colors. Finally, three eyes were on their head, One in the center and one more on either side.

The crowds moved past one Taruk and then the next. Drake could hardly fathom that creatures like this could be tamed, or for that matter ridden in a race. Drake looked to the left and then to the right, admiring all the different Taruks as not one of them was the same in build and stature though different breeds seemed to have different colors or patterns to them.

"What do you think?" Lily asked.

"They look like amazing creatures," Drake admitted, his eye drawn to a pure white Taruk on the left.

Drake studied the white Taruk, its deep colorful eyes permeating into his soul. He could hear the creature's deep breathing and careful movement as it stood to its feet. A tap was felt on his arm but he hardly felt it as he found himself drawn closer to the animal.

A growl came from the beast and then it opened its mouth, spewing fire towards Drake. The heat stung his eyebrows and sweat formed on his forehead. Drake fell back, flailing for a moment. The Taruk looked away and Drake looked up to the person who had caught him.

He was sure his face showed his surprise when he saw that it was Aiden who had caught him. The man who had helped them escape from Bucklebeary was now standing before them, battle-scarred and worn, but very much the same man. He helped Drake away from the Taruk.

"These are dangerous creatures, Mr. Thomas. I know you haven't seen one before but keep your distance."

"How do you know I haven't seen one?" Drake asked in a whisper. The others were still out of earshot.

"I know many things, Drake Thomas. Many things that people think I shouldn't know."

"But yet you know?"

"Indeed. Make sure you keep your distance from the Taruks in the future. Not all of them are as nice as Elohim here."

"It has a name?" Drake asked.

"Well of course he has a name. All Taruks have names!" Skander exclaimed as they rejoined the group.

"If he has a name someone must own him right? Who does he belong to?" Drake asked."

"He's mine," Aiden said. Now all their faces were showing surprise.

"You're a Tarukai?" Lily asked.

Aiden nodded. "I am. Surprised?"

"A little. So what were you doing in Bucklebeary?"

"Helping some people who needed my assistance. It doesn't matter what race is or isn't coming up, if someone needs my help, then I will be there to help them. Even if it means that I lose everything."

"But you're a Tarukai! You must have it all. Could you really lose all that? I'm sure the money you make is more than I could ever dream of," Skander asked him.

"I'm sure it is, but I came into this world with nothing and I am content to leave this world with nothing. I keep enough to get travel supplies and the rest I give away. I could compile a stash of wealth if I wanted to, but what would be the point? You're probably heading to Ariamore after this right?"

"Yes," Drake answered. "Where do you have to go after this?"

"Anywhere I want. I'll find a place that needs help and do what I can."

"All this small talk aside do yeh think yeh can win the race tomorrow?" Ellizar asked.

"Everyone thinks they can win it. Whether it's Lathon's will is not for me to say."

"You've heard of Lathon?" Drake asked.

"Everyone has. Some people just don't pay attention to him as much as they should."

"What happened in Bucklebeary? To the people I mean," Lily asked.

"They survived. Most of their possessions were destroyed in the battle that continued into the next day and night but they persevered and their enemies were destroyed. They'll be alright now. The Borags are after you, not them."

"Where on earth is this conversation going?" Skander asked. "Is there something that I don't know?"

"It's a possibility," Aiden answered, piquing Drake's interest once again.

"Lily, is there anything that I don't know?" Skander asked.

"We'll talk about it after we're done touring the Taruks," Lily told him. The answer seemed to satisfy Skander for the time being and they continued on their way leaving Aiden and his Taruk, Elohim, behind them. They looked at the other Taruks and riders, none of which seemed to have the same relaxed feel as Aiden and Elohim had. The other Tarukai were harder in their expressions and less friendly.

The other Tarukai were dressed in fancy clothing and jewels and anything else that might suggest prestige and fortune, while Aiden looked no different than he had in Bucklebeary and his Taruk looked as normal as he did. Drake had to admit that he found the difference comforting. They were a light in the darkness. A welcomed change in the world. They sought no reward and kept no reward which he gathered was not how the rest of the Tarukai operated.

When they had finished their tour, they entered back into the city, entering in the *Mossy Haven* a while later. Willard and Miles had vanished from sight but no one seemed to be particularly concerned about where they had gone.

They told Skander of Drake's secret but kept most of the facts to themselves, not wanting any more people to know than was necessary at this point. Rohemir showed up later in the day, not saying much about where he had been or what he had been doing.

Drake was the last one to fall asleep that night, wondering what the future held. His past was still a mystery to him but he was hopeful that in the days that lay ahead, he would be able to figure out once and for all where he was from and who his parents were.

His mind pondered them for a couple of moments. Were they worried about him? Did they want to see Drake and hold him tight as badly as he wanted to hold them? The past was a mystery and the future was out of his reach at the moment, leaving him with only one choice.

He would live in the moment he had been given and take what life dealt him as it came. This was the only moment he could do anything about. He couldn't change the past and he couldn't see what the future held, so he could only change the situation he was in at present.

Drake fell asleep and his dreams welcomed him as they flooded his mind and brought him visions of things that he didn't understand. Some of them weren't even visions but sounds and smells of things that should be familiar to him. Right now they were nothing to him, just a dream, a pleasant long dream.

XIII   MEZUTOR

ily's voice was the first that Drake heard in the morning. As soft and gentle as it was supposed to be, he couldn't help but notice there was a sense of urgency and impatience in her voice. She stood next to the side of his bed looking more impatient than she sounded.

"Come on sleepy head! You don't want to miss the Mezutor because you were sleeping!" Lily exclaimed shaking him again.

"At least this time it would be because he slept through it and not because he took a tumble over a waterfall," Ellizar pointed out. Lily nodded her agreement.

"What time is it?" Drake asked, noticing that everyone else was dressed up nicer than usual. Gwen and Lily wore matching dark blue dresses, that made each of them look like royalty. Ellizar was dressed in slacks, a shirt, and a tie, which looked unusual on him, but he still wore it well.

"The race starts in an hour and a half," Gwen answered. "Usually common folk don't get to go to championship races! Make sure to dress your best. For the other races you can show up wearing anything, but to the World Cup you'd better look good. Rohemir bought us these clothes, we have some for you too. I'm still not sure where he gets all his money, but wearing clothes like this I can hardly argue." She did a spin and Drake couldn't help but smile at the sight.

"Well what are you waiting for? Get some clothes on! The Mezutor is waiting for us!" Lily exclaimed. Drake dressed as quickly as he could, putting on a nice burgundy-colored shirt and a pair of slacks.

They entered into the bustling dining hall where Baron and his staff went here and there faster than Drake had ever thought possible. They found Skander and Rohemir, dressed nicely and waiting for them, with breakfast already ordered and on their table.

They quickly finished their breakfast and took what shortcuts they could find to get to the stadium faster. They came to a large stone gateway with many doors and gates. They handed in their tickets and were allowed to enter the main grounds.

Inside, many merchants frantically called out to the masses, selling what items they could. Lush gardens, fountains, and small ponds were laid about the path to the main entrance. The path twisted throughout the grounds, eventually bringing them to an impressive courtyard, which was built alongside the back of a large hill, made entirely of rock.

A large gateway welcomed them into a tunnel, which led them deeper and deeper into the mountain. The tunnel melted away and they stood in awe at the size and scope of the stadium.

Grandstands towered far above them, stretching to the left and the right. A wall with a heavy mesh fence separated the crowds from the chasm beyond. The bottom of the great chasm was filled with sharp rocks and boulders, and on the other side of the chasm was another set of stands just as big and long as the one they were in.

"This is amazing!" Gwen cried. Drake nodded his agreement, too stunned to speak.

"It's rumored this stadium was built to hold one hundred thousand," Rohemir answered. "Every year the Mezutor stadiums seem to get bigger, which is just as well. Some people, come hundreds of miles just to see this event."

"This is beyond anything I could have imagined," Drake commented. Taking in the sights, the colors, and the atmosphere of the Mezutor.

"Just wait until the race begins," Lily told him excitedly. Gwen also seemed to bubble with excitement as she had never even been allowed to see a Mezutor before, no matter how small or large it had been.

They found their seats and for the next hour, they watched the seats fill to capacity, forcing everyone else to stand along the fence and the aisles.

A loud horn sounded from the top of the stadium and, as if on cue, every person in attendance erupted into thunderous cheers. Gwen pointed up and to the left where the first of fifty shapes were coming into focus. It didn't take Drake long to figure out that it was the first of the Tarukai coming into the arena. The Taruks and their riders swooped low and did a small twirl in the air, passing by all the fans before taking their place on a smooth part of the ground just in front of them. One at a time the Taruks and their riders came in, introduced by heralds who were stationed every hundred feet. Although the cheering was constant and you could hardly hear what they were saying, the heralds continued to announce the names of the Tarukai and their Taruks, and where they were from.

The moments went by faster than they realized, but finally, a white Taruk appeared in the sky. The roar of the crowd grew until it was such a yell that it shook the stadium. Aiden flew his Taruk, Elohim, lower and slower than the rest of them, still dressed in his battle-worn clothes. He circled around and took his place in the back of the starting grid.

"Looks like he's popular?" Drake inquired to Skander.

Skander nodded. "I've seen a couple of races with him in it and it's no wonder he's popular. He's the best Tarukai that I've ever seen. Plus, he has a white Taruk and do you see any other white Taruks?"

"No I certainly don't," Drake answered.

Aiden climbed off and stood next to Elohim. An important-looking man entered onto the arena floor and held a hand to the exuberant crowd. Everyone became silent, and then the man pulled a wand out of his robe. He muttered something and then spoke, his voice magnified so all could hear it.

"Ladies and Gentlemen, I welcome you to the sixth hundred and thirty-fourth Mezutor Championship!" The crowd erupted into cheers. "We're all glad you could make it and I'm sure we'll see a fantastic race today!" The man looked to the Tarukai before continuing. "I want a good clean race, with no foul play. You've all been chosen because you are the best Tarukai in the world. Now it is your turn to prove it!

"You will race for three laps over the ten-mile long course and believe me when I say that this course is not going to be easy. You have been allowed to walk through the course but you have not been allowed to fly through it. Riders mount your Taruks!"

The crowds erupted once again as the riders climbed on their Taruks, some of them mounted with poise and class, while people like Aiden just climbed on and took their seats in the saddle that was on their backs. The saddles were simple, with just a couple of leather straps that went around the chest and neck. There were stirrups but no reigns.

"How do they steer?" Drake asked.

"I think they do it mostly by thought," Ellizar answered.

Drake's attention was on Elohim who unexpectedly looked at Drake. Time faded around them, but this time the sensation drew him in. A whisper came through the air, soft, gentle but also dangerous.

'*Be ready*' the voice said.

Elohim turned his gaze from Drake and the sensation faded.

"Something's going to happen," Drake whispered, Gwen looked at him, concern in her eyes.

"What do you mean? How do you know that?" Gwen asked.

"I think Aiden's Taruk just warned me. Is that possible?"

"I don't know anything about Taruks except that they're large and they can breathe fire." Their attention was diverted back to the scene in front of them and the one lone man standing in front of them, waiting to start the race.

"Riders to your mark!" the man held up his wand, jumping back a couple of feet and smacking his colorful cape when the Taruk to his left let out a single puff of flame. The crowd laughed and the starter shook his head. "Let's try this again. Riders to your mark!"

The stadium became deathly silent. Everyone held their breath in anticipation.

Green sparks erupted from the tops of the stadiums, sparkling on the way down.

The Taruks extended their powerful wings, climbing into the sky and moving at speeds that Drake could hardly fathom. The wind from their great wings' flapping pushed them back for a moment. The Tarukai jockeyed for position, trying to climb their way through the pack, meanwhile, Aiden remained in the back.

Elohim looked in Drake's direction and for a fleeting second held eye contact. The Taruk kept on flying in a straight line while still looking at Drake until it became impossible for them to keep eye contact any longer.

His heart felt as if it was going to jump out of his chest as he looked around the massive stadium for anyone who might not be friendly to them. His fear took hold of him as he realized a Spirit could be sitting right next to them and they wouldn't have any clue until it was too late.

Drake could think of nothing else as the seconds passed and turned into minutes. When he was brought out of his thoughts, he found that the first lap had been completed and he was now standing on his feet. Aiden and Elohim were now halfway through the field, having made up some positions.

Without warning, his hand turned to ice and his thoughts went numb. Drake grasped Gwen's hand alerting her. She immediately called for Rohemir who managed to come alongside Drake.

Everyone spoke to him, but Drake had lost all his hearing. For the moment he was alone with the dark voice that whispered unintelligibly in his head.

As though someone had pulled a veil, the voices ceased and the sounds of the crowds came back to him, overwhelming him after having been cut off from it for so long.

"Tell me what's going on!" Rohemir yelled. The people surrounding them took no interest in what they were doing, as the Taruks and their riders came around again. Drake quickly noted that Aiden and Elohim were in the third position now as they started the last lap.

"Someone knows we're here!" Drake exclaimed above the noise of the crowd. "We've been here too long."

"Who knows we're here?" Rohemir asked. Drake's face washed white as the voice entered his head, once again taking control of his thoughts. Drake fought back a moment later, regaining control.

"I don't know, but someone knows we're here and they're after us," Drake answered.

"What are we supposed teh do?" Ellizar asked.

Rohemir was silent and offered no suggestions as each of them realized they were completely trapped.

The roar of the crowd grew louder, suggesting that the Tarukai were on their final approach. Three Taruks and their riders were coming side by side to the line. Aiden followed, quickly closing the gap.

Drake's heart stopped cold when the three Tarukai turned their steeds to face the grandstands. The first opened his mouth to breathe fire but never got the chance as Elohim sent forth a stream of flame that consumed one of them.

The flaming Taruk fell to the ground, violently rolling and flipping until it stopped against the wall bordering the grandstands. At once, the motionless beast changed form, becoming the blue mist that they had come to fear.

The other two Taruks and their riders did the same and all three of them flew toward the stands and burrowed into the rock. The structure was shook violently as the Spirits passed through it and exited on the other side.

Panic consumed the spectators who now swarmed towards the exits that were bogged down with people trying to escape. Hope returned as Drake pointed out seven flames in the distance just to their left. The flames struck the ground next to Drake and when the flames subsided, Rade and his six companions stood.

"Grab on!" Rade exclaimed, extending a hand. Each of them took the hand that was extended to them and they were lifted from the crumbling grandstands. Drake looked around him in wonder, as they were surrounded by mist and flames, yet they were not burnt.

The streets were now filled with panic as soldiers arrived and tried to make sense of what was happening. Rade and his companions quickly landed in a back alley, which was empty of people at the present. Up above, Spirits blanketed the sky, terrorizing the people of the city.

"Get out of sight and stay there until things settle down!" Rade ordered. "They're looking for you and if they find you, it will be the death of us all!"

"What are you?" Drake asked, "Are you Spirits as well?"

"We are Korazin, we used to serve the leader of Grimdor, but now we do not stand with them. You do not have to be afraid of us!"

The Korazin streaked up into the sky where they seemingly went to battle with the other Spirits which had doubled in the past couple of minutes. Rohemir quickly led them away through back alleys and roads that were foreign to them.

"Aren't we going back to The Mossy Haven?" Lily asked.

"It's too dangerous," Rohemir snapped.

"Without our weapons, we won't last very long as it is," Lily argued.

"We have to get into hiding. We can see about getting our weapons later!"

"Drake," Gwen whispered. Drake looked at her briefly. "We're not that far from The inn. It's just on the other side of that building!"

He looked at Rohemir and the others who hadn't heard what Gwen had said.

"Come on," Drake replied. They quietly veered to the left and rushed towards the Mossy Haven. They weaved in and out of the frenzied crowd, traveling around the inn, until they found their room. "Rock."

Gwen handed him a fair sized rock and Drake whipped it at the window. The glass shattered and they made quick work of wiping away all the glass. Drake jumped through the window and hastily handed weapons to Gwen.

Almost as soon as Drake jumped back out the window they were attacked by Spirits and knocked down. The weapons were scattered, though Drake and Gwen managed to pull their swords from their sheaths.

The Spirits landed in front of them and took the form of guards, attacking with fury and vengeance. Drake and Gwen both blocked the attacks.

The thunderous call of a Taruk filled the sky. Torrents of flames came from Elohim's mouth, consuming several Spirits, while the others scattered.

"Come on!" Aiden hollered. Drake and Gwen grabbed the weapons and scrambled onto Elohim's back. Soon they flew over the city. The sky behind them was dark with blue mist as three more Spirits rushed towards them. Elohim ducked and twisted, managing to lose all but one of them. Drake looked to the left where the mist was, noticing that half of it had taken the form of a person while the other half was still a cloud of mist.

Aiden pulled out a knife, golden in color, and threw it in the direction of the mist. The Spirit changed course and vanished into the city out of their sight.

"What did you throw?" Drake asked.

"Just a knife," Aiden answered. "It probably wouldn't have done any harm to him, but he was afraid of something else."

"Apparently," Gwen replied, giving Drake a knowing look. They flew for another minute or so until they landed on a large building and climbed off. Aiden said something to Elohim who quickly rose into the sky and disappeared into the chaos.

"Where are we going?" Drake asked. Aiden led the way, climbing down the stairs that were built into the building.

"We're going to a secret hiding place," Aiden answered. "It's been a long time since I've been there but I'm sure everyone else will be here."

"You seem to know a lot."

Aiden smiled. "I've been around a long time. You might be surprised at the things that I know, but let's not talk about that now. Right now we have to get you out of sight and figure out what to do."

They walked and came into a section of the city that was abandoned. The remains of a house and buildings sat in front of them. They carefully crept through the overgrown yard and fence line until they came under a tree where a trapdoor was hidden. They made their way down into the hole, finding a maze of tunnels and corridors, long abandoned.

Drake and Gwen exchanged looks but kept their thoughts and words to themselves as they were finally led to a larger room. Rohemir and everyone else were in the room as well as the two wolves, Willard and Miles.

"Foolish to go back for weapons," Rohemir scolded.

"Sorry," Drake replied.

"You could have gotten yourself killed! You are more important than weapons, Drake Thomas. You are the most important weapon! Without you, we have no hope of ever figuring out who Shedaros is. The races of Men and Elves would never be united because you wouldn't be able to tell us who Shedaros is! You gave us a good scare today, do it again and I'll give you something to be scared about."

"Sorry," Drake replied.

"Back off Rohemir. He was thinking beyond the moment. You can't be mad at him for that, "Aiden defended.

"Yes, I can!" Rohemir fired back. "He had no clue what he was doing!"

"If he is as you think he is, then maybe he did," Aiden pointed out. "Either way, it would not have been wise to continue without weapons, not against these enemies."

"Fine!" Rohemir cried, unofficially conceding that Aiden had won the argument. "How are we going to get out of this city? Do you have any ideas?"

"The harbor is already in lock-down due to the Mezutor, that's certainly not going to change now. I'm sure the gates will be locked until order is restored. Even then, I think they won't open the gates for another two days. I certainly wouldn't," Aiden said.

"They won't get a chance to," a voice called from one of the tunnels that branched off. A moment later seven figures came through the darkness and into the light. It was the same seven Spirits that had saved them on two different occasions now. The leader of the Korazin stood with the others staggered behind and to either side of him, their signature rings, glowing brightly on their hands. Rohemir seemed to shrink back and for some unexplained reason the leader of the Korazin, Rade, looked at him long and hard.

"You have news?" Aiden asked.

"Yes, and none of it good," Rade answered. "First though, introductions. My name is Rade, leader of the Korazin, former allies, and now enemies of Grimdor. We were on our way here and discovered the Spirits, but we also spotted a large Borag army making their way in this direction. With their speed and their stamina, they will be here by morning and will destroy the city until they find this man." He pointed a finger at Drake.

"How did they cover so much ground so quickly?" Drake asked.

"They're Borags. The Spirit's role in this joint attack effort is to hold us here until they can kill us," Rohemir answered.

"The Borags are destroying everything in their path, they've already wiped out three different villages along the way," Rade said.

"The war is coming sooner than I thought it would," Rohemir stated. "Do you think if we get to Ariamore we'll be okay?"

"I think you'll be safe for a little while, but there's no telling for sure," Rade answered. "The leader of Grimdor is still gathering his loyal ones and building up his forces. He brings war to many nations at once, but I don't think he believes he's strong enough to march into Ariamore at the moment."

"Let's hope you're right," Rohemir replied.

Rade turned back to Aiden. "We mustn't tarry. We must get all of you away from here as quickly as possible. There's only one path that will do that."

"It is a path that we were already planning to take, but now the vessel that is hired is likely impounded and can't leave," Lily told him.

"You'll need to find a new ship, one that isn't already in the harbor."

"Do you know of any?" Skander asked.

Aiden thought for a moment. "Rade, if you can find a ship then I will find a way to get us there."

"Why can't these Korazin just fly us there? Getting us out of the stadium wasn't a problem," Rohemir pointed out.

"Short distances we can do that. The curse upon us will not allow us to carry people for much longer than what we did today. Plus we'll attract too much attention and would therefore endanger anyone directly with us."

"Of course," Rohemir reluctantly acknowledged.

"We'll go see if we can find a willing participant," Rade replied. Aiden nodded.

"Look no further," another voice said. A tall elf strode into the room, from the same tunnel the Korazin had come out of.

"Everyone I would like you to meet Atruss," Rohemir started. "Though I'm not sure why he is here. Certainly, it will be an interesting tale."

"I was deep in sleep last night when I had a vision of a Makkura. I was told to turn my ship about and head back to Revly," Atruss replied. Drake watched everyone's reactions carefully.

"Your ship isn't impounded?" Drake asked.

"Correct, we are anchored ten miles north of here. No one has seen us."

"We can walk to the ship?" Drake asked.

"I wouldn't try it," Aiden answered. "We'd have to make it through all the guards and the gates and then not get caught while we get on the ship. The best way is the way that I will arrange."

"Should we ask what that is?" Gwen asked. Aiden smiled.

"Let's just say I have some friends in the Mezutor who would donate their services for the evening. We escape on the Taruks. Have the ship underway, and we'll join you. We'll sail away, hopefully, without too much trouble."

"I've never flown on a Taruk before," Ellizar answered. "It's unnatural teh leave the ground."

"If you'd like, you could stay and become a permanent part of the ground," Skander replied.

"On second thought, flyin' wouldn't be that bad."

"We'll wait until midnight!" Aiden declared. He turned to Atruss. "Once we're in the air, we'll have to find your vessel and let us know of your location before we start our escape. The rest of you sit tight and try to relax."

Within a couple of minutes, everyone had vanished into the different tunnels all carrying out the plans that had been made. They sat in silence, not talking for what felt like the longest time. Drake wished once again that he could have a normal day, but so far that idea seemed to be nothing more than a dream.

The hours faded and so did his mind as he silently thought about everything that had happened. Ariamore occupied his mind, hoping when he got there it would be as good as everyone said it would be. Sleep overtook them as the day turned into night.

XIV — A GATHERING STORM

The city was finally quiet, momentarily forgetting the troubles of the day. Drake stood alongside Rohemir with the others asleep behind them. Aiden and the Korazin hadn't shown up yet, but Rade had come by earlier and told them everything that needed to be known if they were going to successfully escape.

"Rohemir, how is it that the Spirits are killed by fire?" Drake asked. "You said they could only be killed by your special dagger."

"So did I, but I forgot one rule. Fire can also kill them, it has to be a hot fire though, hotter than any other. Therefore a Taruk's fire can kill them and the Spirits themselves can kill each other. If it wasn't for the Korazin helping us tonight, I doubt we would really stand a chance at getting out of here in one piece."

"Why do Rade and the Korazin appear as fire in the sky when all the other Spirits appear like mist?"

"The Korazin are cursed to not be able to live like a normal Spirit might be able to. A Spirit in the form of blue mist can go anywhere without being seen, to some extent, but Spirits who are forced to take the form of fire cannot, because everyone knows where they are."

"Yes, but why are they cursed?" Drake asked.

Rohemir shrugged. "I'm a bit foggy on the details of Rade's history. Perhaps the Korazin were cursed by the Spirits themselves?"

"Sounds confusing," Drake replied. Rohemir smiled weakly.

"Unfortunately nothing is as simple as it seems. I could stand here and tell you hours and hours of things that I know about prophecies and what might lay ahead, but I can't predict the future. The only thing that I can guarantee is that when we get to Ariamore you will be safe."

"Can you guarantee that?" Drake asked. "The Borags and Spirits clearly have no fear of marching into other nations. They'll be here by morning, what's to stop them from attacking Ariamore?"

"They know in their hearts that Lathon is greater. Yet there's still a part of them that wants to be more powerful. They will be held at a distance by their fear for some time, but eventually, they will come marching into Ariamore. Long have the Elves been known for their skills in battle, far surpassing the skills of Borags. They are afraid of the Elves. They know they will need a much larger force to take the Elves than the rest of the land," Rohemir explained.

"Where do the Spirits come in?" Drake asked. "I remember someone saying that Grimdor was formed by people who didn't agree with Lathon, but what about the Spirits? Did they just show up? Where do they live?"

"If you look at the map again, you'll notice that there is a nation that is drawn on the map but there is no name on it. That is the Spirit's nation. People of the world like to pretend it doesn't exist. Therefore it is not named. It's just an empty dangerous stretch of land that no one travels.

"But now, those dark spirits wander the earth, doing their master's bidding and looking to Ariamore for the one person who can put an end to their very existence if he chooses."

"Shedaros?" Drake asked, Rohemir nodded.

"Yes indeed," Rohemir answered. "Lathon wasn't the most powerful king of all time for nothing. We believe that he conceived a son in a woman who had never known a man. I helped in the escape of that son many years ago."

"Who is Shedaros?" Drake asked.

"We never learned his name."

"And somehow I'm part of all of this and they want me dead?" Drake asked. He looked behind him surprised to find that the others were still asleep on the floor.

"Yes, they want you dead, because of the mark on your hand. They know where you are and they know the longer they wait, the harder it will be to kill you. They'll take the risk if it means they win."

"I hope one of these days I can live a normal life."

"Extraordinary events only happen to extraordinary people Drake Thomas. You were chosen for this spot. You may not know why and I may not even be able to come close to guessing the purpose, but there is something deeper behind life that binds us together in our belief."

"Lathon right?"

"That is what people from Ariamore believe. They look to the future while everyone else looks at the present and the past. The Borags and Spirits are consumed by the past. They wish they had done things differently, but their greed and their pride have consumed them to the point where nothing will soften their hard hearts. Overall you can assume the same thing about the rest of the people in the world, except for those who choose to join Ariamore."

"People from Ariamore sound like they're something else," Drake observed.

"Indeed they are my friend. You cannot say you follow Lathon unless you *follow* Lathon. Lathon was the most kind and compassionate king the world has ever known. It is our job to imitate him and live the same way so that the world may see what makes us different. You understand?"

"I think so," Drake answered. "So it's almost like a part of you dies when you reach Ariamore because you have to change how you live when you join. That's why the Borags and the Spirits are so afraid to attack."

"You are correct Drake Thomas. The will of Lathon is far beyond the reach of our minds. It moves in the world and speaks to us but that's all we can figure out."

They were stopped from their conversation as the seven Korazin appeared in the tunnel.

"Wake the others, it's time to go!" Rade announced. Drake did as he was instructed. "Everything's ready. We have located Atruss's ship, *The Blackmorr* twenty miles down the coast, and ten miles from shore."

"How will we get out of the city without being seen?" Gwen asked. "It is even possible?"

The Korazin shrugged their shoulders.

"I have my doubts, but we can always hope that we'll get lucky. But first put these on." One of the Korazin opened a bag and pulled out some dark cloaks as well as shirts and pants which were thrown onto the small table next to them. "If we are discovered by Spirits they won't be able to tell who's who, quite so easily." They changed into the clothes, and when they were done they looked nearly identical. Each of them now wore black shirts, cloaks and pants. On the girls the pants were too big and had to be awkwardly tied, and their hair had to be pinned up. When they were done Drake had to admit that unless the Spirits got really close, they wouldn't be able to see the difference.

Rade led them down a different tunnel than they had been in previously. Carved out of dirt, it was cold and damp, with a damp chill in the air. A few minutes later they came through a trapdoor that brought them into a building they didn't recognize. The Korazin carefully concealed the entrance, before continuing.

"Where are we?" Drake whispered.

Rohemir looked around as if trying to remember for himself. "Somewhere near the north side of the city, but beyond that, I can't tell you anything else."

"It's an old storehouse," Rade replied. "Comes up about five minutes from the Taruk stables."

"At least we don't have very far to go."

"Not far at all, but that doesn't mean it's not dangerous," another of the Korazin reminded. "This place is crawling with so many guards that it took us twice as long to get here as it should have. Hopefully, we will be able to get there in a reasonable amount of time, or else we'll have to relocate the ship."

They entered the empty streets keeping in the shadows whenever possible. Drake followed behind Gwen, with one of the Korazin right behind. The sky was filled with dark menacing clouds, stealing away the last shred of hope that remained within Drake. The darkness may provide them cover, but it also made him uneasy.

They continued, their footsteps echoing until the ground beneath their feet turned to dirt. They picked up the pace, getting nearer to their destination which was now in sight.

Seeing no guards, they walked into the opening. Drake recognized it as the Taruk stables they had toured the day prior. They carefully walked in between the two rows of cages that were filled with sleeping Taruks.

Aiden stepped out from the darkness that concealed him. He let out a sharp whistle and six Taruks and riders came out and lined up in a row. Elohim stood at the front, tall and proud, looking just as magnificent as ever. The other Taruks, though they were a touch bigger in size, were nowhere near as elegant and powerful as Elohim seemed to be.

Their eyes connected as they had earlier, but this time that was all that happened as Drake stared into the deep blue eyes. Aiden stood at the front of the line and the riders of the other six Tarukai bowed as they approached.

"Glad to see you all made it here safely!" Aiden exclaimed. "We don't have much time. One person to each Taruk, don't worry about the Tarukai they're all on our side." Drake climbed on Elohim and Gwen took the Taruk directly behind.

Drake felt strangely safe sitting atop the great beast. He had ridden a horse and now here he was sitting on a Taruk. Aiden stood in front of the group, with the seven Korazin standing next to him.

"One Korazin to each Taruk," Aiden ordered, "One of the Korazin will come just a few seconds behind Drake and me. If anyone challenges us we'll give them a good fight before they capture us." All seven of the Korazin moved next to the Taruk they chose to guard and transformed themselves into Taruks with two riders on top of them.

"At least a dozen Spirits are guarding the city so be ready, confrontation is inevitable. We will split up once we're in the air. Do whatever you have to and we'll see each other next on the deck of the *Blackmorr*."

Aiden came forward and bounded onto Elohim, giving a final nod to all the others. At once, all the Taruks used their muscular legs to thrust themselves into the air, climbing higher and faster than they could have ever imagined. Drake held on for dear life, too scared to do anything else at the moment.

Elohim flew with confidence and strength as though he could see things that Drake and Aiden couldn't. They circled back around letting the others pass by them as they entered the menacing clouds that would hopefully hide them. Even Drake had a hard time making out the shapes of the other Taruks.

"We've been spotted!" Aiden yelled. He pointed to the left where blue mist was faintly visible in the sky. The mist shifted and changed shape as it came towards them. All at once, the twelve Taruks in their group split up, heading in six different directions leaving the blue mist in a temporary state of confusion. Only a moment passed before the mist split into six different entities and flew after each of them.

A flash of light came from Drake's left and narrowly missed him as Aiden shoved him down on his stomach. The light collided with Aiden but didn't seem to have any effect on him.

"What just happened?" Drake asked above the noise.

"They're using magic, that's what the light is."

"How did it not hurt you?"

"It did hurt me," Aiden answered. "Elves can use 'magic' remember, or at least something similar."

"What do you mean something similar?" Drake asked, as more flashes filled the sky around them.

"We don't use wands and spells and curses like everyone else does. In the ancient scrolls, Lathon said 'You do the natural and I'll do the supernatural.' We may want something to happen but we can't make it happen, not by ourselves. Lathon has acted to save us."

Drake's attention was diverted to the right where the Korazin flying behind them collided with the Spirit that was attacking them.

They were nothing but a falling shape of blue mist and fire as flames flashed between them. They struck the ground and only the Korazin came back into the sky.

"Are the other riders who are helping us Elves?"

"Yes, that's why you don't see them using wands." Fire and sounds of pain echoed from all around them. More light illuminated the sky. Rohemir, who could be faintly seen to their left, pulled out his wand and yelled loudly in a language they didn't understand. He released attack after attack from his wand.

Eventually, the Spirits retreated into the darkness.

The sky became still, with nothing but their breathing and the noise of wings and wind to be heard.

Drake peered over the side of the Taruk, the vast ocean to their right as they flew along the shoreline. Aiden watched the ground as if he was studying it, searching for something.

Screams filled the air. A Taruk fell and two shapes could be seen falling right beside it. Drake's mind hardly had any more time to process what was happening as Elohim was knocked sideways in the sky. Drake grasped for something to hang on to.

Aiden grabbed him by the arm, keeping him from falling off. Another Spirit, disguised as a Taruk had flown into their side. Elohim cried out in pain as the claws of the Spirit cut into Elohim's hard flesh. Aiden and Drake both clung tight to the saddle, as Elohim fell out of the sky, pulling the other Taruk with him.

Elohim opened his powerful jaws and released a stream of flame. The Taruk immediately let go but was unable to do anything else but fall to the ground as the fire from Elohim's mouth consumed their enemy.

Drake and Aiden's celebration was short-lived as something struck their other side, sending them over the edge of Elohim. They flailed for a moment falling about ten feet until they splashed into a small brook that ran through the forest.

"Lucky the brook was here!" Drake called to Aiden who was already standing on the bank.

"Watch out!" Aiden exclaimed, pointing to another Spirit that Elohim had set on fire.

The Spirit (in form of a Taruk) fell onto the ground. A shock wave of flames raced from the point of impact, rushing towards them, and then as if it had hit an invisible wall, spread around them, and kept going.

With no hesitation, Aiden ran towards the fire in front of them. The flames recoiled, forming a pathway for them to run through. It stayed formed long enough for them to run past and then it filled back in.

They escaped the flames, immediately noticing blue mist filled the sky above. The Spirits burrowed into the ground and dirt flew up from the impact spots, restricting their view. When their vision cleared they could see the blue mist had taken the form of men which were now in pursuit.

"We've got six of them!" Drake exclaimed. "What are we going to do?"

"Run!" Aiden answered. Drake flinched as something hit the ground behind them. Light flashed all around as the magic that the Spirits were using struck the ground, sending dirt up into the air.

Drake came to a halt as six more men appeared in front of him. He looked at Aiden unable to hide the fear that was running through him.

"You have no escape!" one of the Spirits said. The voice was different, seeming to break into his very soul and eat away at any confidence that had been present.

Drake's heart cried out when a Borag came forward with Gwen. A knife was at her throat, and her clothes were in tatters.

"If you try anything the lady's dead!" the Spirit yelled, holding Gwen by the hair.

"What is your business with us?" Aiden inquired.

"Who are you?" another Spirit asked. Aiden looked into the eyes of the leader, who seemed to cower.

"My name is Aiden of Avdatt."

"We have no business with you, only with this one over here," the Spirit answered, motioning towards Drake. The Spirit drew a wand, leveled it at Aiden's chest and muttered something so fast that Drake couldn't understand it. A blast of light flooded from the end of the wand but never reached Aiden as the light ricocheted and struck the Spirit that had fired the attack.

The force of the impact launched the Spirit from his place on the ground, his wand slipping from his grasp. Drake dropped to the ground, avoiding a different magic attack from the next Spirit who stood right in front of him.

He frantically searched for the wand that had been dropped, but Aiden found it first. He held it in his hands and snapped it with ease. The Spirits in front of them vanished in the blink of an eye.

Drake sprang up from his spot and wrapped his arms around Gwen. She shook in his arms and both of them wished this horror could be over. Aiden pushed them forward as the trees splintered and began to buckle finally crumpling like paper as an invisible force of great strength began to destroy the large trees towering overheard.

They ran, narrowly escaping the falling trees. The sky above was filled with numerous Spirits that landed behind them and took the form of men, giving chase.

"What now?" Drake asked as Aiden urged them forward.

"We have to get to a clearing so we can find Elohim."

"You think he's still alive?" Drake asked.

"He's alive. I can feel it!"

They turned, and made for the shoreline, which was visible through the trees. Fire raced through the sky as the Korazin passed overhead taking out the Spirits who had appeared in front of them.

Three Spirits who had managed to evade the Korazin, stood before them, each of them pulling back their wands.

A thunderous sound shook the forest as Elohim sped through the sky, spewing flames from his mouth. The fire consumed all three of the Spirits before they could do anything.

Elohim landed and Aiden helped them climb on. Soon they were in the sky, bringing the cool air of the sea to greet them. The shoreline quickly became nothing more than a small black shape on the horizon. The wind picked up and rain began to fall around them.

Finally, a great vessel came into view, the bow pushing through the stormy sea. The sails were full and the crew hurried around the ship, doing everything possible to keep the ship on course. Elohim announced their presence as they raced towards the ship.

"How are we going to get on?" Drake asked.

"We'll have to jump off!" Aiden yelled, getting ready. Drake and Gwen both sat on the edge of the Taruk, following Aiden's lead as he shoved off Elohim.

The trio were submerged into the cold ocean water. They surfaced a couple moments later, gasping for breath and looking at the great ship rushing towards them.

They swam toward a rope that was lowered and when took hold, they were lifted from the sea. When they were able to grab the railing, a couple of sailors helped them get onto the deck. Drake pulled Gwen to him and they clung to each other.

"Welcome to the *Blackmorr*," one of the sailors greeted. A streak of fire appeared in the sky. The Korazin landed on the deck, and the fire vanished promptly, giving way to the form of a man, as they expected.

"We made it," Drake said.

"That is good news, but no one else has," the Korazin replied.

"What do you mean no one else has made it?" Gwen asked.

"No one else made it." They turned around to see Atruss coming towards them.

"Then I'm going to go get them," Aiden replied, starting to move toward the side of the ship. Drake stepped forward and grabbed his arm, stopping him from jumping over the edge.

"Take me with you," Drake pleaded. "I want to help them."

"You are no help to the world if you're dead Drake. Let me do this, I can get them back in one piece." Drake knew better than to argue and instead went to Gwen's side. Aiden jumped over the edge of the ship, splashing into the water below.

The Korazin that had landed on the *Blackmorr*, took flight again, transforming into flames that trailed through the air. A few moments passed as they watched Aiden swim away from them.

Elohim dove under the surface of the water, coming up a moment later with Aiden on his back as the two of them rose high into the sky and vanished from their sight.

Atruss came near Drake and Gwen and quickly pulled them below deck where they were given towels and dry clothes, but neither of them could find the energy to change at the moment. The waves pounded into the vessel and rocked it endlessly. As exhaustion threatened to overtake them, they lay on one of the many hammocks that swayed with the ship and listened to the sound of the storm.

The sky showed no sign of the coming dawn as Aiden and Elohim descended toward the water's surface. The shoreline and the forest came into view, an eerie silence hanging in the air.

His heart leapt for joy when he spotted small dark figures running through the forest. He could see the light from the magic that the Spirits were using and he could hear the screams of the others as they tried their best to escape their enemies.

Aiden grasped the pommel of his sword and flexed his hand as Elohim heard his thoughts and dropped out of the sky at a frightening pace. Elohim opened his powerful jaws and let out a sound so great that it shook the trees below.

Fire came from Elohim's mouth, and the trees in front of them were set ablaze. A moment passed before, Elohim tucked his wings in and did a flip, dumping Aiden off into the forest. As planned, Aiden did a twist and landed safely on a large hill that rose above the rest of the terrain.

The Korazin landed next to him and together they bounded down the hill, toward their enemies who were chasing Rohimer and the others. A group of Borags appeared on the ridge, giving them pause.

As if equally surprised by their presence, the Borags halted. Their armor shimmered in the dim lighting and the grotesque face and eyes looked at them with hatred and anger.

"How'd they get here so fast?" one of the Korazin asked.

"The whips of their master no doubt," Rade remarked. "Unnatural." Rohemir, Ellizar, and Lily finally reached them, each of them looking like they had been through a dozen wars.

"Three of you, take the others to the ship, the rest of us will try our skills here and see how many of these foul creatures we can take down by ourselves."

"Four against fifty?" one of the Korazin asked. "Those are some interesting odds. I'm not sure they're ones that you can win with."

"I'm not planning on winning, but if I can kill fifty then it's fifty less to torment the people of Revly. Lathon will be with us," Aiden answered.

Without another word, three of the Korazin led the company away from the inevitable fight.

A lone Borag came to the front of his soldiers, brandishing his sword and letting out a hideous cry. Aiden and the Korazin matched the Borags and both sides rushed into the vale between them. Surprised by their boldness, the Borags panicked, when swords were raised against them. They fought their opponents, slaying Borag after Borag as more soldiers came into the forest.

The roar of Elohim shook the forest and at once Aiden and the Korazin fled from the battle, racing back up the hill. Elohim's sharp massive claws were extended as he crushed the Borags beneath him. Aiden quickly ascended onto Elohim and moments later they were airborne, the Korazin also in the form of Taruks.

As they flew away they found themselves in silence. Undisturbed, comforting silence. The smell of salt water overwhelmed them as they lost sight of the coastline.

Finally, the *Blackmorr* became visible in the storm. The great ship bobbed up and down in the waves as the rough waters tossed the vessel around mercilessly.

The call of a Taruk filled the sky. A lone Spirit, (having taken the form of the Taruks), flew directly towards them. Elohim didn't turn from the enemy and didn't hesitate. Instead, he flew straight at them, not changing his course or slowing down in the slightest.

Elohim climbed slightly into the air, using his massive claws to grab one of the Taruk's heads and yank him backward. Aiden dropped from Elohim, free-falling into the water. The two Taruks flailed in the air and then plummeted into the churning ocean.

Beneath the surface of the water, the two Taruks battled with each other clawing and breathing fire. Elohim let out a stream of fire, which looked green in the water that was all around them. The heat from the fire evaporated the water, drying it up for a second until more water rushed into the area.

Aiden swam towards the boat and grasped a rope that was lowered to him. He climbed up to the deck, watching the battle between the two Taruks. Without warning silence filled the sea. Every member of the crew paused, looking over the edge.

At last, Elohim soared out of the water, his claws clenched to his opponent, the other Taruk was limp and disfigured to the point of no hope. Finally, Elohim released his opponent, letting him fall into the murky depths.

Everyone aboard the *Blackmorr* watched in awe, though the sea still churned. Elohim was lost from sight as the wind and the rain fell around them.

"What just happened?" Lily asked.

"I'm glad it's over," Ellizar said. Many shook their head in agreement.

"Our enemy is wounded but not killed. I expect that we'll see him again in a few seconds," Aiden stated, with such certainty that everyone, even Atruss was shaken.

"You sure know how to cheer someone up," Gwen snapped.

A moment passed as Aiden's words came true. A rumbling in the sea made their ship tremble. They cautiously moved to the railing, staring into the dark murky water that surrounded them. Another rumble echoed through the water.

"It's moving towards the bow!" Aiden yelled. The rain seemed to get heavier, so hard now that the bow of the ship could not be seen by Atruss who was at the stern. Aiden and Drake both moved towards the front.

Everyone was thrown to their knees as the *Blackmorr* was thrown from its course. The cracking and splintering of wood filled everyone with fear.

"What do you think it is?" Drake asked.

"A Spirit of some kind, what form it's taken I couldn't begin to tell you." Aiden helped him up as they stood together at the bow of the ship. A wall of water broke upon the bow, knocking them down to the main deck.

A shrill cry, eating away at whatever confidence remained. A sea serpent now stood in their path. Tall and overbearing, it loomed over them. The world slowed and dark strange whispering entered into Drake's mind.

Unable to resist, Drake stood to his feet and began moving toward the front of the ship. The next moment, Aiden had shoved him to the ground and the sensation and voice that had been whispering in his mind vanished.

Without warning, the sea creature moved to the left and thrust itself into the water, creating a wave twice the size of any they had experienced so far. The wave hammered the ship, ripping crates and boxes from their spots and threatening to wash everyone into the sea. The sail was ripped and the mast was cracked in several places.

Drake frantically searched for Gwen and found her floundering against the side of the ship, barely hanging onto the railing. He reached out to her, beckoning her to take his hand.

She grabbed his hand, but slipped with her other hand, nearly pulling Drake over the edge and into the water. They struggled for a moment before he finally managed to pull her back onto the deck.

Another deep rumble came from under the sea as the sea creature rose up in front of Gwen and Drake. Fear took hold of the crew as they realized their doom was near. If the sea creature was to throw itself onto their starboard side, the ship would be broken in two and they would drown.

Aiden came alongside them and Drake scooped up a spear that was lying on the deck. The sea monster in a move of finality pulled back its head and lunged towards the *Blackmorr*.

Drake hurtled the spear and struck the creature. The serpent recoiled, shrieking loudly. A moment later, they watched as lightning came from the serpent and it was destroyed. Another shrill cry escaped before collapsing into its watery grave.

The serpent was lost from sight and for several minutes the ship was silent, half expecting their opponent to come back out of the water. Several minutes passed and still, there was no sign.

"You did well," Aiden commended, getting up from his spot. The sea churned and the rain still poured down, but the monster had been defeated.

"Thanks, I think," Drake said, a weak smile on his face.

"When will this storm end?" Skander asked.

"Not for a long time my friend. We're entering, the most dangerous part of the ocean. It always storms in the Sea of the Spirits," Aiden informed them. "It'll be the most challenging thing we've ever encountered. Men's hope will fail and the strength of the Elves will be tested. Together we may persevere, but not if we go it alone. We must stick together and defeat the darkness in ourselves if we are to face what lies ahead."

"What lies ahead?" Gwen asked.

"Whatever our enemy wishes to give us," Aiden answered starkly. "It'll be the Sorcerer's best chance to kill us before we enter Ariamore and are out of his reach."

"Can't we go around the Sea of the Spirits?" Drake asked. "Is that such a bad thing?"

"The Kassar River, but it would take more time than we have," Aiden answered. "We will face the evil that awaits us in the Sea of the Spirits. Avoiding it will do no good. Trust in something bigger than yourself and then you will find your new strength...the strength to defeat the evil that has ruined this earth."

"Repair the ship the best we can!" Atruss yelled, above the rain. "Then we sail to our fate in the Sea of the Spirits."

The waves pounded against the side of the *Blackmorr*. The vessel was tossed this way and that, in a storm that had far exceeded the strength that they had imagined. The crew scrambled about the deck, trying with all their might to keep the *Blackmorr* afloat.

Feeling it was too dangerous to return to port, they had repaired things to the best of their ability on the sea, and ever since they had been trapped in the tempest of a storm that threatened to send them to their death.

Wave after wave crashed over the bow, and crew members desperately clung to anything that couldn't be swept away. Never in his life had Rohemir seen a storm like this. He had done what he could to keep the ship afloat, using every bit of magic he knew to protect them. Still, they were helpless against the storm that seemed to gain strength and intensity with every mile they sailed.

Water poured into the holding area below deck and the crew desperately rushed to bucket the water out. The Korazin worked alongside everyone else, doing what they could against the wind and the waves.

It had been three days since they had entered the Sea of the Spirits, yet somehow the morale of the crew had not withered. Rohemir clung to the railing, working his way to Atruss's cabin at the stern.

Rohemir entered the cabin and then closed the door. Directly ahead was a beautiful desk with Atruss behind it. Lanterns were lit and hung from the ceiling, swaying with each wave that tossed them about. Atruss was intently studying some maps and charts.

"Have we traveled far?" Rohemir asked.

"Not far enough for my liking," Atruss answered. "It's impossible to get our heading with these storm clouds. We may be sailing to our death if this storm doesn't let up soon. All we're doing is riding waves and many of our supplies have been tossed to lighten the ship. I agreed with the decision to come into the Sea of the Spirits but I am certainly having second guesses. It would seem a dark power is trying to keep us here. I just wish our enemy would show himself instead of giving us all these obstacles."

"The fact that he has not shown himself likely means that he is not strong enough to show himself," Rohemir concluded.

"Either that or he's confident that he can destroy us without leaving his lair. The fact of the matter is we only have two days of extra food to spare due to the storm. If we don't start making some significant progress by tomorrow night we have to sail north to the mainland and do what we have to so we don't sink or die of starvation."

"I never dreamed that the storm would be this hard to push through. You would think that we might have gotten better at sailing through this disaster, but we haven't."

"Thank you for stating the obvious!" Atruss snapped. "Some things are beyond our control."

"I might be able to use magic to calm down the storm, or to give us extra speed," Rohemir suggested. Atruss looked up.

"You know how I feel about you using your 'magic' Rohemir," Atruss reminded. "For you to use 'magic' you have to give up a piece of your soul and in my estimation, there is never a time for that."

"The Elves use it frequently," Rohimer insisted.

"The Elves do miracles and everyone else tries to imitate them with magic."

"Agreed," Rohemir said. "What of Drake's use of magic? What do you say to that? He easily took down that sea creature a few days ago. He's a human and he used magic as though he didn't even have to think about it. How? Has he been trained in the magical arts? Humans do it all the time and you say we lose a part of our soul when we do. The only people that it comes naturally to are Elves, he is clearly not Elvish. What do you think of Drake Thomas?"

"I think he's a very interesting person," Atruss answered. Rohemir gave him a suspicious look. "I don't suspect foul play."

"You don't?"

"No," Atruss replied. "If he was a Spirit or a spy the Korazin would surely be aware by now. His memory being gone is strange and the use of magic is unusual, this I admit. But he has the mark, he has been chosen by Lathon in some way. Even if it's not clear."

"You take it as blind faith?"

"I trust the wisdom of Lathon," Atruss corrected.

"Is that your opinion?"

"Am I wrong? You say he used magic, I say Lathon acted on his behalf."

"You don't real-"

"Think it through Rohemir! Honestly, think it through. He bears the mark, he has been chosen by Lathon. Why would Lathon not act on his behalf and kill the sea creature with a little *'miracle'*?"

"You think the one who will prepare the way for Lathon, Sherados, would have the ability to do miracles?

"Wouldn't that make sense?"

"The whole situation puts me on edge," Rohemir admitted. "I don't know what to expect from him."

"If I were Lathon and I wanted to unite two races that had been separated for a millennium I think I would send someone who had similarities to both races. A Man who could do magic as Elves do and bore the mark of Lathon as a sign to the people that he is who we believe him to be," Atruss explained. "I do not doubt that Drake Thomas is either Elyay or Sherados himself. Time will reveal the truth. For all we know Drake Thomas could very well be Shedaros."

"You bring up an interesting point and there's only one way to find out for sure."

"I will not allow you to invade his mind!" Atruss exclaimed. "We are going to sail to Ariamore and once there, we will have many meetings regarding everything that's happened. I'm sure the religious sect will take an interest in him, especially the Farsees."

"Sometimes I wish that Elves had more insight than Men. Maybe then we would be better able to prepare for the future."

"The only insight we have is the ancient scrolls of Lathon and the Prophets. Other than that, we have no special knowledge of what this time in history will bring."

Rohemir opened his mouth to speak but never got the works out as a knock came at the door.

"Enter," Atruss said. The door was opened and Aiden walked in, sword by his side. He was soaked to the bone, looking as though he had been outside in the rain for years.

"Good evening," Aiden greeted.

"Good evening," Atruss replied. "How are the men doing? Are we in trouble of losing them to the storm? If you take my meaning."

"They're hungry but other than that they seem to be in good spirits. There are a couple that are starting to unravel a little and lose faith, but for the most part, they seem to be finding strength."

"Their motivation is very interesting," Rohemir commented. "I know they are good sailors, but they are aware that we've gone nowhere in the past day or so correct?"

"They are aware, still something seems to be driving them," Atruss answered.

"Perhaps it is because they think they are with Shedaros or Elyay," Aiden answered. "Their faith and hope are inspiring, but I fear that may vanish in the coming days if we don't start moving."

"I'm going to wait one more day and if we don't start making some serious progress then I'm calling it off and we're going another way. Any news of what's happening on the mainland?" Atruss inquired.

"Revly has come under attack and has been conquered. Elohim did several flyovers of the city and the surrounding countryside and saw nothing but smoke and destruction," Aiden said.

"Do you think they have figured out that Drake isn't in the city anymore?"

"They attacked the city anyway. War is inevitable whether we like it or not."

"What can we do to stand against them if we are not ready to fight?" Rohemir asked.

"We do our best and prepare to fight and make a stand for what is just and right in this world," Aiden answered. "We give them a fight to remember and show them once and for all that *we* will not be overcome, but we will triumph over the evil that threatens the nations."

"The council will make ready preparations for an army to be created, although it will likely be spring before anything official is done, thanks to the Farsees. They will likely be the people who oppose the move if there is one," Atruss informed.

"Why am I not surprised?" Aiden asked.

"Aiden, I know you may not get along with the Farsees, but you must entertain them," Atruss started. "They hold a great deal of influence among the people. If the Farsees turn on you, they will do everything in their power to get rid of you. Just keep your cool. They might stand in the way of creating the army, but in time I'm sure they will see our side."

"We don't have time for them to debate the future of the world! Our enemy seeks to destroy us now, and all the religions in the world won't save us from them. Only Shedaros will have any power."

"If the Farsees heard you speaking like that they would likely have you put to death," Rohemir said. "Are you saying you don't believe in the ancient scrolls of Lathon?"

"The scrolls I believe in, the Farsees on the other hand, no. They preach about following Lathon's example yet they are nothing more than hypocrites. I've watched them and how they act when people aren't around. I don't approve. It's what you do when no one's looking that matters."

"Still they lead the people-"

"That's enough gentlemen," Atruss interrupted. "This bickering is pointless. We all have our views and opinions, let's keep them to ourselves for the moment. We will cooperate with the Farsees until we have reason to do something else. We *will* create this army."

"Creating an army is a step in the right direction," Aiden agreed. "However when we reach the shores I really must be on my way. I have business to attend to in other parts of the world, and now that the Borags are officially on the move. I think there is work to be done."

"We understand, and may I thank you again for standing beside us and lending a hand in this dark storm."

"It's no problem at all," Aiden answered. "I'm glad that I can be here to offer hope to the crew. My shift is over so if you'll need me I'll be sleeping."

"How can anyone sleep in a storm like this?" Rohemir asked.

"Either try to sleep or drop over dead from exhaustion," Aiden pointed out.

"Very well. Try and get some sleep," Atruss ordered. "Thank you once again for everything you're doing."

"Don't mention it," Aiden answered. He left the cabin. leaving Rohemir and Atruss to their thoughts for the moment.

"What should we do when we get to Ariamore?" Rohemir asked. "If Drake Thomas is using magic, should he be trained? It appears that he didn't mean to use it, which means that he may be like the Elves in that respect. If it happens in front of the Farsees then I'm sure they will want to train him."

"Let us not worry about that now," Atruss said.

"But what is to be done when we get to-"

"Rohemir! What you need is a good night's rest! It doesn't do good to worry about the future. Let things unfold the way they are meant to unfold. There is a plan in all of this; we should just get out of the way and let it be, otherwise, we'll screw something up. When we get to Ariamore we will figure out the next move. I will suggest that we train Drake Thomas and his friends with the necessary skills to make them excellent fighters. They seem good, but against our enemies that will only get them so far."

"Perhaps you haven't seen Drake fight, but he also seems to have a gift for fighting. He has been taught nothing yet he fights as if he's been fighting for years. Each second that passes I grow more and more suspicious about him."

"Enough of this talk for tonight. I'll see you in the morning Rohemir." They said their good nights and Atruss blew out the lantern and left the room. Rohemir stood in the darkness thinking about everything that had happened in the past couple of days before leaving the cabin himself and moving below deck to the sleeping quarters.

Drake lay in his hammock, with Gwen asleep on his shoulder. Ellizar and Lily were slumped in the next hammock.

"Good evening Drake," Rohemir greeted. Drake's eyes went wide and then focused in on Rohemir as he looked up. Rohemir smiled warmly and Drake smiled back. "How are you doing?"

"Tired," Drake answered. "Tired, yet I can't sleep."

"This is quite the storm that we're going through."

"It's not the storm that's keeping me awake...I'm just worried about everything. It seems as if everyone wants me and I don't know why. If I knew my past it would make the present and the future much easier to live with."

"I wish I could say that I understand what you're going through but I don't," Rohemir answered. "I am surprised that nothing's come back to you in the past weeks that we've been traveling."

"I'm remembering something, but nothing more than flashes of light and water. I just hope when we get to Ariamore I'm not locked up as a nutcase or something like that."

"I wouldn't be bringing you all this way just so you could be locked up. I wouldn't worry about what the future holds. I know in my heart that there is a purpose and meaning behind everything that's transpired, just sometimes we're not that good at understanding it."

"I wish I could see the future."

"No, you don't. If you could see the future, terrible things could happen, because the future is always in motion. You might see one thing and then have to figure out how to get there and in doing so you might make a choice that would lead you down a different path completely. You've been put on this path for a reason, maybe it's time you embrace it."

"Maybe." Drake fell silent staring into space again. "Rohemir, can I ask you a question?"

"Certainly."

"When we were in Revly I saw a bird, a very unique bird. I can't shake the image from my head. It was bald, having no feathers. It was kind of black with claws on its wings. If I had to take a guess I'd say it was about the size of an owl. Have you seen a bird like that before?"

"No," Rohemir answered. "But that doesn't mean it wasn't there. For whatever reason your eyes have been opened to what ours cannot see. It's just another thing that makes you unique."

"I think the bird recognized me," Drake replied. "I haven't seen it since."

"Very curious," Rohemir answered. "Don't worry about anything, for now, try and get some rest, otherwise you'll be in worse shape than you are now."

"Can't you just use a spell on me and help me get to sleep," Drake replied. They both laughed.

"No, I try not to use magic unless I'm in a life-threatening situation."

"We seem to always be in a life-threatening situation, whether it's a storm or being chased by our enemies."

"Worry not, soon we'll be able to rest. Our enemies won't enter the borders of Ariamore. Speaking of magic how did you use it?"

"Use what?" Drake asked.

"Killing the sea monster? Some kind of magic happened. How did you do that?"

"I used magic? I thought someone else caused that. I just threw the harpoon. That's all I know."

"Very well, why don't you get some sleep and I'll see you in the morning."

Rohemir moved to the stairs and walked out into the storm, not noticing a featherless bird, like Drake had described, sitting atop the ship watching everything.

Drake opened his heavy eyelids, unsure of how long he had slept. The inside of the ship was empty except for himself and one other person, who was asleep in their hammock. The waves still pummeled the vessel and water came pouring in through a crack that had appeared in the upper deck.

Drake walked towards the stairwell and stepped into the storm, which had grown more fierce. The sails had been folded up to avoid them being damaged any further and although some of the crates and supplies had been tied down, he could see that several ropes had snapped and the supplies swept out to the sea.

Drake carefully made his way towards the front of the ship where Gwen was working with five other people, trying to pull a rope tight around a beam. He came alongside and helped hoist a crate from the lower deck. To Drake's surprise and alarm, as soon as it was set on the deck, it was pushed over the side of the ship where it was lost to the sea.

"There's not much more we can throw over," Gwen admitted bitterly. Drake didn't reply but understood fully what she was saying. For the first time, they wondered if they would make it out alive.

They carried out the orders they were given and together the two of them lost all sense of time as the waves never ceased to come. The sky remained dark and full of mystery as the sea churned, tossing the ship in every direction except the one they wanted to go.

Each wave laughed at them. Each swell jeered them and whispered dark thoughts in their mind. With his hope almost diminished Drake looked longingly into the horizon for something that would offer a sliver of hope that they would be leaving the storm behind him.

"Hey! I can see land!" Drake yelled. Atruss was the first one to rush to the front of the battered ship, looking in the direction that Drake was pointing. He studied it a little longer, only seeing the dark shapes for a moment at a time as the ship bobbed up and down in the storm. Atruss turned to all the crew who could hear him.

"Turn this ship towards the north!" He ordered. "There is something over there, we can only hope that it's land!" The sailors did as he said, and the ship slowly began to turn toward the black shape that Drake had seen. The wind increased and the waves shoved them in the direction of the black shape, picking up more speed than they had planned on.

Within no time the black shape had grown into a large city which was now towering over them. Buildings jutted up out of the sea like teeth waiting to send them to their death. Atruss frantically yelled out and ordered them to turn around, but it was too late.

Everyone was brought to their knees as the *Blackmorr* struck one of the small buildings. The crunching of boards reached their ears as they floated backward a little ways and then were pushed forward by the next wave. This time they struck the side of the rock that they had struck the first time. The ship lurched to the right, before rushing forward towards the next building that stood in their way.

"Get Aiden from below deck!" Atruss ordered.

Leaving Gwen, Drake had bolted from his spot to the stairwell that led to the lower deck of the ship. Drake searched the area, seeing Aiden sleeping on his hammock.

"Wake up!" Drake said, shaking him vigorously. Aiden showed his surprise noticing the water that covered the floor. Water splashed over the floor as seawater entered through a hole that was only a foot or two above the water line. as he took notice of the inch of water that covered the floor.

"This is new," Aiden said standing to his feet.

"A small hole on the starboard side, above the water line," Drake explained.

"What's going on?"

"The ship is falling apart!" Drake exclaimed. "We're in a rock field of sorts and we're hitting all of them. I didn't think it was going to end like this."

"End?"

"We're going to sink if we keep this up!" Drake exclaimed, watching Aiden's eyes fill with a light he hadn't seen before.

"Where's your faith?" Aiden said. He motioned for Drake to follow him as they approached the stairwell.

They were thrown into the stairs as the vessel slammed into another building. The hole in the starboard side became larger allowing more water to come in. They scaled the stairs and then came to the bow of the ship as Aiden looked out over the storm and the buildings in front of them.

"There's no way we're going to get out of the storm!" Drake cried above the noise of the waves and the rain.

"Curse this storm!" Aiden exclaimed. Even as he finished speaking the storm subsided and the sea became calm. The rain was no more and the clouds vanished from the sky leaving only the stars to shine down on them.

The moonlight shone on the water and their hearts were left to ponder what had just happened. When the sea was completely calm Aiden looked at Drake with a smile on his face.

"I don't see a storm." They laughed and the crew let out shouts of praise and cheers.

"It appears we're not goin' teh sink after all!" Ellizar exclaimed.

Everyone was knocked down as they struck another rock. The bottom of the ship was torn and splintered beneath them as they went over the rocks beneath. Their speed dropped and they were thrown forward as the ship came to a rest.

"Well that was good," Skander replied standing up on his feet. The ship had now come to a rest leaning sideways in the shallow water. Boards and planks of wood, as well as some of their supplies, floated below.

"I think we're sinkin' now," Ellizar stated.

"The *Blackmorr* is lost. We seem to be in some lost harbor, land is not far off. Gather what supplies you can carry and get to shore!" Atruss ordered.

They went to shore, bringing all the supplies they could manage in the darkened skies. They made sure to be in the cover of trees, and also within the walls of the ruined city that awaited on the mainland.

After an hour or two of work, they had gathered most of the remaining supplies that weren't damaged or spoiled and started a fire in the ruins. They kept it small, but even at that, it gave hope to their weary hearts.

Rohemir and Atruss walked through the abandoned city for an hour or so, trying to figure out where they were, but the crew talked and laughed, more relieved than ever to be free of the storm that had nearly killed them. Drake looked over at Aiden who smiled back at him, instilling a sense of mystery in Drake.

Who was this man that the waves seemed to listen to him?

There was a chance that everything that had transpired was nothing more than a coincidence. That Aiden had come to the bow of the ship, and the waves had stopped on their own. Drake doubted that as a serious possibility though.

Then again maybe *he* had stopped the storm from destroying them and just hadn't realized it. After all, Drake had apparently used magic to kill the sea monster.

He laid down next to Gwen and let his eyes fall shut, as his exhaustion pulled him into a deep sleep. A vision filled his eyes as he slept and Drake was unable to pull away from it. In the dream, the bird was there. The same bird that he had seen in Revly. It was featherless and kept looking at him as though it knew something that he didn't. Finally, the vision ended and he was left to sleep in peace.

Drake stirred to see the campfire, which was now a pile of ash. Everyone else was still fast asleep and the sun was high above them, suggesting it might be midday.

The *Blackmorr,* battered and broken, still sat awkwardly on the rocks, a permanent reminder of the storm they had been delivered from. Remembering this, Drake drew a deep breath and said a prayer of thanks to the God who had saved them.

The ruins spread out all around him, inviting him forward. Drake explored level after level until he came to the very top level of what had once been a beautiful city. The green forest bordered them on three sides as the top of the city joined with the forest.

As he stood at the citadel, Drake felt something was wrong. The sun was warm, and the view was amazing. Nevertheless, the forest was silent, without a bird or chipmunk to lighten the heavy air.

A rustling sound caught Drake's attention and when he turned, he saw a lone bird sitting atop one of the broken spires. The bird was featherless and scraggly looking, identical to the one he had seen in Revly. It looked in his direction and cocked its head when it spotted him as though it was surprised to see him standing there.

The bird pushed off the tall spire and opened its wings. It climbed into the sky and swooped down, landing only ten feet from him. It continued to look at Drake as if it was trying to figure out what he was. A moment or two later the bird took flight, vanishing into the trees.

Drake entered the trees, hoping to catch sight of the bird again. His efforts proved successful as he would find the bird, only to have it take off and then be found again, like a cat with a mouse.

Drake followed until he entered a small clearing in the forest. The trees and their canopy of leaves provided almost complete shade and at first, he didn't notice a Taruk lying in the opening, curled up like a cat would be.

The bird he had been following flew into the sky and landed on a branch, seeming content to sit there. Drake turned his attention towards the sleeping Taruk, fully aware he probably shouldn't approach, yet he felt as if he should.

It was the strangest thing that Drake had ever felt. Aiden had warned him once about going near a Taruk. Memories of what had happened last time flashed through his head. The Taruk was all white, but not a shiny white like he would have thought. The moments passed and Drake's heart was stirred.

This was Elohim, Aiden's Taruk. The Taruk yawned and then picked up its head. With a single bound Elohim climbed onto all fours inviting Drake to come closer.

Drake moved forward and Elohim did the same, and when they were close enough Drake held out his hand and Elohim touched it with his large nose. To his wonder the Taruk stood there, seeming content, allowing Drake to pet him.

They both stared at each other, not saying a word, but each knew what the other one was thinking and feeling. Drake no longer felt any fear as he petted Elohim's nose.

"You are a brave man Drake Thomas." Drake whirled around to see Aiden standing by the trees. Drake backed away from Elohim.

"I'm sorry, I didn't mean to do anything it's just that-"

"Don't apologize. It's a rare person who can approach a Taruk twice and live to tell about it. That kind of person, in my opinion, is destined to have a Taruk."

"What would I possibly do with one?" Drake asked.

"You can do many things with them. You could become a Tarukai like myself. You could join an army and destroy the enemies that seek to destroy all that is good in the world. You could use them as transportation if you wanted. It would be completely up to you."

"You said it's a rare person who can approach a Taruk. Why am I able to?"

"I can't answer that," Aiden answered. "As much as it is your choice to pick a Taruk and care for it, the Taruk also has to choose you. Taruks won't even hatch until they know of a person they want to choose. When a Taruk is thinking about choosing someone it'll watch that person for a very long time."

"How do they know? How can they do that?"

"It's how Lathon made them Drake," Aiden said. "Taruks are quite extraordinary; they can know things from a very long way away. They can keep their eye on someone from one end of the earth to another without even having to work at it. They know what you are doing and that's how they can keep an eye on you."

"So, if you're being watched by a Taruk, you'd better be on your best behavior all the time; not just when you think he's around."

"Indeed, and that's where many people fall short. All Taruks are different and they're not very trusting of people. It is usually dangerous for others to approach. You though seem to have no problem doing so."

"Why don't Taruks trust people?" Drake asked. "Not like we can harm them, they're powerful creatures-"

"They were once very hurt by humans," Aiden told him. "It was a long, long time ago but the Taruks lived here with everyone and would not hesitate to show themselves and their mighty power. But, when the union of Elves and Men fell apart, the humans decided they didn't want the Taruks around anymore. They hunted all the Taruks they could find.

"Since then the Taruks have been scattered all across the world, trying their very best to only show themselves to people who want to see them. Their population has improved over the centuries, and the Mezutor is proof of that, but overall they still don't trust humans very quickly.

"The Elves were the only people who fully embraced and welcomed the Taruks. That is just another reason why people fear coming to the borders of Ariamore. They think that thousands of Taruks would devour them in a second."

"Are there Taruks in Ariamore?" Drake asked looking towards Elohim.

"Not many. The only Taruks in these parts are used in the Mezutor, other than that there isn't one to be found."

"How did you get Elohim then?"

"Most people have to buy theirs, they go through the process, express interest in a Taruk, then the Taruk watches them, and so on. However, I found Elohim in the forest near Seredath a few years back."

"You just found him?"

"That's right. I just stumbled across him while I was hunting one day. He was sleeping in the forest, he was much smaller then. It was as if he knew I was coming and had decided to wait for me. That's how I got him and he's never left my side since. Nowhere else in the world will you find such a noble, majestic, and caring creature. The union between the Taruk and the person who owns him is one that nobody understands. Elohim seems to like you."

"Aiden, have you seen that-"

"You're asking about the bird right?" Aiden asked. Drake nodded. Aiden looked up in the trees and spotted it. "I can see it too. You're not going insane."

"What kind of a bird is it? It seems to be following us."

"I'm not exactly sure," Aiden admitted. "I've seen it on several occasions in my life."

"It seems as if it's keeping an eye on me," Drake started. "I'm not sure why or how I know that, but it seems to show up when I don't expect it."

"Maybe you have someone watching over you," Aiden suggested. Aiden moved around to Elohim's side, petting the soft skin that covered the Taruk. As Drake looked closer he could see hard scales beneath the Taruk's short hair.

"Can I ask one more question?"

"There's no crime against asking a question if you need to know the answer."

"Last night when we were in that storm...the waves, when we went up onto the deck...they stopped and it was like the storm had never existed. How did you do that?"

"Nothing says I did."

"I think you did," Drake answered.

"Perhaps I played a small part in stopping the storm, but how I did it I cannot say."

"You don't know?"

"Some things are better left unsaid," Aiden replied. "Don't worry about it. You'll see many unusual things in this world Drake and if you worry about everyone you'll go insane. Things happen a certain way for a reason."

"So you're not going to tell me how you did it?"

"I'm Elven, perhaps that has something to do with it," Aiden suggested. Drake's mind burned with a dozen more questions that didn't have answers. Something about Aiden was different from everyone else that Drake had met. Aiden seemed to be hiding something, but he couldn't guess what it was.

Aiden turned from him and climbed onto Elohim's back. Elohim, who had sat down while they had been talking, stood back up onto his powerful legs, looking at the sky, ready to take flight any moment.

"Where are you going?" Drake asked.

"To figure out where we are. Probably in an hour's flight time, we can figure out our approximate location. Do you want to come with us?"

"You mean to fly with you?"

"Yes, this time not in a getaway. I promise it'll be much more relaxing."

"Is Elohim okay with that?" Drake asked.

"I wouldn't have asked you if he hadn't suggested it." Drake climbed on and Elohim pushed off the ground sending them into the sky at a more relaxed pace than the last time they had flown.

Their clothes were pressed against their bodies as they flew for a period of time that Drake didn't measure. The forest continued, remaining as silent as a tomb, the only change was that the trees now had some color in them, showing signs of the coming fall. They looked down unable to spot any house or village.

Finally, Aiden pointed in the distance in front of them where a rock structure jutted up out of the forest below.

"I know where we are now!" Aiden exclaimed. They turned and flew back the way they had come landing in the forest clearing once again. Drake climbed off following Aiden who led them back through the ruins where the others were starting to wake up. Rohemir and Atruss stood on the far side.

"Good morning everyone," Aiden greeted.

"Good morning. I'd say we have to get out of here but I haven't got a clue where we are," Rohemir said.

"You are in the land of Giahon. For those of you who don't know anything about Giahon it's generally a nation that is popular with Giants," Aiden answered. "I'd be careful about wandering through this land any more than you have to, Giants aren't the friendliest sort. Nice if they like you, but if they hate you, I'd watch out. They have quite a temper. Their kingdom may be next to Ariamore but I'm sure they won't be friendly if they spot you here."

"Why are there no birds in the trees?" Gwen asked.

"Giants aren't particularly fond of birds or anything that makes noise, besides themselves. They have good hearing and they can hear things from a very long way away. They'll hear you before you hear them," Atruss explained.

"So when yer travelin' through Giahon yeh won't hear anythin'?" Ellizar asked.

"Only the ranting and ramblings of a dwarf who doesn't know what to think about life," Lily piped up. They tried not to laugh as Ellizar turned and shot Lily a look and Lily looked all around them at the forest appearing not to notice the stare.

"Blasted elf kind," Ellizar replied.

"Where exactly are we in Giahon?" Skander asked.

"A lot farther west than you would have liked to be. The best I can figure it, you're about three hundred miles west of the border of Ariamore," Aiden answered.

"Three hundred miles?" Atruss asked, looking at the shipwrecked vessel they had been traveling on. "Amark," an elf looked at him. "As Navigator, I hope you don't take this wrong, but you're fired."

"I got us to land in record time didn't I?" Amark asked a weak smile across his face.

"Yes, but we were all under the impression that we hadn't moved anywhere in three days. Now it appears we not only made it through the Sea of the Spirits in record time, but we also ended up tremendously off course."

"Not even a dwarf could screw up that much!" Ellizar exclaimed with a laugh.

"That's because people would never let someone four feet tall navigate a ship in the first place," Lily fired back. Ellizar threw down his cup and stood to his feet.

"Blasted elf kind! Why must yeh always pick on poor Ellizar? I'm nice teh yeh all the time and yet look at the treatment I get."

"Just relax Ellie, I'm only teasing, and I only tease the people that I love."

"What do yeh do with people like her?" He asked everyone else. "Elves are supposed teh be intelligent. You'd think she'd be able teh call me by my name and not by Ellie!"

"Are you guys finished?" Gwen asked. They all laughed and Ellizar looked at them strangely for a moment before breaking into laughter himself. "So, what do we do now?"

"We start making our way towards Ariamore as fast as we can and hopefully we can do it without alerting anyone to our presence," Rohemir replied. "It's going to be a harder journey though, no horses for any of us."

"I have to be going," Aiden declared. "I wish I could accompany you to the border of Ariamore but I have business to attend to elsewhere. Dangerous business. I will need the Korazin to come with me."

"Where are you going that you need to take them?" Atruss asked. Aiden smiled.

"I need to get into a certain city undetected. I'm headed towards the nation of Grimdor, the capital of Grimdor to be exact."

"I'm not even sure I want to know," Lily replied.

"You're more foolish than I thought," Rohemir replied. "I've been held hostage in the capital of Grimdor before and I don't think getting in undetected is going to be even remotely possible. I tried and I ended up captured for a month."

"That's why I need the Korazin. I believe with their help we can get in where no one else can," Aiden told them.

"We would be honored to fight alongside you," Rade, the leader of the Korazin answered.

"I'm glad to have you on my side," Aiden answered. "We'll be leaving immediately. I'll tell you the plan as we get closer."

"I wish you all the blessings and speed one can wish you on a death journey like you're about to set out on," Rohemir replied. They said their goodbyes and followed him to the clearing where Elohim sat waiting for Aiden. The Korazin took off into the sky taking the forms of Taruks'. Elohim pushed off into the sky and the group vanished from sight.

"Let's waste no time in getting to Ariamore. Until we're there we aren't safe," Atruss said. They made their way back to their camp and picked up their belongings, only taking what they could carry.

They walked for hours, the silence of the land unnerving them. No one spoke as they continued, hoping they were quiet enough to not be heard by the Giants who may be roaming the land. The day faded and gave way to night when they made camp in the forest.

The second day went faster than the first. How far they were traveling none of them had a clue, all they knew was that they still had a long way to go. They spoke a little bit, but for the most part, they stayed quiet still not wanting to raise suspicion.

On the third day, the shoreline continued stretching out in front of them no different than it had previously. The landscape was becoming much more interesting for them to look at. The shoreline was bordered by hills and cliffs, and gradually the coast became rocky and hard to traverse. The hard sand they had walked on up to this point had completely vanished.

The nights came and went and they found themselves chilled to the bone by the bitter air that rolled off the water and brought with it fog that generally soaked everything in the morning.

It was two more nights before they came into sight of a town of any sort and even at that, the town was larger than they would've liked.

They camped far outside of the city, watching for an evening before deciding to go in early the next morning. It was only Rohemir and Atruss who entered the city, seeing that they knew how to act around Giants so as not to arouse suspicion. They came out with supplies and they set out shortly after noon, walking at least another twenty miles before they came to a stop that night.

Their home for the night was a large ruined castle that seemed to be more eerie and unnerving than anything they had come to up to this point. The castle was overgrown, with trees jutting up here and there and vines of every kind and color wrapping up and down the walls. Pieces were missing from the walls and the towers were crumbling and broken.

They ate a quick meal and then fell to sleep one by one, except for Drake. His eyes searched the heavens for answers but found none. The moonlight shone down above him and he was left alone to ponder his thoughts.

He laid there for hours still unable to even feel the slightest bit tired. He tossed and turned several times before his thoughts were shattered by a faint roar that echoed through the night. Drake's heart skipped a beat as he looked up towards the top of the ruined castle where the sound had come from. He got up and walked into the ruined city.

THE DUNGEONS OF GRIMDOR

Aiden led the seven Korazin, cleverly disguised as Borags, through the barren and desolate landscape of Grimdor. They had been walking for two days, hoping and praying that they wouldn't be discovered along the way.

Aiden had been to Grimdor on several occasions, but never to the capital city of Iscariot. Of the three Borag cities that were above ground, this was by far the largest. Rade and the Korazin, who had been here before, had described Iscariot as a place out of the abyss. The dark black rock that the city was built out of rose from the ground like a tombstone marker, stealing away all hope of ever escaping.

They scaled a large rock hill and then scrambled to find cover as the walls of Iscariot became visible. The parapets were ominous and topped with cruelly shaped jagged points on the towers and spires. Torches lined the outer wall, which stood forty feet above the ground. Beyond that, they could make out an inner wall, and beyond that, they could make out three tall spires, reaching hundreds of feet above the rest of the city.

"Where would the dungeons be?" Aiden asked.

"One of those spires in the center," Rade regrettably admitted.

"What's the best way to get in?"

"The only time I've been in this city, I walked through the gates," Rade admitted.

"We are in the form of Borags. We could just march Aiden through the city gates as our prisoner," one of the other Korazin suggested.

"We will fool the eye, but only at a quick glance," Rade replied. "We can't take a chance on a Mage or other people who deal in the Dark Arts being able to tell that we're Spirits and not Borags. If it was any other Borag city, perhaps, but this is different."

"What of the drain tunnels?"

"They always have guards watching. Even if we can walk up them we'll be shot full of arrows before we can blink."

"What other way is there?" one of the Korazin asked.

Aiden smiled weakly. "How about the sewage tunnel?"

"Disgusting and gross for sure," Rade confirmed. "It's going to be awful but they won't have anyone guarding that."

"If they do then they're really twisted," one of the Korazin added.

"It should work though," Rade said. "I know where they are, follow me."

Horns bellowed through the night and the cry of a great voice cast an eerie presence over the land. The stone and metal gates of Iscariot creaked noisily as if they hadn't been opened for some time.

A great host of Borags began marching out of the gates, bringing with them siege towers and other weapons of war. They spread out, moving in many different directions and an hour later there was no sign that the armies of Grimdor were done being unleashed.

It was clear now that the rest of the world had been blinded by the person who had united the nations of Grimdor and Vernal (the nation of the Spirits). The Sorcerer wasn't building his strength, he *had* built his strength. He had done so in silence and in secret, now declaring himself.

Rade carefully led Aiden and his companions around the city, using rocks and other natural formations to hide them from sight if it was necessary. A while later they reached their destination.

The ground dropped off and formed a deep crater that was empty at the moment. Twenty or thirty feet off the bottom of the crater many tunnels and shafts opened up in the rock.

"As crazy as this idea is, it might actually work," one of the Korazin said.

"We're going to have to free climb to the opening," Rade explained. "We'll go first, since we are currently Borags we'll use our claws and climbing abilities to create enough cracks and ruts in the rock that you can climb."

"Lead on!" Aiden exclaimed. The Korazin didn't waste any time using their razor-sharp claws to dig into the rocks and scale their way to the top, reaching the small ledge just outside the opening. Aiden followed in their path, using the footholds, cuts, and gashes that had been created by the claws that Borags were known for.

Aiden finally reached the top, putting one hand up over the ledge. He froze, looking up at three Borags who stood directly in front of him.

"What are you waiting for? It's just us!" Rade said. Aiden breathed a sigh of relief as he pulled himself up onto the ledge.

"Sorry. I forgot what you looked like," Aiden replied.

Rade held a finger to his lips. "At the end of this tunnel, there may be guards. They hastily moved down the hall, trying to remain as quiet as they could, despite their boots splashing through small puddles of sewage. Rade stopped them and then motioned to two of the Korazin. They slowly strung their bows.

At once they darted around the corner. The Borags who were standing guard never got a chance to make any noise as the arrows landed in their throats and slumped to the ground.

They moved the guards to the side and tried to hide them as best they could, only then realizing the stench that this tunnel had. Several minutes later they came to a fork in the road as the tunnel split off into several directions.

"Which tunnel do you think it is?" one of the Korazin asked.

"Probably the one that smells the worst, which would be this one," Rade deduced. They moved down the tunnel, which seemed to get smaller as they went. Finally, they came to the end of the tunnel where it turned and went straight up.

"Allow me," one of the Korazin said. Aiden moved out of the way as one of the Korazin grabbed his bow and an arrow, firing it into the narrow tunnel. The arrow flew up towards the top of the shaft and then ignited sending light into the shaft. Different tunnels could be seen branching off in every direction.

They moved backward as flames spread throughout the entire shaft. When the flames subsided they found that the shaft had been cleaned by the fire and didn't smell anymore. Aiden silently thanked them and the Korazin began climbing, making footholds for Aiden who followed behind them.

They reached the top of the shaft and climbed into one of the tunnels. Rade once again took the lead, lightly running down the tunnel until an opening appeared in front of them. The top half of the tunnel was gone leaving them to be seen by anyone who looked in their direction.

The large spire that they were headed for towered over them.

"Ten more minutes," Rade estimated, knowing Aiden's question. Walkways and bridges stood between them, taunting them to find a way to the prisons. Several guards could be seen, which the Korazin promptly spotted, stringing their bows carefully.

"How are you going to get them without making too much noise?" Aiden asked. "If they fall over the edge someone will raise the alarm.

"Don't worry about that," Rade reassured. "These are special arrows." Aiden watched as the three of the Korazin stepped out from behind him and loosed the arrows that they had prepared. They aimed them high up into the sky. The arrows climbed and then descended at just the right time. The arrows hit the guards and caught fire, black flames incinerated the Borags within a second until nothing but a pile of ash remained and floated away in the wind.

"Glad you're on my side," Aiden replied. The company carefully made their way out of the tunnel and then dropped over the edge, falling onto another bridge, which was thankfully clear of any Borags. They traveled along the narrow ledge of the wall, jumping slightly, landing on a bridge that was at least twenty feet wide and eighty feet long, seeming to bypass the city as it went over the top of the whole city from one tower to the next.

They began running not even pausing as more guards came into view. The Korazin fired more arrows turning them to ashes before they could alert anyone. The confusing maze of stairs and bridges continued until finally, the tower was before them. The number of guards was more than they had planned, with six guards standing and waiting.

The Korazin aimed with the last of their fire arrows and let them loose. The guards fell to the ground and the Korazin took the place of the incinerated Borags.

"How long do you need?" one of the Korazin asked.

"Give me ten minutes, and then start making some noise. Wait for Elohim to make the first move though." The Korazin nodded their reply and Aiden moved inside, his eyes adjusting to the darkness.

His eyes focused on two guards who stood, one with his sword drawn while the other was ready to release an arrow at him. Aiden bolted from his spot, jumping in between the two guards and then jumping to the left as the arrow that had been aimed at him was released. The arrow missed him and hit the other Borag who fell to the ground.

Aiden pulled his sword and swung it once. The other guard fell and Aiden grabbed the keys and a torch from the wall, climbing up a large spiral staircase. Several prison cells were along each side of the tower until he came to a metal door, which stood out from all the wooden ones he had passed.

Aiden fumbled with the keys trying the first of the twelve locks, finally getting it after several tries. He moved onto the second one, surprising himself when the next eleven locks popped open just by his touch.

He pushed open the door and moved into the dark cell. His torch illuminated the darkness, bringing into view a tray of old and moldy food and a frail figure of an elf who sat curled up in the corner.

Aiden knelt next to the elf and put a hand on his shoulder. The elf stirred, alarm in his eyes for a moment. His friend's eyes softened a moment later.

"It's been a long time," the elf said.

"Indeed it has been, so long that I'm not sure how you ended up here."

"Life certainly has some interesting twists, this is just one of them," the elf answered. He was skinny, with barely enough skin to cover his bones as he stood. "I don't care what you want to know, it couldn't have been so important that you had to break into Iscariot."

"I thought it was," Aiden answered. "Where is it?"

"Where is what?" the elf answered.

"You know what I'm talking about."

"How do I know this is you and not just some Spirit in the form of an old friend of mine? I've been tortured by the Spirits on several occasions."

"Ask me something," Aiden told him. "Anything you want." The elf pondered the request for a moment.

"What were the last words that we said to each other?"

"We have to find them both," Aiden answered. A light came into the elf's eyes.

"So, what is so important that you felt you had to break into Iscariot just to talk to me? I'm not even sure how you got in. I can't break myself out," the elf, Rigmar said. "Not to mention you smell horrible."

"It's a long story."

"Always is," Rigmar said. "To what do I owe this honor?"

"I know what you were supposed to do. Were you successful?"

"More or less, but I can't guarantee anything," Rigmar replied. "After we last talked I got some friends together and everything went as planned. It was our escape that went badly. I'm the only one who got away. I traveled for months, trying to lose those filthy Borags. Taking the hardest paths I could think of. I cheated death several times and managed to keep myself alive. I was sure that I had shaken them from my trail.

"But I was wrong," Rigmar continued. "When I finally figured out where I was, I made my way into the borders of Giahon. Come to find out, I was being chased by Spirits the whole time. How I managed to stay free was, truly and without a doubt, only because of the work of Lathon. I hid the egg and then I was captured and brought here. I have told them nothing."

"So the egg is in Giahon?" Aiden asked.

"Yes, it is. We can't allow the Sorcerer to find it. If he finds it, he will grow more powerful than he already is. He already has an army that is larger than any other I've laid eyes on."

"So the Sorcerer intends to reveal himself? I've suspected as much. What does he call himself these days?"

"Don't ask me to repeat that name," Rigmar answered sternly.

"Very well, we'll just call him the Sorcerer," Aiden agreed.

"I know the name, but the very thought of it brings all the visions of my torture back to my eyes and haunts me every second of the day. He is more real and deadly than I wish to recount. He personally tortured me on several occasions wanting to know where I hid the egg."

"Where is it?"

"I'm not even sure where in Giahon it is. I was just traveling and decided that it looked like a good place. Ruins of some kind, other than that I couldn't tell you anything."

"Even if he finds the egg, he will not get everything he wants," Aiden stated. Rigmar's eyes lit up with questions.

"Are you saying we know where the wizard's staff is?"

"It was found and is now hidden, safely out of the Sorcerer's reach."

"I wouldn't be too sure of that," Rigmar objected. "He's powerful. I do not doubt in my mind that he's going to search every inch of this land until he can find it and claim it as his own once again. He needs two things to destroy everything good on this green earth. If he finds them both, I'm not sure what hope would remain."

"There's always hope," Aiden told him. "It just might not come in the way that people expect. Several new developments might change the fortunes in the coming war."

"And what is that?"

"A man has been discovered bearing the mark of Lathon. He is the one to make the way for Shedaros. The one who will first recognize the king who has come back to reclaim the throne and save the rest of the world." Rigmar's face lit up.

"He's here?" Rigmar asked, disbelief sounding through his voice.

"He's in Giahon right now. He's on his way to Ariamore even as we speak. Even though the enemy of the world seems to have an impossible strength, it seems that the races of Elves and Men have some hope in these dark times."

"How long has this been known?"

"I met him a month and a half ago when they came to the town of Bucklebeary, needing healing."

"If he's here that means that Shedaros is among us even now. We always suspected that he made it out of that city alive when the elf kings came to visit, but he seemed to have just fallen off the face of the earth. What if he's right in front of us and we are just too blind to notice?"

"Perhaps he is," Aiden suggested. "Either way Ariamore is in a tight spot. There's not much that one nation can do to stand against its enemies. There have to be some big changes if Ariamore plans to stand through the coming storm."

"At least we think the same, unfortunately getting the council, or more accurately the Farsees, to think like we do isn't going to be easy."

"It has to be done, otherwise we are all going to die," Aiden answered. "Trust me, when I get back to Ariamore I plan to have a little chat with the Farsees and see just what is going through their heads."

"You have more guts than I do."

"I'll start looking for the egg and hopefully I'll be able to find it before the Taruk is loosed on the world. If the Sorcerer gets his hand on that, his strength will double."

"At least now we have some hope," Rigmar answered. "Now, apparently you got in here without being seen, but I've always noticed that the real trick is getting back out without being noticed. How do you plan to do that?"

"I've enlisted the help of some friends," Aiden answered. "Korazin."

"Korazin?" Rigmar questioned, giving Aiden a long hard stare. "You trust them?"

"With my life," Aiden said. "As far as getting out I just have to wait because Elohim will be showing up and making some noise in just a couple of minutes."

"I nearly forgot about Elohim. The last time I saw him was about a week after you found him in the forest."

"He's much larger now than he used to be," Aiden replied, they both laughed. "Do you want to come with me? I intend to get out of here alive, getting you out wouldn't be that much harder."

"I can't go," Rigmar answered. "I'm far too weak. I would never be able to keep up with you, or hold a sword up should I have to fight. If they see someone missing in the prisons they will know that someone was here. At least if it's only you escaping they'll think that Elohim is just a stray Taruk who happens to like destroying their city."

"Well said," Aiden answered. A thundering roar shook the tower. They both moved to the narrow window. They searched the moonlit sky for any sign of Elohim and finally spotted him coming from the east. He clenched a boulder in his claws and descended low to the ground opening his jaws and releasing flames, which incinerated a number of the Borags that were exiting the city.

Elohim flew up into the sky and released the boulder, letting the rock crash and roll in the city streets. Elohim flew towards them careful to avoid the arrows that were loosed at him. He landed on the top of one building, dug his thick powerful claws into the rock, and then took off into the sky.

The top of the building was ripped from its place and then crumbled to the ground as Elohim released the roof that he held in his claws. The rooftop crashed down onto more troops and broke through the walls of several buildings which were then set afire by Elohim. A moment later Elohim was racing towards their tower.

"How exactly are you going to get out of here?"

"Just stay down and we'll be alright."

Dust and debris began to fall from the roof above them. They both looked up, Elohim's large claws sliced their way through the roof of the building. A section of the ceiling of the tall spire was ripped from its place, revealing the moonlit sky. Elohim changed course again and dropped the section of the roof over the city, breaking and crushing it in his claws as he went. Orders were yelled out on all sides and horns were blown all across the city.

"Are you sure you don't want to come?" Aiden asked.

"Get out of here while you still can!"

Aiden didn't hesitate, going back out the cell door and locking it. Sounds of turmoil filled his ears and he could hear shouting and loud crashing noises from the stairwell he was in. He sprinted down the stairs, forced to draw his sword and defend against several Borags who were starting to come into the stairwell.

Aiden burst out the door, his heart dropping when he was grabbed from behind and pressed up against the wall. He reached for his sword, but his hands were pinned. Borags surrounded him, their foul breath making him gag.

"Us again," the Borag told him. Aiden felt relief flood through him like a river.

"Rade, I'm glad you told me that or I would've just killed you thinking you were one of them."

"I'm sure you would have, but now we have to get out of here and the best way to do it is to make it look like we're chasing you. After all, we are supposed to be Borags."

"Agreed."

"We'll give you a head start," Rade replied. They released him and Aiden began sprinting down the confusing maze of bridges and alleys. The commotion could be heard all across the city as Elohim caused more destruction.

Behind him, the Korazin gave chase, in the form of Borags. He moved to the left narrowly avoiding an arrow that was loosed from somewhere in front of him. Aiden looked to one of the tall spires where a Borag yelled out orders and blew on a horn. The sound radiated through the night.

"They know what we're up to!" Rade exclaimed.

"I know. Create a perimeter!" Aiden said. The Korazin immediately did as he said, changing into the form of fire. They raced ahead of him, creating a wide circle of fire that burned and destroyed everything in their path. When finally the circle of fire was complete, the Korazin hit the ground and took the form of warriors.

A roar filled the sky, as Elohim saw the ring of fire, stopped the destruction he had been doing, and rushed toward the spot. The Korazin stood inside the ring of fire, using their abilities to damage the city and the troops charging toward them.

The Borags raced towards them and the Korazin tried to keep them at bay with the fire they had started. The heat and the smoke seemed to get thicker and hotter with each second that passed, pushing them further and further back until they only had enough space for Elohim to land. The Korazin exchanged several glances.

"Something's not right!" one of the Korazin exclaimed. "We're losing control of the fire! Borags can't use magic."

"Then how's it getting larger?" One of the others asked. Aiden pointed in the distance where a lone figure was coming towards them. The Borags had broken rank letting the person pass through. All they could see was a silhouette coming towards them, his identity masked in flames and the surrounding shadows and darkness.

Elohim flew towards them, releasing another plume of flame from his mouth. The person coming towards them was unhindered as the fire recoiled and then spread to either side instead of hitting its desired target. Elohim swooped low and landed in the clearing waiting only a moment for Aiden to jump on his back.

Elohim pushed off from the ground and the Korazin took flight, creating one large beast which was engulfed in flames. The creature changed form again and it turned into a Taruk which then flew over the city igniting everything in fire as they went. The Korazin devastated the city and split up, each one going in a different direction as they continued to set the city ablaze.

Finally, they pulled up and changed form again into Taruks and vanished into the sky, eventually joining back up with Aiden. The entire city was repaired within seconds after they were gone.

Aiden looked to see the Korazin in the form of Taruks and riders next to him. "He fixed the city as though he was only playing with a toy."

"I do not doubt that the figure we saw at the end was nothing more than the Sorcerer himself," Aiden said.

"We were fortunate to be able to escape," one of the Korazin said.

"Fortunate, not to mention lucky," another Korazin replied.

"Luck is just a loser's explanation for winning," Aiden replied. "Back to Giahon!" They flew into the night looking behind at the torches illuminating the land below them as the Borags set out to devastate the cities of the earth.

XVII · BELVANOR

Drake kept his hand on the pommel of his sword, searching for the source of the rumbling, which had become more frequent. He carefully traversed the ancient stairwells and corridors, entering room after room, all of which looked the same.

Had this city been inhabited, Drake could imagine how beautiful this city would have been. His heart was stirred as he looked at the workmanship that had been put into the intricate carvings over the doorways and windows.

Once again the rumbling echoed through the night sky. Drake continued, coming to the top of the wall. Down below he could see the glow of their campfire. For whatever reason, it seemed as if he was the only one to hear the strange sounds.

Questions filled his mind and began to burn inside his soul as he wondered why it was that he hadn't been able to sleep. Was this nothing more than an elaborate trap?

Drake felt his blood run cold as the scar on his hand slowly turned to ice as it had done on a couple of other occasions. Drake fell against the wall and slid to the floor, losing control of his mind.

Memories of the Mezutor filled his mind. His thoughts were not his own and a dark and powerful voice whispered inside the dark places of his mind. He listened to the voice for only a moment and put all his efforts into trying to break free from the voice that was taking control of him. In an instant, the voice stopped, and a moment later his mind cleared.

Drake stood as the smell of smoke awakened his senses. Despite the wind, the smoke seemed to be moving against it. He quickly looked at the trees, noticing they were also swaying and blowing in the opposite direction than the smoke.

From here a lone staircase rose to the very citadel of the castle. A light glowed from with. The tower was circular and tall, and the very sight of it made Drake's blood run cold.

He walked until he came to the top of the tower where a dull red light glowed. He walked into a small room, which was circular and tall with nothing else in it except for the strange object in the middle of the floor..

A large stone, burgundy in color, glowed brightly in the desolate chamber. Steam rose from the large stone and lines, highlighted with orange, ran up and down the length of the object.

Drake crept forward, mesmerized by the scene.

The stone creaked and groaned, shaking wildly at times. The familiar rumbling that had drawn him to this tower, was coming from the stone itself. One minute faded into the next and how much time passed, Drake didn't know. The stone grew brighter, and the rumbling became more frequent. Even the lines that ran up and down, seemed to have multiplied.

Completely taken by the stone, Drake touched a finger to it.

Fire flashed through his mind and an explosion, without fire, destroyed the top of the tower. Drake was thrown from his spot and fell onto the hard floor.

He sat up and looked to the center of the broken tower, unable to see the stone this time. Instead, only steam rose from the spot which looked as if though it had been burning for a hundred years. The rocks were now black and the entire area was littered with hundreds of small shards of rock that had exploded.

Each of the pieces was the same shape and size and still glowed the same red color that it had before the explosion. Steam came from them, but they were cool to the touch.

Drake's thoughts were interrupted by the sound of clicking, like someone walking up stairs behind him. He looked around but saw nothing. Drake tried to get up but found that his strength hadn't returned to him.

The clicking finally ceased, and so did everything else. His mind faded and he lost all control of what he was doing, held in place by some invisible force. After a minute, a new sound started, this time sounding like metal on metal.

Drake felt his pulse quicken as the sea of shattered rock pieces began moving toward the center of the tower. The pieces flipped and slid across the floor of the tower until all of them were in the center of the room, emitting heat and small traces of smoke.

The pile of shifting rocks stopped moving, their steam rising into the night. Drake found the strength to stand and could have walked away but he chose to stay, determined to see what would happen next.

The pieces began to shift again, seeming to melt into one another, forming a shape Drake didn't recognize. The shape was small and appeared as if it was something that wasn't fully formed or grown yet. It shivered in the cold and looked at Drake through its small empty eyes.

A few more of the pieces moved from their spots and created another layer, this time it became much bigger and clearer. Drake could make out legs and a long neck and the head was clearly defined. More pieces moved and then more pieces moved until finally the last of the pieces moved to the creature which was growing larger and larger with each layer.

Fear filled Drake.

The shape of a Taruk had formed in front of him. A single black spot was in its chest and strange whispering and scratching came from beneath Drake's feet. Drake lifted his foot, where one last piece of stone had been trapped. It flew to the Taruk and put itself in place.

As if awakened from a great sleep, the bright fire-orange color that had dominated all the rocks had vanished and became the familiar skin of a Taruk. The beast shifted and stirred from its slumber, quickly rising to its feet. It was already large and powerful. It stood proud and tall, as though it had been waiting for this moment.

The Taruk turned its gaze to Drake and didn't look away. It was only a second before Drake wished he had never come to the tower. Unlike Elohim, this Taruk's eyes left you confused and disoriented.

Drake looked at his hand, aware that his scar was starting to go cold again. He opened his palm further, allowing the moonlight to hit it and illuminate the ice crystals that had formed in it. The great beast backed away and looked at it and then at him, seeming to have concluded something about Drake.

Drake jumped in surprise as the Taruk shook the land with a deafening roar. He bolted from his spot, jumping the entire flight of stairs that he had come up. He ungracefully landed at the bottom and then dove out of the way as the Taruk's powerful tail destroyed the wall he was standing against.

The Taruk leapt into the air, spreading out its massive wings and easily getting ahead of Drake who was running as fast as he could in the opposite direction.

Drake froze with fear, as the Taruk glared menacingly at him. If it was possible he even thought the beast was smirking at him, taunting him even.

"You won't win," Drake said calmly, though he didn't understand where the words were coming from. The beast trembled slightly, its eyes narrowing on him, turning dark with their hatred towards him.

"You won't win!" Drake declared again. The creature, now frustrated, swung its tail wildly and let another powerful note ring out. A moment later the beast pulled its composure back together, sitting tall and magnificent, but still glaring down at Drake.

Somehow Drake knew what the Taruk was thinking.

"You ask me how my friends have not come to my aid yet?" Drake asked. He knew he had guessed correctly. "They will come."

The Taruk shifted again as if to say, *'And if they don't?'*

Drake pondered the answer knowing it to be true. "You may have a spell over this castle, to keep others from hearing your call. But I know a name greater than all names. A single name so powerful, your pathetic spell will be shattered like waves on a rock."

The creature shifted his eyes, looking harder and thinking many dark thoughts. Drake studied the Taruk who seemed to be stumped. For many minutes their contest continued, each of them willing themselves to win their contest.

Suddenly the beast sat tall and looked to the path behind him.

"Those are my friends!" Drake said. The Taruk roared in frustration, opened his powerful mouth, and let fire spew from it. The fire scorched everything in its path, narrowly missing Drake as he ran past the Taruk and then hid around the nearest corner.

Rohemir and Lily ran up the path. The Taruk's confusion was only momentary as he shifted and then opened his jaws to release more fire. Rohemir shoved Lily at Drake and rushed to meet the Taruk.

"Go to your master you foul beast!" Rohemir roared. The Taruk and himself stood face to face, but the Taruk was not moved. "Get the others and get out of here while there's still a chance!"

Flashes of light streaked through the air as Rohemir flicked his wand at the great beast. The Taruk flicked its tail and white light shot from it. The beam of light hit Rohemir in the chest and threw him back against the wall, Drake and Lily were standing against. Rohemir's wand flew onto the hard ground, vaporized by another flash of light that came from a flick of the Taruk's tail.

The Taruk opened his jaws and fire raced towards them. Drake closed his eyes, expecting to die. Instead, when they opened their eyes they found that they were standing amid a great wind, which wrapped around them, protecting them from the fire. They were now in a dome of fire, large enough for them to stand in comfortably. The fire was like a wall before them, but they weren't burning.

Drake and Lily looked at the phenomenon in wonder, while Rohemir did nothing but stare at the great beast. Lily put a hand on Drake's arm and pointed into the flames. A robed figure came towards them and stopped just before his features came into view.

The man held his arms open, a great staff in one hand. The fire rapidly recoiled leaving them to stand in the cool night. Drake and Lily looked towards where the man had been standing but saw no one there. Just the Taruk who was cowering and backing away from them.

The Taruk pushed off the ground and took flight disappearing to the north. Rohemir shoved them down the alley.

"What just happened?" Lily asked.

"Shut up and run!" Rohemir yelled.

They ran through the winding alleys and stairways until they came to their camp where everyone was fast asleep. Rohemir angrily woke up everyone.

"How did you know where I was?" Drake whispered.

"I didn't, I was exploring the same as you," Lily said.

"What was Rohemir doing then?"

Lily never answered that question as everyone was now awake and asking more questions then they had answers.

"We have a Taruk on the loose!" Rohemir boomed. Everyone was taken aback by his rage.

"I see no Taruk," Atruss retorted.

"It flew to the north!"

"Then we have nothin' teh worry about, 'cause we're going east!" Ellizar exclaimed.

"Giants hate birds and things that make noise!" Rohemir clarified. "If the giants are aware-"

"Your ruckus will alert more than a single Taruk flying rogue through the sky!" Atruss reprimanded calmly.

Rohemir took a deep breath, attempting to sound calm. "Drake, as soon as we are in Ariamore I demand to know everything that just happened."

"How far are we from Ariamore?" Drake asked.

"Three or four days walking. Let us hope we go unnoticed!"

"That's enough Rohemir!" Atruss scolded. "We are alive, let's focus on that. We will get to the border as fast as we can. I will send word of the situation ahead so that everyone is prepared."

"Send a message?" Gwen asked. "How?" As if on cue, the two wolves known as Willard and Miles appeared out of the darkness. A message was written and tied to their necks. As if they understood what they should do, they ran into the east, lost from sight.

"Haste will be needed in the next few days, but more so, quiet will be vital. There's no telling what a Giant will do if he finds out we are the source of the noise."

They set out immediately, running at the beginning and walking when they needed rest. The night gave way to day and they lost all track of time and distance as they put league after league behind them.

Further inland, they could faintly see smoke rising from distant villages and cities. Once the smoke could not be seen, they made camp for the night, nearly collapsing on the ground. Drake didn't find it difficult to sleep that night, falling into his dreams the moment his head hit the ground.

They were awakened sooner than they would have liked and ate a small but satisfying breakfast and then they were off again. They all managed to keep up pretty well with Ellizar usually pulling up the rear.

"Curse this runnin'!" Ellizar exclaimed. He came to a stop as did they. He took a moment as he tried to catch his breath. "This dwarf isn't goin' any further until he gets some rest."

Rumbling filled the sky and a strange and unusual cry echoed through the land. Ellizar's face wasn't the first to wash white but it was the most amusing as he looked at them and smiled weakly.

"Then again, a few more miles won't hurt!"

The rumbling and the tremors continued for the next two days, never seeming to get any closer, but also never getting any further away. They traveled as fast as could be managed, looking over their shoulders far too often.

By the fourth day, the tremors were a constant rolling thunder and everyone knew it wouldn't be long until danger was imminent.

"How close are we?" Gwen asked. They had stopped for just a couple minutes, filling their canteens in a spring.

"I'd say we're within five miles of the border. We've made incredible time," Atruss said.

They continued on their way, each step feeling like a mile as their lungs and legs both burned like fire. Without warning the source of the tremors became visible.

Behind them nearly a mile, the horizon was filled with a legion of Giants, intending to crush the ever-slowing traveling party. A renewed sense of urgency came to them and by some miracle, they were able to keep ahead of the Giants with neither side gaining nor losing ground on the other.

"There's the border!" Skander yelled, half laughing. Drake looked up to see tall pillars fifty feet in the air. The pillars were carved in the likeness of great elven kings of a long-lost age.

Fifty horsemen came out of the trees and let the tired company pass before drawing their swords and rushing to meet the giants.

They watched for only a minute, now realizing the poise and furry of the Elvish race. Soon the remaining giants scattered and ran back the way they came, cursing as they did so. They didn't stop until nightfall when each of them easily fell into a deep sleep.

In the morning they were met by the same Elvish warriors who had defended them the previous day. They were given horses that were now without their riders as they traveled further inland.

Drake and Gwen shared a horse, both of them grateful for the break from running, but they took little comfort in this as plans for battle were openly discussed.

"Will the Giants come looking for us?" Gwen asked.

"Giants do not take defeat easily," Atruss said. "Many got away at the border. I do not doubt once they bring their wolves, they will track us and bring more warriors with them.

The trees towered above them. Unlike the other forests they had been in, this forest felt younger. A few stray leaves drifted to the ground having already turned colors bringing to their attention the coming change of season. They had been traveling for almost two months since they had left Fiori, and to finally be near their destination was a welcomed feeling.

The forest ended and gave way to lush meadows, which were home to livestock and the occasional farm. The meadows gave way to hills and climbed steeply but then rolled gently down the other side. Drake looked into the distance hoping to catch a glimpse of their destination, but instead, all he saw was a cliff of green which was ever growing in the distance.

"Are we near our destination?" Drake asked. Rohemir looked back and smiled.

"We are nearly there. We could have reached it by the shoreline if we had wanted to."

"And we didn't why?" Gwen asked.

"If we were to continue going up the shoreline it would have been a lot more open and the Giants would've been able to track us easier," Atruss answered.

"What's going to happen when we reach the city...what's it called?" Drake asked.

"The city is called Belvanor, which means 'to believe' and likely a great battle will follow," Rohemir answered.

"Another bat'le?" Ellizar asked. "After all of this runnin' and travelin' I was hopin' fer some rest."

"Evil does not rest and therefore we can't rest. I'm not sure what the battle will look like or how we'll survive, but we must try," Atruss declared.

"What do you mean you're not sure how we'll survive?" Lily asked. "Surely there is more than just these warriors in Ariamore?"

"Yes, but it's a small army," Atruss answered. "Ariamore has withdrawn from all political matters in the world. I do not know how we will fare against an army that is so large."

"So we have no hope of surviving then?" Skander asked.

"The Giants are so big," Drake noted. "How are we supposed to stand against them?"

"All of the obstacles that stand in our way are huge, but it is our determination to overcome them that separates us from everyone else," Atruss replied. "I think you will find that the people of Ariamore are very different from everyone else that you've met up until now."

"As long as they're nicer than the people in Fiori," Drake said.

"Don't worry, I can assure you they're nicer than that. Most of them anyway," Atruss answered.

They rode for another hour and the land changed once again back to the same flat forest that they had first entered. The trees seemed to get larger and larger giving off a sense of security and history to the area.

Cliffs rose on either side of them, rising hundreds of feet above them covered with flowering vines. The flowers on them were vibrant purples and whites with a couple of reds mixed in. Drake looked at them in wonder as it was the end of autumn and still, they bloomed as if it was spring. The birds still sang in the trees, their songs reaching into the forest.

"What is this place?" Drake asked.

"It's called the grass canyons," Atruss answered.

"I've never heard of grass canyons before," Gwen replied.

"That's because it's not a natural land formation," Atruss started. "Back in the days of Lathon he created a fortress so complex and difficult to break into that no army has ever breached it. He made piles of dirt, to be a maze of valleys and ravines. They have since been covered and planted with vines to camouflage the city to the point that if anyone came and was looking for the city with ill intentions they wouldn't be able to see it. However, in our case, they will be able to find us because of our scent.

"There's only one way to get through the grass canyons and to the city itself without spending hours and hours going up over the steep hills and down into the ravines and that's the way we will go. I expect that our enemy however will not be that smart and will climb over the hills, which will not only give us more time but also tire them out before they get to us."

They walked for a while longer, turning left and then right, walking in the valleys that were to either side of the steep hills and cliffs, all of which were covered in flowering vines.

Drake and Gwen lost all sense of direction until they rounded one last corner and came into a clearing nearly fifteen miles wide. Dead in the center of the clearing was a rock larger than any they had seen up to this point. To the south, they could see the coast

"Is that Belvanor?" Gwen asked.

"Do you like it?" Atruss asked a gleam of light in his eye.

"I've never seen anything like it," Drake answered. "The whole city is in a rock?"

"Not in a rock, carved out of the rock," Lily corrected. "I've heard of it but I never thought I'd see it for myself."

"Leave it teh the Elves teh come up with such a ridiculous notion. Imagine carvin' the rock out of the city, most people, certainly the Dwarves would have carved the city out of the rock."

"We prefer to do things anyway but the way the Dwarves do them. Why do you think we're so tall?"

"Blasted elf kind," Ellizar exclaimed. "They can't just let yeh have a moment. They always have teh give their input."

"Ellie, my sweet dear, that's only because Dwarves demand that Elves give their input."

"That's ridiculous!" Ellizar exclaimed, he turned to Drake. "What do yeh think?"

"I think I agree with Lily on the part about Dwarves wanting people's input."

"Bah, who needs yeh? First off, in response teh yer statement Lily, yeh not only called me Ellie but yeh also called me a 'sweet dear' as a dwarf I should be insulted."

They laughed and kept on walking, getting closer to the city. Guards paced the walls and pointed them out to other people who ran and then blew into large horns that were built into the city walls. The sound shook the valley.

In reply Atruss grabbed a small horn from his belt and blew through it, announcing their arrival to those who were listening. The gates of the city were opened and the portcullis was raised. Several riders came from the city and escorted the group through the gates.

The streets lay to the left and right. Shops and houses, like everything else, were carved out of the rock. The outer walls were as the rest of the canyon had been, covered in flowering vines. The streets were all stone and ramps led up to other sections of the city.

People stood waiting for them. Guards stood at attention, their weapons by their side as well as several official-looking people. They walked down the path a few feet until finally, a woman came through the crowd.

"I was wondering when you would show up!" the woman exclaimed. Atruss hastily dismounted his horse and greeted the woman with a kiss. "We've heard many things regarding your travels here and were worried sick."

"I know, and I'm sorry for the delay my dear. Much has happened," Atruss replied. "Everyone, I would like you to meet my lovely wife, Gabrielle. She is much smarter than I am, that's why she stayed to keep everything running while I went off trying to do other business. We will worry about formal introductions later when we all eat supper. For now, I'm afraid that we must work out the details of our defense."

Gabrielle gave him another kiss and they small-talked for another minute before she disappeared as fast as she had come leaving the group to themselves. Rohemir and Atruss talked quietly for a minute or two before turning to the others and several of the guards that were waiting for their orders.

"Captain!" Atruss started. "Unlock the armory immediately and fit every able-bodied man, dwarf, elf, or giant in the city that can fight. Give them as much training as our time allows. If these are Giants that we're going up against they need to at least know the basics of swordsmanship."

"Put Mr. Thomas here in charge of teaching one of the classes. He seems to know more than the average person when it comes to fighting in a battle," Rohemir suggested. To Drake's horror, it was agreed without his input.

"I want scouts to leave immediately. Keep watch for the giants. They will come, it's just a matter of when," Atruss said calmly.

Much to their surprise, they found that word had spread quickly and when they arrived at the armory there was already a long line of people waiting to receive weapons.

A key was brought and the armory was unlocked allowing the captains and guards to get inside and begin handing weapons out to other people. Drake helped hand out the weapons and within an hour they had been distributed and fitted to all the people who had shown up. Drake was given some chain mail, which he put on, grateful for the protection.

All the newly fitted troops were led outside the city walls and lined up in formation as the captains and guards as well as Drake quickly taught the people what they knew about fighting. Drake had never taught anyone to fight before, at least not that he could remember.

He had fought against Borags and Spirits, but somehow fighting against the Giants would seem a little more daunting than he would have liked to admit.

Lily had hastily and against her will, been put in charge of the archers, who were practicing at the shooting range, and was teaching them as best as she could. Drake just for fun tried to shoot one of the arrows at the target, and quickly discovered why he wasn't an archer.

Training for the day ended and Drake and the others were led back into the city and through the beautiful winding streets, to a large palace that was built at the very top of the city. The palace was made out of the same rock as the rest of the city. A flower garden was to either side of them, lining a path to the marble doors that waited for them.

They reached the massive doors which swung inwards. In front of them for the next five hundred feet, giant pillars lined the path. A majestic throne sat empty. It was made of gold and far more beautiful than anything Drake could have ever imagined.

A moment later they entered a large room, complete with basins of steaming water, the finest soaps and perfumes, and everything else was waiting for them as they were left to bathe and rid themselves of all the dirt and grime they had been carrying with them for the last two months.

Their old worn clothes were taken from them and they were brought new clothes which looked much richer than anything they were used to. Drake couldn't help but smile when he saw Gwen and how beautiful she looked in the new dress she had been given. Her dress was white, trimmed with a pale blue. Her hair was done up by some other people who came in, treating them like royalty.

When they were ready, they were escorted to a large dining room that sat empty except for three people, Rohemir, Atruss, and Gabrielle. Drake was taken aback by Rohemir and Atruss who both looked like new people compared to the ones they had been traveling with. They took a seat and dinner was served to them.

They talked about their travels on the way to Ariamore and Drake answered a few questions that were about him or directed towards him, but other than that he kept quiet, content to sit back and listen.

Drake watched how everyone interacted with each other as the conversation progressed, hardly able to take his eyes off the woman next to him. With each second that passed Gwen seemed to be more and more beautiful, stirring his heart.

"You look much better than when you first arrived," Gabrielle told them. "I hope everything is to your satisfaction."

"Better than anything we could have imagined," Drake answered. "Thank you for lending us these clothes."

"These clothes are not being lent to you, they are being given to you. You five will likely have to attend several high-end meetings and things of that sort, so if you're to impress the higher-ups you have to look the part."

"We have to try and fit in with them?" Lily asked.

"I think my wife misspoke," Atruss started. "An unfortunate curse of being in leadership is that within the higher societies, some people think they are higher up than everyone else. If you don't look the part they won't even give you a first glance, let alone a second. It's not the way I like it and I'm desperately trying to come up with a way to get rid of that attitude, but for the moment I've been unsuccessful. For the most part, everyone gets along, as you may or may not have picked up on when you walked through the city gates."

"I did notice that," Gwen answered. "This whole city seems to have a different feel about it. The whole nation, really."

"Indeed, the nation *is* different. Although I must say I'm not too crazy about how it is different sometimes."

"What do you mean?" Drake asked.

"The problems are usually with a particular group, we call them the Farsees, they're the religious leaders. They supposedly remind us to keep and follow the ancient teachings of Lathon. The trouble is they're very hypocritical and seem more arrogant and cocky than anyone should be. They've created so many extra rules that it makes me sick. The Farsees think because we're chosen by Lathon and that Shedaros will one day come and live among us; well, they seem to think they are entitled to everything and anything they want. They have much pride in the fact that we haven't had to fight in any wars and frankly, I doubt they will want to vote for a permanent army."

"If we don't we'll die," Lily replied. Atruss shook his head.

"I know, but their pride won't let them. Pride can be the doom of all men and the Farsees and most of the higher-ups are living examples. They have power, and with them in the picture, I'm not sure how long we'll be able to keep the walls of this city standing and our citizens safe."

"You worry far too much about the Farsees, Atruss," Rohemir started. "They are only out to do good; after all good is a point of view."

"I disagree," Drake said. The table fell silent. "Good is not a point of view."

"Then what is it?" Rohemir asked.

"The northern star does not change its location even if I've turned my back on it," Drake said. "Only through the lens of Lathon can things be judged right or wrong, good and bad. In the end, I imagine it will not matter what our personal opinion on any matter is. It matters how the good judge will rule it. I might have justified my heart and thoughts on killing my family, but we all know it goes against the character of Lathon."

Drake fell silent, everyone seemed to be smiling at his words.

"Like Mr. Thomas is saying, I do not agree with the Farsees on many, many things," Atruss stated. "As I see it, this nation not only has a responsibility to itself but to the other nations of the world. If we sit back and only protect ourselves then what good are we doing anyone? The world will not be able to stand against the coming darkness. The only way we'll survive is if we come together and build each other up."

"Well said sweetheart," Gabrielle said. "What ideas do you have?"

"I have ideas, none of them good," Atruss answered. "These people are not trained or seasoned enough to properly and effectively defend our walls and keep the enemies out like we need to. I'm afraid that our walls will be breached."

"I have an idea," Gabrielle said. "We all mutually agree that we cannot hope to hold our enemies at our walls because we do not have an army big enough correct?" They all nodded. "In which case I suggest that we use the surroundings that we've been given to improve our chances."

"Use the canyons to our advantage?" Skander asked.

She nodded her head. "Exactly."

"It's not ideal, but it's certainly got the element of surprise!" Atruss exclaimed.

"This still won't guarantee victory, but I agree that it does sound promising,"

Rohemir replied. "It'll be harder for us to fight on the uneven ground but it will also make a small army feel and look much bigger than what it is."

"That's the idea," Gabrielle said. "We use the ravines and cliffs and hills to our advantage, drawing enemies into them and then dealing with them as we see fit." Atruss motioned for one of the guards to come forward from his post in the corner.

"Tell all the commanders to report to the palace within the hour. I'm not sure how long we have until the Giants' army comes crashing through the walls, but we have a new plan and need to fill them in immediately."

"Yes sir," the guard replied.

"Drake I've been meaning to ask you a question," Rohemir started. "You don't have to accept this request if you don't want to. We are in great need of a leader and since you bear the mark of Lathon I can't think of a better reason to have you lead us into this battle."

"I don't think I'd be comfortable leading an army by myself. Therefore I decline the request. However, if I was to have someone with me then I might accept it."

"You may choose anyone you wish," Rohemir answered. "I've seen you fight. There is something about your skill with a blade that sends chills through me. I hope that you will be able to inspire our army, and give them the courage to stand proud and defend their homeland."

"Courage?" Drake asked, pausing for a second afterward. "You think I have courage? I think you're mistaken. I feel more fear than I believe any normal person does. You expect me to give the army something I don't have?"

"But you do have courage Drake," Gabrielle started. Drake looked into her deep brown eyes, getting caught in her gaze. "I may have never seen you fight, but I can see in your heart that you have more courage than any of us. Courage is not having no fear, it's having the guts to stand up for what you believe even amid fear. It's not caring what other people think of you even though they may hate and despise you. That is what courage is. Going out of your way to make a difference, even if it costs you your life."

Drake fell silent exchanging glances with the other people at the table. The silence continued for another minute or so until finally Drake looked back towards Gabrielle and nodded his reply. Smiles came across their faces.

"Very good. You may choose any person to stand next to you and give you advice or whatever," Rohemir replied. "Now I also have to ask a favor of a couple more of you. Lily, I believe your use of a bow could be quite useful in the opening stages of the battle, we would like you to lead the archers and spear throwers."

"I will do what I can to hinder our enemies," Lily answered confidently. Both Drake and Ellizar knew she was hiding her fear.

"And what would yeh have a dwarf do?" Ellizar asked. "I'm certainly not goin' teh sit on the sidelines while some elf and human lead us into bat'le."

"I understand perfectly Ellizar," Gabrielle replied. "And I have a plan for you too. If I know a dwarf well enough, you're probably not going to be anywhere but on the front lines; am I correct?"

"Yeh are correct!"

"Then it's settled," Gabrielle replied, a smile on her face. "You will be in the same group as Skander. I have something special planned for the two of you." Ellizar smiled and then laughed.

"I like somethin' special. Do I get teh find out what it is yet?"

"We will tell you in just a few moments. Drake, you may choose who you want to stand next to you to lead the army, because that will shape the rest of the battle plans."

"I would love to have one of you standing next to me in the battle," Drake started. "But do you have other places you'll need to be?"

"Yes but you've forgotten that there's three of us at this table," Gabrielle replied.

"You're going to fight?"

"The time to sit on the sidelines and let life happen as it may has passed. Something has changed in the past few months, I have felt it in the trees and heard it in the air. The birds whisper of some great thing that is about to be done, yet they also tell me of an evil that is now spreading over the world. I cannot sit back and watch this land be destroyed without knowing that I did whatever I could to help. If you would ask me I would accept the position with great honor. Atruss, dear, don't try to talk me out of fighting with the army."

"Hon, I learned a long time ago that arguing with you over something like this is useless," Atruss replied, turning back to Drake. "Your decision?"

"I would like Gabrielle to stand next to me. Where will Gwen be?"

"Very near to you if you wish."

"I do wish that," Drake replied.

"Very good. We have already sent out scouts to try and locate the approaching army so we know approximately how much time we have to deal with. I have a plan but it's a little complicated and will require some time to set up," Gabrielle announced. "Go now and rest while you can. I would ask Ellizar and Skander to stay behind for a moment, while we suggest our plan to them."

Ellizar's face lit up like they had never seen before. He looked at Lily and laughed.

"How about this, in an Elvish city and nation, a dwarf is honored with the privilege of knowin' the attack plan before an elf. And yeh say that Elves are the privileged ones!"

"I never said we were privileged Ellie. However it may interest you to know that I don't have to be told the plan because I already know the plan, that's how superior Elven wisdom is."

"Blasted elf kind! Yeh don't know what the plan is!"

"True, but it was fun teasing you," Lily said.

"Be gone with yeh!" Ellizar said teasingly. They left the room and the doors were closed as they made their way to the rooms they had been given. New clothes and armor were waiting for them. They tried on the new additions finding both weapons and armor surprisingly light, yet they were told it was stronger than any armor they had seen up to this point.

They put the rest of their battle gear on, with guards on their forearms and shins and a breastplate that would hopefully protect them in the coming battle.

The group stood before each other hardly able to recognize the warriors they saw in the mirror.

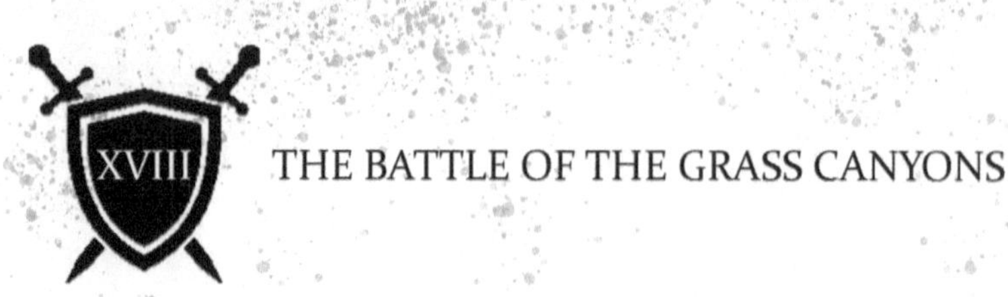

THE BATTLE OF THE GRASS CANYONS

rmies of Giahon approached, the vibrations shook the grass canyons and with it, threatened to steal the resolve of the army that had turned out. Given the little time and supply of weapons, only six hundred fully armed warriors had been managed.

Scouts and spies had spent most of the day trying to locate the Giant's army and finally brought reports that the army that they would be facing could be as large as a thousand Giants.

Drake sat atop the horse that had been provided to him. Gabrielle sat on her horse next to him, sitting tall and proud. Her horse's stature was much the same and seemed to be the most flawless horse that Drake had ever seen. Gwen stood behind him, on foot, nervous as he was, but ready to do her part.

Lily stood to the other side of him, having left her company for a brief couple of moments. The archers stood along the entire crest of the canyon ridge. Lily's bow was still on her back as she paced quietly.

"Do you think Ellizar and Skander will be okay?" she asked Drake in a whisper.

"If anyone can do what they were assigned to do, and live to tell about it, it would be them. Ellizar has more spirit than the entire army of Giants."

"I hope so. Those are my closest two friends in this world. If anything happened to them, and I wasn't with them to help...I don't think I would ever forgive myself."

"Don't worry about them dear," Gabrielle said. "Worrying won't change anything. They will come back. I can feel it in the air." Lily seemed to be comforted by the simple words and went back up the hill to the archers, who numbered fifty at the most.

The army behind Drake was barely trained. Some of them he doubted had ever picked up a sword in their life before this. There were a few Dwarves, Men and Elves, and some children that looked as if they were only twelve years old at the most.

"You nervous?" Gabrielle asked him. Drake nodded and took a deep breath. "It'll be okay, that's why I'm riding with you. We'll fare just fine against the army."

"I wish I had your faith," Drake said, his horse shifted anxiously.

"You just have to believe in something greater than yourself. Seeing you have the mark of Lathon I wouldn't think that would be that difficult for you."

"I know I have the mark, and I know it means something, but my memory isn't what it should be and I only know what I've been told the past couple months. I certainly don't think that I'm worthy of leading an army of any kind."

"You will find strength Drake Thomas," Gabrielle told him.

"How do you know?"

"Lathon is the king of the impossible. Through him all things are possible. The mark on your hand offers hope to all of us. For years the Elves and anyone associated with them have been despised in the eyes of the world because we *do* believe in Lathon and the fact that he would send a king to live among us and one day rule. The stories of the past have turned into fiction in people's eyes, and they no longer believe. They see us as a bunch of unintelligent idiots, who believe in fairy tales. Now that you're here with the mark, you've offered hope to all of us."

"If only I could offer hope to myself," Drake replied. "Then maybe I would feel a little better."

"Things happen for a reason and what that reason is I couldn't begin to tell you. I can't see the big picture. But some can."

"Do you think that we stand a chance against the Giants that are coming?" Drake asked. Gabrielle's eyes met him and held his gaze.

"Yes, I do. I think we stand a good chance."

"Hopefully Skander and Ellizar are okay. They don't exactly have the safest job in the world."

"I may have only known them for a little while but, due to the stories that I've heard I'm sure they will have no problem with the assignment that they've been given."

"Lily would be heartbroken if anything ever happened to Ellizar."

"I suspect you would feel the same way if Gwen were to die tonight." Drake shot her a look. "Don't worry, it's not very obvious," Gabrielle whispered. "I just have a way of sensing these sorts of things. It's part of how the Elves were made."

Drake looked in either direction at the line of troops. Rohemir and Atruss were fifty feet away from him, also on horseback. The troops shifted uncomfortably as the vibrations coming through the ground were now getting louder and more frequent. Eventually, it became a steady role of thunder as the Giants approached from somewhere in the darkness.

Ellizar waited in the darkness, looking twenty feet to his left and nodding at Skander who sat in the brush just like he did. Even though he knew they were only a half mile away from Drake and the army, it seemed like a thousand.

Torches illuminated the forest floor as the Giants blindly followed the path that snaked its way through the canyons. The Giants neared, likely to go right past them and continue through the maze of canyons that they had passed through earlier.

Ellizar and Skander moved to their left, standing alongside trees that had been notched, to the point where a simple push, would send them toppling to the ground.

Together they shoved two of the trees into the valley. The trees fell onto the Giants running below. Many at the front of the army were crushed beneath the massive trees.

The remaining Giants spoke in their own tongue as they tried to figure out what had happened. Skander and Ellizar came together at the crest of the steep hill. The darkness hid most of their identity, but they were noticed by the general who stalked forward.

"Hey yeh bloody idiots, we're up here, and what are yeh goin' teh do about it?" Ellizar asked, shouting through the valley. "Oh yeah that's right yeh can't do anythin'. Everyone knows Giants are unintelligent."

"I resent that remark," Skander replied.

"Yer elf kind, so stupidity doesn't apply teh yeh. They on the other hand are as dumb as a bag ov rocks! So what yeh goin' teh do with us? We can fall a few more trees if yeh would like us teh?"

Skander and Ellizar exchanged looks, waiting and anticipating what the Giants would do. Silence plagued the valley for a moment until the unspoken order to attack them was given. The entire Giahon army charged up the steep hillside.

"Our plan worked!" Ellizar rejoiced. "It looks like they mutually agreed teh come after us."

"In which case we should run!" Skander exclaimed. Several other trees that had been notched, were broken with the vibrations of the Giant's feet and fell onto the army. The Giants halted at the top of the canyon, each bringing out a bow.

"Watch out!" Skander warned. Skander dropped to the ground, narrowly avoiding a volley of arrows that had been sent in their direction. Ellizar laughed as they went over his head.

"Oh yeah, that's right! That's how we Dwarves are superior!" Ellizar exclaimed. "We're so-"

Ellizar soon found himself tumbling down the hill as he tripped on a log that was in his way. Skander laughed as he pulled Ellizar to his feet.

"I see them!" Lily exclaimed. Drake looked carefully, seeing Ellizar and Skander coming over the top of the canyon directly across from them. Ellizar and Skander took their places as Giants began to appear over the canyon wall. Lily and her archers sent a volley of arrows toward the army.
The commander of the giants came to the top of the hill, while the rest of the army spread to either side.

"Valiant effort, citizens of Ariamore!" the commander boomed. "You have done well, but I have only this to say to you; we have waited for the day when we would finally topple your nation and destroy every last one of you, and now that day has come. We have been ordered by the Sorcerer himself to destroy every last one of you.

"None of you will leave this battle alive! And when we're done here we will march to your city, break down your walls, and slaughter your families! Forever ridding the earth of you miserable people!"

"I don't think so," Drake yelled back. The Giants laughed, mockingly.

"Oh you don't?" the giant asked, amused. "And who are you to stop us? We are twice the height of you. We could kill you in our sleep. However, since you are so brave, perhaps you would be inclined to a different arrangement." Silence came over them. "We are far superior to your small army and do not fear you at all. Just to make things a little more interesting why don't we have a duel? I will use no weapons. You may use whatever you wish. If you can defeat me, my army will vanish back into Giahon and you'll never hear from us again. What do you say?"

All eyes were on Drake as he wondered about the proposal that had been made. He looked down at the leader of the army who waited for his reply. The odds were against them. A slight sound echoed through the air, distant and faint, but good enough for Drake to hear it and know what it was.

They would be alright.

"You might as well attack. You'll lose either way." The Giants laughed, a thunderous roar escaping as they began running into the canyon.

"Arrows!" Drake yelled. Lily's group released arrows sending them through the air like invisible daggers taking out countless Giants.

Gabrielle and Drake drew their swords and everyone else did the same as they ran down to the valley. The two sides crashed together and the sound of people crying out in pain became commonplace.

The battle continued as both sides suffered losses. Drake's limbs burned and his mind was numb from battle. His horse had been lost, leaving him to stumble around the canyon and pretend that he knew what he was doing.

Drake was knocked to the ground and his sword was scattered, leaving him defenseless as the commander of the Giants towered over him. Drake tried to move towards his sword but was kicked in the side a moment later.

"What do you say to my agreement now?" The giant asked. "Let's fight right here and now. I will hold to my word if you beat me. You may use anything you wish. What do you want to do?"

Drake looked around at all the people who had been killed, considering the proposal. Suddenly the deafening call of a Taruk shook the valley. Drake looked to the right, seeing a white dot rushing towards them.

"You lose!" Drake exclaimed. The giant laughed, but never got the chance to say anything else as fire consumed him, coming from a white Taruk which was already past. The fire continued to rain down, splitting the battlefield and consuming enemies who stood in the way.

Elohim flew over the battlefield and then swooped low, grabbing troops in his massive and deadly claws and then letting them fall to the ground. Aiden jumped off and came running towards him.

"Why don't we draw our swords together?" Aiden asked. They raised their swords and attacked their enemies. The time faded and their hopes began to rise, noticing that there were far more Giants that had died in the battle than anything else.

Drake swung his sword slaying the giant in front of him and turned his attention toward the troops that were on the hill. Several Giants left the main group, walking to a large tree. Together, they grabbed the trunk and the tree out of the ground, throwing it into the valley.

The tree crashed into the ground and then burst into a hundred different pieces all of which struck the army of Ariamore. Drake narrowly missed being struck as another tree was sent in their direction.

A giant came hurtling towards him and threw him backward. Drake quickly rolled out of the way, narrowly missing a sword that had been swung in his direction. Drake jumped to his feet and took a swing at the giant, missing by a mile, and instead found himself scrambling back to avoid the sword again.

Drake whirled around but never got any farther than that as the blade of another Giant's sword slashed him in the arm. Drake dropped his sword and yelled out in pain. He fell to his knees, looking up at his captors.

A moment later, the Giants fell dead, Their heads were severed by the blade of a soldier who had come up behind him. Drake looked up, Aiden standing where the Giants had been.

"You alright?" Aiden asked. Drake nodded and picked up his sword, determined to fight with one hand. "I've got an idea on how to turn our fortunes in this battle."

"I'd love to hear it," Drake replied. They darted out of the way as another tree was hurtled in their direction. It sent debris everywhere.

"Just stay with it, don't give up, I'll be back in a minute," Aiden said, running into the canyon. Elohim flew around the entire battlefield and continued to spit out flames.

Drake faced his next opponent, raised his sword in the air, and let it find its target. His sword pierced the giant but didn't seem to faze him at all as the giant whirled around with his big club and smacked Drake. Drake was thrown backward, his sword was lost again. The giant pulled his sword back and Drake thought he would die until he was saved by a single arrow that pierced the giant.

Drake fought to remain conscious, his mind foggy and slow. Somehow, finding the strength, Drake stood, but was promptly struck from behind. The chain mail protected him, leaving him winded but not hurt. He took swing after swing unable to get any closer to disabling his opponent.

A cry came from behind Drake as Ellizar came running in and vaulted off a fallen log, with his battle axe in hand. He smashed his axe into the Giant's neck, as they both tumbled to the ground. Ellizar was thrown a few feet away but was quickly to his feet. He grabbed his axe, then looked at Drake and smiled.

"That's right, that's another point fer the dwarf!" Drake smiled and found his strength again as they lost track of time as one giant looked like the next.

Drake's mind slipped away, weariness took over him and finally, he slipped up allowing his opponent to get the upper hand. He was knocked off his feet and fell backward and hit his head on the ground.

The canyon was silent except for the giant in front of him. Only one more giant was separating them from victory and yet it seemed like the biggest obstacle in the world. Drake stood but was struck in the face.

The giant swung but his sword was stopped by Aiden who had once again come to his rescue. The giant matched him but eventually was defeated. Silence filled the canyon.

The light on the horizon was starting to grow brighter. The fires that Elohim had started still burned, but had now died down, having spread no further than it had when it had been started. Drake looked to see some soldiers standing, while others kneeled, trying to aid comrades or themselves. Sorrow overcame Drake.

Drake reached for his arm and then pulled his hand away, blood covering it. He had cuts on both arms, one across his face, and another on one of his shins.

Aiden sheathed his sword and came over to him, extending a hand.

"You alright?" Aiden asked.

"I am now," Drake answered, trying to smile. "Lucky to be alive."

"You can say that again. I'm not sure why you were put in charge of leading the army into battle but if I may say so that wasn't a very wise thing to do. No offense."

"None taken," Drake replied. "I wasn't very sure of the decision either, but it was offered and everyone was waiting for my reply. What was I supposed to do?"

"Make the choice that you want, and not be influenced by what other people think."

"You really think it's that easy?" Drake asked.

"Yes, I do. It all depends on how pleasant you want your life to be Drake Thomas. If you bow to everyone's wish and command and try to live for their approval you'll end up nothing more than a pathetic shell of a person who doesn't know who he is or what he can do. Living for the approval of others is useless, in the end, they die the same as you."

"I'll have to remember that."

"Who was it that suggested you lead the army?" Aiden asked. "Please don't tell me you volunteered for the position."

"No, I didn't do that."

"Good, otherwise I'd have to worry about the size of your head," Aiden replied. Both of them let a laugh escape them.

"It was Rohemir who suggested me for the job and I foolishly accepted."

"Rohemir?" Aiden asked. "Well, I think there will have to be a little chat with Rohemir as soon as we can find him."

"Don't get mad at him," Drake pleaded.

"I won't get mad at him, Drake. Getting mad is another thing that doesn't do much good in this world. But I will talk with him and see what he was thinking. Who knows in times like these if he really thought you could lead, or if there was a larger plan behind all of this."

"Are you suggesting that Rohemir might be with the bad guys?"

"You have to look at all the evidence before you make any kind of a judgment. I'm not suggesting anything Drake, all I'm saying is that all avenues have to be observed no matter how slim the chances are."

"I wish I knew why people were so interested in me. I have a scar on my hand. So what? Why am I being hunted like this and when will it stop?"

"It probably won't stop Drake," Aiden replied. "People like you, who are set apart either by choice or by something they've done, are likely to have lives where rest, peace, and serenity are not things they often find. For the most part that is. The people of Ariamore are exiles. Elves, yes, but they are also exiles from other nations because of what they believe. They may not be at peace with the rest of the world, but they can sleep easier at night. They have peace on the inside where it counts."

A somber silence settled over them as they walked through the battlefield, which was covered with the horrors of war. For those who had loved ones in the battle, Drake could hardly imagine what they would be going through. How had he been lucky enough to live when so many others had been killed?

Drake looked again at his hand, studying the three slash marks that had changed his life ever since he had woken up on the side of the river. He still had to figure out what they meant, but he grew more and more curious with each day that passed.

The rustling of leaves in the trees above caught his attention. There he saw a black featherless bird sitting on one of the branches. The bird was the same one that had been following him all this time. Featherless and scraggly looking, it sat atop the tree and looked down on everything. Strangely enough, the bird seemed to express the same sorrow and pain that Drake felt. They continued walking, appearing to have no set course as they moved through the canyon.

"I'm glad you came back. I thought you had other people to help after your trip to Grimdor?"

"Oh I did, but what I discovered in Grimdor was far too great for me not to return. As it was I showed up right on time. We have bigger problems on the horizon."

"Do I dare ask what they are?"

Aiden shook his head. "Just wait until we get the battle cleaned up and everything else taken care of. I know there are going to be a lot of meetings in the days to come. Hopefully, they lead us in a direction that will do us good."

"Anything's better than where we are," Drake answered.

"Not always. You must constantly think things through and let the Spirit of Lathon guide you if you're to make a good judgment about things. Hasty decisions will get you nowhere." A moment passed. "I hate war," Aiden finally said.

"You hate war, yet you're good at it," Drake pointed out. "Where's the logic behind that one? If you hate war then why do you fight like an expert?"

"Because it's necessary if I'm to survive in this world. If I wander through this world, hating war, yet if I won't fight for what is good and right then I might as well not even be alive. We are all called by Lathon, to stand up for the weak and the poor. The rich don't need our help. At least they think they don't."

"Every time I think I have something figured out, you say something that ruins it," Drake noted. "Is there anything else that I don't know about you?"

"I'm not a big fan of winning the approval of others," Aiden answered. "I won't say too much about that, except to say when we meet with the council and the Farsees, you won't see me trying to impress them." Drake opened his mouth to speak but was prevented as his name was shouted from behind them.

Drake turned around only to be met with a mouthful of hair as Gwen threw herself into his arms. Drake held her tight. They held each other for several moments, kissing each other.

"Looks like someone had a secret," Aiden said with a smile.

"You found us out," Drake replied.

Aiden laughed again. "Don't worry, if you don't want anyone to know then I won't say a word, you're secret is safe with me."

"We'd sure appreciate it," Gwen answered. Her hair was messed up and matted with dried blood from her enemies as well as some mud.

"I was starting to wonder where you had gotten to," Drake answered.

"I almost didn't think I was going to make it," Gwen replied. "I was an inch from death so many times I lost count, yet something gave me the strength and the determination to keep going even when I wanted to give in and embrace death with open arms."

"Has anyone seen Ellizar?" Lily asked, frantically running up to them. Drake and Gwen looked at each other and then at Aiden.

"We haven't seen him," Gwen answered. "But we haven't found him among the dead either." Silence passed as sorrow filled their hearts, each of them considering the possibility that Ellizar was dead.

"Blasted giant!" Ellizar's voice echoed from behind them. "Why can't yeh just get off of me and let me up!" Lily's face lightened as she took off running towards the sound. Drake and Gwen followed closely, while Aiden continued his trek across the battlefield.

They finally caught up with Lily who had now come to a stop and was laughing hysterically. They looked down at the corpse of a dead giant who was sprawled over the ground with Ellizar pressed beneath him. None of them could stifle a laugh.

"Blasted elf kind!" Ellizar exclaimed. "Leave it teh an elf teh stand there and laugh at yeh when yeh're in a moment ov need."

"How did this happen?" Gwen asked. Ellizar's face lightened as he tried to hide a smile.

"Well, ah, it seems that during the battle I got a little bit carried away. Yeh see that small cliff just above us? Well, I wasn't thinking about what I was doing and so I ran and jumped in front ov the giant and then I killed him. That's when I first noticed there was a drop-off there. I fell over the edge and so did he, he landed on my axe, killing himself and leaving me pinned here."

"Leave it to a dwarf to have this problem," Lily remarked.

"Blasted elf kind." No one spoke for a moment as Ellizar looked around at them, his impatience growing. "Don't just stand there get this big lug off ov me right now!"

They moved the dead giant and then helped Ellizar off the ground. He managed to stand up straight and then grabbed his axe, which was embedded in the Giant.

"That'll wake yeh up!" Ellizar exclaimed. Lily embraced him in a hug and then they all followed suit, leaving the dwarf with a funny expression on his face.

"Weird custom, giving of hugs. We don't do it much in dwarvish culture, but you know what? I think I like it."

They started walking through the canyon once again. Skander joined them, looking to be injured the most out of any of them with a broken arm and a bad cut across his forehead.

"There you are!" a woman's voice echoed from behind. Drake was the last one to turn around and see Atruss and Gabrielle coming near them. "You are all safe and well?"

"As well as we can get seeing we've just been through the largest battle that we've ever seen," Skander answered. Atruss nodded.

"We were very fortunate."

"What now?" Gwen asked.

"Find anyone who is still alive, get them out of the valley, and take them to the healer's tower. There the injured will be able to find rest and comfort. Post guards to alert us if any Giants should come wandering into the grass canyons again. We'll send a group back for the dead bodies."

"Where do we go after that?" Gwen asked.

"Go to the bed you were given and sleep!"

They parted ways and searched through the battlefield more carefully now, for people that were injured to the point that they couldn't walk by themselves.

Ellizar and Lily found a man and helped him walk back to the city, having to help him almost more than they could, as one of his legs had been crushed beyond hope of healing.

Drake and Gwen fell further behind with the person that they were carrying. He was alive but unconscious and Drake for the most part carried him on his back except for the occasional break where he and Gwen would both carry him. The man was a great burden and finally, they stopped to remove his armor. With their load lightened, the journey became easier for all three of them.

By the time they had pulled the last of the living from the grass canyons, the sun was shining brightly. The city lay before them, gates open. The flowering vines that covered the walls of the city caught the light and reflected it, making it one of the most beautiful sights Drake had ever seen.

They made it to the healing tower where they left the people they had rescued. Their wounds were dressed and then they made their way up to the top level of the city and into the chamber they had been given. They once again found hot baths waiting for them, which were welcomed with open arms as they undressed and sunk into the water.

When they had all bathed and dressed again, they made their way to the beds that had been prepared for them and laid down, falling into a deep dreamless sleep.

XIX — THE HEALING TOWER

The city was silent, but somehow it was different. More haunting and eerie than Drake remembered experiencing before. He looked from one side of the lavish room to the other. Gwen, Lily, Skander, and Ellizar lay in their beds to either side of him.

Drake climbed out of his bed and dressed, making his way out into the silent hallway which would either take him out to the world around him or to the main meeting room where Gabrielle and Atruss likely were.

Drake grabbed his cloak and went to the right, observing the exquisite detail that had been put into everything. If the Elves were known for their skills in battle, he wondered if they were known for their attention to detail in design?

He exited the palace greeted by the cool autumn breeze that moved through the city. He stared at the buildings and the empty streets. The more Drake walked the more he realized that he must be the only person awake. For the moment he was on his own.

He walked mindlessly through the city, guessing by the height of the sun that it was midday or a little after. He wandered to the third level, standing atop the wall and looking out at the field and then the canyons beyond, where smoke still rose from the trees.

He walked to the healing tower surprised to find everyone asleep there as well. The only sound was the breathing of the patients, who far outnumbered his fears.

He looked at the first person, and then the next and the next, hoping that one of the faces would spark a memory from his past. He desperately hoped that his memory would someday return to him, but for now, he was left to live without it and struggle through the situations at hand only to hope that in the future he would remember.

Drake stopped at the sight of a thin black-haired man, who had suffered a broken leg and arm. A stirring in Drake's heart gripped him. Though his mind was void of memories of this man, there was something familiar about him. Drake studied him for the longest time, finally deciding to sit down in the chair and wait for him to wake up. He was well-built and fairly tall. His face was hardened but at the same time, peaceful.

The time passed and finally, the man began to stir, moaning slightly as he shifted. He looked around and then stopped when his eyes met Drake.

"You're no doctor," the man greeted. Drake smiled.

"No. I'm not." The man looked at him strangely.

"Good morning," Drake greeted. The man nodded and looked around.

"More like afternoon isn't it?" the man asked.

Drake nodded. "I guess it is, although no one else is up to prove that it's not morning."

"Can't argue with that," The man said sitting up and leaning against the headboard as best as he could. "Do you have a name?"

"Drake Thomas." Drake held out a hand to the man and he looked at it cautiously, as if something bad was about to happen. Drake kept his hand extended and finally, he grabbed it.

"You have two names?" the man asked. "That's very unusual."

"Tell me about it."

"My name is Tremin."

"Pleasure to meet you."

"Same here," Tremin replied. "I must say, I'm a little shocked that you have two names. I had heard rumors up until now, but to actually meet you, it's a nice surprise. All these years I thought there was only one person who had two names."

"There is only one person who had two names isn't there?" Drake asked.

Tremin studied him for a moment.

"There's always been rumors of another person with two names. A strange person that one is. She's an outcast for the most part, not many people talk to her. I went in her shop once and that was enough for me."

"Maybe I'll have to go see what she's like."

"Are you a freak like she is?"

"Depends on your definition of freak, but either way someone has to have a friend. Just because she has two names doesn't mean you shouldn't talk to her."

"You must be new around these parts," Tremin said decidedly. "No one goes to her shop. Everyone's afraid of her."

"That's silly," Drake replied. "I'm sure that she's a nice woman once you get to know her."

"Think what you want Mr. Thomas," Tremin replied, bitterness in his voice. "She lives on the east side of the city, supposedly because the sun looks better from there. She's a freak and that's all there is to it. The sun looks the same no matter where you are."

"Maybe she's talking about the sunrise?" Drake suggested. "I choose not to make any rush judgments before I meet someone."

"You'll be thinking the same thing if you ever met her."

"I guess we'll just have to wait and see won't we."

"I guess so."

"Where are you from?" Drake asked. "Have you always lived here?"

"No, I only recently moved here a couple of years ago. Until I moved here, I lived in Idumea. I just came back from visiting some friends a month ago."

"I passed through there a couple of weeks ago," Drake stated.

"It's a small world. Perhaps we crossed paths a hundred times and never noticed each other."

"Perhaps," Drake admitted looking behind him as the front door opened. One of the nurses came in and another woman followed. Drake's heart nearly leapt from his chest as he saw Gwen come in. She kissed him and then sat in an empty chair beside him.

"Who's the woman?" Tremin asked. Drake introduced the two of them, unable to help but notice that the man was studying her with an interest that Drake couldn't place. The more time that passed the more nervous Drake became. A sudden urge to know more about this man was growing in his heart.

"What's the matter?" Drake asked, finally breaking the man's stare.

"Nothing, she just looks familiar, and I must say I'm a little jealous. I think you have the most beautiful woman in Ariamore."

"You're too kind," Gwen answered. They stayed for several more minutes. Drake's heart warned him of a danger that was near at hand. They said their goodbyes and left.

"Good morning you two," a voice greeted from behind.

"Good morning Rohemir," Gwen greeted. "I see you made it through the battle unscathed."

"One of the few and for that I am very fortunate," Rohemir answered. Drake looked him over, only noticing a few minor scratches and cuts, nothing compared to what they had suffered. "Not all were given the same fortunes."

"At least we survived. Of course, if another army shows up at our doorstep we can't even think of holding them," Drake replied.

"I hate to admit it, but you're right. There's not much we can do if another army should come, but I highly doubt that we'll be in any danger for a little while."

"Why do you say that?" Gwen asked.

"Food," Drake answered. "Everyone has harvested all their food for the year and therefore can last through a siege or attack much easier. If he waits until spring, there won't be as much food to feed the people he's invading. If he comes, it will be in the spring and he will bring his army with him, no doubt."

"I hope someone else has a plan as to how we're going to survive because right now I don't see much hope," Gwen answered.

"The council will be holding many meetings in the next couple of days. The outcomes, I'm quite confident, will offer hope to those who have none."

"We don't have to be in these meetings do we?" Drake asked.

"No. The council and the Farsees may wish to speak with the five of you briefly, but I don't think that you'll have to stay in the meetings all day. You are free to do as you wish," Rohemir answered. "Look around the city, help with the cleanup effort. Just make sure that when the day is over you are in the city walls because the gates will be closing at sundown from now on."

"Are you part of the council?"

"Yes and no," Rohemir answered. "I stepped down about three years ago. However, I am always allowed to sit in on the meetings and give my input. They still seem to like me. I won't argue. I've always enjoyed the meetings and discussions that get going."

"Someone has to," Drake commented.

"Some people are wired for it and others aren't."

They walked until they reached the outside world where the cool sun greeted them. The streets were now beginning to show signs of life. Drake's heart was broken as they walked the streets seeing dozens and dozens of people who hadn't been able to fit into the healing tower. They lay on beds that were off to the side of the street, with a couple of nurses checking on them.

"I will have to leave you here and catch up with you later," Rohemir announced. They said their goodbyes and watched as he vanished from their sight, into the ever-growing crowd of people.

"Something isn't right," Gwen said.

"If only we could figure out what it is," Drake replied. "Each day a threat grows closer in my mind. The worst thing is, I don't think the others see it."

"Do you think we should mention it?"

"They have to make up their own mind, we can't force them to come to any conclusions," Drake agreed.

"Wise words Mr. Thomas." They turned around to see the source of the voice this time was Aiden. High in the sky they could faintly see Elohim flying over the surrounding area.

"How much did you hear?" Drake asked, suddenly afraid.

"Everything, but you don't have to worry."

"What do you think about the matter?" Gwen asked.

"I think there are many mysteries in the world and this is merely one of them. I think that it is best to sit back and thoroughly examine all the evidence and facts before making any kind of decision. Too many times people rush into judgment and end up screwing something up."

"Makes sense," Drake replied. "What are you doing today? Are you going to be in on the meetings as well?"

"Only if they say they need me there," Aiden answered. "I'm sure at one point or another I'll be called in to give my side of the story, but until then I will be more than happy to *not* be a part of the meeting. I have a heart for helping people, and whether it's cleanup or healing, I will do what I can."

"I wish I had a heart like yours," Gwen said. "I want to help people also, but I feel as though I'm too small to do anything of importance. Have you ever felt that way?"

"Many, many times," Aiden answered. "There is not a person on the earth who hasn't felt that way. I've been there and it was a challenging time for me. But for those who put their trust in Lathon, we can find a discontent for certain things."

"Discontent?"

"Let me put it this way. When you look around the world and you see all the problems in it, what makes you so mad that you can't help but do something? Even if it's as small as talking to someone who usually sits alone. That's discontent. When you can't stand it anymore, that's when you find who you are."

"How is putting our trust in an ancient king supposed to help that?" Drake asked, he feared for a moment he had offended Aiden.

"That's how a lot of people in the world feel Drake Thomas, but the question we have to ask ourselves is how did Lathon live? He was the greatest king to ever rule the world. He did so with a loving hand and a kind heart. He united the world and held it together for a great number of years. But as you've pointed out he is now dead, in some ways.

"You see, when someone great like that is in a position to do some good they should do it. In Lathon's case, he affected the world in such a way that everyone around him wanted nothing more than to be a carbon copy of him. They tried to emulate him in every way and show the same kind of love and compassion that he had. They have taken hope in the prophecy when he said that there will be an heir of Lathon that will come to rule as Lathon once did."

"So why is the world in the shape it's in, if there are so many people trying to be like Lathon?" Gwen asked.

"You two have a knack for asking questions that I love," Aiden told them with a smile. "People these days are self-serving. I hate when I look at the nations and what they've become. They say that they're loving and will help other people, but most of them, not all, but most of them, help only themselves and are no different than those who are out in the rest of the world. There will come a day in the future when this nation will be divided by that."

"What are we supposed to do if the nation is divided?" Drake asked. "We won't be able to stand against Grimdor's army by ourselves."

"Maybe not, but I think that there are hundreds of thousands of people all across the world who feel a discontent about the shape the world is in, but feel as though they can do nothing. When Shedaros comes forward, I think many people will finally have the courage to stand up for what they believe."

"I hope when Shedaros comes forward we'll all see him. Somehow I'm supposed to be the one to first recognize him? I don't know how I'm supposed to do that."

"Watch everyone you meet carefully Drake Thomas, Shedaros could be right in front of you."

"That's the part that scares me the most," Drake admitted. Gwen nodded her agreement. "I could have talked to him already today, yet I have no idea who it is."

"Just be calm and take it one day at a time, when the time is right there will be no guessing or uncertainty about it."

"If it wasn't for you I don't think I would be here now. You've saved my life several times over and I don't think I've ever thanked you for doing it."

"You can thank me if you wish but if you want to thank me, help someone else. Doing so brings joy that few people ever experience." They walked for a while. More and more people entered the streets, most of them going to the hospital to hopefully find their loved ones alive instead of dead.

"Drake, I would suggest you take some time today to get yourself an owl or a small bird of some kind. We use them for sending messages to each other."

"Why do I need one?" Drake asked.

"Someone's going to say that you do, so it would be best to buy one before you have to."

"Where do I get one, when I don't have any money?"

"I've got a friend on the east side of the city that might be able to do you a favor or two."

"Is there any specific shop, or am I just wandering blind?"

"The name of it is *The Wingy Wares*. I'm sure you'll be able to spot it right off the bat once you get there."

"How am I going to spot it so easily?"

"Trust me on this Drake." Silence passed for a few moments before Aiden bowed out, leaving Drake and Gwen to be alone with each other.

THE WINGY WARES

Drake and Gwen walked for hours, not going in any particular direction, just enjoying each other's presence as time got away from them. Drake soon found that they had made their way to the east side of the city, and much to his surprise he didn't know how they had gotten there.

Besides Gwen, nothing else existed.

They searched the shops many times over, looking for the one called *'The Wingy Wares'*. As hard as they looked they didn't see anything, leaving them to wander through the city.

His eyes were drawn to a featherless bird flying through the sky. The bird slowly descended and then landed on top of a small building that was narrow and pressed between two other buildings.

While the buildings to either side were fixed up nicely and looked as though a rich person might live in them, the one in the middle was just the opposite. The white paint that had once covered the building was nearly gone and parts of the roof and the building were sagging. There was a porch on the front of the building, which was worn and old-looking.

"What's wrong Drake?" Gwen asked. Drake didn't answer right away, still staring at the building in front of them as if it held some hidden beauty.

An old worn sign hung crooked on the front door.

The Wingy Wares – Open

"This is the place," Drake finally answered.

"This? It's a mess! How can this be the place?"

"It's a mess on the outside, but I have a feeling that the inside is something completely different."

"Are you sure? We don't know who's in that shop. It could be a killer or a Spirit. What if the person inside turns out to be some kind of a freak?" Gwen asked.

"I don't think that's the case," Drake said, taking Gwen's hand and gently leading her toward the front porch. The boards creaked and groaned under their weight. Drake reached for the handle but found that the door opened itself, gently swinging open. No one stood on the other side of the door.

Drake walked through first, taking Gwen's hand. Drake was drawn towards the shop, with a curiosity that he hadn't felt before. Gwen on the other hand was shaking like a leaf, trying to bring herself to take the next step.

The door closed itself a few moments later leaving them in a beautiful house. Just as Drake had suspected the inside of the house was nothing like the outside. The wood floors were nicely polished, and the walls and railings on the stairs were covered with flowering vines that at first glance looked similar to the vines that covered the walls of the city.

Although they were similar to those in the grass canyons, the blossoms on these flowers changed colors, changing from one color to the next within a matter of minutes. Some were red and others were purple while others still were vibrant blues and pinks and any color you could imagine.

They were both captured by the beauty as they took another step forward. They paused only momentarily as the vines extended from each wall and created an arch for them to walk through. They walked through and the arch disassembled itself.

Dozens of shelves stood along the wall, each of them filled with unusual-looking knick-knacks and artifacts that Drake couldn't hope to recognize. Large stones sat on some shelves while others were filled with plants of unique nature. Birds flew all around the building, letting their songs echo through the house.

"This is amazing," Gwen whispered. A light mist came down from the ceiling, watering all the plants. The mist landed on them, but only the plants got wet.

"Hello," a woman's voice said from behind. They turned to see a tall woman, maybe six feet tall, standing in front of them. Her eyes were a vibrant sapphire and her hair was brown. She was dressed in a bright yellow dress, which had a dark green lace pattern along the edges. She looked into Drake's eyes, her own seeming to light up when she saw him.

"Sorry, we didn't mean to enter, we just-"

"It's no problem, this is a shop that people buy things in so it only makes sense that you came in. I know that the door opened itself. It does that all the time."

"It does?" Gwen asked. The woman nodded.

"You'll see a lot of unusual things around the shop and that's just one of them," the woman answered. Drake looked at the woman in front of them. Oddly, he noticed that her dress seemed to be changing colors in a similar fashion as all the flowering vines that covered the walls.

"You're wondering about my dress aren't you?" the woman asked. Drake's face clearly showed the surprise that he felt inside.

"Forgive me, it just seems to be changing color."

"Yes, all my clothes do that regularly. It's a special fabric that I created myself. I figure with all the colors out in the world why should I choose just one to be my favorite? This way I get to see all the colors."

"That's...interesting," Gwen answered, trying to pull Drake away towards the door. Drake didn't move.

"Who are you?" Drake asked.

"My apologies for not introducing myself, my name is Isabel Rachal."

"So is it Isabel or Rachal?" Gwen asked shifting nervously.

"I have two names," Isabel answered. "Why my parents gave me two names I can't begin to guess, but then again they weren't the most normal people you might ever meet."

"I can't imagine," Gwen replied. "I think I'll be waiting outside." Gwen pulled away from Drake and left him alone with Isabel. Drake watched as the door opened itself and then closed again as Gwen left. Drake turned to Isabel, seeing pain and sorrow on her face.

"Are you alright?" Drake asked. She shrugged her shoulders.

"I always hate it when people leave my shop."

"I guess it makes it pretty hard to make a living."

"That's not why I cry. People take a look at me and then think I'm a freak and take off running. I've been used to that kind of treatment my whole life and it never gets any easier for me."

"I can't imagine that it would," Drake replied. "My name is Drake. Drake Thomas." Isabel's eyes lit up with curiosity.

"So, after all these years, I'm finding out that I'm not the only person with two names?"

"Like you, I'm not sure how I ended up with two names, all I know is I have them."

"I guess I knew that," Isabel replied. Drake pondered her reply. "What brings you to my shop Mr. Thomas?"

"I was just looking around the city, and this shop seemed to catch my attention."

"Really?" Isabel answered. "Almost everyone walks right by and doesn't notice the shop or even glance at it. What brought you here?"

"A friend of mine, and a bird which I saw outside."

"A bird?" the woman answered. Drake nodded. "What did it look like?"

"Featherless, kind of scraggly looking. I've never seen a bird like it before, it was very strange. I've been seeing it here and there, it seems to be following me."

"Yes, he tends to follow people who are interesting to him."

"He?" Drake questioned. Isabel nodded.

"I would like to claim him as my bird because he's very special to me, but I don't know where he came from. He came to me in a time of sorrow and hasn't left me since. I'm not even sure what kind of bird he is. I've looked through all the books that I could find and I've come up blank. He is very curious though. Since I'm not one of the most popular people in the world he goes out and flies all over and tells me what he sees. People always wonder how I know the things I know, it's because of him."

"So, he's like a spy?" Drake asked.

"I suppose in some ways, however, because only certain people can see him that makes it a lot safer for the both of us. From what I hear you've seen your fair share of action lately."

"I'm not sure I like being watched all the time, but I suppose I can't tell you anything new because he told you everything, correct?"

"He did tell me a lot. When he told me that you had two names, I was quite excited. Any idea how you ended up with two names?"

"I'm not sure, yourself?"

"My parents were quite eccentric. My mom wanted to name me Isabel and my father wanted to name me Rachal, so I ended up with both names. They were nice people, my father was human and my mother was Elvish, which is why even though I look human I can use Elven magic. It's quite a perk. I'm not very good at it though."

"You're not?" Drake asked looking around her shop and all the interesting things. "It looks like you're pretty good at it to me."

"Thank you," Isabel answered. "But don't let this fool you. I've had many, many accidents over the years. The first time I tried to put the flowering vines on my walls, I ended up with Haverine Vines. They're a kind of vine that eats anything they see. It was a couple of months before I was able to enter again. They finally ate each other and then I was able to kill the only one that was left."

"Did you know that you had planted the wrong vines?"

"Not for a week or so, until my closet of clothes started disappearing," Isabel answered. "I love to experiment and I suppose I get that from my mom.

It was the death of my parents though."

"How's that?" Drake asked.

"They were trying to make this new kind of stew, named *Taruk's curd*. They managed to make it correctly, which is a miracle in itself, but at the last minute, they tried to add some green peppers and the whole house exploded. I was only six at the time and I was at someone else's house so I lived."

"I'm glad you lived or else I'd be talking to no one right now," Drake replied. Isabel let a slight laugh escape her, walking further into the store.

"What is it I can do for you Mr. Thomas, you must be looking for something in particular?"

"Please call me Drake."

"Very well Drake. What are you looking for?"

"I was looking for a messenger bird of some kind. I need to get one so I can be reached at all times?"

"Good idea, you definitely need protection. I might have the thing you need here."

"Really?"

"It's a possibility, I don't have many owls, but I'm sure I'll have something just as good if not better. Maybe I'll be able to find one similar to the featherless bird. Then hardly anyone would be able to see it."

"That would be great."

"Come with me." Drake followed Isabel, noticing that her dress had changed colors again and so had the flowering vines. His mind tried to sort out what had happened, as he noticed that Isabel's hair and eyes had changed color as well.

They moved through the twisting maze of stairwells and hallways, with Isabel glancing behind her now and then, seeming to study him with interest. They reached the top floor of the house, which appeared to have an open roof on it. The sun was shining and the birds sang in the vines. Light snow came down from the ceiling, which was made to look like the sky.

"This is amazing," Drake said, hardly able to get the words out. "It's a shame that people don't come in here more often."

"It took me many years to figure out how to do all of this. I've always loved the snow. People are often so quick to judge by the outside, they miss the beauty that's inside."

"I won't be making that mistake again," Drake replied, noticing that Isabel was looking at him funny. "What?"

"Sorry, I just can't help but notice how much you look like them."

"Like who?"

"Like your parents. They're very nice people."

"You know who my parents are?"

"Don't you?"

"I seem to have lost my memory, I don't know who they are or what they look like."

"I'm sorry to hear that. Your parents are amazing people. They along with your cousin have come in here before. Your cousin sees me regularly. I don't remember their names, but you do look like them. You have the build of your father and the eyes and hair of your mother, who was always quite radiant."

"You can't remember their names?" Drake asked. Isabel shrugged her shoulders.

"After years of being an outcast and having no one come into my shop, I learned to stop learning people's names because they never cared to remember mine."

"And my cousin?"

"I can see the resemblance, though few others probably would. Anyway back to the task at hand." They came to large shelves and countless cages of birds and owls of every kind."

"I thought you said you didn't have many owls?" Drake asked.

"These are all owls that the normal shops wouldn't sell, due to their unique nature. I took them in and gave them a home. So, as far as everyone else is concerned, I don't have any owls."

"How are they unique, or should I not ask?"

"Touch one." Drake carefully reached through the wooden rungs of the cage and touched a small dove that was flawless white. Immediately following his touch the bird burst into flames, leaving only a pile of ashes.

"What just happened?"

"Don't worry, he'll be back tomorrow. They're meant to explode or do something spectacular unless you're the right match for the bird."

"So I don't choose the bird, the bird chooses me."

"Correct. Never really understood it, but they're a bit like Taruks in that sense. How about this bird?" Isabel opened a nearby cage and let a fair-sized parrot come out. It landed on her shoulder and looked at Drake kind of funny. Drake reached out to touch it and barely got a finger on it before the bird screeched and flew through the air, wildly flapping its wings. The bird lost control and flew into the wall, sending a puff of feathers into the air. When the feathers fell to the ground they noticed that the bird wasn't there.

"I guess that's not the bird for you," Isabel replied with a laugh. "Should we try another one?" Drake went to answer but found himself unable as his eye caught on something by one of the far shelves. Drake's curiosity got the better of him as he cautiously approached the object. It was larger than anything else in the room, probably weighing at least a hundred pounds. Although it had at one time been sitting on the shelf, it now sat below them. The birds all watched him with interest as he approached the large stone.

The stone was a dark green, with white light coming from inside of it. Drake knew immediately what it was and felt fear run through him as he reached out and touched it.

"A Taruk egg?" Drake asked.

"Yes. I'm not sure exactly what kind of a Taruk egg it is, but there are more than just a few mysteries about this egg. First of all, I found it sitting in the back of the shop when I purchased it. I wasn't able to find any records of where it came from. It was just there. It was no larger than a small stone when I moved into my shop. It also seems to know what I'm saying."

Drake replayed what had happened with Elohim. Aiden's words flashed through his mind reminding him that Elohim had seemed to have a connection with him and that maybe he was meant to have a Taruk in the future. Drake felt his heart surge and then search for something else inside himself, as the egg held his attention.

He recoiled his hand and stared at it, Isabel watching him. A few seconds passed before Drake turned away and looked at Isabel, his eyes conveying the fear he was feeling.

"We can look in a different room if you would like?"

Drake nodded and they went through room after room, and at the end were unable to find anything remotely close to one that he might be able to have. When Drake touched the birds he could never predict what would happen. One of them sparked into fireworks which then rose to the ceiling and exploded, another created a tidal wave that soaked them, and another lost all its feathers, leaving just one of them atop its head.

When finally Drake got tired of trying all the other birds he excused himself and stepped out into the streets, surprised to find that the day had vanished and now it was early evening with the sun slowly setting on the horizon. He searched up and down the streets, hoping for some kind of a clue as to where Gwen had gone. The streets were now bustling with people and Drake walked with the crowds, finally making his way back to the bed he had been given.

No one else was there, but for Drake the thought of sleep welcomed him. He lay down trying to process everything that had been said in such a short amount of time. In a matter of minutes, he fell asleep.

XXI · MANY MEETINGS

Rohemir waited with the Farsees and all the council members who were anxious to get started. The Farsees shifted uncomfortably. They had been waiting for ten minutes and still, there was no sign of the guest of honor who had been asked to sit in on the meeting.

Rohemir looked in Atruss's direction, noticing that he seemed to be as calm and collected as ever, as though he wasn't concerned. Rohemir wasn't sure what to think at a time like this. They had barely managed to survive an attack that they had no business living through, and now they were ready to discuss their next move and they couldn't because they were waiting.

A few minutes later, the doors to the meeting chamber were opened and Aiden walked through. Red flags immediately went through Rohemir's mind. The guest of honor had arrived, but not how they would have expected him. Aiden strode into the room, dressed as he had been during the battle. His weapons were still on him and his clothes were worn and dirty.

The sight was almost too much for Rohemir to handle as anger swelled in his chest. Several council members and Farsees exchanged glances, and shared in Rohemir's outrage, clearly not approving. Aiden took a seat as though nothing was out of the ordinary and patiently waited for the meeting to start.

"Sorry I'm late," Aiden started. "I was helping some of the people in the healing tower and I lost track of time."

"We certainly wouldn't have minded waiting a few more minutes if it meant that you were a little more presentable," one of the Farsees, Confius, remarked. The others nodded their agreement.

"My apologies," Aiden said. "I thought it was what was on the inside that mattered, not the outside appearance of something." Confius shifted uncomfortably once again.

"Let's get started," Gabrielle interjected. "We are here to discuss the future of this nation. The survival of our people, the chosen ones of Lathon, is about to be threatened."

"The world is changing and with it, we shall also change or else we will be destroyed in the days to come," Atruss added. "We must decide our next course of action."

"I say we create an army immediately," Aiden said. "We survived the attack by the Giants, but barely. If we wait any longer we're only going to be hurting ourselves. There is a powerful Sorcerer that controls both the nations of Grimdor and Vernal. I know this for a fact because I saw him when I recently visited Grimdor. The world will fall into his clutches unless we do something."

"We can't do anything," one of the council members said. "We can barely defend our walls let alone help all the other people. We might as well acknowledge that there's no way we can stand against this *Sorcerer*. He's too strong. Somehow he has built up his forces and is on the move? There is no hope in the future, we must just accept our doom and wait for it to arrive."

"You people might be content to sit back and watch the world fall into the clutches of evil, but I won't have any part of it," Aiden fired back. "We're talking about people's lives here, their homes, their villages, the people themselves. Would you want them to sit back and not help you if you were the ones being attacked?"

"We're the chosen ones of Lathon, we will not be attacked and overcome. We must trust in that," another person fired back. "Or do you now doubt the power of Lathon?"

"I do not doubt anything," Aiden responded. "All I'm saying is that Lathon said this day would come and now it is here. He would want us to pick up our swords and rush the gates of Grimdor for the sake of every person on this earth. Why should he save people who don't want to save themselves? We must help them."

"I agree with Aiden's motion," Atruss said. A couple of people rolled their eyes.

"You two think that we should run into a battle we can't possibly hope to win and do what? Attack the nation of Grimdor? We might as well commit suicide. We have no hope of ever standing against them," Confius replied.

"If we have no hope then why are we gathered here? If we have no hope then we should all leave now and accept our doom," Aiden said. "There's always hope and it comes in the form of the prophecy of Shedaros."

A person across the room laughed. "I'm Elvish and I've lived here for many years. Even I doubt the prophecies! Lately, they've become something for people to listen to, something for children rather than actual people. We all know what the prophecy said and if you think that it all happened then you're just as crazy as the next person."

"I know they are real," Rohemir answered. "I was there on that very night when I helped Shedaros escape from Masada. He is in the world. Now we must wait for him to come forward and present himself to us."

"And what happens until then Rohemir?" another council member asked. "What if he never comes? What happens if he was killed in a battle several years ago? By Lathon coming and living among us he subjects himself to the same struggles that we face. If you ask me, that is nothing that a king should do."

"Perhaps he came to earth the way he did so that he might be one of us," Aiden suggested. "To share in the suffering of the world and feel the pain and show that pain to the people, so that they might look to him to see what he does in the hard times. I believe that Shedaros lives among us even now."

"Then you're fools!"

"Perhaps," Atruss responded. Silence followed his statement. "Still we *must* discuss our plans for the future. We must create an army and do it quickly."

"There shouldn't be any rush," another of the Farsees replied. "I doubt the Sorcerer will attack us before the winter comes, that gives us several more months to prepare something."

"We don't know that he won't attack us," Atruss pointed out. "The fact of the matter is he might get the Giants to descend on us once more. We can't hope to hold them off again. We barely did it the last time."

"It still takes time to create an army! Surely you realize that?"

"But why waste any of that precious time?"

"Because we have far more time than you seem to think. You realize how many cities and nations stand between us and the Sorcerer. It might as well be a million miles. The Sorcerer will be weakened by all the battles he has to fight along the way, by the time he reaches us, his force will be small."

"Don't be too sure," Aiden told them. "I was recently in Iscariot and was witness to an unthinkable force leaving that Hellish fortress known as Iscariot. A force far greater than anything you could imagine. It was probably three hours and still, the line of Borags marching from the city walls was flowing. Our enemy is strong and he seeks to kill anyone who stands in his way."

"Even if we create this army, there's not much we can do. We'll be able to defend our walls and that's it, and I highly doubt the effort will do any good if the forces of Grimdor are as numerous as you say they are."

"That's why I make the motion that we attack immediately after the army is created," Atruss suggested. Laughter went through the room. "Why do you laugh?"

"Why do we laugh?" Confius asked. "You realize what you just said? You said that with our little force, we are somehow supposed to attack the greatest force the world has ever known! We would be much safer here, you must realize that! I'm certainly not going to stand on the front lines and let the only defense this nation has, be wiped out in battle."

"Maybe you don't have a heart but I do!" Aiden exclaimed. "Even though almost everyone here cares about clothes and status, I'm not here for personal gains. I'm not sure why I was chosen to be the guest of honor in this meeting, but I'm here, and if there's no one else in this room who will fight for what is good and just in this world, then it looks like I'll be fighting alone. Don't you see? The Sorcerer wants us to stand alone and be worried only about ourselves, because if we're alone then we're much easier to defeat. Too long has this nation sat on the sidelines and wasted away into a state of nothingness.

"We sit back and let people talk about us, and you know as well as I do that their talk isn't good. Yet, we let it continue and do nothing to fix the reputation that we've received. The world views the Elves and anyone who believes in Lathon, as a bunch of self-centered, condemning brats that care only about themselves. I'm sick of it. It's as simple as that. If we want to stand a chance against the forces that align themselves against us, then we have to get off our lazy butts and do something. Faith without good deeds is dead, that much is clear."

"The other nations have not called for our aid! Why should we rush to their side when they would not come to ours?"

"Because we have to start somewhere. They won't call for our aid because of the conclusions they've formed. They think we're going to sit back and let them fall, if we show up at their walls to help them fight their battles, I think their alliance might be with us. The more we help other people, the more they'll help us and in the end, we *can* stand against the Sorcerer with more hope and strength than he could have fathomed. We have to come together otherwise we are just making ourselves easy targets for him." The council fell silent for several moments.

"Aiden is right, we must form an army and use it to help the people if we are to have any hope of surviving any future attacks. I'm sure there will be many in the days to come," Atruss stated. "I push for the creation of an army immediately, we can use the winter to train the army and prepare and plan for the war that will follow." Nobody objected and the motion was carried and approved.

"Perhaps this would be a good time to also discuss what we are to do about the Sorcerer himself?" Rohemir suggested. Every head turned and focused on him. "We know that he needs two things to rule and destroy all that is good in the world. His Taruk and the Wizard's Staff. The tools of destruction for him. We already know that the Taruk has been released in an interesting turn of events. I fear our days are numbered."

"Perhaps I'm wrong Rohemir, but didn't we find and hide the Wizards' Staff?" Gabrielle asked.

"We did, but how can we be sure that he won't be able to find it? It may be hidden in the middle of nowhere, in a place that can't possibly be found, but what if he does? What are we going to do against the reckless hate that now threatens to consume our world? If he finds the staff I'm not sure we can even hope of surviving."

"If we are to be attacked," Aiden started. "And the armies of Grimdor come crashing through the gates of this city and every other city in the world, then there's only one thing to do. Rush out to meet it and give it a fight to remember. Trust that Lathon will watch over us. We can't let our worries stop us from doing good, when we let our worries control us we become useless. I would say leave the staff where it is and let things unfold as they may."

"The Wizard's Staff is one of the most powerful and destructive weapons ever created. It wears on your mind and seeks to influence people around you and fill their minds with its poison. Forgive me Aiden, but I have a hard time sitting back and doing nothing," Rohemir replied.

"I understand. Nonetheless, if we make a move we might give away our hiding place." The others nodded in agreement.

"With that order of business done, there is only one more urgent matter that needs to be discussed," Atruss announced. "As we all know by now, Rohemir was traveling, almost two months ago he came across a man who was anything but ordinary. His hand was marked with a scar that we all know too well. We managed to get him here, but barely. He seems to fight as though he's experienced, but he remembers none of his past.

"Although he is a great fighter, the battle that we just lived through was hard on him and his friends. They've never fought for so long in their lives. I suggest that these five people who traveled here with Rohemir, take fighting lessons that will improve their chances in the days to come. I think that if they are better at fighting, they should be the ones to lead us into battle, with Aiden assisting as well."

"Why with Aiden assisting?" a council member asked. "I have no problem with it, but he's a Tarukai, that's his big claim to fame. Why is he so worthy of leading us into battle?"

"Aiden is both wise and cunning, fast and smart, full of all the traits that our army must have if we are supposed to live through the year. Putting him in charge along with Drake would be the best move we could make in this war. Drake can't fight this war alone and until Shedaros comes forward we need someone to help guide us. I know Aiden's been in many battles previous to the one we had last night. Are there any objections?" Atruss asked. "And if there aren't any objections, will Aiden accept?" Silence filled the room once again.

"Yes, I will accept. I want nothing more than to help the world in waging a war against the Sorcerer. It would be my honor to lead us into battle when the day comes."

"Very good," one of the council members replied. "We will begin the recruiting process for the army immediately. We will pick only the best people to be brought here to be trained for battle."

"Why only the best?" Aiden asked. "There are more of us in this world than just the best people. I think that we pick out the best, but if someone comes forward and wants to fight, then they should be allowed to. With the size of our existing army, I can't see it hurting our chances any."

"What if they should die in battle?"

"Then they will die knowing that they got to be a part of something great and that they contributed to the effort, which in the end is the best thing in the world. To know that they tried when others wouldn't come forward, to know that they stood when the world didn't have the courage to. That's what this is all about and the people who aren't *'the best'* deserve to have that chance as well.

"Well said Aiden," Atruss agreed. "I second his motion, and if anyone here objects to that motion you might as well give yourself up to the Sorcerer right now. I think this is another thing that will be a deciding factor in the war ahead." A few seconds passed before someone else spoke.

"I was going to inquire about one of the people that you brought here to Ariamore. You know the one I'm talking about," the man started. "This person looks very familiar to me, almost as if I've seen her in the past. I'd like to know why she looks so familiar, perhaps it's just my imagination but haven't we all seen this woman before?"

"I have seen the woman you speak of and I know exactly what you're saying. She does look familiar and every second that I look at her I'm reminded of the past that haunts us. We can only hope that no one ever figures it out. If they do then we might have another problem on our hands," Gabrielle replied.

"There's a prophecy that we all know too well. We may have never fully understood the words but I think that they would make sense if you applied them to the woman."

"It is not for us to decide this woman's purpose and destiny," Aiden told them. "The future is always in motion and if you've read the same prophecy that I have then you know as well as I do that it isn't clear what will exactly happen after that moment. Will this woman learn some things about her past that will haunt her? Yes. However, that doesn't mean she will be joining the Sorcerer."

"I'm afraid you've lost me altogether," Rohemir admitted. "What prophecy are we talking about?"

"One that is nearly forgotten by the world. It's so small and seemingly unimportant that we have never been able to make sense of it," Atruss answered. "I don't think it ever will make sense. Let's move on to other business."

Drake woke, quickly noticing everyone else's empty bed. He dressed and made his way to the large dining room where breakfast had been prepared. Skander sat talking to his sister whenever she wasn't humorously arguing with Ellizar. Gwen sat across from all three of them, not saying a word, seeming to be lost in her thoughts. Drake came forward and sat down next to her. Ellizar finally took notice of him as he began to fill his plate with food.

"Sleepin' beauty's final'y awake!" Ellizar exclaimed.

"Yes, I am awake. What did I miss?"

"That's an interesting question," Lily answered. "I think you should ask Ellie that question. Oh, that's right he can't remember!"

"Blasted elf kind!" Ellizar exclaimed. "I don't know what she's talkin' about. All I can say is that the followin' story is a crafted piece that they're makin' up."

"Do tell?" Drake asked. Gwen nodded.

"Let's just say after you went into that strange shop yesterday, I met up with them and had a very interesting time," Gwen started. "So interesting that I think Ellizar should be the one to tell it."

"I'm not tellin' a story that didn't happen," Ellizar replied.

"That's because you can't remember it!" Lily exclaimed. "It seems that he and I were taking a walk around the grass canyons. As luck would have it we were looking to see if there was anything that we could help with. A smaller tree that had started to be ripped out of the ground by the Giants decided that it was going to fall. I got out of the way but one of the branches smacked Ellizar in the helmet and pushed him to the ground.

"Then the funny part happens. I help him up and we start walking and it appears that Ellizar has amnesia. All day we were walking around the city, and all day he remembers none of it until this morning."

"So he couldn't remember who he was?" Drake asked, amusement etched on his face.

"He remembered the basics, who he was and who we were," Gwen answered. "But anything else and he's clueless."

"I am not! They're makin' it all up."

"I've never actually seen a case of amnesia before but it was very interesting because he was asking the same questions over and over again," Lily explained.

"What questions?"

"I think the most popular one was, 'Are you hungry?' he must have asked us that twenty times in an hour. I was about ready to smack him upside the head. Then the other two most popular questions or comments that he repeated over and over and over and over were 'I love trees' and my personal favorite for teasing sake 'Are you my wife?' I had half a mind to say yes just to play with his little head," Lily said with a laugh.

"Don't listen teh them Drake, they made up the last question. Imagine a dwarf marryin' an elf? Talk about a fun'y lookin' couple."

"They say opposites attract," Drake pointed out.

"Who asked yeh?"

"Ellizar, I think you asked that last question more than the other two combined. Either you didn't like the answer Lily was giving you or you didn't remember the answer," Skander said.

"I always hate how yeh guys pick on me the most just because I'm the short one. Yeh tall people look down at poor Ellizar and say, let's make fun of *him* today."

"You make it so easy," Lily commented. "By the way, I might point out that for once since we started this journey you were the bloody idiot."

"Such abuse I take. I'm not sure why I hang out with people like yerselves."

"We're not sure either, although we all have our own opinions," Skander replied. "So how was your day yesterday, Drake?"

"Interesting, but not nearly as interesting as yours was from the sound of it. I ended up in a strange shop called *The Wingy Wares* on the east side of the city."

"That's what Gwen was saying. Apparently, it was a little freaky for her," Skander said.

"It was different, but once you got inside the woman was quite nice. Mysterious but nice. I almost think that I've seen her somewhere before this. She tried to get me a bird but I didn't get one."

"What was so different about the shop?"

"Mostly the shop owner. I can only suggest that we take a trip over there today so you can see for yourself. She seemed to know who my parents were."

"Really?" Lily asked.

"Yes, she couldn't recall their names but she seemed to know who they were. She said that I looked like them. She also mentioned something about my cousin, whoever he is."

"Yer cousin?" Ellizar asked. "So after all this time, we might final'y begin teh find out something from yer past."

"I was very interested to talk to her. Even if she couldn't remember anything specifically about my family, the fact that she seemed to think I had one was enough to give me hope."

"We'll have teh take a trip over there and see what there is teh see. This time I'll remember it!"

"Are you sure about that Ellie?"

"Quite, I only have a poundin' headache and that's from yeh callin' me Ellie, it has nothing at all teh do with being smacked in the head by a tree."

"That's true, you were crazy before you were hit in the head." They listened to the argument continue as they finished their breakfast and left the building behind them. They stood on the top level of the city looking down at the land which was just now starting to wake up.

Sunlight poured into the valley, steam rising from the buildings as the frost that had formed on them the previous night was now burning off. Drake looked to the east, his mind lost in confusion as he could see smoke in the air.

"You see that smoke on the other side of the city?" Drake asked, he pointed in the direction of the smoke.

"It looks like the same area we were in yesterday," Gwen replied. They made their way through the streets until they came to the same shop that he and Gwen had been in the day before.

It looked the same from the outside, except this time the windows were opened and blue smoke drifted out of the windows.

"Mr. Thomas I would like a word with you!" a voice exclaimed. They all turned around to see Isabel, her dress black with white lace designs this time. Her hair was loose and fell carelessly down over her shoulders.

"Is something wrong?" Drake asked. Isabel stared at him and crossed her arms.

"You just about wrecked my house this morning! Thank you very much."

"How did I wreck your house? I haven't been here yet this morning."

"Oh you wrecked this house trust me. I haven't done any testing or experimenting to even come close to doing the damage that you did!" She turned and motioned for all of them to follow. They did so and entered The Wingy Wares.

Some of the furniture was smashed and damaged, several sections looked like part of the floor and walls were burnt and destroyed. Glass was all over the floor.

"What happened?" Gwen asked. Isabel's face showed amusement.

"Let me show you," Isabel answered leading them to the third floor. They were surprised to find that the other two floors were damaged the same as the first. They rounded another corner and they all gasped and came to a stop right in their tracks. In front of them, twenty feet away, was a Taruk, standing tall and proud. The Taruk looked in their direction but was unable to come forward as Isabel had somehow made a cage with the flowering vines that covered the walls.

The creature stomped wildly and then sat down, looking at Drake and not shifting his gaze. Drake approached the animal.

In a single bound, the Taruk rose to its feet, shaking the entire house and punching another hole in the floor with one of its powerful feet. The Taruk came up to the gate and touched Drake's hand which was extended towards it. The Taruk was dark green with lighter green stripes. The eyes were bright red.

"Where did you get him?" Drake asked.

"Where did I get him?" Isabel asked. "This came from the same Taruk egg that was sitting on the floor yesterday. He may not look like he was born last night but he was. He almost incinerated my room. It took me three hours to contain him so he couldn't destroy anything else."

"At least yeh got him contained," Ellizar commented. Isabel shot him a look and Ellizar fell quiet.

"How is this my fault?" Drake asked.

Isabel rolled her eyes. "You touched the egg yesterday! It may not have seemed like very much of a problem, but as you can see we now have a big problem. I have a Taruk in the house and he won't fit through the door!"

"What am I supposed to do?" Drake told her. Isabel rolled her eyes again.

"It's your Taruk, you'd better do something."

"His Taruk?" Gwen asked. "How is that possible?"

"Taruks are selective. They will stay in their egg for years unless they see someone that they're interested in. Drake was chosen for this. I'm not sure how else to explain it except to say that it's Drake's Taruk and he'd better get it out of my house while I still have a house standing."

"You, Drake Thomas, are full of surprises," Lily commented. "Does anything about your past come back to you now? Not just anyone ends up with a Taruk, for free. Someone's watching over you. Maybe it'll help solve the mystery of who your parents are?"

"I don't think a Taruk would choose me just because of my parents. I think they're smarter than that."

"Trust me, Drake Thomas, you're not the first person to have ever gotten a Taruk from me," Isabel replied. "I had two eggs, one of them was stolen from me a very long time ago. I'm not sure where it is or where it went but someone stole it, and didn't return it."

"Usually when people steal something they don't return it," Skander replied.

"Somehow we have to get it out of here. Do you have any ideas?" Isabel asked, ignoring Skander's statement.

"Can I see the Taruk," Drake told her. She gave him a knowing look and then proceeded to unlock the gate that had been formed by the flowering vines. He took a step closer to the Taruk. Isabel and the others waited from the other side of the gate.

Drake took one step at a time until he stood before the magnificent beast. He touched it on the nose and the Taruk shivered as though a chill had run up its spine. Drake stroked the soft, but hard-as-nails skin.

Ever since he had awakened he had wanted to feel that he had a reason. There *was* a reason that he had no memory of the past, there *was* a reason that he longed to help people when he didn't know how to help them. He had felt so small and powerless at first. This Taruk was living proof that something bigger than himself was watching over him and guiding his every move.

The Taruk moved backward and then shoved off the ground, crashing through the ceiling as though it was made of paper. Within seconds the beast was nothing more than a speck.

"You really owe me now!" Isabel cried. Drake smiled weakly.

"Sorry, I'll fix it or work it off if ever I get a job," Drake answered. "Where's Ellizar?" They searched the room for another moment or two until they finally spotted him entering one of the rooms with a dozen different birds, sitting in cages. He was talking to them and not paying the rest of them any mind as he reached out to touch one of them.

Drake and Isabel yelled out their warnings but it was too late as the entire shop was filled with smoke and fire as an explosion shook the building. The smoke cleared and Ellizar came into view, standing in front of the cage that was now filled with a bouquet of flowers. Smoke and ash covered Ellizar.

"Oops!" Ellizar exclaimed. The bird reappeared moments later, looking just as it had before it exploded.

"What kind of a bird is that?" Lily asked.

"All the animals in this shop are unique," Isabel explained. "If you find one that doesn't explode then you can have him. I must warn though that there could be many more explosions should you continue."

"Which is why my friend here isn't going to touch any more of them, right Ellizar?" Lily asked moving towards him. "After all the last thing we need is for you to end up with amnesia again."

"I'm never goin' teh live that one down am I?" Ellizar asked. Drake leapt out of the way as his Taruk came back through the roof, looking twice as large since they had arrived. The Taruk looked at Drake, inviting him forward. Drake climbed on its back and the Taruk stood to its feet.

"How do you fly these things?" Drake asked.

"You communicate with Taruks through thoughts," Isabel stated.

"Let's see how this goes. Who wants to come for a ride?" Drake asked. Gwen came forward while the others remained where they were. Drake reached down and grabbed Gwen's hand helping her up. She wrapped her arms around his waist and held on tight as the Taruk pushed off the ground.

The building vanished beneath them. Drake looked over his shoulder into Gwen's eyes seeing a light and a love in them that he hadn't seen before.

They flew for an hour as Drake practiced talking to the Taruk through his thoughts. The ride was not the smoothest at first but the longer they flew the better it went.

They lost all track of time and direction, enjoying the freedom of flying on a Taruk. They eventually came to rest on an open hilltop, where they talked and laughed, not having a care in the world. The day faded and they started a fire, looking up at the stars shining brightly.

The night grew long and finally sleep overtook them and they both drifted off to their dreams. His Taruk was curled up next to the fire, making sure to breathe more fire if it started getting cold or dying. Drake woke only a couple times during the night and only once did he wonder if there was another reason the Taruk had brought them here.

Eventually, Drake was unable to sleep anymore as he began to hear sounds in the forest.

The sound of people walking by them.

The sound of hammers in the distance.

Drake wondered if his imagination was getting the best of him. From the sky, they had seen no sign of anyone or anything that could have found them.

Crunching leaves awakened Drake in the middle of the night. Gwen still slept next to him and his Taruk slept on the far side of the camp, unaware of the noises.

For the next few minutes, all was quiet, but then he heard the same sound again. He stood and began to move towards the area the sound had come from, cautious about traveling too far in the fog that had settled over the area.

He looked down and to the left seeing a footprint barely visible in the dirt. The sound came again, this time from behind. Drake spun around seeing nothing, but still heard the footsteps as they came closer to him. Drake crouched in some brush, hoping that whoever was near would pass him by. The footsteps neared and then passed by him again.

Footprints appeared in the dirt and then kept going as though the person was invisible. A few minutes passed and it happened again, this time five or six sets of footprints were seen trekking into the forest.

Drake waited for them to pass and then quickly scrambled back to Gwen and shook her awake. Her eyes fluttered open and following his prompts, they were both ready within a minute. Drake moved over to his Taruk and laid a hand on its side.

The Taruk's big eyes looked towards him, seeming to understand everything.

"What are we looking for Drake?" Gwen asked.

"People are going by the camp but they're invisible. I don't know who they are or where they're going."

"Is it even possible for there to be invisible people?" Gwen asked.

"Not that I know of, but I'm sure there must be some Sorcerer who made a way to make people invisible."

"Quiet!" Gwen urged. They both heard more footsteps coming near them. They watched as the footsteps appeared in the dirt like they had the previous times and then continued. Drake led the way and Gwen followed closely behind him as they were swallowed by the forest.

They walked for hours until the forest began to get lighter. The fog that surrounded them showed no signs of lifting, but even having grey light to walk through was better than nothing. They followed the invisible people, hoping that they were getting somewhere close to their destination.

The forest disappeared and instead wrapped around a clearing. Drake and Gwen both stood with their mouths wide open. The fog still hung on the hillside, carefully concealing what was on top of the large hill.

A castle stood in front of them, easily matching the size and magnitude of Belvanor. Drake was the first one to take a step forward, soon followed by Gwen who found the courage after he did. The footsteps continued inside and then disappeared. Drake and Gwen moved to the path which was covered with grey cobblestone brick. They made their way up to the massive gates, which were wide open. They looked in, seeing nothing but old buildings and carts of supplies. The footsteps could still be heard echoing throughout the entire structure. By the sound of the footsteps, Drake would have to guess the castle was full of people.

More invisible people walked by them and seemingly joined the others.
'Drake.'

Drake looked around, wondering who had said his name. He looked at Gwen, silently conveying the fear that was now ragging inside his soul.

'Come away from there, it's too dangerous! We'll go in there later but we have to wait for a little while. If they see you then we have bigger problems than we had previously.'

"Who-"

'Don't speak they can hear you. They can't see you, however. Just think what you want to say and I'll be able to hear you. Don't try to tell Gwen anything, my friend's telling her exactly what I'm telling you.'

'Who are you?'

'Never mind that. Go a mile and a half to your left and we'll be waiting for you. You'll be safe there.'

'How do I know I can trust you?'

'Because we've met before and I didn't kill you then so I won't kill you now.' Gwen gripped his arm and their eyes met as they both turned to their left and walked a mile and a half into the forest. The forest was very different from the section that they had been walking through up to this point. This one was full of hills and steep ravines that made the going slow and difficult.

The time passed and the distance they had traveled didn't seem to be getting any longer as one hill led to another hill which was larger than the previous one. The fog was clear on top of the hills and dense in the valley, adding another obstacle as they both wondered how they were supposed to find the people who had spoken with them if they couldn't see.

'Welcome.'

"Where are we?" Gwen asked aloud.

'Right where you need to be, you're safe. Like I said previously, walking into that city in the middle of the night would have been very foolish.'

"That's a little backward isn't it?" Drake asked. "In most cities, people sleep during the night."

'Nothing about that city is normal Drake Thomas.'

"You know my name?" Drake asked.

'Yes.'

"Show yourself," Gwen said her voice wavering in the pale light.

'We're coming down the hill right in front of you. Don't be afraid we're not going to hurt you. You've seen us before.' Drake and Gwen studied the foggy landscape in front of them.

"This feels like a trap," Drake whispered. Gwen stared ahead, looking again for something that might have been missed. Drake started to move but was stopped by Gwen who pointed to the top of the hill.

A wolf stood tall and proud, barely visible through the dense fog and dim light. The wolf looked in their direction and held their gaze, unmoving as though it was searching them for something.

The wolf looked away and then looked to their left. Drake and Gwen followed the wolf's gaze, fear flooding through them once again when they spotted another wolf standing only ten feet away from them. The wolf looked at them and then up to the one on the top of the hill.

'It's them, you can come down now.' The voice said. Drake and Gwen both searched their surroundings for the person who had spoken.

"Who said that?" Gwen asked, gripping Drake's hands so tightly it nearly cut off his circulation.

'I did.' Gwen followed the voice looking to the left where the wolf now sat. They were soon joined by the other wolf who made his way down the hill and stood in front of them.

"You can talk?" Drake asked.

'Yes, we can talk, only to those we choose to talk to though. Most people would freak out if they came across wolves that could talk.'

"I can't imagine why," Gwen remarked. The wolf in front of them laughed without moving his lips and talked the same way.

'I have a funny feeling that you don't remember having met us before, so allow us to introduce ourselves again," the wolf in front of them started. 'My name is Willard and this is my friend Miles. Do those names ring any bells for you?'

"Willard and Miles?" Drake asked. "What are you doing here?"

'Could ask you the same thing,' Miles replied. 'We like to travel quite a bit, after all, we're wolves; we can usually get away with things that most people can't. We've traveled thousands and thousands of miles and we've got so much knowledge in our heads that it hurts sometimes. Up until now, we're the only ones who know anything about the city that you stumbled across.'

"What kind of a city is it?" Gwen asked. "I've never heard of invisible people before and I don't think we even know where we are."

'First off, to answer your question about where you are, you are about three hundred miles northwest of Belvanor. How you ended up here we haven't a clue. This is still a part of Ariamore, but it's a more deserted part. Even though there are a lot of people in Ariamore who support Lathon, there are just as many that have set out to do their own things, carrying out unthinkable acts in the darkness.'

"So these people are rebels?" Drake asked. Willard and Miles both looked at each other for a moment or two.

'It's a complicated story,' Willard started. 'I'll try my best to condense it for you. I'm sure by now you've heard the history of the Borags and Spirits?' Gwen and Drake both nodded. 'It seems even this beautiful nation of the Elves, the nation that creatures like us call home, has its own dark history. Though the Elves were blessed and beyond doubt as to the existence of Lathon, rumored followers of the Sorcerer, rose up and tried to change a few of the things they didn't like with the system and government that Lathon had set up. So they sought to overthrow him.

'It was an ugly affair, involving civil war, but they did succeed in pushing Lathon out of nearly everything. Loyal friends held steadfast the belief in the heir of Lathon that would one day reclaim the throne and rule forevermore.'

"Shedaros?" Drake asked, the scar on his hand burning in his mind.

'Correct. After the uprising was over the rebels ruled for ages until they were overthrown and a new government was set up by three Elven kings, who to this day are among the most famous of the Elven-kings. They went traveling and returned three years later with a story that gave new hope and vision to the people of Ariamore and the people of the world.

'Not wanting to risk another civil war, rather than push the rebels away or deal with them directly as they probably should've, they decided to do what they thought was the next best thing. They made them invisible. The city you *have just seen, even though it looks as if it's old and abandoned, is anything but. We've watched it as it rose higher and higher into the sky and now it's the fortress it is today. The people who live within the walls are invisible to the normal person and cannot do them any harm. The only catch to this invisibility thing is that when you walk into the city gates you become visible to them. You still can't see them.*

'They move only at night, hoping to be forgotten by the world and they've succeeded. There's not just one castle like this there are six castles like this, throughout the world.'

"You said that these people are 'invisible' to normal people?" Gwen asked. "What does that mean? We saw their footprints. Does that mean we're not normal?"

'If you've thought that any part of you was normal up to this point then you've been fooling yourselves. We know many people, Gwen and Drake, and your names come up a lot in the conversations, and not all of them are from the good guys so to speak.'

"I don't understand," Gwen started. "We know Drake has the scar, and that's what makes him different and interesting to the Sorcerer, but do you know something about me that I don't know?"

'It's complicated,' Miles answered. *'Have you ever heard any of your past?'*

"Just that I was found on the doorstep," Gwen answered.

'There is much that you don't know then, and we're not the right people to tell you the truth. All we'll say on the matter is that there's more to you than meets the eye. You have a history and it's a pretty ugly one.'

"Would you tell me what it is?" Gwen asked. "I want to know."

'Let's just say you're a vast difference from the rest of your family and that difference is fascinating to some people.'

"What do we do now?" Drake asked.

'Once it's about noon the people of the invisible city will go to sleep, we'll be able to walk through the city without being seen.'

"Why do we have to go in there?" Drake asked.

'It's the easiest way to get back to where you came from. There's something you'll have to see and remember for the future.'

"Can the Sorcerer see the city?"

'No. They are hidden from his view for the time being. Until he can acquire the items he needs. Once he does they will be freed from the invisibility spell and he will be stronger than before.'

They didn't speak letting the silence grow between them. Hunger gnawed at Drake and Gwen. Willard and Miles tried their best to bring them food that they could eat, but all they got was a few leafy plants and some wild berries that were growing next to a small stream.

When Drake and Gwen were finally awakened, the sun was high above and the fog was gone and the leaves all lay on the floor of the forest, covering it completely.

Willard and Miles were already standing at the top of the hill. He was both anxious and scared to see what Willard and Miles had to show them. Gwen grabbed Drake's hand, easing their fear a little bit. He looked up to the tallest spire that was in the middle of the building seeing a flag flying high in the air even though there was no wind.

They walked by smoldering fires from the blacksmith's shops. The smoke rose into the sky and then vanished when it got above the city wall. Their footsteps echoed off of every inch of the walls, yet the sound seemed to contain itself.

Willard and Miles led the way through the confusing maze of streets and bridges until they came to a stop outside a set of large doors. They stood about ten feet tall and looked like they weighed a hundred pounds apiece.

'We're here.' Willard said. *'In the bottom of this spire is something few people have ever seen and for good reason. But you need to see it for yourself.'*

"How do we get in? I'm sure these people, even if they are invisible, have locked the gates to the keep."

'Yes, they have. When the city was being built they purposely built the doors and gates so heavy they could barely be opened. Only when you said a password could you get them open. Not a bad idea really.'

"I assume that you know the password?" Gwen asked.

'She's a smart one Drake I'll give you that,' Miles replied, they both smiled. 'We know all the passwords. We also know that they don't have to be verbally spoken but only by thought.'

"What's the password?"

'An ancient form of a name that people wouldn't want to say. Murok!' Nothing happened for several seconds as though the door was trying to process the word that had been said.

The door slowly slid inwards without making a sound. In front of them, a dark chasm waited. Cool moist air came out of the castle, certainly giving the appearance that there was no one living there. Drake started to take a step forward but Miles stepped in front of him.

'Don't say a word in here. Think your thoughts.' Drake and Gwen both agreed and entered into the darkness letting the door seal them off from the outside world. Once their eyes adjusted, they could see that the chasm was nearly twenty feet wide and at least that tall. Huge pillars ran up to a balcony that was ten feet above them. A few faint torches glimmered in the darkness, but none of them too brightly.

Willard and Miles began walking to the left as Gwen and Drake followed close behind. They walked for a good half hour before they finally came to a large stairwell that descended downward.

They began walking down the twisting stairwell, going down flight after flight of stairs until finally, they came to another door, this one smaller and not quite as grand as the ones they had seen up to this point. Willard and Miles stood to either side of the door speaking the same password they had the first time. Without a sound the latch on the door lifted itself and they were allowed to enter.

The door creaked and groaned, the sounds echoed off every inch of the castle. They entered another hallway, this one narrow, only wide enough for one person to get through at a time. Gwen went in front of Drake coming to a stop when she reached the end of the hallway.

Enormous statues stood to either side, carved in memory of the ancient kings that had once ruled over one part of the land or another. Drake looked past the statues to the room that lay ahead.

Tall floor-length mirrors stood all around, mounted perfectly on the wall and touching the ground. Drake and Gwen counted seven mirrors in all, and in the middle of the room a rock cauldron that stood no more than four feet high.

Drake ran his hand along the trim of one of the mirrors and then reached out to touch the glass. He stopped short, noticing that he didn't see his reflection in the mirror.

He looked into the mirror, seeing a large room similar to what they were standing in, except he wasn't in this one. Drake's mind started to spin as he reached out to touch the mirror and felt his hand slide through the glass as though it wasn't there. Drake pulled his hand back and looked to Willard and Miles who, if it was possible, had smiles of amusement on their faces.

'What are these?' Gwen asked, through her thoughts.

'These are the Sorcerer's mirrors,' Willard answered. *'Dangerous and deadly tools that he can use. In the days of long ago, this was how he kept in touch with his loyal troops, kings, leaders, and so forth. Remember when I told you that there were six other castles like this one? Each one has a room like this and that's what you see in the mirrors. This is a very dangerous room to be in for that very reason. If one of the leaders that is loyal to the Sorcerer was to enter then he would be able to see us.'*

'So this is how the Sorcerer can get messages to his people so quickly?' Gwen asked.

'That's right. All he has to do is look into his cauldron and he can see every one of his kings, and he can tell them what to do whenever he wants.'

'You said this city was made invisible by the elf kings? If that's the case why are there Sorcerer's Mirrors inside them?' Drake asked.

'The history of every city is complicated," Willard said. 'It's unknown to us if the elf kings or anyone in the city even knew these were here. Right now these mirrors are virtually useless if the Sorcerer doesn't have everything he needs to gain the power necessary to control the mirrors.'

'What do you mean?'

'He needs his Taruk and the Wizard's Staff to have full power, but with these mirrors, he would break the curse of invisibility that's been put on this city and use it to his will.'

'How?' Gwen asked.

'In addition to being able to see and hear his leaders from anywhere they also are portals of a sort.'

'So could we go into these other castles from here?' Drake asked.

'Yes,' Miles answered. 'He could as well. He could march his whole army through here if he wanted to, but right now he can't.'

'We have to hope that he doesn't find the Wizard's Staff.'

'Rumor has it was hidden a little while ago, but those are only rumors.'

'So what does the cauldron do?' Gwen asked stepping towards it. Miles stood in the way growling and baring his teeth.

'This room is dangerous enough as it is. There is nothing harmless about these cauldrons. If you look into the water you might as well surrender to the Sorcerer now! The water that is in them is a special kind of water, a kind that only he can make. If you drink the water, a person cannot refuse his orders. Unless you wish to be a slave to the Sorcerer for the rest of your days do not look into the cauldron. The ancient kings of these castles drank the water. They were unable to refuse a command.'

'What does the middle mirror do?' Drake asked, pointing to the mirror right in front of them. Even though the rest of them were filled with images of every kind this mirror showed nothing. It was full of black space.

'This one will show you anything you wish to know, for the most part. Now if *the Sorcerer knows that you're using it then he could twist whatever vision you see when you look into it. I doubt he knows that we're here. Think of a place, anywhere that you've been up until this point.'*

'How about Fiori?' Gwen asked. The mirror gradually began changing with light coming into the dark space in the mirror. An image became visible and they were able to look into the remains of the Lily's hometown. Even months after the fact, small amounts of smoke still drifted into the sky, a constant reminder of the terrible force that had struck the village and town. The buildings were nothing more than piles of rubble, with a few walls still standing acting as grave markers.

'Can we go to these places as well?' Drake asked.

'If you want to go there, think of the place and walk through, but be careful. The last place that you think before you walk through the mirror will be visible the next time someone wants to use the mirror.'

'So if we think of Belvanor and then walk through they'll be able to see it?' Gwen asked, even as she spoke the name, the city came into their view.

'Maybe we should go back to where the Taruk is. From there, no one will be able to see anything, at least not cities.'

'Is there anything else we should see while we're here?'

'I don't think so, but be very careful of what you do when you're walking through the mirror. If you even think for a split second of another city they'll see it and then there are problems.'

Gwen and Drake both nodded, walking towards the mirror together. They thought about their landing spot and it came into view, the Taruk was sitting and patiently waiting for them. Drake and Gwen were both relieved to find that the Taruk was all alright.

They walked through the mirror, Gwen first and then Drake. The world spun and light flashed all around them as the ground rushed towards him. Drake crashed onto the ground and moments later Willard and Miles came walking through, apparently better at using the mirrors than they were.

"That went well," Drake stated standing up and looking around for Gwen.

His heart nearly stopped when he spotted Gwen lying on the grass ten feet away from him. Blood colored her skin and clothes as a thousand cuts and scrapes covered her body from head to toe.

Drake ran forward and held her head in his arms. Her clothes were torn and tattered and her auburn hair was already matted with blood. Willard and Miles surrounded the two of them, looking towards the woods and growling.

"What just happened?" Drake asked.

'She was seen in the mirror!' Willard answered. *'She was seen and attacked! How you managed to escape unseen is beyond me. We're in danger if we stay here. You have to get her back to Belvanor while she's still alive.'*

"How though. I ended up here flying on the Taruk and I didn't know where I was going. How am I supposed to tell him to get back to Belvanor?" Drake asked.

'Think where you want to go and he'll take you. Now get out of here before you get yourself killed!' Drake began to move and then froze in his tracks, as a throwing knife embedded itself in the ground right next to him.

"What just happened?"

'Someone from the city followed us and is shooting at you, they're invisible remember?'

Drake carried Gwen towards the Taruk, dodging several more arrows as they landed just behind him. He managed to get Gwen up on the Taruk and held onto her tight as he took Willard's advice and thought about the destination that he wanted to go to.

The Taruk pushed off the ground and unfolded its massive wings, quickly lifting them into the air. The ground faded beneath them. Willard and Miles were lost from his sight as he looked to Gwen who still was motionless. Her eyes were open and blank, staring straight ahead into the open space.

If the Sorcerer gained his strength and carried out his plan with every ounce of his power, there really was no hope. Their days were numbered, and for the first time, Drake was worried about what would happen.

The fortress of Belvanor appeared below them. Gwen was unconscious, her blood staining everything red. They had been spotted from miles away and much to Drake's relief they hadn't been shot down because they had a Taruk. The Taruk swooped low out of the sky and landed twenty feet in front of the castle walls where everyone came, dropping what they were doing and rushing to help the two of them.

Drake's mind drifted in and out of the situation as he watched them rush Gwen away, leaving him standing in the middle of the clearing. His heart was a mess of emotion as he stood trying to process everything. A screech echoed through the sky, pulling his attention to the air above him. Elohim swooped low and landed right next to Drake and his Taruk. Aiden dropped off the side and came running towards Drake.

"Is everything alright?" Aiden asked.

"I don't know. All I know is they took Gwen away about ten minutes ago and I was left here alone."

"You are never alone Drake Thomas, you'll do good to remember that. Lathon is always here and watching out for you."

"He is?" Drake asked.

"Have I ever steered you wrong?"

"No, it's just that sometimes I wonder if everything I hear about Lathon can be true."

"It's true, if anyone should know that it would be me. There's something bigger behind this, behind all of this. We'll just have to figure out what it is. What happened?"

"Long story short we ended up in the middle of nowhere and then we ran into Willard and Miles, two wolves, then we ended up in this room of mirrors."

"Room of mirrors?" Aiden asked.

Drake nodded. "Does that mean anything to you?"

"Maybe. I can't help but notice that there's a rather large Taruk sitting behind you."

"That's how Gwen and I got so far away from here. There was a Taruk egg in the shop you told me about on the east side of the city. It exploded and the next day I somehow acquired a Taruk. Not sure how it happened or what I'm supposed to do with it but I have a Taruk now."

"Consider yourself fortunate Drake Thomas," Aiden said. "I've told you before, people dream of having a Taruk. What is its name?"

"I don't know Isabel, the shopkeeper, didn't say."

"She wouldn't know what the name of it was, because it wasn't hers to name. If this Taruk is truly yours all you have to do is name it and it will follow you until the ends of the earth."

"What am I supposed to name it?" Drake asked. "Is there a wrong name for a Taruk?"

"Just listen to your heart Drake. If you give it a name from your heart then it will always be the right name." Drake pondered all the ideas that floated in and out of his head. The moments passed and turned into several minutes as Drake was glad to have something to take his mind off Gwen and the condition she was in.

"How about Destan?" Drake asked. "It was destiny that gave him to me in the first place. Is that a good name for a Taruk?"

'Yes.'

"What was that?" Drake asked, wondering if Aiden had heard the voice as he had.

"I told you that there was a connection between Taruks and their riders. Your Taruk won't speak a lot of words, they rarely do, however, they know what you're thinking and you know what they're thinking. It's a unique connection."

"So does Elohim speak a lot?" Drake asked. Aiden nodded.

"Sometimes, and then other times I can hardly get him to say a word."

"Do you have any idea why he took us so far away like that?"

"The one thing about Taruks is that they tend to go crazy after being cooped up for too long. I've been into Isabel's shop before and I've seen the egg as it grew bigger and bigger. The best I can estimate, the egg was twenty-five years old. After being cooped up all that time I'm not surprised that Destan took off like he did.

"There's so much I need to learn," Drake replied.

"In time you will. The more you learn the more patient you'll become. Anyone who rushes into anything without carefully thinking through all the options is going to have more trouble than they bargained for in the future."

"What's happened since we were here last?" Drake asked.

"Not much. The call for all able-bodied people to come to Belvanor for training has been put out, within a week they will be arriving and then the training will begin. You, Lily, and Ellizar along with Gwen have been promoted, but I'll tell you more about that later. We're already beginning plans for a large-scale attack on Revly next spring."

"Why that long?" Drake asked.

"Because the council and the Farsees doubt that the Sorcerer will expect us to attack then. Once winter gets here he won't attack us, so if we get a city that he's taken right when the snow is gone then we've caught him by surprise."

"You don't think that he'll attack this winter?"

"The council doesn't think he will. Atruss and myself on the other hand think there's something else going on that we can't see. It troubles our hearts and warns of danger and betrayal that might lay ahead."

Aiden and Drake passed the city gates. People moved about the fortress, trying to move on from the battle that had taken place. Mysteries still surrounded the battle and nothing would be known for certain, for some time.

Drake's mind was fixed on the castle they had discovered. He had briefly told Aiden about the mirrors, as he trusted Aiden almost more than anyone else at the moment. Aiden seemed to always be looking out for him and had a heart that Drake hadn't seen in anyone else. There was no way that Drake could ever hope to pay him back for all the times Aiden had saved his life.

The two of them walked until they came to the healing tower. They were greeted by Lily who wrapped her arms around him. She pulled back and Ellizar came forward holding out his hand. Drake grabbed the hand and then pulled Ellizar into a hug which got a humorous response from both Ellizar and Lily.

"Gave us a mighty scare there Drake!" Ellizar exclaimed.

"I gave myself a scare. Destan took off and carried us away. I didn't know what I was doing."

"You'll have to tell us all about it," Lily said.

"Don't worry I'll tell you everything that happened later, but I want to know how Gwen's doing."

"Not very good. What happened teh her?" Ellizar asked.

"I wish I knew. We were just trying to get back to the Taruk and when we did she looked like that."

"Speakin' ov yer Taruk, there is a *very* livid shopke'per who would like teh have a word with yeh as soon possible."

"I can't imagine," Drake replied. "Do you know where she is?"

"Drake, I know you probably want to be polite and all that, but I think this is one time you should probably wait for her to cool down before you approach," Lily advised.

"I know. I was asking so that I would be able to avoid her."

"I was about teh suggest that we have the doctors look at yer head," Ellizar commented with a laugh. Lily just smiled.

"I think that they should look at yours, but they won't take the time to because they know that you don't have anything in there," Lily teased. Ellizar frowned and shook his head, muttering something in dwarvish.

"I wish I could think up a good comeback fer that, but on this one yeh beat me, elf. But never again shall a noble dwarf like Ellizar fall teh an elf."

"No, but apparently, you'll speak of yourself in the first person," Aiden pointed out. "Since, I doubt you will be able to see Gwen until they treat her for her injuries, might I have a word with you?"

They left the healing tower and made their way to a modest little house in the middle of the town. Aiden motioned for them to take a seat and fixed a pot of tea which simmered as he poured it into their cups.

"For the past two days, I have been buried in meeting after meeting of the council. Although I may not agree with all the decisions that have been made I do agree with the ones I am allowed to tell you. Keep in mind you do not have to accept the positions that are being offered to you."

"Positions?" Lily asked. "Like jobs?"

"That's correct. None of you are normal people, therefore your jobs will not be normal. What I mean is, instead of merely being assigned to build something you will be in charge of building it. You've moved up on the list because of your incredible feats."

"What incredible feats?" Drake asked. "We were nearly killed a hundred times in our quest to get here and you or Rohemir always ended up saving us when we were in trouble. I'm not a hero."

"No you're not," Aiden agreed.

"If I'm not, then why do people treat me like I am?"

"People will do what people will do, they want something they can believe in. Little do they know, if they put their trust in Lathon they would be a lot better off. Just because you have a mark on your hand doesn't make you a hero, like they think it does. What makes a hero is what goes on when people aren't looking at you. That is what makes people a hero or a fraud. You cannot truly be a hero unless you put your hopes into something greater than yourself and never waiver from the truth."

"What are yeh sayin'?" Ellizar asked.

"Drake, you have a scar correct?" Aiden asked, Drake nodded. "Do you know how you got the scar?"

"No."

"Are you willing to concede that there might be something greater behind everything that has happened? That *maybe* that scar on your hand is no accident, even washing up on that river was no accident." Silence followed. Drake carefully considered everything before nodding in agreement. "Do you believe that there is a reason and a purpose and that events that have unfolded have happened for a reason? Do you believe that Lathon, lived and that he has a plan to save this world again?"

"Up until now, I've only played along with whatever people have said about me or told me," Drake started. "But it's been two months and finally the other night I decided to myself that there must be a purpose behind this scar. I still don't know what I am supposed to do."

"I tell you this Drake Thomas, if you believe that in your heart and never let it waiver, you will be a great leader. You will be an example of what a follower of Lathon can and should be. People have named the four of you, heroes. But are you worthy of the title? Something to think about in the days to come.

"Now that I've accidentally run off into that little tangent, I'll get the conversation back to what I intended to talk to you about," Aiden continued. "Drake, you were put in charge of the army during this last attack. It was a bad decision on Rohemir's part and it nearly cost you your life. The council has ordered that the five of you begin training in swordsmanship. It is plain to see you know the basics of fighting, now you need to have the endurance and techniques that will allow you to fight for hours without rest and without getting beaten down to the point that you can't do anything.

"As soon as Gwen is well enough to travel, you will be going to the city of Remnda. I will be at Remnda with you, most of the time. It's a city near the sea, that should be out of the way and is the last place in the world that the Sorcerer would think to look for you. He would expect you to be kept in Belvanor, which is why we can't risk having you here.

"You will be educated in the ways of the world. Geography, History, Politics, Culture. This is not a training that the majority of the council or Farsees think is necessary."

"Then why are we to be trained this way?" Lily asked.

"Because to help a person you must know the world they come from. How they see things. Then, you can begin to figure out how they must be helped. Catch a man a fish and you feed him for a day, teach a man to fish and you feed him for a lifetime," Aiden said, looking to Ellizar. "What do you think so far?"

"I think, I won't have a clue what I'm doin' but I'm willin' teh give it a try," Ellizar declared.

"Good. The second part of what the council wishes for you is as follows. Drake, you will be in charge of a regiment in the army and you will be educated in everything you need to know. Gwen will also be put in charge of this. Skander and Ellizar will be put in charge of creating and building a new weapon I thought up. One that might catch our enemy by surprise."

"Ah, it sounds like a job good fer a dwarf like me!"

"You don't even know what it is yet," Skander pointed out. "For all you know, it might be throwing manure at the opposing army." Ellizar frowned and looked at Lily.

"Yeh guys are related! What's the weapon we'll be buildin'?"

"That has to remain a secret until you get there, but trust me it'll be right up your alley. And so that leaves Lily." He turned to face her. "Lily your skill with a bow is great, and it has not gone unnoticed. You will be in charge of the archers and catapults, but you all will be educated in what the others are learning. Should something happen, you need to cover for the other person."

"What about Destan will he be coming?"

"Yes, he will be trained by me and Elohim. In this part of the world, a Taruk would be used in the Mezutor but that was never intended to be their purpose, if you take my meaning."

"I think I have an idea," Drake replied. They laughed and drank their tea as they tried to learn more about what they would be doing when they reached Remnda. As hard as they tried, Aiden wouldn't tell them anymore, saying that he had already told them more than he was supposed to.

At length, they left Aiden's dwelling and made their back to their rooms, quickly falling into their their dreams. Drake woke up several times throughout the night, his heart warning him that something was wrong.

The threat tormented his mind and threatened to drive him mad. As if in connection with the threat, a whisper filled his mind. Drake ignored the voice, instead reminding himself of the blessings in his life.

The voice became distant, as though its power was diminished. He opened his eyes to see everyone else sleeping peacefully. Drake laid his head down and finally was able to fall asleep.

Gwen wanted to cry out in pain. Her jaw was clenched and her eyes were shut, regretting every breath. She had stepped through the mirror like she had been told. Then, flashes of light filled her mind as well as a voice that was more horrible than any she had ever heard.

She had been defenseless as the dark voice yelled out command after command and the flashes of light became more and more intense. She had felt the life draining from her and then she had seen only darkness.

The world around her was brought into focus. She was buried beneath a blanket and new clothes sat next to the bed, but at the moment she couldn't find the strength to put them on. She looked to the left and then to the right, focusing on the person in the next bed, fear taking hold of her.

It was Tremin, the same black-haired man whom she and Drake had spoken with the last time they were in this tower.

As if it was rehearsed Tremin began to wake. Gwen hastily closed her eyes, hoping he would think she was asleep. Despite her best efforts, Tremin looked and her and smiled. He didn't speak to her for several minutes, choosing instead to eat the food that had been provided.

"Good morning," Tremin finally greeted her.

"Good morning," Gwen answered.

"You were the center of attention when you arrived yesterday. It seems everyone can't figure out how you got so injured."

"I'm not even sure how it happened."

"It happened to me once, still don't completely understand it myself," Tremin reflected. "You walked through one of the mirrors right?"

"Mirrors?"

"Yeah, the Sorcerer's mirrors. Come on, you can't end up in that condition doing anything else. The time it happened to me I would've died if it hadn't been for a person who was traveling in the area. He saved me."

"I'm not sure what to say," Gwen replied.

"Who says you have to say anything?" Tremin reasoned. "I just told you something about me, that's all. It's a shame though. You were so beautiful; you still are, but it'll be a while until you're as gorgeous as you were. You look familiar to me, have I met you before?"

"I doubt it," Gwen answered. "The only place I've seen you before this is in the hospital a day or so ago."

"At least that's the only time you can remember. You never know, maybe we met a couple of years ago and aren't aware."

"I doubt it," Gwen answered, letting the conversation die out. The doctors came and treated her numerous wounds again and again. Her mind shut down and she stared ahead, hardly knowing what she was looking at. She had been beaten as a slave and she had been abused in ways that she wished she could forget, but this kind of pain was something new, even to her.

She longed to have Drake by her side and hold his hand, letting the simple touch of his hand take away her worries. She waited for him to come until she drifted off to sleep.

The sleep brought some relief, but it was also filled with terrible dreams. In the dream she kept walking through the mirror over and over, bringing back the pain and the fear she had felt the first time.

She could feel each cut she had received, she could feel the cool grass beneath her as she lay, unable to do anything. The cool breeze swept through the forest and Drake's voice could be heard yelling, but she couldn't make out the words.

Then a different voice entered her head.

This one was familiar and despite her heart warning her about it, it sounded completely fine and normal. The seductive voice was speaking to her but Gwen still couldn't make out the words. She studied the image in her mind a little harder, thinking that she might be able to see the source of the voice.

The world around her changed and then she was in a large castle. Dark clouds threatened rain. One lone torch hung on the wall, casting light into the dark dank room. A few pieces of furniture were to either side of a man who stood looking out the window. Gwen tried to approach the window with her mind and found that she was able to move closer, but no further than five feet from the window.

An army lit by flames, snaked its way out of the city and into the distant mountains. The man in front of her was dressed in black and even though she couldn't see his face she perceived that his face was covered with a graying beard. He had a full head of hair that came halfway down his neck. He was taller than Gwen only by a few inches.

She tried to speak but found that her voice was gone. Without warning the man turned around and faced her. Fear consumed Gwen and light flashed through her mind as the man noticed her.

Without speaking, he came closer and Gwen's fear became almost unbearable as the man looked directly into her eyes. His face was hardened and his eyes were filled with malice and disdain. Gwen shifted awkwardly.

The longer they looked at each other the longer she realized that she in some ways held a resemblance to him. The man swung a fist at her but she never felt any pain as the attack seemed to pass through her.

Her heart cried out to leave and finally, the vision faded and she found herself waking in the hospital bed once again. Tremin, whom she had grown to fear was asleep, while the man from her dreams still haunted her.

She was pulled out of her thoughts by the sound of Drake calling to her. To her left she could see Drake and the others all coming her way.

"Feelin' better are we?" Ellizar asked. Gwen nodded and tried to move, reminded of the ever-present pain.

"Better but not good," Gwen replied. "I can't remember a time I was in more pain. I wish I could come up with an explanation as to what happened."

"We all wish that, but even Rohemir can't come up with any good ideas as to what caused it," Skander announced.

"You told Rohemir?" Gwen asked Drake. Drake shook his head.

"We didn't tell Rohemir, but he found out. I told Aiden, he's the one we trust."

"Trust? You don't trust Rohemir?" Lily asked.

"It's not that we don't trust him, it's just we're not sure if we should," Drake started. "He's got us this far but when you look at the past events, it just makes us a little uncomfortable."

"I don't sense anything, I think the two of you have overactive imaginations," Skander replied.

"That might be so, but either way..."

"Have they said how long until they'll be able teh get yeh out ov here?

We're in fer some big changes when the time comes," Ellizar said.

"Big changes?"

"Yes, but you get your rest and we'll worry about that later. The sooner you get better the sooner we can get out of here," Drake started, hesitating a moment later. "Oh and if our dear friend Isabel comes along and asks if we were here would you mind lying, because I think she wants to kill me."

"Once again, I think you're overreacting I doubt she wants to actually kill you," Skander replied.

"Drake Thomas!" a woman's voice bellowed from the entrance to the hospital wing. They didn't have to even look to know that Isabel had found them. Drake grimaced and Gwen joined the others as they tried not to laugh.

"Isabel!" Drake greeted, forcing a smile to his face. "So nice to see you again! How is The Wingy Wares?"

"That's what I've come here to talk with you about Mr. Thomas. You may think that just because I have two names and you have two names that you can get away with certain things, but not this time!"

"I did get the Taruk out of your house. There might have been a little damage, but it can't be that bad can it?" Isabel's dress turned dark black with red trim and her hair also turned black as if it was expressing on the outside what she was feeling on the inside.

"I *can* live with a hole in my roof. That's easily repaired, but there are some things that I *can't* fix. For example, I can't fix a house or shop that isn't there!"

"What do you mean it isn't there?" Drake asked.

Isabel rolled her eyes. "Thanks to Mr. four foot tall over there, I now have no place to lay my head. I had to sleep in the gardens. Which wasn't too bad, because as you may have noticed by my shop I do like gardens, but back to the point, the dwarf blew up my shop."

"How?" Drake asked, Ellizar shrugged his shoulders.

"Still a mystery teh me."

"He started messing with all my birds and he touched one and it destroyed everything except for us and the strange bird that brought you there. So now I am a proud owner of a pile of ashes! You owe me big time...or at least the dwarf does."

"What are we supposed to do?" Drake asked.

"You and your friends are going to be very skilled builders when you're done rebuilding my house!"

"We're leaving in a week," Drake announced, forcing a smile on his face. Isabel wasn't amused.

"I guess that means you only have a week to fix it then doesn't it?" Isabel asked. "I'll meet you at my house...let me amend that...my pile of ashes and ruins, in an hour to discuss the fine details and begin working."

As though all the rage had left her, Isabel's hair went back to its normal color and her dress changed to a light green tone that was both pale and beautiful. She turned and walked in the other direction, leaving them as though nothing had ever happened.

"I think we should try to fix the shop just so she doesn't kill us."

"Agreed," Lily replied. "I vote that Ellizar does most of the work seeing that he caused the explosion."

They talked for several more minutes until they were ushered away by the doctors and nurses who once again treated Gwen's injuries. Gwen was left by herself, with nothing to do but keep a watchful eye on Tremin who was sleeping next to her, despite it being the middle of the afternoon. The doctors left her and a few more people came by and talked to her. but her heart was saddened when Drake didn't come back. A while later, she allowed herself to smile, knowing that by now he must be busy building Isabel's new shop.

Darkness settled over Belvanor and finally, Tremin allowed himself to look up and down the rows of beds and then to Gwen who was in the bed next to him, fast asleep. Tremin threw off the covers and slipped on a dark cloak, which was carefully tucked under his bed.

Without a sound, he crept out of the hospital wing, past the rows and rows of sleeping patients. The moon was high and the crisp autumn air ate through his cloak like a knife.

Keeping to the shadows he made it to the city gates, where a few soldiers sat at their post. He had watched the schedule of the guards meticulously, learning their patterns and schedules. It was nice to know that even with the attack, nothing had changed.

He slunk into the shadows and waited until, just as he had known, the guards left their post, temporarily leaving the city gates unattended. He carefully crept to the gate, struggling to move it. The struggle was short-lived as it was pulled open by five people waiting on the other side. They carefully closed the gate and then entered into a dark stable that had horses and all the other supplies.

"Uniforms," Tremin said. He threw his comrade's uniforms from their supplies. "We'll be able to get into the hospital wing without question." They mounted their horses and entered the streets dressed as soldiers.

Within minutes they were at the Healing Tower.

The company dismounted and Tremin motioned the others to follow him. Once inside, they came alongside Gwen, who slept peacefully beneath the covers, her face relaxed.

He pushed a hand over her mouth and held it there. She jerked awake, kicking and trying to free herself. Tremin quickly produced a knife and held it to her throat. She immediately stopped.

"I wouldn't try anything, sweetheart," Tremin whispered. "I will not hesitate to slit you from naval to nose if you defy me!" He pulled her from the bed, securing her wrists. His other men came alongside and surrounded her. She had no choice but to come with them.

They exited the tower, pausing when they saw that their horses were missing. Tremin cautiously stepped backward. A moment after that a hand had grasped his throat. The rest of his men heard the commotion and immediately picked Gwen up and disappeared.

The man holding Tremin's throat relaxed his grip, allowing a little bit of air to go to his lungs. His head was turned to face his captor but in the shadows, his features were a mystery.

"Very interesting development wouldn't you say?" an elf asked. Tremin didn't reply. "What are you doing here?"

"You're not supposed to be awake," Tremin informed. The elf smiled.

"I thought it would be best if I was tonight. What am I missing Tremin? What have I not figured out? I can't for the life of me figure out why you would be taking Gwen as your prisoner... certain people are higher up than she is. It doesn't make any sense."

"It makes sense to me, that's what matters!" Tremin spat.

"Who ordered that she be kidnapped?" the elf asked. His heart quivered as the face of his captor, Aiden, was revealed in the full moonlight.

"You're a smart person figure it out for yourself," Tremin fired back. Aiden thought for a moment.

"I know the answer to that question, but what I don't know is why the Sorcerer himself would be interested in a girl who was nothing more than a slave. Why not take Mr. Thomas?"

"Perhaps because Gwen was easier to take than Drake?" Tremin replied with a sly grin on his face. Aiden's face lightened as if understanding something that he hadn't before.

"You're an interesting person Tremin. Until recently, I thought you were nothing but a loyal guard who had gotten injured during the fighting. However, we found you when we were helping the wounded. I've searched my memory and I don't remember seeing you at all before or during the battle."

"Perhaps your memory is failing you!" Tremin fired at him.

"We both know that it never does."

"You weren't even here at the beginning of the battle!" Tremin pointed out. Aiden's face and expression were unwavering.

"I didn't have to be. I still know what went on and what happened. I know you weren't here. I can see it in your eyes. I can feel your fear. There's a reason things have unfolded this way and I *will* find out why things are happening the way they are tonight. You stay put while I go and get Gwen back."

"Good luck," Tremin replied. He swung at Aiden and twisted out of his grasp. Aiden lost his grip and Tremin made a mad dash for a darkened alley.

A dwarf stepped in front of him, axe at the ready. Tremin darted to the left, avoiding him, and barreled through an elf. The elf was knocked off her feet by the force. He continued running, unable to get any further from Aiden who was gaining.

Tremin cursed and looked over his shoulder, but then was knocked to the ground by a horse and rider who had run into him. Tremin knew his name.

It was Drake Thomas.

Within a moment he was pinned down.

"Good work Drake," Aiden said, tying his hands and feet together. Several more horses trotted into the alley, one bore the elf and dwarf he had passed, while the other horses held strange riders. Whether they were elvish or human he didn't know, but his fear took hold of him.

"Take him to the dungeons and make sure to guard him," Aiden ordered.

"It will be done my Lord!" the leader said, nodding.

"Thanks, Michael," Aiden said. He quickly turned to Drake.

"Go to the west gate," Michael said. "That's where they entered and that's where they're headed. If you have any chance of getting Gwen that's it. Now go!" Drake, Lily, Ellizar, and Aiden all spurred their horses forward, vanishing from their sight.

It was several minutes before Drake and company came to the west gate as Michael had told them. Rade stood before the gate, his purple ring glowing brightly in the night. The gate was now wide open. Everyone followed Aiden's lead as he dismounted and came alongside Rade.

"Sorry, Aiden," Rade started. "We failed you. We could sense their presence immediately. We didn't want to tip our hand too soon. We just waited too long."

"Go catch them now," Aiden suggested. Rade seemed to consider it, though some great mystery was still concealed.

"I failed."

"You fail when you quit!" Aiden declared. "You have the skills to catch them and get Gwen back to safety."

"Drake and the others need training. Get them to Remnda as fast as you possibly can."

"Probably a good idea," Aiden concluded. "After all, if they can't find us they can't bother us."

"Correct, and if they're using Gwen as bait you won't play into their hands."

"I just hope that nothing happens to her if we don't go after her right now," Drake lamented.

"This is one time you'll be better off doing nothing," Rade replied. "I don't think the Sorcerer wanted her for bait, but rather for something else."

"Any ideas what that might be?" Aiden asked.

"If I knew that I'd know everything. I'll do what looking I can and I'll try to figure out the answers for you. You on the other hand get out of here and I hope I don't see you back here for a very long time. Get to Remnda and learn what has to be learned. War is nearly on our doorstep. They have to know how to fight."

"We'll leave at first light and we'll take the Taruks with us, that'll get us there in a matter of hours not days," Aiden agreed. Rade took the form of flames and carried himself through the sky towards another part of the city. Aiden thought Elohim's name and within a moment the powerful Taruk landed in the street.

"Pack your belongings and prepare to leave, we leave at first light. We'll need the use of Destan as well, Drake."

"I don't know where he is."

"Just think what you want him to do and he'll do it."

We need you here at first daybreak Destan, if you can hear me. As if in response to his request he felt something stir in his heart. It was faint at first but it was enough for him to know that Destan had heard him and would be there when he was needed.

"What are we going to do about Gwen?" Drake asked. "We can't just leave her."

"That's exactly what we are going to do. We are going to let the Korazin do an investigation, while we begin your training. Be ready and don't worry about Gwen."

"Easier said than done," Lily replied. "I've known her my whole life."

"I understand, but it's for the better." They all agreed and went their separate ways while Aiden made his way to the citadel where Atruss and Gabriel were sleeping.

He entered the palace and came to Atruss's door. He spoke the password and the guards let him enter, announcing his presence to him and his wife who had been in a deep sleep.

"What just happened?" Atruss asked.

Aiden quickly recounted everything that had happened.

"Get them out of this city and to Remnda as quickly as possible," Gabrielle instructed. "I'm not sure what the future holds but the army will have to be ready by spring."

"I'd plan on being ready before that. I have a feeling that the Sorcerer won't wait that long to attack us. Especially now," Aiden replied.

"You think he would be so bold as to attack in the middle of the winter?" Atruss asked.

"Our enemy is too smart to sit back all winter and give the people a chance to attack him. I think no matter what the weather is he will have a force strong enough to cripple any resistance if it's not properly set up. I'm sure with each of his armies there are many sorcerers capable of making the traveling easier for his troops," Aiden argued.

"Unfortunately, I cannot deny that you may be more right than you even know," Atruss started. "We have received word that Borag armies are marching in multiple nations. There's no way that any person, Borag or otherwise, could travel such a large distance in such a short time. The only theory that we can conclude is that our enemy has either created a Borag race that doesn't tire or that he has some other power that is giving them strength."

"It'll make the fight that much harder," Gabrielle added. "We all know that there are people who are going to make a push to give our armies the same protection."

"Then let them leave," Aiden replied. "It sounds harsh, but we know what we believe to be true and we all know that many things are going on underneath the surface that Lathon would not stand for. Perhaps this war will be a good chance to sort out those who are true followers of Lathon and those who aren't."

"But how will we manage to have a force if our homeland is divided?" Atruss asked.

"Do you think that in all the earth, only those who live in Ariamore believe in Lathon? I believe with a passion and a conviction that there are people in the other nations of this world we live in who know in their hearts that there's something better. Taking a stand like this will give them the strength to come forward. What our enemies think is weakness, we will find a strength far greater than any force the world can send at us."

"Next time the council brings up the subject of putting someone else on the council I think I will suggest that you just take over. Your wisdom astounds me," Atruss replied.

"I'm just thinking as Lathon would think. I have to try my hardest to set the example that he set for us. Maybe if we all modeled ourselves after him this world would be a lot better off."

"Can't argue there," Gabrielle replied. "This world has changed. The people have taken Lathon out of everything and forgotten that he even lived. In his memory, we will live our lives and show the world a little bit of the light that shatters the darkness."

"I'll take them to Remnda first thing in the morning and they'll begin their training. I have a few other ideas that are probably better left unsaid at the moment."

"No doubt a result of something you've discovered during your travels?" Atruss replied. Aiden smiled.

"Perhaps," Aiden answered. "Also, I know there's still a bit of work to be done on Isabel's shop, and she'd be livid if Drake left without repairing it. Could you see that it is repaired?"

"I will assign men to the task first thing in the morning, which I'm guessing isn't far off." None of them could suppress a smile.

"In that case, I'll let you two get the rest of your sleep now that I've ruined it for you," Aiden stood up and walked to the door. "In a couple of weeks have the shopkeeper Isabel come to Remnda, she has something I'd like her to tell Drake and the others."

"I will do as you wish. Good night my friend."

"No. Good morning."

The Adventure Continues...

DRAKE THOMAS

-BOOK 2-

DECEPTION OF MERDERICK

TYLER SVEC
JORDAN SVEC

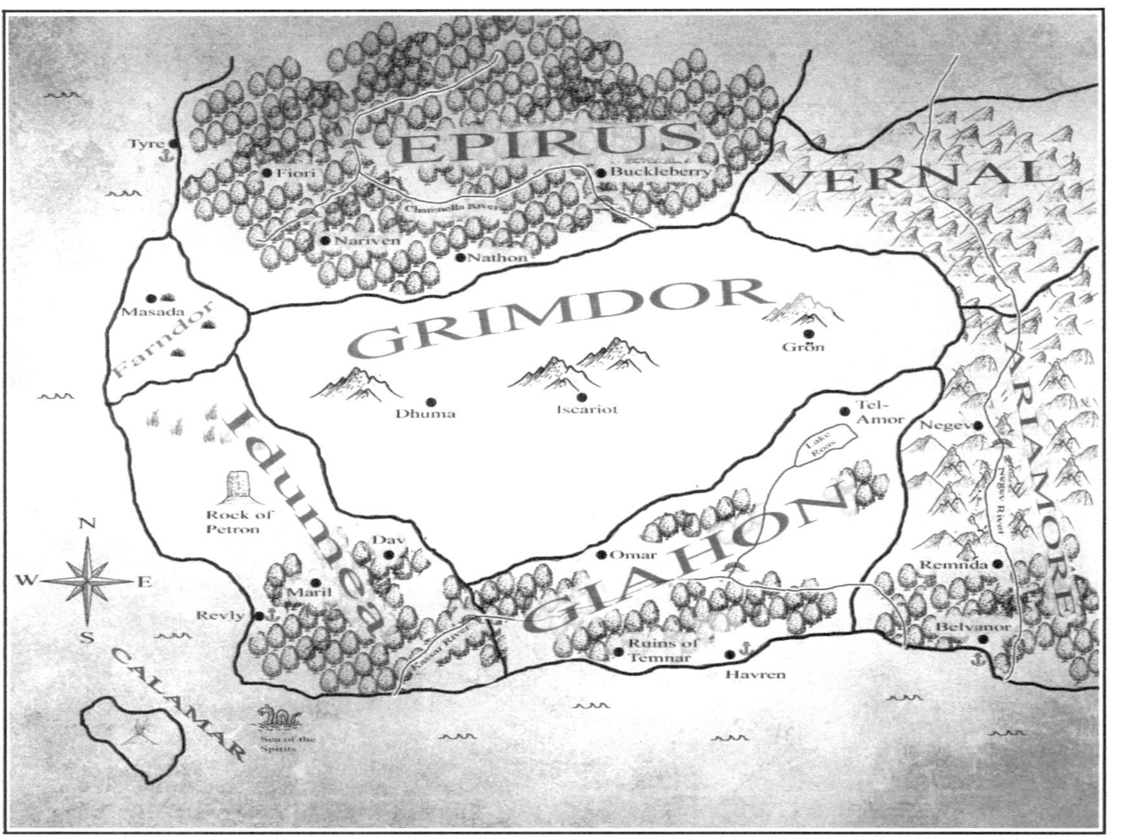

EPIRUS
VERNAL
ARIAMORE
GRIMDOR
GIAHON
Idumea
Farndor
CALAMAR
Tyre
Fiori
Buckleberry
Charnella River
Nariven
Nathon
Masada
Gron
Dhuma
Iscariot
Tel-Amor
Negev
Lake Rein
Rock of Petron
Dav
Omar
Remnda
Maril
Revly
Ruins of Temnar
Havren
Belvanor
Negev River
Kesan River
Sea of the Spirits
N
S
E
W

STORIES/REFERENCES

Pg. 7-8 : The star and asking permission to search the city.
Based off Matthew 2

Pg. 11 : Prophecy given is taken from Micah 5:2

pg 17 : The virgin birth

pg 17 : Gifts of gold, frankincense, and Myrrh

Joseph and Marion flee : Taken from Matthew 2:13-23

Pg 29 : All the children under 2 are killed. Taken from Matthew 2:16-18

Pg 84 : Adonai. Hebrew word for Lord.

Pg 104 : Tower of Seru is Tower of Babel Genesis 11

Pg 171 : Elohim. Hebrew word for God.

Pg 213-214 : Aiden calms the storm. Taken from Matthew 8:23-27, Mark 4:35-41 & Luke 8:22-25

About the Authors

Tyler Svec is a farmer in Northern Michigan who first started writing in high school. In the years that has followed, he has written 7 novels. He is happily married to his wife, Jessica, and they have five kids together.

Jordan Svec lives in Northern Michigan with his wife and two children. By day he works along his brother (Tyler) and together they collaborate on the ideas that go into the Drake Thomas series.